COLOR YOU IN

EMS STATION 1: BOOK TWO

K. EVAN COLES

For information contact: http://www.kevancoles.com

Book and cover design by K. Evan Coles

Edited by Rebecca Baker

Why are the hot guys always straight?

EMT Gus Dawson is off men, thanks to his jerk of an ex. He's set his sights on a promotion to paramedic and being the first amputee to hold that title for the city of Boston. Gus doesn't care that his new rookie partner thinks he'd do the job better. Or that the straight, married dad is all wrong for him.

Madoc Walters never imagined he'd have to restart his career. But he'll do whatever it takes to make a better life for his daughter, Val. Even if it means playing rookie for a hotshot who'll get a promotion Madoc deserves more. A guy he can't stop thinking about no matter how hard he tries.

In spite of the rivalry, the partners strike up a friendship, supporting each other after Gus is injured and Madoc's ex-wife abandons the family. But when crushes become real emotion and Gus bonds with Val, will Madoc be ready to stop playing it straight?

For my son, who makes me laugh every single day and is surprisingly patient with my endless questions about internet slang.

Enormous thanks to Randall Jussaume and Sue Philips, who generously donated their time to help fix my words, and to Rebecca Baker, the editor ninja, and Barb Payne Ingram, my proofreader and EMS expert.

Love, love is a verb
Love is a doing word

- *Teardrop*
Massive Attack

If you're always trying to be normal,
you'll never know how amazing you can be.

- Maya Angelou

ONE

FRIDAY, *March 31, 5:35 P.M.*

MY KINGDOM FOR COFFEE.

Gus Dawson stared at the station's coffee machine like it held the secrets of the universe. Not that he needed anything particularly existential from the thing as it sputtered and hissed; he just wanted to feel marginally more awake.

His cup filled, he settled at one of the canteen's tables and pulled a pencil and small drawing pad from his shirt pocket. Before he could begin sketching, a tug on his pant leg had Gus leaning over and peering at the small black cat messing around with his bootlaces.

In practice, Princess Lemonade Small Void Kitty belonged to Boston EMS Station 1 and the crews and admin staff cared for her as a team. But Gus had been the one to rescue her from a flooded-out basement and give her a home, and everyone knew she was really his. Gus paid Lemonade's vet bills and made sure she was well groomed and had toys and snacks she liked, and the bed-slash-box she used for sleeping sat in the corner of the changing room next to his locker.

Lemonade was just as attached to Gus, haunting him like a playful shadow through the station, her orange eyes aglow as she rode on his shoulders or perched atop his right foot when he sat, almost like she understood he was metal and plastic from knee to toe on that leg and impossible to injure.

"Quit it, you," Gus chided her, unsurprised when Lemonade ignored him, but then a casserole dish of burritos appeared before Gus, all luscious and cheesy. Gus worked hard not to drool as his friend Connor plunked down in the seat opposite.

"Help me eat these," Connor said amiably. "Judah used sweet potato and re-fried beans and the chipotle cream sauce you like."

Gus's stomach let out a yowl he was sure could be heard from space and he happily helped himself. "You are a prince among men," he said, "and please tell your man thank-you from me."

"I will. Your new partner starts tonight, yeah?"

"Yup. Walters from Station 5 in West Roxbury. He's been there since he finished the Academy program."

"Another rookie, huh?" Connor smiled at Gus from beneath his thick beard. "You ready to shape another young mind, Coach?"

"Sure. As soon as I'm more awake." Smirking, Gus stuck more burrito in his mouth. "Honestly, I'm hoping this rook doesn't need his mind shaped."

Gus was counting on it, actually. He liked working with rookies and the last two he'd had under his tutelage, Lucky Guzman and Amaya Monroe, were not only outstanding EMTs but had become friends. Walters was a different kind of rookie though, coming to Boston EMS after several years riding trucks in King County, Washington. Station 5 was far enough south of downtown that Gus couldn't remember having ever seen Walters at a scene, but on paper the guy had more experience in emergency medicine than Gus. That was a stroke of luck Gus hoped meant he'd spend less time training his new partner and more on preparing him to take Gus's place on Ambulance A1.

Because Gus had his own plans to progress his career and would take every advantage to make it happen.

Someone nearby cleared their throat and when Gus glanced up, there was an absurdly attractive human looking right at him. Beautifully chiseled features. Dark hair lying in soft curls. A small smile that hit Gus square in the chest.

Happy Friday to me.

"Hi," the hot human said, expression warm. "Are you Dawson? I'm Madoc Walters."

Gus stopped chewing. This hot human was his new partner. And here Gus probably had burrito on his face.

Wiping his mouth with his napkin, Gus stood, accidentally dislodging Lemonade in the process. He muttered a quick apology she dismissed with a glare, then looked back up at Walters—literally, because the dude was several inches taller than Gus's own five-foot-eleven, had very pretty blue eyes, and was built like a brick shithouse.

Gus thrust out his hand and smiled. "Gus Dawson, and welcome, it's good to meet you."

They sat down, Walters taking the empty seat between Gus and Connor, who extended his hand over the table.

"Connor Devlin," he said. "I'm on P1 with Lieutenant Parks." His shy smile widened when Walters set an insulated lunch bag on the table along with a travel mug emblazoned with a glittery rainbow-striped pony. "I know a little guy who'd be all over that mug."

Chuckling, Walters patted his cup, his cheeks flushing adorably. "It was a birthday gift from my daughter," he said. "Valerie loves anything rainbow and sparkly, and this year she's been really into these ponies."

And ho, that was interesting. Because Walters wasn't wearing a wedding ring, so maybe it wasn't too much to hope this big, beefy dude was a single dad who also happened to play for Gus's team.

"Of course, Val also wanted a pony cup for herself," Walters said. "So, her mom had to buy two."

Well, boo.

Gus bit into his burrito and figured it was just as well. He was off men at the moment, thanks to his asshat of an ex and, as senior tech on A1 and Walters' supervisor, keeping things professional was in both their best interests.

Still, why were the hot ones always straight?

Conversation at the table stopped dead when the station's alert system sounded.

"Ambulance A1." The dispatcher's voice echoed through the speakers overhead. "Person down at Devonshire and State. Male, early twenties, experiencing dizziness after a possible blow to the head during an assault. 32-B-1, patient is alert and talking. Code Two, just lights."

Gus caught Walters' eye. "Pony up, Rook—it's time to go."

They quickly gathered their stuff and took off for the ambulance bay, Gus calling back a thank-you to Connor for feeding him.

"You want to drive?" he asked Walters as they jogged into the garage.

"Happy to," Walters replied. "I live in the Seaport and I know this neighborhood."

Fancy.

The Boston Seaport sat less than a mile from the station in

South Boston's Waterfront district and was one of the city's more expensive neighborhoods. Walters could also walk to work, unlike Gus who'd battled ten miles of horrendous traffic tonight between his sister's place in Hyde Park and Downtown.

After confirming with the dispatcher they were en route, Gus crammed the remains of the burrito into his mouth while Walters raised the garage door and eased them out onto Purchase Street. They zipped past the massive firehouse that sat next door, and Gus raised a hand to the cluster of firefighters washing the big engine truck in the drive, smiling at the shouts he got in return.

"Sorry we didn't get to cover anything," he said to Walters. "But this is probably as good a way as any to get to know each other."

"True." Walters guided the truck onto Pearl Street. "So, you know I'm not a rookie, right?"

"Yeah." Gus glanced out the window on his right. "That was for Connor, really," he said. "You're not the first probie I've been partnered with, and he likes giving me crap about shaping the next gen of EMS."

"Got it. But I'm not a probie."

"Except you are."

"Um, no."

"Um, yes," Gus said. "All Academy recruits remain on probationary status for the first year, regardless of prior experience."

He watched Walters' right eyebrow rise and bit back a grin. Gus really was uncommonly fond of being a pest and among the crews he'd worked with, to tease was to love. But sadly, his new partner didn't seem to have much of a sense of humor because the big lug actually rolled his eyes.

"That's just a technicality," Walters said.

"Agreed," Gus replied. "A technicality that is still totally happening."

"Except it doesn't have to. *Technically*, I have more experience than you and I don't need you treating me otherwise. I got enough of that from the fossil I was stuck with out in West Rox who acted like I was a damned toddler."

Now Gus was the one raising his eyebrows. The 'fossil' Walters had been partnered with at Station 5 was Billy Lord, a guy with twenty years of service and a talent for guiding new recruits. He'd missed the mark with this probie, however, who thought nothing of mouthing off to a supervisor he'd known for less than an hour.

Turning to the Toughbook tablet mounted on the truck's dash, Gus looked over the call details. He didn't have time just then to figure out what had crawled up Walters' ass and died and instead thumbed the talk switch on his radio.

"A1 on scene," he said as they turned onto State Street.

This section of the city was old with crooked streets and wonky intersections already clogged with evening traffic and pedestrians, not to mention piles of dirty snow left over from a series of blizzards that had buried the city only a month ago. But there was no missing the police cruiser parked outside the landmark Old State House, and Walters eased the ambulance up behind it.

They grabbed the jump bag and gurney from the back cabin before Gus led the way over to a knot of onlookers who'd gathered.

"Hi, folks, Boston EMS," he said. "Can we get in here, please?"

People peeled out of the way until it was just a young man on the ground and a cop squatted beside him. Officer Don DiChico, a grizzled veteran Gus knew well, looked up at Gus's and Walters' approach.

Gus exchanged a nod with him. "How we doin', Don?"

"Gus, this is Adrian." DiChico straightened up. "Says he got jumped by some other kids coming off the train. He's got a goose egg on the right temple and some scrapes, and he says he's not feeling too hot between the headache and dizziness. He doesn't think he lost consciousness."

Gus took a knee beside his patient on one side, Walters the other. Adrian was a good-looking guy with medium-brown skin and curly hair, and he appeared younger than dispatch had reported, probably only in his late teens. The abrasions along his right cheekbone and outer edge of his eye were clearly fresh, and the bump on his temple bloody.

"Hey, Adrian." Gus kept his tone easy. "I'm Gus and I'm an EMT, and this is my partner, Walt."

Walters cocked his ridiculous eyebrow again. "It's Madoc," he said, frowning slightly at Gus's shrug.

Sorry, not sorry.

"Can you tell us where you're hurting, Adrian?" Gus asked.

Adrian eyed him warily, knees hugged to his chest. "My head aches like hell."

"Okay. You just chill and we'll take care of you." Gus caught Walters' eye. Time to figure out how well this guy knew his stuff.

They checked Adrian's pulse and pupils while Gus asked him questions, and though the kid responded readily, his gaze stayed down and he tensed up whenever Walters touched him or the police officers got close.

Gus frowned to himself. Maybe Adrian didn't like uniforms. Specifically, being surrounded by white guys in uniform. Especially a dude as big as Walters, whose biceps bulged under his jacket as he worked and—

Focus, Dawson.

"You're not in trouble, Adrian." Gus kept his voice low. "We just want to make sure you're all right."

"I know." Adrian let go of his knees and sat cross-legged, hands in his lap, and that was when Gus spotted the Pride pins on his jacket.

Setting his right hand over Adrian's, Gus made sure the braided leather cord he wore on his wrist was visible, its rainbow-striped clasp facing up.

"We're here to help," he said. "The officers, Walt, and me."

Adrian exhaled slowly through his nose. "I know," he said again, but this time he didn't look away. "Thanks."

"Of course. Let's get you up." Gus patted Adrian's hand. "You ever been on an ambulance before?"

"No." A doubtful sound came out of Adrian. "Head feels swimmy, y'know? So, if I puke on you, you can't be mad."

Gus chuckled. "How about you vom on my partner and not me, since I'm wearing new boots?"

That earned him a glare from Walters, but the moment felt lighter as they eased Adrian to his feet. Until Walters moved to grab the gurney and the color fled from Adrian's face.

Gus had just enough time to brace himself before Adrian bent over and emptied his stomach onto Gus's feet.

FUCK THIS FUCKING DAY.

Madoc stepped back, his own stomach churning as Adrian vomited. Hearing people heave always made him want to puke too, despite his years on the job.

Adrian let out a pitiful groan. "Oh, shit."

"Nah, that's barf, dude," Gus teased gently. "Ooh, you got me good."

"I'm so sorry."

"It's okay, hon. Just hang on to me while Walt grabs the gurney." Gus snapped his gaze to Madoc's and Madoc got his ass in gear.

His new partner was *very* different from Billy Lord, who'd carried a steady, low-energy vibe that paled against the charisma practically crackling off Gus Dawson. On paper, the dude had far less experience than Madoc, but he clearly knew his medicine and was incredibly composed, seeming unbothered as he managed the heavy jump bag and a patient several inches taller than himself, all while wearing puke on his boots.

"Don't be upset," Gus said to Adrian, his voice soothing as the cops and Madoc helped him get Adrian settled on the gurney. "I've been barfed on plenty and I'm sure Walt has too. All you need to do is chill while we take care of you and talk to Officer DiChico about how you got hurt. You think you can do that?"

Adrian nodded. He was crying now, fat, silent tears rolling down his cheeks as the gurney was loaded into the truck. His hand shook when he accepted a wad of tissues from Madoc, but he seemed more trusting of Officer DiChico who asked Adrian to walk him through what had happened.

With their patient distracted, Gus turned his attention to Madoc. "What are you thinking?" he asked.

"I wouldn't say he's altered, but the memory loss is concerning." Madoc watched Adrian for a couple of beats. "Add in the vomiting and vertigo, and I'd say concussion."

Gus nodded. "Same. Let's get him to Mass General for an eval. You drive."

For a second, Madoc wanted to balk at Gus taking point without any discussion. He'd treated concussions dozens of times over the course of his career and he could do it again now. But one look at Adrian's tearstained face and the way he was hanging on to Gus's hand kept Madoc quiet. Adrian obviously trusted Gus, and Madoc was not going to put his ego in the way of what his patient needed. *Especially* after already letting his big mouth get away from him.

Heat flashed across Madoc's cheeks. He'd known Gus had been teasing when he'd called Madoc a rook and a probie—the smile in his eyes had been visible across the truck's cab. But Madoc *hated* having to repeat his probationary year when he was already an excellent EMT, and he'd let Gus's snarking burrow its way under his skin.

"They were calling me a fag, said I was polluting their air," Adrian muttered. "Then I was on the ground and people were asking me if I was okay."

DiChico nodded. "I'm real sorry that happened, Adrian—the kids who jumped you are shitballs. I'm going to give your name to the Civil Rights Unit, and they'll send a detective who'll talk to you and start an investigation."

"M'kay." Biting his lip, Adrian looked back to Gus. "Am I going to be all right?"

Gus gave Adrian's arm a gentle squeeze. "Yes, you are."

He kept up the easy patter during the ride, soothing Adrian's nerves while Madoc did his best to keep the trip smooth.

"They were calling me a fag. Said I was polluting their air."

Madoc checked the screen on the dash that displayed the surveillance feed from the patient cabin. "How we doing?" he called, loud enough to be heard through the small window behind him that connected the truck's cab to the back.

"Our boy's hanging in there," Gus called back. "Said you have pretty eyes."

"Dude." Adrian groaned. "Why you running your mouth?"

Gus laughed. "Because that's what I do, hon. This is Walt's first shift working with me, you know."

Madoc snorted. "My name isn't Walt."

"Yes, it is!"

"Ass."

Still, Madoc was smiling as he guided the truck onto the MGH campus. Until he caught himself thinking that Gus was the one with pretty eyes.

Oh shit, that isn't good.

Madoc had been attracted to women since his early teens and genuinely liked everything about them. But every once in a while, a guy would pique an interest in Madoc that he didn't truly understand. He'd find himself considering the guy, even admiring him. A muscled forearm beneath a rolled-up shirt sleeve. Strong, blunt-fingered hands. Broad shoulders or a devil-may-care smile. Eyes shaded rich brown and lit with gold that crinkled a little at the corners the way Gus's did when he grinned big.

Madoc stifled a grunt. Why did his brain do this to him? And with his new supervisor too, which was just adding a whole different level of problem.

The ED's managing nurse, Lashawn, waved them toward the back left side of the massive triage space that made up a large portion of the floor.

"Hey, y'all—we're going to put you in bay three." She looked toward the nurses' station next and hailed a dark-haired nurse Madoc recognized. "Mark, you're with Dr. Thomason."

Nurse Mark fell in beside Gus at the back end of the survey and the two exchanged a quick smile before Mark turned to Adrian.

"Hey, Adrian, my name is Mark," he said. "You just hang in there and we're going to have you feeling better in no time."

A slim doctor wearing navy scrubs and a stethoscope jogged up as they entered the treatment bay and a whirlwind of activity commenced, the team transferring Adrian onto the bed, bodies swarming in a practiced dance. The doc re-checked Adrian's vitals, then ordered fluids and pain relief before promising he'd be back soon to check in. He'd slipped back out past the privacy curtain when Adrian reached out to Gus.

"Can you stay?" Adrian murmured. "Don't want to be here by myself."

Gus took Adrian's hand. "I've got to get back out there, hon. But you're not by yourself—Mark and the doc will take care of you." He nodded at the Pride pins on Adrian's jacket. "You're in good hands with them until your bro can get here, I promise.

"Also-o-o," he drew out the word teasingly, gaze sliding over to Mark. "Mark knows where all the best food in this place can be found because he's worked here forever. So, if you get hungry, just say the word and he'll work his magic."

"I am fairly magical." Mark patted Adrian's shoulder before he looked at Madoc. "It's Madoc, right?" he asked.

"Yeah, hi," Madoc said. "I'm Gus's new partner."

"Well, good for Gus." Mark's sly expression had Gus rolling his eyes.

"Down, boy," he chided. "Walt's got a wife."

Mark sighed. "Such a pity for our people, Super Gus. Though probably a blessing for you." He cocked an eyebrow. "You're not allowed back in here until those smelly boots are clean, by the way—I don't care how stupid hot your partner is."

Wish I'd stayed out in the truck.

Cheeks warm, Madoc walked off, aware of Gus scolding Mark though he sounded more amused than irritated. And whatever, Madoc didn't need to be bros with a new partner he didn't plan to work with for very long anyway.

Except ... he wished he'd corrected Gus about the whole being married thing, rather than ignoring what now felt like a giant-ass elephant in the very small truck.

"Grabbed a few things we always run low on," Gus called as he approached the truck's back bumper. "Just give me a minute to get the barf off my boots and I'll put it away."

Remorse itched at the back of Madoc's neck. "I can do it, no problem," he said, pausing in his efforts to clean the cabin floor. "I'm sorry about the puke, by the way. I should've seen that coming."

"Eh, no worries." Gus set an armful of supplies down, then bent to untie his boots. "It wouldn't be a day ending in 'y' if we didn't get splashed with bodily fluids at some point."

Madoc smiled wryly. Good to know his new partner wasn't the type to get petty over a little vomit. And Gus'd been so good with Adrian, reaching past the kid's distress with kind words and a turn of his wrist to show off his Pride colors. Connecting with the same easy candor he was showing Madoc now. Communicating instead of just talking.

Straightening up, Madoc carried the mop back to the closet. "Do you think Adrian was afraid of me?" he asked. "I caught him flinching and wasn't sure how to take it."

Gus had taken a seat on the bumper and shot a somber look at Madoc over his shoulder. "You're a big dude and that might have been a factor, but I doubt it was the only one at play. Being queer can make everyday life tough for guys like Adrian and me, even in places that are supposed to be liberal and open. You learn to keep your guard up and it's not always easy to know who you can trust."

"I hate that," Madoc said. "It bothers me knowing patients are sometimes afraid of the people who show up to help them."

"Agreed," Gus replied as he wiped down a boot. "But not everybody's reality works the same way. And let's not forget the kid had a head injury so he wasn't himself regardless."

After stowing away the supplies Gus had brought back, Madoc exited through the rear doors, skipping the bumper and jumping straight to the ground. Madoc automatically glanced down as he moved though, and that was when he noticed Gus's socks didn't match.

The left sock was a standard issue black number that covered Gus's ankle and disappeared beneath the hem of his dark brown cargos. Gus's right sock was short, however, stopping just below his ankle which ... wasn't an ankle. Or not one made of flesh and bone anyway but instead fashioned in matte black metal that shone softly under the remains of the day's light.

That's a prosthesis.

The thought went off in Madoc's brain like a lit match thrown into a box of fireworks. And when he met Gus's level stare, words tumbled out of his mouth before his brain could catch up.

"Jesus, man. Were you going to tell me?"

TWO

"WERE YOU GOING TO TELL ME?"

Scorn licked along Gus's insides as he watched his new partner work very, very hard to maintain eye contact. He hated these moments and the comments they often brought out of people when they got a look at Gus's prosthesis for the first time.

"What the heck happened to you?"

"Damn, bro, you're inspiring!"

"I would delete myself if that happened to me."

People made snap assumptions about amputees. Decided without even speaking to him that Gus was lesser or broken or deserved a gold star for not giving up on life because he was missing a part of his body.

"I lost it to a shark," Gus said to Walters, voice dry as fresh gauze. "Ran into a Great White while I was surfing out on the Cape."

Walters goggled at him. "A *shark*? Seriously?"

"No."

Those pretty blue eyes turned hard in a flash. "What the hell, man?"

Gus shook his head. He was used to people being weird about his leg. Most had little experience with amputees in their day-to-day and carried notions about mobility and quality of life that had them convinced Gus couldn't be physical—vital—while also missing a limb.

But Gus *had* expected more from Walters. The guy was a health professional for fuck's sake and had no business shoving his discomfort back onto Gus.

"Do you do this with your amputee patients?" Gus asked. "Make them feel shitty for having lost limbs?"

The color drained from Walters' face. "No. I would never talk to a patient like—"

"So, just to me then—that's nice." Gus went back to wiping his boot. "I'd have told you about my leg when I felt like it. Because that is my right and you being uncomfortable with my body is *your* problem not mine."

"You're right." Walters had a hand in his hair when Gus glanced up. "I'm sorry."

Gus eyed him narrowly. "For being an ass or because I called you out?"

"The first one. I've never worked with someone who uses a prosthesis before and my ... my mouth got ahead of my brain."

Gus stuck the soiled wipe into the waste bag and grabbed another. "I get the feeling that's a thing with you, huh?"

He didn't care that he sounded salty. Gus did *not* want to be having this conversation right now or a partner who was prone to dumbassery, and if he wanted to die mad about it, he would.

Walters surprised Gus by nodding. "It can be. Sometimes when I'm nervous I start blabbering, and I'm definitely nervous tonight because I need this partnership to work."

The admission coupled with Walters' red face loosened the knot in Gus's chest slightly. It wasn't an apology, but it was an honest answer and Gus appreciated the candor.

Gus gestured toward his right leg. "I'm BTK at the midway point on the tibia," he said, knowing Walters would understand Gus meant his amputation had been done 'below-the-knee' and about halfway up his shin. "I wear a prosthesis on duty so I can drive and handle anything this job throws at us. Yes, I live with a disability, but it doesn't get in the way of me being me."

In truth, Gus'd put in hundreds of hours re-learning how to move and function with his prosthesis and adjusting his gait so he could walk without limping. But he didn't want or need praise for passing as 'normal' or succeeding at just living his life, so he didn't bother explaining any of that to Walters.

"I've been lucky making my prosthetics work," Gus said instead. "I can play sports and do my job, and when I'm promoted to paramedic, I'll be the first amputee to wear that badge for Boston EMS."

Walters blinked once, then nodded. "I didn't know you were looking to move up to an ALS truck."

"I've got my certs and finished my field training. Just waiting for a spot on P1 to open up."

Gus left it at that. By now, Walters would know the ins and outs of becoming a paramedic for Boston EMS; that positions opened up rarely and required months of classroom work, hospital rotations, and shadowing other paramedics. Getting it all done around regular shifts on duty and life was always challenging, but if an EMT wanted to ride an Advanced Life Support truck like P1, you did the work and hoped a slot came along sooner rather than later.

Gus'd dropped his boots to the ground and was disinfecting his hands when their radios beeped again.

"A1, what's your twenty?"

Walters thumbed the talk switch on his unit. "A1 at MGH," he replied to the dispatcher. "You can show us as clear."

"Copy. We have a possible eye injury at 26 Kingston Street. Female, twenty-three years of age, struck in the face by a glitter bomb. 16-A-1, moderate vision loss due to particulate. Subject is conscious and responsive, Code Two with lights only."

They went to the cab, Walters behind the wheel again to give Gus time to get the right boot back on over his foot, but Gus noticed his partner was frowning. "What?"

"Is a glitter bomb what it sounds like?"

"Yup. That address on Kingston Street is Mister Moves, a male burlesque club where glitter bombs are a thing." Gus smirked at Walters' headshake. "I'm thinking it's bachelorettes pre-gaming the show since it's still early. Anyway, I'll take point and—"

Walters put a hand on Gus's arm. "Hey, I can handle it. I promise you that I am good at my job."

Acutely aware of the palm pressing heat through his uniform's sleeve, Gus quirked a smile. "Okay. I still say it's safer for me to take point."

Walters dropped his hand. "Gus."

"Walters." Gus parroted his partner's warning tone and basked in the withering expression it earned him.

"Knock it off. What do you mean by safer?" Walters pressed. "Do we need cops for backup?"

"Jesus Murphy, no." Gus laughed. "The last thing we need are more uniforms. Just follow my lead and we will be fine."

Walters hit the ignition but not before glowering at Gus in a way that had the back of Gus's neck heating.

Fuck, angry Walters is sexy.

"I need to know what we're walking into here, Gus."

Walters said. "I have a daughter to get home to, and I need to know if I'm going to be safe."

Gus's heart gave a strange little jerk. "I would never knowingly put you in harm's way," he said. "As for what we're about to walk into, let's just say the glitter-bomb crowd isn't dangerous but it's possible they'll think we're part of the show."

Walters' mouth opened and closed again. "But why?"

"Well, you're stupid hot, just like Mark said, while I am a fucking delight," Gus said, "and we're dressed in first-responder uniforms. If we have a cop with us, those women will eat us alive in the nicest way possible."

"What is my life?" Walters muttered, cheeks fiery as he steered the truck onto Cambridge Street.

The scene was indeed a bachelorette party tucked away in a private room at Mister Moves. The place was festooned with pink and silver balloons and streamers and the crowd of young women who descended on Gus and Walters was delighted to find men in uniform in their midst before a bouncer gently herded the partygoers toward the bar.

Their patient, Gabby, was seated at the back of the room and *coated* with pink and silver bits. The shit was in her ear and nasal canals for God's sake, though the skin around the eye sockets was cleaner than Gus had expected.

"How you doin', Miss Gabby?" he asked. "And what happened here?"

"I don't even know," she grumbled. "I was just setting up the party favors and boom, glitter got everywhere!"

"Is the blood on the tissue in your hand from your nose?"

"Yeah. I wear glasses." Gabby waved glitter-encrusted frames in the air. "They smacked into my nose, and it hurt like a motherfucker."

"The glasses did a good job of shielding your eyes." Gus pressed his fingertips lightly against the sides of Gabby's nasal bridge. "Nothing feels broken, but how's your pain on a scale of one to ten?"

"I've been drinking since noon so I'm going with a fairly medicated three."

"That's ... cool, I guess." Gus exchanged an amused glance with Walters, then froze when Gabby leaned over and slipped her arms around Gus's neck.

"Your voice is *sexy*," she said, "and wow, you smell really nice! Just don't make me go to the hospital, okay? This is my best girl's party and I don't want to miss it."

Walters hollowed his cheeks, doing his best not to crack up, but then a blonde sporting a tiara with '*Same Penis Forever*' spelled out in rhinestones across its front dashed over and he legit snorted.

"Is she okay?" the blonde asked, voice pitched loud over the music and chatter of partygoers.

"I'm fine, Ash," Gabby said against Gus's neck. "These nice boys are taking good care of me."

Gus eased Gabby back into her seat, but as he and Walters used saline and gauze pads to wipe off the glitter, the party-goers at the bar got progressively louder.

"Atta girl, Gabs!" one of the girls shouted. "You already got two guys on their knees!"

"Threesome!" another bellowed nonsensically, the rest quickly taking up the chant, hooting and hollering while Ash and Gabby shushed them through their own cackling.

Laughing themselves, Gus and Walters sat back on their heels.

"All right, Miss Gabby," Walters said. "Let's see those peepers."

Her damp lashes fluttered a few times before Gabby opened her eyes and broke out in a huge smile.

"Guy-y-y-s!" she exclaimed, trying to hug both Gus and Walters at the same time. "Thank you for freeing my eyeballs!"

Gus barked a laugh. "How do you feel, girl?"

"I feel amazing!" she exclaimed, dark eyes only a little bit reddened as she planted a kiss on his cheek. "And so ready for drinks!"

"BRUH, you've got glitter in your hair."

"And you have a fork in your butt, so quit judging."

Gus leveled a look at their patient, Perry, who did indeed have an actual utensil sticking out of his left buttock, and the two shared a chuckle that had Madoc smiling too.

Over the course of this wildly uneven night, he'd come to understand his new partner delighted in being a pain in the ass. Luckily, Gus was also a baller on the job and great with his patients, unfailingly kind in the face of hysteria, incoherence, and abuse as he provided top-notch care. Gus also seemed to have only one mode, *On*, which kept him in near-constant motion and made it easy for Madoc to forget his new partner was missing part of his leg.

Something he was happy to do if it meant *never* thinking about how badly he'd bungled the discovery of Gus's prosthetic.

"How'd you fall into the dishwasher?" Madoc asked Perry.

"Tripped." Perry hissed as Madoc and Gus eased him onto the gurney. "Tried to catch myself on the way down but everything went to hell and man, my landlord's gonna be pissed."

"Can't you just pull the fork out of his bum?" That was Perry's girlfriend, an attractive young woman named Nora.

"Unfortunately, no," Gus replied. He and Madoc had arranged Perry on his right side and were busy securing him with the gurney's straps. "There are arteries in the buttocks connected to the main blood supply in the body and even slight damage can be dangerous."

"Ooh, drama."

Madoc wondered at the girl's odd tone. Granted, a fork in the butt was rather comical, but her apparent disinterest after what Gus'd just said struck him as odd. And then Nora was *right there* at Madoc's side, standing just slightly too close.

"Where are we taking him?" she asked.

We?

"You don't need to come," Perry said before Madoc could answer. "I doubt it'll take long."

Nora scoffed. "Please. You know this'll take ages. I'll go grab my shoes."

She was undoubtedly right. Even at this late hour, Perry was looking at a couple of hours in an ED, whether he ended up needing a bandage and tetanus booster or more intensive care. But then Madoc saw Perry's knuckles go white around his phone and an alert went off in his brain.

"You can't ride with us." Madoc put a sheepish expression on for Nora. "Only immediate family are allowed in the ambulance."

"Oh, yeah?" Expression arch, Nora looked at Gus. "Since when?"

Gus was looking at Madoc though, and Madoc looked right back. A friend or family member was always welcome to ride along, provided the patient wanted them. *This* friend gave Madoc a weird vibe, however, and he didn't want her near Perry.

Trust me, he tried to tell Gus with his eyes. *Trust me to know my patient.*

Gus's expression shifted subtly, and he gave Nora a small

smile. "It's a new policy," he said. "Non-family members aren't allowed in the trucks anymore."

For a second, Nora's expression faltered. But then she smiled, and unease prickled up the back of Madoc's neck.

"Pretend I'm his sister," Nora said. "It's not like anyone's going to ask."

"Maybe not, but I don't mess around when it comes to patient care." Gus'd stopped smiling and now turned to Perry. "Where's your wallet, buddy? Let's grab it on the way out."

Perry blinked. "Um. My backpack's on the bench by the door."

"I'll bring it," Nora began, but fell silent again at Gus's quelling look.

"You can't ride with us, ma'am," Gus said, tugging the gurney and Perry toward the exit. "You're free to follow however you want to get there, of course."

His cool tone—the 'ma'am' Gus'd used instead of a more playful 'hon' or 'Miss Nora'—sucked the air out of the room. And when Madoc glanced down at Perry, his patient's body was rigid, almost like he was holding his breath.

"What do you think the police would say about this?" Nora asked, her tone very casual. She'd folded her arms over her chest though, and her mouth was a straight, tight line. "I mean, EMTs aren't allowed to turn people away, are they?"

Gus stopped the gurney just inside the door, and now he looked almost puzzled. "We're not turning our patient away, ma'am. If you're also injured, I'll get dispatch to send another ambulance ASAP." He set his hand on his radio. "Or ask for Boston PD and you could talk to them now."

Madoc bit back a smirk. Nora could complain to whomever she wanted about not being allowed to ride, but the cops always had the ambulance crews' backs and not one of them was going to argue with Gus or Madoc over how they chose to manage their truck.

"I'm good," she said airily, though her face grew pinched when Gus bent to grab Perry's backpack. "You still haven't said where you're taking him."

Madoc waited until they were out in the hall before answering. "We need to assess Perry's wound," he said, "and then we'll make a decision."

Silence followed them down the hall though Madoc felt Nora's gaze on the nape of his neck all the way to the elevator. He didn't glance back, knowing Gus had his six, eyes flicking every so often over Madoc's shoulder to where Madoc knew Nora still stood.

Once aboard the truck, they locked themselves in the patient cabin, then got to work cutting away Perry's pants and underwear so they could swaddle his lower half with a blanket.

"Do you or Nora own any firearms, Perry?" Gus asked. "You're not in trouble, but I need to make sure you and my partner are safe."

"We don't have any guns." Perry's voice sounded distant. "Did you grab my bag?"

"Yup." Stepping forward, Gus picked the navy backpack up from where he'd set it on the captain's chair, then startled the shit out of Madoc by pulling a pair of running shoes out of it. "Scooped these up on the way out." He set everything down on the gurney beside Perry. "You don't want to be walking around in socks once you're released."

Perry pressed his lips thin.

"What happened tonight, Perry?" Madoc asked gently. "Did she hurt you?"

"Sorta." Eyes squishing closed, Perry dropped his head onto the gurney. "I did fall into the dishwasher. But only because we were arguing and she pushed me."

Disgust left a bitter taste in Madoc's mouth. He treated victims of domestic abuse far too often in his line of work, and his heart went out to every one of them.

"I'm sorry to hear that," he said, giving Perry's shoulder a squeeze. "Has she hurt you before?"

"Yeah, but not like this."

Settling himself on the bench by the gurney's left side, Madoc studied his patient. He hated the defeat he glimpsed on Perry's face. Knew Perry was battling a very specific kind of shame because his abuser was a petite female who looked perfectly harmless while Perry himself was taller and stronger. So, Madoc kept his voice gentle, knowing Perry badly needed to feel safe and heard and absolutely not judged.

"Nora shouldn't be hurting you ever, Perry," Madoc said. "You understand what I'm saying?"

Perry's nod was jerky. "I just ... I don't know how it started."

"I hear you," Madoc said. "And it's not your fault that it did."

He talked a little about domestic abuse resources while he and Gus checked Perry out, but it was only when Gus radioed back to dispatch for police backup that Perry shook off some of his daze.

"What's going on?" he asked, looking from Gus to Madoc. "Why is he calling the cops?"

"In case Nora or someone else followed us outside," Madoc replied simply. "We won't know until Gus opens the doors and steps out, and he just wants to make sure we're all safe."

Glancing at Gus, Madoc spotted the glitter shining among the strands of his brown hair. They'd been finding pieces of the stuff all night on their clothes and skin, but damned if it didn't suit Gus somehow. The straight slope of his nose, which was strong without being harsh. His lips, pursed as he listened to the dispatcher, so different from his wide smiles because Gus was one of those generically good-looking guys whose face was absolutely transformed by emotion.

Madoc's asshole brain shouldn't have noticed any of that of course, so he shoved it all aside and put his focus on helping his patient.

He felt kind of buzzed as he sat on the truck's back bumper outside Mass General after the transport though, his gaze on the still-dark sky and his breaths turning to smoke in the chilly air. Madoc had made it through his first shift riding A1 with no patients dying, and that was a win in his book.

Gus strolled up, holding a tray with their travel mugs in one hand and a brown paper bag in the other.

"Got you some go-juice," Gus said, bending slightly at the waist to get the tray in front of Madoc. "Didn't know how you take it, so I picked up creamer and sweetener and stuff."

"Thank you." Sighing, Madoc took his mug and some plastic creamer cups from the tray. "I need this after that mess of a call."

"Dude, I know." Gus settled himself on the bumper too. "I got a strange vibe from the girlfriend straight away, but what tipped you off?"

"Their body language. She got too close to me at one point and Perry kind of froze. And when you said she couldn't ride with us ..." Madoc shook his head. "Her expression was weird."

Gus hummed. "That was good work back there," he said. "Your instincts were great, and you handled a strange situation very well."

"Thanks." Madoc turned to doctoring his cup of coffee with creamer. "Listen, I want to apologize for my earlier terrible attitude. I know you know Billy Lord was my last partner, and we did okay working together. But he treated me like I didn't have years on the job, and it got to me, maybe more than

I realized." He looked back up at Gus. "I'm a great EMT, Gus, and I don't need to be handheld, you know?"

"I do. Billy's old-school in ways true rookies need him to be, but I get that you're different." Gus tipped his head left to right, expression considering. "I'll give you space when I can," he said at last, "but you're still a recruit and I'll be your supervisor for the next four months. There may be times I override you and maybe you're not going to like that. Just understand that it'll never be personal."

"Good to know," Madoc said without hesitating.

He couldn't argue Gus's point when, fair or not, Gus was senior to him and that was simply all there was to it. Besides, Madoc had more apologizing to do if he wanted to get a decent evaluation out of this partnership.

"I'm also sorry I was weird about your prosthesis," he said, his face heating again. "I was caught off guard and—"

"—your mouth got away from you. I get it." Gus regarded his cup for a beat, frowning softly. "It was never going to be a simple thing to tell or show you, Walters, no matter what. But now you know, and you can decide how you feel about it going forward."

Madoc frowned too, unsure what to make of Gus's words. What was there for him to decide about Gus's prosthesis? The dude was an amputee, and it wasn't like he had any choice about using one. Right?

"Will you tell me if I say the wrong thing?" he asked. "I don't *want* to mess up with you and I know it's not your job to educate me about your life, but I probably will say stupid stuff because I don't know what I don't know."

"That's ... very honest of you to admit," Gus said. "And I get what you mean. So yeah, I'll tell you if something you ask or say comes off as not cool."

Smiling slightly, he dangled the brown paper bag he'd

brought out with him between Madoc and himself. "I brought you a peace offering in *bolos*."

"In what now?"

"Portuguese muffins, also known as *bolos levedos*. Trust me, they'll change your life. Take them home to your fam," Gus said. "All the kids I know love *bolos*, especially if butter and jam are involved."

That was thoughtful.

Bemused, Madoc accepted the bag. "Thank you. I'm making breakfast for Val this morning and these will be fun to try. You sure you don't want to keep some for yourself?"

"I ate two while I was waiting to pay," Gus said with a chuckle. "I'm slutty for baked things, bread and cake in particular."

He walked off, moving at a more relaxed pace than he had all night. And boom, Madoc was aware of Gus's leg and prosthesis again, a host of questions he'd never had about a partner hitting him all at once.

Did the remaining part of Gus's limb cause him pain? How long did he wear his prosthetic every day? Did he switch out the style of foot depending on his activity? How had he gotten so good at walking and working with it?

"Yo! Ground Control to Walters, come in, Walters!" Gus called back. "You ready to ride?"

"Yup!" Standing, Madoc jogged around to the passenger side and popped open the door. "Sorry, just got a lot on my mind."

Gus started the truck with a smirk. "Do your thinking later, guy. We still need to hose this beast down and vacuum up ninety-five thousand pieces of glitter."

THREE

THE LOFT WAS silent when Madoc let himself in at just past 6:00 A.M., but he'd only just hung his jacket on a hook by the door when the light thud-thud-thud of small feet reached his ears. Turning, he caught sight of Valerie clad in pajamas and a sparkly purple tutu that bounced as she ran, her dark curls coming loose from the braid she wore down her back.

Crouching slightly, Madoc opened his arms and grinned as his girl flung herself at him. His fatigue from the long overnight shift disappeared, replaced with joy as he swung her up in his arms.

"Welcome home, Daddy!"

Chuckling, Madoc cuddled Valerie close. "Thank you, my honey," he replied. "Did you have a nice sleep?"

"Yup." Valerie settled her cheek on his shoulder. "How was your work? Did you meet your new partner?"

"Work was good and yes, I met my new partner. His name is Gus, remember?"

"Uh-huh. Is Gus nice?"

"He's super friendly and knows a ton of stuff," Madoc replied. He headed into the loft, unsurprised when Valerie kept her head down. She loved to sleep and rarely got up before her alarm unless it was to greet her dad. "Gus also keeps a kitty at the station and her name is Princess Lemonade."

"No way!"

"I swear, it's true. I'll take a picture of the kitty when I go in tonight."

Madoc deposited his bag and his daughter on the kitchen counter. Just thinking about Gus—all dark eyes and expressive face, a smile in his voice when he tossed out those damned nick-names—had the back of his neck going hot. But Valerie wanted to tell Madoc all about her night and that was a terrific distraction.

"Kenny Baker and Lucie came over an' we played cards and the Poop Bingo game with Uncle T," she said. "And after they had to go home for dinner, Uncle T and me cooked veggie sausage and rice and we saved you some!"

"Thank you for thinking of me. Did your mom eat with you?"

Valerie shook her head. "She went out. How come you're shiny?" she asked, one hand coming up to pat Madoc's hair.

"Shiny?" *Oh.* The glitter. "Well, there was an incident." Madoc waggled his eyebrows. "And it involved every piece of glitter in the city."

He launched into a sanitized tale about Glitter Bomb Gabby, omitting the booze and raunchy bachelorettes, and Valerie took it all in, her expression rapt. Madoc had just handed her a pony mug of hot chocolate when she spied the brown paper bakery bag sticking out of the top of his backpack.

"What's that?" she asked.

"That's from Gus." Madoc plucked the bag up and handed

it to her. "He sent you some *bolos levedos,* also known as super-tasty Portuguese muffins."

"Ah!" Peering into the bag, Valerie smiled. "They're breads," she mused, "and they smell yummy! But, Daddy? What is a Pork-a-cheese muffin?"

As predicted, she went wild for the *bolos,* which were wonderfully fluffy and delicious with just about anything: butter and guava jelly, sliced fruit and cheese, even leftover sausage and rice.

"Yum," Valerie mumbled around another mouthful. "I love this a lot."

Her uncle Tarek emerged from his room then, and though he fixed himself his usual green juice smoothie, he too failed to resist the siren call of fresh bread and took up where Valerie left off when she headed to her room to get changed for hockey practice.

"I hate that you brought these into my life." Tarek glared at the half-eaten muffin in his hand. "Are they really from a hospital bakery?"

"Yup. My partner picked them up for Val."

"And this new partner is cool?"

Madoc nodded. "He knows his stuff and seems extremely smart. Great with the patients. He's got fewer years on the job than me which I don't love, but I'm sure I'll get over it."

"If you say so," Tarek said around another mouthful of bread. "Anything else?"

"Not sure what you mean."

"Well, what's he like? Married with kids? Born and raised here or a transplant like you? What'd he do before he was an EMT?" Sitting back in his seat, Tarek leveled a knowing look at Madoc. "Most critically, is he a hockey guy or one of those nerds who watch baseball?"

"Well, I know he used to be a firefighter, but we didn't get into sports or anything like that," Madoc replied. "Gus and I were out the door two minutes after meeting and stayed busy all night. Like, eating dinner in the truck on the way to a shooting kind of busy. Not a ton of time for small talk, you know?"

Except that wasn't strictly true. Gus'd come out as a gay man and amputee within the first hour of their shift, talking about both with a grace Madoc could hardly fathom. Meanwhile, Madoc had talked a little about Valerie and complained about Billy Lord, then acted like a jackass over Gus's prosthetic because he sucked at life.

The smile he gave Tarek felt more like a grimace. "How'd it go here last night?" he asked.

"Smooth as butter. Noels had a client dinner and then a thing at the casino over in Everett, so it was just me and Val."

"I hate that she spends time there."

"I know." Tarek rubbed a hand over his dark auburn hair. "But she was home before 2:00 A.M. and she's an adult."

"An adult with a gambling problem who blew all our money at casinos."

"I *know*, Madoc."

Guilt prickled through Madoc at the bite in Tarek's tone but damn it, sometimes the guy acted like Madoc had moved his family across the country just for the hell of it.

Tarek sighed. "Look, I get that you have concerns and they are totally valid," he said more gently. "But Noels has been in recovery for over a year, and we can't watch her every second. You wouldn't want to if you took the time to make some friends."

"Rude." Madoc made a face. "You know I have friends."

"Val and I don't count and neither do co-workers you don't see off duty." Tarek smiled. "I understand that you need to be here for Val, but you should also have stuff going on in your life that isn't about work or childcare. Get out there and be social, man."

Madoc poked at the remains of his breakfast. He knew Tarek genuinely wanted to help. But Tarek was also likely looking for something or someone to focus on that would distract him from his own troubles, namely losing the two loves of his life, ice hockey and Tim Slattery.

Hockey fans understood the game had been important to Tarek McKenna; he'd made the game his life since he could walk. But no one apart from Noelene and Madoc knew Tarek had felt the same level of passion toward his teammate and friend Tim, or that Tim's untimely death two years ago had shattered Tarek's carefully controlled and closeted world.

Madoc felt for his friend, who was still nursing a broken heart in secret. But he wasn't about to offer his own personal life up as some kind of diversion.

"I don't have a ton of bandwidth to be social," Madoc said. "Moving out here meant restarting everything and I barely have time to breathe between the job and Val and the field work I need to complete. Honestly, I don't mind having all that to focus on, because God knows, I'm not ready for dating. But, if it makes you happy to know that I'll work on the making friends part, I promise I will."

Tarek shook his head. "Work on making *yourself* happy, doofus, and I'll be satisfied. Now can you please grab your kid so I can run drills with her?"

Madoc went to the room Tarek had set up for Valerie and found her by the closet, dressed in her hockey shirt and underwear with a bright purple Converse sneaker clutched in each hand and the tutu puddled on the floor.

"Are we not wearing pants today?" Madoc asked, nodding toward her bare legs.

Smiling, Valerie shook her head at him. "Of course, I'm

gonna wear pants—don't want my bum to freeze when I go to skate, Daddy! But I have to find my ladybug track suit first."

Ah.

After the tutu, a navy velour tracksuit embroidered with ladybugs was Valerie's favorite thing to wear. Madoc had put it in a basket of clothes that needed washing before he'd left for work the night before, however, and knew his daughter's search would be in vain.

"It's in the laundry back at our place," he said, going to the closet and pulling a pair of hockey pants off a low shelf. "But I promise I will wash it while you are at practice so you can wear it when you get back."

Valerie made duck lips with her mouth, but took the pants Madoc offered her. "M'kay," she said. "Can you braid my hair? And remind me to tell you later I love you?"

Madoc gave her a smile. "I can do both of those things. And tell you I love you lots right now."

"I love you lots too, Daddy."

They got Valerie into her hockey pants and her hair braided, but as they trooped back to the kitchen, they ignored the closed door across the hall. That was Noelene's domain, a space Madoc hadn't stepped inside since he'd moved his stuff and the bulk of Valerie's into a two-bedroom unit located three floors down from the loft.

GUS EASED his prosthesis off with a grunt. Using it was like wearing a tightly laced shoe that started midway down his right shin, and taking it off always felt strange at first, the sensation of his short limb being 'freed' intense to the point of pain. The prosthesis made Gus exquisitely aware of how his stump was responding to any number of factors, too: weather and air pressures, the layers he wore to pad his skin—even the time of day and his diet affected his level of comfort.

"Hey, rock star." Connor strolled in, long blond hair free from the tactical braid he wore while on duty and flowing halfway down his back. He sank into the seat beside Gus. "How you doin'?"

"Doin' fine," Gus replied. "Just gearing up for some laundry. Did I thank you already for loaning me your washer?"

Connor shrugged. "You know the invitation is always open."

They'd eaten breakfast after shift with the crews who worked the downtown neighborhoods, then come back to Connor's North End apartment so Gus could skip the drive out to Hyde Park.

"Hey, did you invite Walters to breakfast?" Connor asked. "I was hoping he'd be there."

"He had a family thing." Gus set his leg on the floor and began peeling his socks and the silicone liner from his stump, his nerves prickling as the cool air met his skin. While his amputation scar was long healed and had lost most of its color, its edges were sometimes sensitive, and Gus smoothed over the skin with his fingers. "Said he had to get home and make breakfast for his kid, so I didn't bother asking."

"Cute." Connor smiled. "Ask him for next time."

Gus made a noncommittal noise. Connor and the nightshift crews just wanted to get to know the new guy. The trouble was that Gus still wasn't sure what to make of his new partner himself.

Moody and mouthy by turns, Walters had warmed up when he'd found his groove, as if a power source had switched on inside him. He and Gus had started to 'click' at that point and ended the night working as a team instead of each in their own world. Which was all fine, except Gus didn't dig the idea of working with someone who ran hot and cold. Who maybe had a chip on his shoulder over reporting to someone junior to him. And who'd definitely been weirded out by Gus's prosthesis.

Connor mussed Gus's hair. "I'm gonna go pass out. You need anything?"

"Nah, I'm good." Gus flexed and straightened his knee a few times. "I'll crash after I get through the wash cycle."

"Judah's brother's out of town, so you can take his room," Connor said as he stood. "Just watch out for the dog, because he'll try to get up on the mattress with you and he's not allowed."

Said dog appeared as if summoned, a giant Irish Wolfhound called Hank, who parked himself by Gus's knee and did his best to look pitiful. Gus ran a hand over the dog's big blue-gray head.

"You heard me, mutt." Connor eyed the beast. "No beds and be nice to Gus."

Hank kept Gus company while he tended to his short limb and cleaned his liner, a silent, furry sentinel. Gus loaded the washer with clothes, then set to work on some drawings, but he must have been more tired than he realized, because out of nowhere, he found himself on his back and blinking up at the ceiling from beneath the soft blanket that usually lay over the back of the couch.

Oops.

Sitting up, he located his crutches and Hank, who'd camped out on the floor by the couch. They made their way to the kitchen where Connor and Judah were sorting through a mound of Boston EMS browns at the kitchen table, some of which Gus knew on sight were his.

"Dudes," he chided. "You didn't have to do my laundry."

Judah, bless him, just grinned. "Mornin', Super Gus!

Connor had stuff to wash too, so I figured I'd keep going instead of waiting for you zombies to rise."

Gus fixed himself a coffee, then joined the others clearing away the laundry before they sat down to a fantastic meal of savory potato kugel and salad. When Judah's lunch break ended, Connor walked him and the dog back downstairs to the yarn shop Judah ran with his family and a hollow feeling settled over Gus while he loaded their plates into the dishwasher.

He didn't miss his ex, Ben; Gus was still too pissed off at the guy to feel nostalgic. But he did miss making a home with someone—the easy acts of cooking and folding laundry, or any of the dozens of commonplace chores that transformed an impersonal space into something special. He longed to have that brand of friendly chaos in his life. After he did some work on himself, obviously. Gus wasn't exactly great boyfriend material right now, especially given he didn't even have his own place.

Or control over his own brain either, a problem he discovered after he'd sat down at Connor's table with more coffee and his sketchbook.

Gus didn't always think when he drew, particularly when he was tired and it was easy to simply let the pencil move while images surfaced in his head. He had no trouble recognizing the face on the page before him though, especially the eyes which were deep set and large, framed with thick lashes and full eyebrows. Gus's pencil had rendered the irises a light gray, but he knew they were really a cool steel blue, the exact shade of Madoc Walters' eyes.

And that was ... bad. Gus hadn't meant to draw any part of Walters, not his eyes, nose, or charmingly imperfect teeth. And Gus could *not* be looking any kind of way at the straight, married guy who reported to him and thought Gus's leg was gross.

He resolved then and there not to even think in Walters' general direction unless they were together on shift. Which proved impossible when Connor wanted Gus's impressions of his new partner.

"What did you think of him?" Connor braced a heavy bag against Gus's punches as they worked out at their gym later that day. "I'm guessing he's got skills because you'd have said by now if he was a dud."

"Ha, that's fair. And yeah, Walters is good. He had a career back in his home state and has worked in EMS at least as long as you have." Gus jabbed the bag twice with his left hand, then followed with a right cross. "I think he's smart and knows what he's doing, which should make my life on the truck easy. Not sure we'd mesh away from work, but no one's asking us to."

"Uh-oh." Connor let go of the bag and straightened. "What does that mean?"

Fuck if Gus knew. He'd felt unsettled since leaving Connor's apartment, thoughts about the things he missed in his life chased by the knowledge he'd been sketching his new partner. But he didn't want to talk shit about a guy he'd only just met and would have to deal with for several months.

Quelling a sigh, Gus gestured for Connor to switch places with him.

"Walters doesn't seem like he's one for sharing," he said, walking around the bag. "I know he's married and has a daughter, and that he's looking for some autonomy on the truck, and that's about it. Meanwhile, I outed myself as queer before we had a short, spectacularly uncomfortable conversation about my leg."

"Oh, heck."

"Whatever. The guy was going to find out both things at

some point. My point though, is that I talked about myself while Walters went out of his way not to."

Connor went at the bag, alternating crosses and jabs with a wicked right hook. "Maybe he feels awkward riding with you," he said between whacks. "It's gotta burn being stuck as a recruit again, especially if he knows he has more on-the-job experience than the guy he reports to. A guy who's probably going to get the job Walters wants for himself."

"What do you mean?"

"Liv said he asked her about Stark's retirement and timing around replacing him on P1."

Gus mulled that over. Bobby Stark rode opposite nights from Gus and Connor and, at sixty, was the most seasoned member on Station 1's crews. He made no secret of wanting to turn his annual two-week trip to the Dominican Republic into a permanent gig and a lot of people were waiting for the guy to make it official.

Gus included. A fact Walters knew because Gus had told him so during their shift.

"I can see where he might be bitter," Gus allowed. "But the idea he's even thinking about promotions is absurd. Walters still has to graduate and get his EMT badge, for fuck's sake."

Unless an exception was made for an Academy recruit who was appropriately qualified. Someone like Walters, who had years on the job and, if he were fast-tracked, could easily become eligible for paramedic spots that became available.

Gus had to assume Walters was aware of this loophole in the rules—the dude was smart and experienced and would know what questions to ask. So maybe that was why Walters had stayed quiet when Gus'd mentioned his own plans to ride on P1. Because he viewed Gus as a rival, rather than simply a partner and supervisor.

Well, fuck that noise.

Walking back around to the front of the heavy bag, Gus assumed a southpaw stance and blistered the bag with punches. If the stars somehow aligned and he and Walters became eligible for promotion to paramedic at the same time, one of them was going to have to transfer out to another station.

It wouldn't be Gus. Station 1 was his house, and he wasn't going anywhere.

FOUR

"GET OFF ME, YOU FAGGOT!"

Madoc winced at their patient's snarling. The guy, a monster-sized and incredibly drunk dude who said his name was Dozer, had been on the ground and bloodied from a head laceration when A1 had arrived at the scene outside a popular bar in Chinatown. He'd perked up after being transferred to the gurney though, turning combative and shoving at Gus and Madoc until the police had handcuffed his hands in front of him, a strategy that'd only angered him further.

"Relax." Gus frowned at the wound on Dozer's scalp. "We need to slow this bleeding or you're going to make a mess in my ambulance."

"Fuck your mother."

"Let's leave my ma out of this, guy."

One of the cops standing nearby snorted, but unease prickled up Madoc's neck. Gus had been quiet tonight, not talking much between calls, expression troubled sometimes like he had a lot on his mind.

Dozer jerked his shoulder away from Gus's touch. "I'm

gonna beat your queer ass into the ground you keep feeling me up."

"I want to treat you, not make out with you," Gus quipped. "Besides, you're not my type."

Madoc just managed to haul Gus out of the path of the gob Dozer spat at him.

"Pussies." Sneering, Dozer made a wild grab for them with his cuffed hands, nearly pitching himself off the gurney. "Eat my fuckin' ass!"

"Pass." Gus made way for the advancing cops and pulled Madoc along with him. "This guy has lost *all* of his marbles."

"You good, Gus?" One of the officers who'd peeled away from the scrum approached them. "If either of you want to press charges for assault, you know it's an option."

"We're okay, right?" Gus looked at Madoc who nodded, and together they glanced over at Dozer who'd gone abruptly quiet under the baleful stares of the cops.

"That fool is losing a lot of blood, Andy," Gus said to the cop. "Odds are he'll be too wrecked to do anything once the adrenaline's burned off."

Dozer remained subdued as he was loaded into the truck, his skin slick with sweat and pale to the point it was a sickly shade of oatmeal. He flinched and grumped while Madoc and Gus wound gauze around his head, but didn't fight treatment.

"Feel like shit," he groused. "Head fuckin' hurts."

"That's why we're taking you to the hospital." Gus tried to catch Dozer's eye. "You hearing me, big man?"

"I hear you, fag."

"My name is Gus."

"Dumbest fuckin' name I've ever heard."

"Okay, *Dozer*." Gus rolled his eyes. "Quit flapping your gums and I'll tell you what's going to happen when we get to the hospital."

Officer Andy climbed aboard for the trip to Tufts Medical Center, but Madoc kept watch on the cabin feed to ensure his partner was safe. Luckily, Dozer was too out of it to pose any threat and curled up on his side with Gus's help, cuffed hands tucked under his chin like a child. When the vomiting started, he didn't shy away from Gus's comfort.

"How the hell was that guy even conscious?" Madoc wondered aloud as he and Gus cleaned the epic mess in the back of the truck, the swish-swish of Gus's mopping sketching a pattern in the night air.

"No idea," Gus said with a laugh. "But I guess since his name is Dozer, he gotta be tough."

Madoc chuckled at the way Gus used the local accent on Dozer's name, all flat vowels and a non-existent 'r'. *Doh-zuh.*

"Did you grow up here?"

"Yup. My family lived in Cambridge until I was four, and then my parents bought a house in Brookline so my sis and I could start school."

Gus's fond tone made Madoc smile. "Didn't know you had a sister."

"Donna. I'm staying with her right now, actually. Also, I'm single, no kids, wicked gay, I like the Red Sox, and my star sign is Leo."

Looking up, Madoc found Gus watching him closely. "Okay …?"

"You next, since we're playing twenty questions."

"That's not—" Madoc inhaled deeply, his cheeks catching fire. "I'm trying to get to know you. Since we're partners and all."

"That's not all we are from what I heard." A crease marred Gus's brow. "How come you didn't tell me you were looking to ride on P1?"

Okay, that probably explains Gus's weird mood.

"It seemed like a bad idea," Madoc said. "It was my first shift at a new house with a new partner—talking promotions would have made me look like a jerk. Especially since we both want the spot on P1 and I'm just a *probie*."

Gus wanted to laugh at the disdain in Madoc's voice. "You're only a probie because the rules say you are." He bent back over his mopping. "So, what comes after you make paramedic? Nursing or med school?"

"No." Madoc drew a fresh cover over the gurney's thin mattress pad. "I have no interest in carrying that kind of debt." Again. "Or losing out on more time with my daughter. Getting my medic certs while working full-time has been hard enough and I want to be there for Val."

"I imagine having a child changes your perspective on lots of things."

Gus'd stopped mopping when Madoc looked over and was instead eyeing the floor with a far-off expression. When he looked up and met Madoc's gaze however, Madoc couldn't have looked away if he'd tried.

"I need to know your head's in the game," Gus said. "The guy who knew Perry needed help yesterday and dragged me away from Dozer tonight? I want him on the truck, not someone angling for sexy saves because they think it'll help them get ahead. I get that I'm just a guy standing in the way of a job you want for yourself, but I'm asking you to put your ambition and the rivalry on hold so we can be there for the patients and each other."

Madoc could have told Super Gus Dawson to stick his lecture in his ass. Asked if *he* was ready to put his ego aside for the work. But Madoc had already seen Gus put the job and patients before himself repeatedly in the two shifts they'd worked together so he held his tongue.

"I can do that," Madoc said instead. "I need the promotion

because being a medic will help me give my kid a good life. But I won't let my plans get in the way of the work or being a good partner."

Gus held Madoc's stare a moment longer before he nodded once and took the mop to the closet. "So, why'd you leave Station 5?"

"Traffic." Madoc wrinkled his nose. "It was murder getting to and from West Roxbury every shift, but Val was settled at school, and I couldn't move her."

"Valid. But what if you end up back in West Rox once you're promoted? Or another station that's farther out, like Hyde Park or Dorchester."

"I'll worry about it once the probie status isn't a thing. Besides, you could be the one who gets transferred."

"Sure." Gus hopped off the truck. "But I won't be."

Madoc snorted. His partner was one cocky fucker. Still, it was hard not to admire Gus's confidence.

And the sparkle in his eyes and those ridiculous crinkles when he smiled.

Not that Madoc was looking.

Their radios beeped. "A1, what's your location?"

"A1 clear," Madoc replied, "you can show us at Tufts."

The alarm sounded a beat later, and the dispatcher's voice was tense when she spoke.

"Boston A1, P1, A6, MVA on Frontage Road northbound at the Mass Ave. Connector. Code One, 29-D-1 M, major incident with three vehicles affected, passengers reported trapped. Fire and police are on scene and be advised children are present."

Gus navigated the truck through a thick mess of traffic clogging an elevated section of roadway where two vehicles had a third pinned against a concrete barrier. Police had secured the scene and were diverting traffic, but it was loud and busy with multiple fire and EMS crews at work and news choppers circling overhead.

"A1 on scene," Gus said into his radio. "Who needs us?"

"P1 has two passengers ready to board the Boo-Boo Bus," replied Connor's partner Olivia. "We're in the car that's pinned."

Madoc exchanged a quick glance with Gus. Boo-Boo Bus was the code used for 'ambulance' when working around young children so who knew what the fuck awaited them inside that wreck.

Dressed in heavy turnout coats and orange helmets, Madoc and Gus wheeled the gurney toward the wreck, parking it by the two outermost cars. Gus slid easily into the narrow space that sat between them, but it took a second for Madoc to maneuver his bigger frame into the same space, and when Gus glanced back, an improbable smile lit his face.

"Let's go, Rook!" he yelled. "Get your big caboose over here!"

Madoc barked a laugh. "You're such a dick!"

"And you're just jealous my butt is smaller!"

The car at the core of the scene was a small SUV and badly damaged, several windows shattered and the driver and passenger doors crushed inward. Firefighters from the rescue squad stood ready to peel off the vehicle's roof with their tools, but Gus marched up to the rear of the car and reached in through the hole in the glass.

"Hi, guys!" he said cheerily. "I'm Gus and this here is Walt! How you doin'?"

Reaching Gus's side, Madoc spied a baby in a bucket-style seat, red-faced and crying, gripping Gus's gloved fingers with two tiny hands. Olivia was in the front seat with the unconscious driver, while Connor was in back with the baby and a wide-eyed little girl maybe a year or two older than

Valerie, her body looking incredibly fragile beside his broad frame.

Gus rubbed the baby's tummy. "Did I hear you all want to check out my bus?" he asked the little girl.

"They sure do!" Connor's voice was bright. "I was just telling Lexie and Oskar here that they could wait there with you while we help their mom."

"That's a great idea," Gus said. "We've got toys in our bus and stuff to draw with."

Madoc smiled at the girl, Lexie. "I didn't even know we had toys!" he fibbed. "I bet Gus'll show us if we ask nicely though, and maybe even let Oskar drive the bus."

Lexie furrowed her brow. "Oskar can't drive, Mister. He's just a baby."

Madoc felt more than heard Gus's quiet laughter. "You know, you're right? I didn't even think of that."

Madoc was very aware of the smoke and noise and the firefighters working, traffic still moving on the opposite side of the road and the choppers noisy above them. But time seemed to slow as he and Gus ferried the children away from the car, Madoc in the lead with Oskar in his bucket while Gus carried the jump bag and Lexie.

Once inside the truck, Oskar settled quickly against Madoc's shoulder while Gus comforted Lexie who was shedding tears over leaving her mom. Hand puppets and a stuffed toy shaped like an avocado were pulled from the toy drawer, along with a big pad of paper and a package of colored pencils, and Madoc and Gus took turns distracting the kids while examining them, relieved both were uninjured. Oskar soon dozed off in his bucket, the avocado clutched in his chubby fists, while Lexie sat on the bench, her tears forgotten as Gus covered pages of the pad with drawings. Really decent drawings that were crisp and clever as any professional illustration, and

Madoc smiled at the notion his partner was some kind of closet artist.

"Can you draw a pony?" Lexie had a puppet on either hand and was leaning against Gus's arm. "The kind with a rainbow mane and tail?"

"Sure," Gus replied. "You can color her in however you like. If you don't want to use colored pencils, there are some crayons and markers in the toy drawer too."

"I'll give it to Mama to make her feel better. She was bleeding and the doors on the car are broken," Lexie said to the giraffe puppet on her left hand, sounding very grave.

"The firefighters have special tools to open the doors," Gus said. "I used to work with those guys on the rescue truck and I know they're totally dope at their jobs."

Madoc frowned to himself. He'd heard Gus'd been a firefighter for several years before moving over to EMS, but it was hard imagining how that'd happened when most firefighters were lifers, married to the job unless injury ...

Madoc's gaze fell to Gus's right boot.

Oh.

"Did you used to be a firefighter?" Lexie was asking, her dark eyes on Gus's face now.

"Yup." Gus smiled at her. "But I hurt my foot, so I got a different job and now I drive the Boo-boo Bus for kids who need my help."

Lexie flashed him a small smile in return. "And you draw ponies. Are you gonna draw one for Walt?"

Gus's gleeful expression had Madoc chuckling despite the ridiculous nickname.

"I don't have time to color right now because I'm working, sweetie," Madoc said, "but I have a little girl who loves rainbow ponies, and I'd be happy to give my drawing to her."

GUS DIDN'T KNOW what to think when his partner pulled a small envelope from his pocket. Walters had been pensive since they'd reunited Lexi and Oskar with their mom, a mood Gus understood. Even with a good outcome, treating children was taxing emotionally, their helplessness adding tension to every second on a call. Which was why Gus'd bought Walters and himself some chai lattes and *bolos* from the hospital cafe and insisted they take a short break on the truck's bumper.

"This is from Val," Walters said, holding the envelope out. "Her thanks for the *bolos*. I meant to give it to you earlier but there wasn't time."

Warmth rose in Gus's chest as he looked over an extremely adorable card with a ladybug drawn in crayon smiling at him above a carefully lettered 'Thank you from Val'.

"I love it," he said with a grin. "Will you thank her for me?"

"Of course." Walters bit his lip. "Can I ask about your time as a firefighter? I knew you were with Boston Fire, but hearing you talking about it with Lexie tonight got me thinking about how it wasn't that long ago you had a whole different career."

And a whole different life.

Gus tucked Valerie's card into his breast pocket. "Firefighting was all I knew for a long time," he said. "Wanted to apply to the Fire Academy on my nineteenth birthday but my ma asked me to hold off until after I turned twenty-one."

"Bet you appreciated that."

"I did not." Gus shared a smile with his partner. "I understood Ma and my pops just wanted me safe. They hoped I'd lose interest in firefighting and go to college, maybe get a degree in Fine Arts."

Walters' eyebrows went up. "You like drawing that much?"

"I love it and always have. I never wanted a career in art,

though. I took a bunch of classes anyway while I waited to turn twenty-one and also got my EMT cert because you need one for the Fire Academy."

"That sounds on-brand," Walters said drily, though there was a teasing gleam in his eye. "Your folks had to have known you weren't going to lose interest by then."

"They did. Didn't stop them from worrying, but they and my sister were super supportive." Gus sat back against the truck's doors. "Pops kept after me to get certified as a paramedic. Said it'd be good to have a fallback, just in case, and I did like paramedicine, just not as much as firefighting. We didn't talk about *why* I'd need a medic's cert, though. Until we had to."

Turning his head, Gus met Walters' gaze. "There was a fire in a brownstone in the South End," he said. "The engine and ladder crews had it contained, and rescue went in to extricate someone from the top floor. The staircase collapsed as we made our way down and we fell, all of us."

Walters' mouth dropped open on a soft gasp and Gus turned his eyes on the still dark sky above them. There was too much light coming from the hospital to see stars, but he knew they were up there.

"I lost my leg and one of my brothers that day," he said. "His name was Beni."

"Shit, Gus. I'm so sorry. That fucking sucks."

Gus'd never found the words to adequately describe the enormity of what had happened to him. The terror of feeling the floor open beneath his feet, swallowing him and the crew. Pain like a living thing. Waking up in the hospital to find his career fucked and Beni dead.

Setting his cup on the bumper, he pulled out his phone, aware his hands were shaking as he flipped through his pics to one of Beni in his turnout gear. Beni was brandishing a

Halligan tool and mugging for the camera, all dimples and blithe grin, and the grief Gus still carried smacked into him, so raw it left him breathless. He showed the photo to Madoc who nodded, then surprised the hell out of Gus by reaching over to set a hand on Gus's shoulder. The contact gave Gus something to focus on until he felt less like he might weep or punch the side of the truck really hard.

"Everything changed after that," he said. "Technically, I could have gone back to firefighting, maybe doing a different kind of job inside Boston Fire or for another department altogether. But I didn't want that and was lucky to have family and a partner who wanted to help me figure out what came next." Gus paused. "You're not going to get weird if I talk boyfriends, are you?"

"No." Walters gave Gus's shoulder a squeeze before letting go. "I'm good with you being queer, honest."

Gus nodded. "Ian helped me get back on my feet. He's a nurse and good friends with Mark Mannix, actually. Ian and my folks were there for me while I started over. New leg, new career, new Super Gus life," he said with a smile he knew fell flat based on the regret that crossed Walters' face.

"I'm sorry, man. I didn't mean to make you feel bad."

"You didn't." Leaning over, Gus set his elbows on his knees. "I'm never going to like talking about what happened to me, but I'm not ashamed of my life or my career, and definitely not embarrassed about my leg. You can ask or *not* ask me about it and you and I will be fine."

"Cool." Walters frowned slightly, and a beat passed before he continued. "I do have a question actually, but it isn't about your leg."

"Okay?"

"Do you even like being called Super Gus?"

"Honestly, no." Gus smirked. "But I know you'll appreciate

that I got the nickname when I was a probie with Boston Fire and haven't been able to shake it."

Mischief shone in Walters' eyes when he smiled. "Sorry, not sorry. But I could promise to forget your nickname if you do the same for mine ...?"

"Yeah, no." Gus laughed at his partner's mock pout. "Nice try, Probie, but that isn't happening."

FIVE

MONDAY, *April 24, 6:30 P.M.*

"WHAT IS MY LIFE?" Gus asked the dark hole before him. "And why am I the one with my face in a sewer?"

"Because you said, and I quote, that my 'big ass would get stuck' if I tried," Walters replied from behind him. "Besides, that's a storm drain, not a sewer."

Gus would have flipped his partner off, but he was face down in said storm drain, searching for a lost rabbit while a small crowd of onlookers streamed the absolute fuckery to the internet.

"Quit squawkin' and hurry the hell up!" called a high, reedy voice. "I don't want the goddamned rats eating my Argyle!"

That was their patient, Kathleen, an elderly lady perched on the gurney inside A1 with a bum ankle and a shittastic attitude. She'd come to the park at Post Office Square to walk Argyle, her pet rabbit, a thing one could do with the help of a wee harness and leash built for bunnies. Passersby had come to Kathleen's aid when she'd fallen, but by the time Gus and Walters had arrived on the scene, her pet had hopped off to explore and gotten itself stuck in the storm drain.

"Do you see him?" Walters asked. "Maybe stretch your arm out and—"

"See if a wild thing eats me? No, thanks."

Gus grimaced and inched forward, only to freeze as an unearthly screech filled the space around him and he felt his eyes bug.

"The fuck?" he blurted at the same time Walters asked, "What was *that*?" from behind him.

Wild rabbits lived in the city's parks of course, but Gus doubted they were dumb enough to screw around in the storm drains. Which made it hard not to think about what the actual fuck was in this hole with him as he shone his penlight around. He swallowed as a small thing plop-hopped into the light's beam, its coat dirty and wet and its teeth *very* long. But then Gus caught a flash of unexpected color and knew he was on the right track because no self-respecting wild animal in his city would suffer a zebra-print harness with green trim.

"Hey, buddy." Gus got another piteous cry in return. "I'm sorry about your name. Also, your mom is kind of cuckoo-bananas."

Laughter above from Walters. "Dude, are you talking to the rabbit?"

"Der." Grunting, Gus stretched his body as long as he was able. "Hold my legs, yeah?" he called over his shoulder. "Above the knees so my prosthesis doesn't pop off."

"Oh, Lord." Walters was giggling now. "Hang on a sec while I square off."

Despite himself, Gus had to laugh too. While still somewhat

reserved, Walters had loosened up a lot over the last couple of weeks and he and Gus had a good thing going. Gus had given Walters space when he could, his faith solid in his partner's abilities as an EMT, and Walters had responded by coming out of his shell, laughing and joking more and opening up about his kid.

Gus liked Walters both as a guy and a partner, and he straight-out loved the flow they'd found when they treated patients, a connection that went beyond words with each anticipating the other's next move like they were dancing to music only they could hear.

The partnership wasn't effortless what with the ups and downs of two sets of human moods, and the knowledge of Bobby Stark's impending retirement running beneath everything. Perhaps knowing the job Walters wanted for himself would soon likely belong to Gus fueled Walters' sometimes sullen moods, his hot-and-cold vibe still very much a thing. The guy came alive when he talked about his daughter though, his love for her palpable as he told stories about the kindergartener who played left wing for her U6 hockey team, prized pizza and baking shows, and thought purple glitter made everything better.

That heart-eyed version of his partner was the one Gus liked sketching the most, his collection of drawings of the straight boy he had no business pining for steadily growing.

With Madoc anchoring him from above, Gus put the penlight in his mouth, slid forward another few inches and stretched out both arms, carefully snagging Argyle's harness with his fingers.

"Got 'im!" he crowed around the light between his lips, unsurprised at Argyle's continued shrieking.

The rabbit still let Gus cradle him while Madoc helped them both out of the hole, and the crowd cheered when Gus was vertical again. Kathleen, however, remained deeply unimpressed.

"Quit your showboatin', boyo!" she yelled, her beady eyes trained right on Gus. "And get your dumb ass over here!"

Gus gave her a huge fake grin. "You're welcome, ma'am!" he called, then said out of the side of his mouth to Madoc, "I'm driving."

"What?" Walters asked. "Why?"

"Because *this* boyo's had enough shenanigans for the day."

Glancing down at Argyle, Gus glimpsed a small brown pellet rolling out from beneath the rabbit's rear end and over Gus's arm. The fuck was that?

"Balls," Gus muttered. He and the bunny eyed each other for long seconds, Argyle's tiny nose twitching. Then another pellet came out of its bum, and Gus sighed, long and lusty.

"It pooped on me, Probie," he said to Walters whose face was scarlet with suppressed laughter. "The rabbit fucking pooped on my coat, and I am never going to forgive you."

After returning to the station, Gus changed out his dirty uniform and grabbed a spare jacket from the storeroom, then headed for the canteen where he found firefighters from next door mixed in with the EMS crews watching 'rabbit rescue' videos uploaded by the crowd in the park.

"Ay, Mr. Poopy!" Olivia called out as Gus passed by. "How you doin'?"

"Don't call me that," he warned, then aimed a death glare at Walters who was laughing himself sick. "Bad enough I got all dirty crawling around in a hole."

"You shoulda called in the professionals," agreed Sorenson, a veteran smoke eater from Barbados who rode with the ladder crew. He grinned slyly. "But don't be sad, Dawson. Be hoppy!"

Gus sneered at the slew of rabbit puns that followed, though he only did it for show. In truth, Gus enjoyed hearing the raucous laughter and jokes and seeing Walters and Connor red-faced with giggling. But then Gus's phone buzzed in his pocket and the name on the screen when he checked it zapped all his good feelings.

Ben: *I want to talk.*

Turning his back to the room, Gus grabbed a package of trail mix from a bowl on the counter while he considered what to do next. Ignoring Ben was an exercise in futility when he'd just keep messaging and calling until Gus gave in. A thing Gus would do, because no matter how badly he wanted to block his ex everywhere, he couldn't just yet.

Gus swore under his breath when the phone buzzed with an incoming call.

"I can't talk now, Ben," he said upon picking up. "I'm at work and—"

"Then meet me for dinner," Ben said over him. "We can go out or I can cook, whatever you like."

"No, thanks." Gus set his mug in the coffee machine. "I had a headache for three days the last time we met up and I'm not doing that to myself again. We both know there's nothing left to talk about."

"I disagree. Christ, Gus." Ben made an impatient noise. "We used to be friends for fuck's sake, and I think we could get back to that if you'd just get over yourself."

Gus ground his teeth. "I don't want to get over it. You lied to me, so many times I'm not even sure where to start."

"I did not lie to you."

"My bank account says differently."

"I was going to put it all back!"

"I don't believe you." Ben shut up then and Gus had to close his eyes for a second to center himself. "*That* is why we can't go back to being friends," he said, "because I can't trust anything that you say. All the talking and planning we did—"

"*We* didn't plan anything—that was all you." Ben was scoffing but he sounded hurt. "*Your* plans to play happy family with the kids *you* wanted because everything is always about Super Gus Dawson."

The bitterness in his ex's voice turned Gus's stomach. "And yet you're the one who keeps calling and trying to gaslight me, so maybe ask yourself why that is."

He cut the call, then nearly jumped out of his skin when his partner appeared out of nowhere.

"Jesus Murphy!" Gus yelped.

"*Sorry.*" Wincing, Walters held his hands up, palms facing out. "I thought you heard me coming."

"No, it's fine." Casting a glance around the now mostly empty canteen, Gus grunted softly. "My fault for picking a shitty spot to deal with my ex-boyfriend drama."

"This is the guy you told me about, Ian?"

Gus shook his head. "Ben," he said. "We were together after Ian. And shouldn't have been, ever."

Walters scrunched up his nose. "That bad, huh?"

"That bad," Gus agreed. His smile wry, he resumed his coffee making. "Ben and I were friends before we got together, and I always considered him to be a good guy. But now I wonder if I ever truly knew him or if I just became expert at looking past stuff I didn't want to see."

"I get that." Walters stepped up to the coffee brewer too. "Can I ask what happened between you?"

"Ben ripped me off. As in took most of the money in my checking account and completely cleaned out another we were using to ... it was a nest egg," Gus finished weakly.

He hadn't meant to spill all of this tea with his partner. Wasn't ready to talk to Walters about the family and future he'd wanted either, a future Gus increasingly felt sure he'd have to navigate on his own.

Lemonade stalked up to them then, carrying a banana-shaped toy she favored in her mouth, and Madoc scooped her up, gently chucking her under the chin before he handed her off to Gus.

"Ben invested my money in crypto," Gus said as he got the cat settled in the crook of his arm with her feet up like a baby. "On paper, the investment was worth a fortune. Except the coin was a pump and dump scam and the company and the people who ran it weren't real. After the coin hit a certain price, the so-called executives disappeared with the whole pot of money, and all Ben and the other investors had left was a bunch of worthless virtual currency and no way to recoup the loss."

"At all? The money was gone, just like that?"

Walters sounded horrified and yes, nearly eighty grand of Gus's money had disappeared exactly like that, along with the future he'd planned with Ben.

Unless Ben was right, and Gus'd been alone in his planning.

Gus scritched Lemonade's fur around her collar. "Yep, it was all gone. Which sucks very much, obviously. But the thing that's almost worse is Ben refusing to take responsibility for what he did. He acts like I'm making a big deal over nothing. Like it's ridiculous for me to be angry that someone I trusted stole from me and lied to my face."

"I'm sorry, man." Genuine sympathy filled Walters' face. "Noelene and I have had money troubles," he said. "It sucks so bad having to dig yourself out of a hole. Being broke even for a short time is the worst."

"Yes!" Gus said, then sighed. "Anyway, Ben knows I'm friendly with lots of cops, so he's been paying back the money he took out of my checking account. Both our names were on the nest egg account though, so I doubt I'll ever get even a penny back.

"I'm okay," he added hastily when Walters frowned. "Been staying with my sister to save on rent and most of my medical stuff is covered by my pension with Boston Fire and my health insurance. I worked a ton of overtime for a while and budgeted like it was a second job, but I still had to put some stuff I wanted to do on a back burner. Including school, which really killed me to do."

"School like more training?"

Gus shook his head. "I'm in a program at Bunker Hill Community to get my A.S. in paramedicine. I'd have been finished by now if the shit with Ben hadn't gotten so messy, but I'm hoping to start back up again in the fall."

He and Walters fell silent when the station's alarm sounded.

"A1, person down at 45 Province Street, unresponsive to stimuli," the dispatcher said. "Male, twenty-two years old, 23-C-5, suspected overdose. Code One, police dispatched following reports of an altercation."

Gus and Madoc wasted no time booking it out to the garage. 'Person down' could mean anything from fainting to illness to someone who'd had one beer too many. But like so many cities, Boston had seen a massive jump in opioid-related overdoses and deaths and there was no way to know what shape their patient was in until they laid eyes on him.

Gus didn't notice anything off with his partner at first as they cruised toward Downtown, flashing lights and siren doing a decent job of clearing the way. But then a car traveling ahead of them veered into their lane and Walters leaned hard on the truck's horn.

"Dude, what are you doing!" he hollered with a vehemence that had Gus's eyebrows going up.

"What are *you* doing?" Gus asked. "Road rage isn't a good look on anyone, Walt, not even you."

Madoc muttered something about Gus shutting the hell up, clearly shifting to pouty and fuck it, Gus wasn't going to let the guy stew in his own juices this time.

"What's going on with you, Rook?"

"Can you not just call me by my actual name?" Walters bit out. "It's always Probie and Rook and God, freaking *Walt*."

Gus almost smiled; his partner was really feeling this sulk. "I call you by your real name all the damned time, dude. The nicknames are just for fun."

"Nah." Walters made a quick left onto State Street. "You call me nicknames because you don't respect me. Because you think you're better than me."

Gus's amusement died a quick death. "Hey. I *do not* think I'm better than you."

"Bullshit. I can hear it in your voice when you talk to me. And it's going to get worse once you have that degree and can throw it my face."

For a second, Gus simply stared. Where was this even coming from?

"Are you for real right now?" he asked. "My education isn't about the job or you, Walters. It's about *me*."

Walters scoffed. "Just like everything else."

Abruptly, Gus's brain circled back to his phone call with Ben. *"Everything's always about Super Gus Dawson."* And shit, had he fucked up with Walters?

Gus frowned at his partner. "I don't think I'm better than you," he said again. "Or that you're not good at your job or unworthy of being on this truck—"

"Just stop, okay? I already told you, I don't need to be hand-held and if you just want to go through the motions with me until you're promoted, that's totally fine."

"I don't just go through the motions, ever. I'm committed to this job as much as you are."

"Please don't compare yourself to me." Disdain dripped from Walters' words. "I'm not like you, *Dawson*. I'm not going to make my whole life about work the way you do, because I have a family who needs me."

And you don't.

Gus turned his gaze out the windshield, the siren's muffled wails the only noise in A1's cab as they sped through Downtown. Walters was right—Gus had no business comparing them. Walters had a home and a spouse and a kid and probably plans for the future. Unlike Gus, who was single and staying in his sister's spare bedroom to keep from blowing money on rent, exactly as he'd done sixteen years ago at the start of his career. Except this time, Gus was bunking at Donna's because he'd been too clueless to notice his boyfriend looting his bank accounts.

God, I'm fucked up.

Walters turned the truck onto Province Street and when the flash of police cruiser lights caught Gus's eye, he gave himself a hard internal shake, knowing he had to get out of his own head and stop spiraling.

After easing up to the curb, Walters peered through the windshield. "You see the patient?" he asked.

"No." Gus watched a tall guy wearing a cowboy hat—a truly rare sight in New England—gesture wildly at a uniformed police officer and thumbed his radio's button. "A1 on scene and BPD are present. Are we Code Four?"

"Roger, A1, you are Code Four." There was a pause and then, "P1 ETA in three minutes, additional BPD en route."

"That's weird. Why would they call for more cops?" Walters cut the ignition. The hard edge in his voice was gone, replaced by an uncertainty Gus hadn't heard from him in weeks, probably because it was dawning on him that he'd just accused his supervisor of doing a shit job of managing him.

Frowning, Gus eyed the pub too. "Not sure. Could be there's something going on inside. The dude with the hat sure looks pissed off."

"Yeah." Walters sighed. "Listen, about what I said," he started, but fell silent when Gus shook his head.

"We're not doing this now."

Gus didn't look at his partner. Had no idea what to say now that he knew what Walters truly thought of him. But he could do his job and have Walters' back and maybe that'd make him feel a little less shitty for a couple of minutes.

Focus, Dawson.

Gus popped his door. "I'll take point if it'll make you more comfortable."

Walters practically sprinted around the front of the ambulance to meet him. "I didn't mean you should take point," he said. "I just—"

"Have more in your life than the job, I know." Gus hefted the jump bag onto his shoulder. "I won't write you up if you choose to stand down."

"I want *you* to stand down until we know more. I say we wait."

"For what? Dispatch to tell us we're Code Four again?"

"I don't know." Walters cursed under his breath. "I guess I've got a bad feeling about going in there." He moved like he'd put a hand on Gus's shoulder, but Gus quickly sidestepped him.

"I'm done talking about feelings," Gus said, without looking up. "You want to stay here and wait for P1, you can do that."

SIX

STUNNED, Madoc stared after Gus who'd stalked off, tension pouring off him in waves. What the fuck did the guy think he was doing walking onto a scene without a backup?

His job. The one you said he wasn't good at.

Shame washed through Madoc in a hot wave. Gus's eyes had gone wide as Madoc had laid into him, face slack like he'd been slapped, and Madoc had steeled himself for the discipline he had coming for being so far out of line with his bitching he'd practically left the state. But then Gus had gone oddly quiet, voice flat when he spoke and expression distant, gaze skittering past Madoc like he couldn't stand the sight of him.

And Madoc knew he'd brought this on himself by being a self-centered dick. He didn't even know where the venom that had poured out of him during the drive over had come from. Annoying nicknames and occasional mischief aside, Gus was a *great* partner who not only kicked ass at the work but always showed Madoc respect.

Respect I don't deserve after the things I said.

Hastily, Madoc went around to the back of the truck and

helped unload the gurney. Gus didn't say a word the whole time, his normally expressive face stiff as they wheeled everything over to the pub doors.

The guy in the cowboy hat rolled his eyes. "Come on. That asshole doesn't need an ambulance." He waved wildly at the doors of the pub. "He needs to be arrested for ripping me off!"

Gus looked past the dude to the cop. "Hey, Pete. Patient inside?"

"In back by the restrooms," Officer Pete confirmed. He was a burly guy with deep brown skin and a wry air, though the quelling look he shot at the cowboy hat dude bought them some silence. "White male, young, looks like an OD. There're a couple of girls in there with him, but they're high as kites too."

Inside, the pub was packed but eerily quiet, a strange, spiky energy in the air that set Madoc's teeth on edge. But he knew from one look that the patient they found on the floor in the back hallway was very fucked, his skin slick with sweat and so pale it verged on blue.

"What's your friend's name?" Gus asked the girls kneeling on either side of him, and the one nearest him raised a hand to her dark hair.

"Brendan." Her eyes were huge as she looked between Madoc and Gus, her pupils dilated wide. "We were at the bar, and he went to use the bathroom, but when he didn't come back, we found him like this with some big guy in a hat standing over him and yelling about money."

Gus pressed his fingers against Brendan's neck, then pulled his penlight from his pocket. "Pulse is weak," he said to Madoc before peeling back Brendan's eyelids. "And his pupils are pinpoints." Looking between the girls, Gus asked, "Has Brendan been using opiates tonight?"

"I don't know," replied the girl with the dark hair. "We haven't been together the whole time."

Tucking his penlight away, Gus rubbed the knuckles of his right hand hard up and down Brendan's sternum. "Brendan!" he said loudly. "Time to wake up, buddy!"

An ugly noise came out of Brendan, like a deep gurgling snore that was lodged deep in his throat, and when Gus met Madoc's gaze for the first time since they'd arrived on the scene, Madoc already knew what his partner was thinking.

"I'm gonna hit him with the NARCAN," Gus said, turning toward the bag while Madoc looked at the second girl, a blonde who'd gone very pale.

"Holy shit," she said, staring at Brendan. "Is he gonna die?"

"We're trying to make sure he doesn't," Madoc replied. "We think your friend is OD'ing and my partner's going to give him some medicine to help. What did you all and Brendan take —coke or meth, some kind of upper?"

"It was c-coke," the blonde stammered, tears standing in her eyes. "We've been partying all day, snorted some right before we came in here."

Madoc pursed his lips. He suspected Brendan was speedballing, the coke that had already been in his bloodstream now mixed with a depressant like heroin and God knew what else, the push and pull of the competing drugs throwing his body into a deadly chaos.

The NARCAN spray in one hand, Gus tilted Brendan's head back with the other, and Madoc slid his own beneath the kid's neck for support. There was a crash from somewhere in the bar followed by shouting, but neither looked away from their patient.

Gus inserted the nozzle's tip into the kid's left nostril and hit the plunger, then did the same into the right nostril. "Open your eyes, Brendan!" he called. "It's time to—"

A glass hit the wall at the end of hallway and shattered, the pieces skittering over the floor. Flinching and with the girls' screams in his ears, Madoc grabbed his radio.

"A1, what's the ETA on P1 at 45 Province Street?" he asked.

"P1 is on scene," Connor replied before the dispatcher could. "But half the bar is out here brawling and BPD's trying to clear a path for us to come in."

"They're brawling *inside* the bar too, P1," Madoc said over the yells echoing from the bar down the hall. "And it'd be great if we had some help!"

"Unbelievable," Gus muttered, then flinched when another glass hit the wall, quickly followed by a loud crashing that sounded like falling furniture. "What the fuck is going on out there?"

Madoc glanced over his shoulder toward the bar. "I'll go—"

"*No.*" Gus grabbed Madoc's arm, his face and voice fierce. "Don't you dare move. Those are pub glasses hitting the wall and if you think I'm letting you walk out into that, you're crazy."

After a second dose of NARCAN failed to rouse Brendan and his pulse faded further, they began CPR with Gus performing the chest compressions while Madoc used a bag-valve mask to keep Brendan breathing.

"We'll go to Plan B if we have to," Gus said, his voice strained from his efforts. "Carry him out the fire door and hope for the best."

Madoc bit his lip. Brendan might stand a chance if he got some NARCAN through an IV, but as the seconds ticked by, so did his life.

"Maybe we should—" he started, only for Brendan's body to jerk hard.

"His eyes are open!" the blonde girl exclaimed. "Bren? Are you okay?"

Sweaty and breathless, Gus sat back on his heels with a grunt Madoc could feel. They'd done it—kept this dumbass alive so he could stare up at *them* like they were out of their minds.

"Welcome back, kid," Gus said. "Good job scaring the shit out of your friends and my partner. Can you grab the gurney?" he asked Madoc. "I want to get him off the floor in case we still have to make a run for it out the back."

Body buzzing with its own kind of high, Madoc set the mask aside and climbed to his feet. He'd gone just a few steps when a scream froze his blood.

"GET OFF ME!"

"Yo, I need some help!" Gus shouted. He had his hands on Brendan's shoulders when Madoc looked back, and he grunted when a flailing fist caught him in the face. "Buddy, you gotta chill!"

"FUCK YOU!" Brendan bellowed as he thrashed and fought, the stimulants in his system coming on strong now that the opiates had been neutralized by the NARCAN.

Dashing back, Madoc tried to grab hold of Brendan's legs to keep him from kicking, but it was like fighting two people at once, the kid's bottom half twisting and bucking while his upper half kept throwing punches. Brendan's dark-haired friend scrambled off to the side, but the blonde remained, gripping his left arm hard and screeching at him to chill out.

Then Brendan heaved mightily and jerked the girl into Madoc with a teeth-rattling jolt that sent them both sprawling and left Gus on his own. Pulling his legs into his chest, Brendan kicked out hard in a jackknife move that caught Gus in the chest with one booted foot. Gus yelped sharply but somehow hung on, until Brendan kicked a second time and sent Gus tumbling backward into the wall.

Oh, fuck.

"Gus!" Madoc shouted as thunder crashed into the hallway, more hands helping him secure Brendan, paramedics and other officers swarming around him and everyone speaking at once.

Someone—Olivia, Madoc thought—was talking about sedating the patient, while he tried to get a look through the tangle of bodies to Gus who sat hunched with his left shoulder against the wall, Pete the cop squatted beside him.

That could have been me.

"Go, we've got this," Olivia said in Madoc's ear, and he quickly scuttled his way around the crowd to his partner just as Connor did the same.

"He can't catch his breath," Pete was saying. "I can't tell if he just got the wind knocked out of him or if he's really injured."

"The kid kicked him." Madoc ghosted a hand over the one Gus had pressed against his sternum, his stomach bottoming out. Gus looked awful, his face a terrible shade of concrete gray, and while his prosthesis was lighter than an actual limb, it could easily have torqued his knee or hip when he'd fallen. "Gus?"

"Uh," Gus managed to croak, his eyes watering as he tried to get air. "Am ... okay." Reaching up, his fingers trembled as he pulled Madoc's hand away from his radio and the orange button they used to initiate system-wide calls for assistance. "Mayday for ... 'mergencies," he said on a short gasp.

Pete made a face. "I'd hate to see your idea of an emergency, Dawson, because you look like shit."

Abruptly, Madoc's fear transformed into a fury that scorched his insides. They shouldn't have come into this pub without backup. And *damnit,* Gus should have let go after Brendan kicked him the first time instead of hanging on like a bullheaded asshole who always had to be right.

"Gus." Connor set his hand just above Gus's right knee. "Is your leg okay?"

Gus squished his eyes shut, sending the moisture that had collected in them onto his cheeks. "Y-yeah. Chest ... fuckin' hurts."

Connor patted him gently. "I'm sure it does, hon. Let's get you up so I can take care of you."

Madoc wanted to argue that it was his job to take care of Gus. Yes, Connor outranked him by many degrees. But Gus was *Madoc's* partner. The guy he worked so closely with it sometimes felt like they were inside each other's heads. Who always had Madoc's back and made sure he got home to Valerie after every shift. Who'd taken point on this call and told Madoc to stand down if he didn't feel safe.

That could have been me.

The ride to MGH passed in a blur, Madoc's attention on the dashboard camera every second he could spare as he drove. And it was hard seeing Gus so subdued, clearly hurting as Connor helped him ease off his uniform top and undershirt and applied a cold pack to his ribs.

Mark Mannix met them at the ED's doors, his usual sass nowhere in sight as they wheeled the gurney and Gus into triage. And though Gus was grumbling now about being able to move around on his own, the knot in Madoc's gut didn't loosen at all.

After an X-ray revealed Gus's upper right ribs were badly bruised rather than broken, he was given some pain relief and seemed to breathe easier. He remained stoic as Mark helped him into a hospital gown and applied ice to his injury, but Madoc knew him well enough by now to read pain in his features, despite Gus again looking everywhere but at Madoc.

"That kid could have cracked your skull," Madoc said once

the nurses and doc had filed out. "The way you hit the wall, you're lucky you don't have a TBI."

"I know," Gus said, quietly. "But I don't, and my brain is fine."

Madoc bit his lip. He deserved to be iced out after the way he'd spoken to Gus earlier on the truck. Knew he'd been needlessly cruel and unprofessional and that if Gus wrote Madoc up for being a disrespectful little shit, the reprimand would be deserved.

"Why didn't you want to wait for backup?" he asked anyway. "I know we had a Code Four, but—"

"I made a decision based on the data I had," Gus said over him. "But if you think I'm okay with the way shit went down, you're wrong."

He met Madoc's gaze at last, an intensity in his dark eyes Madoc hadn't expected. "I'm sorry, Walters," Gus said, his lips turning down at the corners. "I put you in a situation that got out of hand, and I know that really sucks."

Madoc's stomach roiled at the words. He didn't want this apology. Gus couldn't have guessed their patient would flip his shit in such a spectacular fashion. He'd been doing his job and trying to help someone who'd desperately needed it.

"I don't just go through the motions, ever."

"What should I tell the commander?" Madoc asked.

"Whatever you want," Gus said, his voice flat again. Closing his eyes, he raised the ice pack and pressed it against his chest. "It was my scene, and I'll take the heat."

The dismissal stung Madoc like a slap. Was this the way things were going to be now? Gus shutting him down at every turn?

"Why did you send me for the gurney?" Madoc asked.

"Because we needed it." Gus opened his eyes. "Because that kid was not in his right mind and—"

"Then you should have said so back there," Madoc bit out. "You had eyes on the patient, and if you had even a second's thought he was going to be a problem, you should have told me. We could have restrained him."

"And you saw the guy too, in case you forgot. Unresponsive after the first dose of NARCAN, which is why I went in with a second. I'm not psychic, *Walt*," Gus bit out, contempt dripping off that wretched nickname. "I can't predict when a patient is going to come at us swinging."

"They're almost always confused and agitated after NARCAN—"

"Which is not the same thing as flipping from blue-lipped and barely breathing to Street Fighter mode. Jesus, kid. Every patient is different, and you should know that by now."

Oh, my God.

Madoc would have laughed at the worst nickname yet if he hadn't been so completely fed up. "No job is worth this," he said, mostly to himself. "I don't have to take this shit from you or anyone."

"All *right*," Gus snapped back with real temper at last. "I don't want to do this now."

"I have to file a report," Madoc reminded him. "You don't want to press charges against the patient, fine, but command is still going to want to know what happened."

"So, tell them. You clearly have an opinion on how things went down, and you can put that in your fucking report."

Gus tensed then, his knuckles going white around the cold pack and his face crinkling up so Madoc's stomach fell right to his feet. Mark was there before Madoc could move though, muttering softly as he fussed over Gus. A big guy walking in *behind* Mark was the one who caught Madoc's attention, however, especially after Gus took one look at the dude and the cold control he'd surrounded himself with instantly thawed, leaving him looking more shaken than Madoc had ever seen.

Holy cats, is this Ben? But why would Mark call him?

Without thinking, Madoc took a step closer to the bed. "You're not the sister," he blurted, instantly regretting the inane comment when the big guy frowned beneath his short beard.

"True, but you shouldn't assume. I'm Ian, the ex," he said, going to Gus's side.

Madoc recognized the name immediately. Ian had been there for the aftermath of Gus losing his leg. Was here for Gus again now, taking up position by the side of the bed. Trying to support Gus while Madoc had wanted to argue.

"Ian's a nurse," Gus said coolly to Madoc, already back in control. "Between him and Mark, I'm in good hands. Head back to the station, Walt, and get busy telling everyone how I fucked up."

An ache burrowed in behind Madoc's sternum as he followed Mark to the nurses' station to sign off on some forms. He hated knowing Gus believed Madoc would throw him under the bus. Even more that Gus was blaming himself for the call having gone bad because Madoc hadn't done shit to convince him otherwise.

SEVEN

THURSDAY, *May 4, 2:15 P.M.*

GUS COULDN'T BREATHE. Heat and darkness crushed into him, a massive weight pinning him down. Shrill chirps from a PASS device sliced the air, an alarm that meant a firefighter had been down for more than thirty seconds. Followed by screams and prayers to whomever was listening.

Pain snaked through Gus, so total it felt alive.

"Gus!"

Gus's heart thundered in his ears. Was that Walters? What the hell was he doing here? The guy wasn't a firefighter for fuck's sake and—

"Gus? Hey, it's okay. You were just dreaming."

Startled, Gus jerked back, eyes flying open as icy fingers of fear wrapped even tighter around his heart. And then the ache in his ribs flared bright and he groaned.

"Fucking *ow*." He tried to hold very still. "Christ on a cracker, that sucks."

"I know it does," Ian said. "You need to unclench or it'll hurt more."

Gus rubbed the sore spot on his chest and worked at relaxing his muscles. He was sore all over, thanks to the trip he'd taken into the wall back at the pub followed by days of sitting around doing nothing. But he was safe. There was no fire or debris pinning him, nobody screaming—dying—somewhere in the dark. He was at his ex-boyfriend's apartment and, aside from ribs that ached like a motherfucker, everything was okay.

Elliott, Ian's giant fluff ball Malamute mix, nosed at Gus's hand with a soft whuff.

"I'm all right, buddy." Gus stroked his fingers over Elliott's muzzle and got a lick in return. "Sorry I scared you."

"You weren't too bad," Ian said. "A little thrashing and cursing, nothing major."

His tone was easy, the way he'd always made it in the past when he'd talked Gus down from his nightmares. But Gus ached in a whole different way hearing him, the loss of the life they'd shared abruptly front and center and fresh in a way he hadn't felt in a very long time. Which was stupid when they'd both moved on, Ian with a new guy and Gus with ... a cat that didn't live with him.

Setting his jaw, Gus let Ian help him sit up and rearrange the pillows they'd stacked around him. He'd been holed up at Ian's since his release from the hospital, too stoned and off balance to stay on his own out at his sister's while she traveled for work. He was grateful for the help and care Ian and his nurse buddies had given him but felt unmoored at the same time. Because Gus didn't belong in this tiny apartment any more than he belonged in his sister's duplex.

Christ, get a grip.

"Connor's on his way over," Ian said. "Wants to check on

you before his shift, make sure we've been taking good care of you."

Gus nodded. "Okay."

There was a pause, and then Elliott was climbing up on to the couch to spread out beside Gus and set his big noggin in Gus's lap, a warm, comforting weight.

"Are you hurting?" Ian had a thoughtful expression on his face when Gus looked up at him. "You've been really quiet."

"I can be quiet."

"But you aren't, typically."

Coming around to the opposite end of the couch, Ian squished into the tiny space Elliott had left him and looked Gus in the eye. "We both know you're not good at admitting when you're in pain, so are you hurting or is this something else?"

Gus scritched a spot behind the dog's right ear. "My pain isn't too bad. But can I ask you a question?"

"Shoot."

"Do I make everything about me?"

Ian blinked, perhaps thrown by the quick topic change, but then a crease appeared on his forehead. "No. I mean, everyone gets self-centered on occasion, but I wouldn't say it's your default. You couldn't do your job if it were," he added. "What made you ask that?"

Gus went to shrug and felt instant regret. "Ow." He took a careful breath and patted Elliott some more. "Ben said as much the last time I talked to him."

"That's rich coming from him," Ian said with disgust. "Remind me why you still talk to that fuckface motherfucker?"

"Because hearing you curse like a sailor is fun?" Gus smiled at the unrepentant gleam in his friend's eye. "Truthfully, Ben still owes me an assload of money and if I block him, he'll take it as permission to stop paying me back."

"Fair." Ian grunted. "I still say you should have filed a

police report and put that shit on blast so everyone knows what he did."

Gus appreciated the sentiment, but he had more important things to deal with than exposing his ex-boyfriend's fuckery on social media. Starting with getting healthy so he could go back to work.

"Lemonade's been sleeping with one of your t-shirts," Connor said over his coffee mug. He'd arrived bearing news from Station 1 and a lemon ricotta cake they'd taken out onto Ian's small balcony. "Also, Walters is working days and riding with Heather while you're off the truck."

Gus whistled softly. "Bet she loves that. Heather hates riding with recruits," he said to Ian, "but she might let Walters live given he knows what he's doing. Working days is gonna suck for his kid-care schedule though, and I'm sure he's pissed at me for that."

"What is it with you and that guy?" Ian asked suddenly. "Monday night, you and he were growling and spitting like you hated each other and I've never seen you like that with a partner."

"They've got a frenemies kind of thing going," Connor said to Ian, grinning impishly at Gus's 'WTF' look. "I figure it's because they're chasing the same job."

Ian's eyebrows went up. "Oh, really?"

"No, not oh, really." Gus flapped a hand at his friends. "Yes, Walters wants on P1, but he's still a recruit and not eligible. As for Monday, please recall I was starting to trip balls on codeine and Walters ... Well, he was justifiably angry that I put his ass in danger by not waiting for backup."

Connor cocked an eyebrow at Gus. "You had backup, bruh —we just couldn't get to you through the mayhem. A *lot* of stuff went sideways on that call, all of it beyond our control."

Intellectually, Gus could agree. There'd been no way to

predict a bar fight would cut Walters and him off from P1 and the cops or that Brendan would react so wildly after the NARCAN. But Connor didn't know Gus and Madoc had quarreled beforehand or that those angry words had sent Gus into a tailspin he'd carried into the pub along with the jump bag.

"Connor's right—the call going sideways wasn't your fault," Ian said. "And if I'm honest, your partner seemed more overwhelmed than angry."

"Totally," Connor agreed. "In fact, I ran into Walters in my neighborhood yesterday and he just wanted to know you were all right."

Gus nibbled a slice of the cake, hardly tasting it over a bitter impulse to scoff and aware he was being unfair. He'd glimpsed genuine dismay on Walters' face back in that Province Street pub. Walters had reached for the emergency button on his radio, a gesture borne from a panic that was surprising in a seasoned veteran like him.

"Why did you send me for the gurney?"

Shit. Was Walters blaming himself for Gus's injury? Thinking that if he'd done something differently, Gus wouldn't have had his ass handed to him?

Gus pursed his lips. *'Hope for the best, prepare for the worst'* was a mantra the crews repeated like a charm to keep themselves safe. But sometimes the worst did happen to patients and crewmates alike, leaving those left unscathed to face the fact that no one definable thing—not luck or faith or whatever force they believed in—could fully protect them from harm.

There were still days Gus grappled with the guilt of having survived while Beni had not. But it wasn't Walters' fault that Gus'd been injured back in that pub any more than it was Gus's own, and he needed to stop them both from blaming the wrong person.

"I'll talk to Walters next week when I'm back on light duty," Gus said. "In the meantime, I need to find a new place to live so if you have any leads, I want to hear them."

"Ooh, I have one." Ian's eyes lit up. "Ground floor studio in Fort Point owned by some friends who moved to Italy. They'll charge you wicked cheap rent *and* the unit is already furnished."

"Yes," Gus said immediately, smiling at his friends' laughter. He'd taken only his clothes and personal possessions from Ben's, and he *really* liked the idea of not having to buy new furniture. "If there's room for me to get around in my chair, I will take it."

He signed a lease two days later after touring the tiny apartment with his ma and a real estate agent. The single room was simple but modern with a high ceiling and ample floor space for Gus's wheelchair when he wanted to use it, plus an ingenious room divider with a built-in couch that converted into a bed. As the building was a scant half mile from Station 1, Gus could bike or walk to work if he wanted, and there was even a public transit line that served the neighborhood, which just made the place all the more perfect.

Less than perfect was sitting behind the reception desk at the front of Station 1, unable to respond to the dispatch alarms.

"Ambulance A1, P1, person down on the roof of 163 Tremont Street, possible cardiac disorder," the dispatcher said through the speaker overhead. "Male, aged fifty-three, 10-D-5, known cardiac history, responsive with difficulty breathing. Code Two, BFD is en route."

Grinding his teeth, Gus flipped the page of the report he'd been reading. While grateful for the hours and pay and the time he got to spend with his cat, Gus wasn't cut out to work in an office, every hour a slow crush of boredom. And knowing A1 was out there chasing calls without him—Walters on a *roof* for fuck's sake—sent guilt crawling through Gus that he couldn't shake.

Until distraction arrived in the form of a young woman holding the street door open for a child carrying a pint-sized hockey stick.

Gus set his tablet aside. The woman was blonde and smartly dressed in a black suit with a briefcase over one shoulder and a purple duffel bag over the other, while the kid was a cute little thing clad in a blue tracksuit dotted with spots of red and had big, curious eyes under a Boston Bruins ball cap.

"Hello," Gus said with a nod. Neither the girl nor the woman appeared injured or in distress and he figured they'd come in by mistake or to use the restroom. "Welcome to Boston EMS Station 1. What can I help you with?"

The blonde's answering smile was tight. "Would it be possible to speak with Madoc Walters? I'm Noelene McKenna."

Gus cocked his head. Noelene was Walters' wife's name, wasn't it? Which had to mean the child regarding him from under the ball cap's brim had to be—

"Madoc's my daddy," Valerie Walters said cheerily. "And he drives a ham-bu-lance."

The kid's grin was *all* Walters, wide and adorably toothy, and Gus gave her one back.

"I know your daddy!" he said. "I'm Gus, his partner on the truck."

"HO-LEE CATS." Valerie's voice took on the earsplitting volume that came so naturally to many young children. "Daddy said your ribs are a mess!"

"They're pretty janky, but I'm getting better." Standing, Gus gestured to his side like a gameshow host. "How do I look?"

"I think pretty good!" Valerie beamed at him. "Daddy was worried, y'know. And he hates working days."

"We all hate it," Noelene said in an agreeable tone. She'd pulled a phone out from somewhere and scrunched her nose at it. "Our schedule is a big house of cards, and one change can topple the whole thing."

Gus imagined a lot of routines had been disrupted to bring Walters' wife, daughter, and a hockey stick wrapped in rainbow tape to the station on a Monday afternoon and damnit, he wished he'd been able to track down his partner to talk.

He extended his hand to Noelene. "Gus Dawson, the guy who knocked down your card house."

Noelene dropped the phone and shook Gus's hand, and the genuine smile she gave him this time changed her whole face. "It's nice to meet you, Gus. I was sorry to hear you'd been injured. This is Valerie," she added with a glance toward her daughter. "Who could maybe take her hat off while we're inside?"

Gus bent at the waist and shook hands with the kid, who had a head full of long, curly dark hair under her cap and really did resemble her dad, though her eyes were warm brown instead of blue.

"Your husband's out on a call," Gus said to Noelene once he'd straightened back up. "I can't say how long he'll be, but we can ask the dispatcher to get him a message."

Noelene's face did something complicated, seeming to freeze and thaw in rapid succession, and Gus got the feeling he'd said the wrong thing.

"I guess that explains why he hasn't picked up *my* calls," Noelene said with another frown for her phone. "I know he gets busy."

"Daddy needs to come pick me up," Valerie said to Gus.

"Him or Uncle T usually pick me up from hockey, but they couldn't today 'cause Uncle T is on a trip and Daddy's at work." She looked at her mom then. "Are you still taking me to school tomorrow?"

"Of course," Noelene replied. "I'll pick you up at your daddy's in the morning, the way I did today."

The child nodded, seemingly satisfied. "I just wanted to check."

Gus offered to take them back to the canteen, his brain racing as he picked the purple duffel up from the floor. Noelene had made it sound like she lived apart from her family, and wasn't that a surprise when Walters had never mentioned being divorced or even separated?

"Mr. Gus?" Valerie eyed him. "Do you play hockey?"

"I'm more of a basketball guy," Gus replied, "and I love baseball. But I'd try hockey if I felt like it."

"Uh-huh. What's the canteen?"

"Oh, um, it's basically a kitchen with a bunch of tables in it for people to sit at when they eat lunch or take breaks."

"I bring my lunch to school," Valerie said. "And Daddy gives me money so I can buy milk and dessert. Do you like butterscotch pudding?"

Gus smiled. "I don't mind it. I think chocolate is better, though. Ooh, or rice pudding, if there are no raisins in it."

"Raisins are gross." Valerie made a terrible face, sticking her tongue out as if she were gagging. "Kenny Baker at school eats them with sunflower butter and celery 'cause that's how his family does Ants on a Log, *and* he chews with his mouth open."

Gus wanted to grimace himself. He'd eaten Ants on a Log a million times as a kid but with cream cheese, thanks very much. And then to add *raisins*? Clearly Valerie Walters needed to examine her friendships.

The kid's face lit up as they entered the canteen, and she

dashed to the seating area with the hockey stick still clutched in one hand.

"Ooh, it's big!" she exclaimed. "It smells like coffee and toast, and I like all these chairs!" Her curly hair bounced as she ran and she waved at the receptionist, Tracie, who'd been on her afternoon break.

Smiling, Tracie waved back before looking to Gus. "How you doin', Gus? You need a hand with anything?"

"Doin' just fine, Tracie, thanks," Gus replied. "When you're done, would you mind getting a message to Walters that his family is here?"

Noelene's phone chirped again. "I need to call my office, Val," she said, frowning when her daughter didn't glance back. "Valerie, are you listening to me?"

"I'll keep an eye on her," Gus offered. "Make sure she stays out of trouble."

Valerie let out a squeal then as if to prove Gus full of shit, but it was only because she'd caught sight of Lemonade, who'd emerged from one of her hiding spots to investigate the new visitors.

"I found the kitty!" Valerie bounced on her toes, her eyes shining bright. "And she's super friendly!"

VAL'S AT THE STATION, pls pick her up.

The fuck? Madoc stared at the message on his phone's screen. That couldn't be right—he wasn't even off duty for another couple of hours.

And in no hurry to get back to Station 1 anyway, when being out in the field made it easy to put off having to deal with Gus, a thought Madoc hated himself a little for having.

He could only imagine how bored Gus was stuck behind a

desk. That seeing a familiar face might cheer him up, despite Madoc and him having parted on not the best terms. Madoc wanted to see Gus, especially knowing Gus'd had to stay with his ex because he'd needed help while he'd been on pain meds. But the idea of meeting his partner's brown eyes and apologizing after *way* too many days had passed in silence between them had made Madoc's words back up in his throat and he'd put it off again and again, aware he was acting like the worst kind of emo brat.

Madoc looked at his dayshift partner, Heather Bennett, over the hood of the truck. "Hey, Heather? I need to make a call real quick. Something's going on with my kid's pickup."

He braced himself for grumbling. While an excellent EMT, Heather wasn't a good match for Madoc, his chaotic personal life at odds with her general lack of patience for … people. But Heather surprised him now with an easy nod.

"I'll go grab a snack." She waved toward a convenience store on the opposite side of the street, the heavy box braids she had tied back in a tactical ponytail swinging gently. "You want anything?"

"No, but thanks. This shouldn't take long," Madoc said. "Pretty sure Val's mom just got her signals crossed."

The problem, of course, was that Noelene's signals weren't crossed at all and she truly expected Madoc to drop everything and pick Valerie up right the fuck now.

"Where *is* Val," Madoc pressed. "Did you really bring her to Station 1?"

"Um, yes? She's hanging out with your partner right now." Noelene frowned at Madoc through his phone's screen. "You know, Gus, the guy who seems to think you and I are still married."

Heat crept up Madoc cheeks. "Noels."

"Fine." Rolling her eyes, Noelene flipped the camera on

her phone away from herself and *there* was Madoc's girl, safe and sound as she sat cross-legged on the floor of the canteen at Station 1 with Princess Lemonade Small Void Kitty and Super Gus Dawson.

Relief washed through Madoc as he watched his daughter laughing at Lemonade, who'd just leaped from the floor onto Gus's shoulder. Gus was hamming it up a little for his guest while the cat kneaded biscuits into his shirt and God, he looked so much better than he had the last time Madoc had seen him, healthy and whole and like his typical cheerful self. He smiled at whatever Val was saying, his eyes crinkling at the corners, and Madoc's heart did the strangest flip.

"See? She's fine." Noelene switched the camera back to herself. "I still need you to come pick her up. I'm due in Back Bay in an hour and since you didn't want to hire a nanny for your daughter, you get to figure this out."

The muscles in Madoc's lower back tightened. He hated the way Noelene talked about Valerie like she was a problem that needed handling. *His* daughter instead of *theirs*, as if Noelene wasn't also Valerie's parent.

Madoc kept his voice even. "I'm still on probation. You know I can't walk off shift unless there's an emergency."

"And what do you call this? "

"Life. We agreed you'd handle the school pickup and drop-off while I'm on days and Tarek's away and that I'd handle everything else."

Noelene sighed. "I know we did," she said more gently. "But you're not the only one with a job and it's not fair that I'm always the bad guy."

"Is that Daddy?" Valerie asked from off-screen, much closer now and her tone petulant, not at all like a child who'd been merry just moments ago. "I want to talk, too!"

"Not right now, Val." Noelene was looking down and to her

right. "The adults need some minutes to straighten things out, so don't go making drama."

"I'm not making drama," Valerie huffed, only for a new player to enter the fray a second later.

"I can keep an eye on Valerie if you need someone to do it, Ms. McKenna," Gus said. "I went off duty a while ago and it's not a problem for me to hang out here with her until Madoc's shift ends."

Madoc's stomach fell to his shoes and hell, he didn't know what to react to first: Gus's offer to kid-sit, Gus calling Madoc by his given name for the first time ever, or the assessing look that crossed Noelene's face.

"You don't mind?" She furrowed her brow at Gus. "I wouldn't ask but I have to—"

"Noels, no," Madoc said over her because what the fuck was she doing? Gus was Madoc's partner, not a wanna-be nanny. "I'm not asking Gus to do this."

Noelene turned the frown back to Madoc. "Why? He offered and I can't miss this meeting."

"Can I give Princess Lemonade some milk?" Valerie said abruptly from off-screen.

"Milk hurts her tummy," Gus replied in his easy way, "but we have these tubes of yummy cat yogurt that she really digs."

"Cats can eat yogurt?!"

"Nah, I just call it yogurt because of the way it looks. C'mon, I'll show you."

A pause followed, Noelene's gaze tracking right as she watched Gus introduce Valerie to the wonders of Lemonade-approved snacks. She'd started to look faintly amused by the time she turned her attention back to Madoc.

"What do you think?" she asked.

Madoc thought Noelene should fucking take care of her

daughter because *parenting* was also her job. But that wasn't fair; Madoc and Noelene had always supported each other's careers and the personal and financial successes of the athletes she represented in her job as a sports agent were important to her in the same way the health and well-being of Madoc's patients were to him. Madoc also felt sure Valerie would be in good hands if they took Gus up on his offer to watch her. Gus was the kid whisperer after all, who charmed young patients with drawings, hand puppets, and the kindest of words, just like he was the guy who'd had Madoc's back every night they worked together.

"Madoc," Noelene said quietly. "We need a solution."

Madoc licked his lips. "I know. I'd trust Gus with Val. But I'd like to talk to them both before you go."

"Ooh!" Valerie said, very loudly from somewhere. "Cat yogurt *stinks*. But the kitty sure loves it!"

Smirking, Noelene brought the phone over to Gus, no doubt assuming the matter was settled. Madoc hadn't forgotten Gus had a life of his own though, or that he was recovering from an injury that could make kid-sitting a six-year-old challenging.

"You sure you want to do this?" Madoc asked him straight-out. "Val's a sweetie but has *lots* of energy. She'll want to run you ragged."

"I can handle it. Although ..." Gus grimaced slightly. "Is it okay that I promised to share some *bolos* with her?"

Smiling, Madoc nodded. "Yes, that's fine. Val likes bread the same way you do, so please limit her to just one or she won't eat dinner tonight."

"Good to know. One *bolo* and that's it."

"Thank you." Madoc paused a beat before adding, "You know I won't hold it against you if you say no, right?"

"Sure." Gus regarded Madoc steadily. "But I can see you're in a bind, and I can help if you want it."

Madoc knew then that this was more than one partner doing a favor for the other. This was Gus making a connection. Extending an olive branch because Madoc hadn't known how.

Steeling himself, Madoc reached out and grabbed it.

EIGHT

GUS TOOK good care of Madoc's girl.

The two were bent over a card game when Madoc got home, and there was pop music playing on the smart speaker in the kitchen. But oddly, there was a cat perched on the arm of the couch, which was weird when Madoc didn't own any pets.

"Welcome home, Daddy!" Valerie dashed over, curls and purple tutu bouncing. "Mr. Gus and me inspected the fire engines next door to where you work! And he drew me some more ponies 'cause he's wicked good at art an' I colored them in so we could tape them up." She waved at the door to her room which was already papered with her drawings and crafts. "Now me and him are playing Slapburger and I'm winning."

"Wow, that's a lot!" Madoc set his backpack and grocery bag on the kitchen island, then swung Valerie up in his arms. "Sounds like you and Gus had a bunch of fun. But what happened to your braid?"

"It fell out on accident when I was at recess."

"By accident, honey."

"*By* accident." Valerie flapped her arms dramatically. "Ms. Jensen fixed it, but it fell out again."

Madoc pushed some of the soft curls off Valerie's face. "How come you didn't ask your mom to re-braid?"

"'Cause you're the best at it."

"Well, thank you very much." He bussed her cheek. "Were you careful with Super Gus like I asked?"

Valerie nodded firmly. "Yup! I didn't call him Super, though."

"I'm sure he doesn't mind. Now." Raising an eyebrow, Madoc looked askance to the couch and back. "Is that the kitty from Station 1 over there," he whispered, "or am I losing my marbles?"

Valerie giggled and took his face between her small hands. "That's Princess Lemonade! Mr. Gus said they're having a sleepover tonight. Did you know she wears a leash and can ride in his backpack? Even when we were on the underground bus! Mr. Gus brought a litter box for her and it's in my bathroom. Ooh, and he told me the story about how she was caught in a flood! She jumped right in the water when she saw him 'cause she knew he would save her." She turned Madoc's face loose. "Do you want to play cards with us?"

"Before you answer, please know your daughter has been destroying me." Gus'd swapped out his beige uniform top for the plain white t-shirt underneath and was smiling. "I had no idea Slapburger was so cutthroat."

Madoc set Valerie down. "Well, I guess you haven't tried Taco Cat Goat Cheese Pizza yet then."

Gus narrowed his eyes. "Is that a game or a food?"

"It's a game!" Valerie zipped back over to Gus. "And it's super fun. Do you wanna play, Mr. Gus? I have cards upstairs in my room at Uncle T's and I can go get them."

"That's okay, hon." Gus nodded at the cards she'd picked back up. "I like the game we're playing."

Madoc turned to his bag of groceries, face growing warm. He dreaded the questions Gus would have for him about Noelene and Valerie. But then Lemonade came over, the tags on her collar jingling softly as she demanded pets, and Madoc indulged her for a minute, aware of Gus and Valerie playing on. Gus played up his continued losses, head tipped back and groaning, and his pile of cards tiny when Madoc ambled back over.

"Will you set the table for dinner, honey?" he asked Valerie. "I left everything on the counter for you."

Gus glanced at his watch. "Heck, I should go. Give me a minute to grab the cat and her stuff and I'll be out of your hair."

"Stay, Mr. Gus!" Valerie grinned as Lemonade crowded against her looking for a little attention. "Daddy's gonna make BLTs and tater tots and they're super yummy."

Madoc smiled at his partner. "You want to join us?" he asked. "Let me pay you in tots and bacon and maybe an ice cream sandwich for dessert?"

Gus set down his cards. "I love tots, actually. What can I do to help?"

They worked together, Madoc frying bacon while Gus made a salad, and though conversation between them could have been stilted given the arguing they'd done a week ago, it wasn't.

"Does Lemonade sleep over at your place a lot?" Madoc asked Gus.

Gus glanced over to where Valerie was batting the kitty's stuffed banana toy across the floor with her hockey stick so Lemonade could chase it. "Yes, though not while I was staying with my sister because Donna's allergic. Now that I'm in my own place again, I figured it was time to get back in the habit."

Wait, what?

Madoc frowned at his partner. "When did you move?"

"Sunday. I found a studio over in Fort Point and my parents and Connor helped me get my stuff from Donna's into town."

Madoc set down the tongs he'd been using to turn the bacon. The historic Fort Point section of the South Boston Waterfront was only four blocks away. Valerie's favorite place to eat was in that neighborhood, along with the kid-friendly museum she begged to visit most weekends, and a micro-brewery Madoc and Tarek sometimes visited for burgers and beer.

"What made you move there?" he asked Gus.

"The place basically fell in my lap through friends of Ian's." Gus dressed the salad with a honey vinaigrette he'd mixed up. "I like not having to rely on a car to get to work, plus the unit is on the ground floor which is nice when I'm using crutches or my chair and, most critically, it's hella cheap."

Despite his casual tone, the tips of Gus's ears had turned pink, and Madoc could tell the admission was costing him. Gus also looked thinner and tired now that Madoc was close to him, with dark circles under his eyes that hadn't been there before his injury.

Abruptly, Madoc needed to make his partner feel better.

"Val's uncle owns this place, and I rent it for almost nothing," he said, shrugging when Gus glanced his way. "We both know I couldn't afford to live here otherwise."

A slow smile curled at the corners of Gus's mouth. "You know, I kind of wondered? Because this place is bougie, yo."

Madoc laughed. "Yeah, I know. Hey, you were rubbing your chest earlier and I wondered if you were hurting. Is it bad?"

"I do hurt sometimes, just not so much I need meds." Gus cocked his head at Madoc. "Is that why you asked Val earlier if she'd been careful with me? Because of my ribs? Or was it because of my leg?"

"Your leg? I didn't think to mention your prosthesis to Val, actually. Should I have?"

"You're her dad, Madoc—you can tell Val whatever you want to about my leg. But I figured you thought I'd have trouble keeping up with her because of it."

Madoc regarded his partner. Six weeks ago, he might have worried about Gus being able to handle Valerie's energy levels when there were plenty of days that she ran Madoc and both of his functioning legs ragged. But working with Gus had reshaped Madoc's perspective on how a body could adapt after limb loss.

Gus had to consider things Madoc typically didn't, like safety on wet surfaces and how level the ground lay beneath their feet. He expended a staggering amount of energy just walking around, his body working extra hard to stay balanced, so he was frequently hungry and running hot. For the rest of his life, he'd work with a prosthetist to ensure his remaining limb stayed healthy and that he got the most out of using prosthetic legs. But any second thoughts Madoc might've had about Gus being able to keep up with *anyone* had been gone by the time their first shift working together had ended.

"I work with you, Gus—I know I have no reason to worry about your leg slowing you down ever," Madoc said truthfully. "I didn't want Val poking your sore ribs though, or guilting you into picking her up when you just came back on duty."

"To sit at a desk, ugh." Gus pulled the tray of sweet potato tots from the oven. "I miss the truck. I guess most people would think that's all kinds of weird."

"We aren't most people." Smiling at Gus's soft laugh, Madoc began constructing their sandwiches.

Valerie had lots of questions when they sat down to eat, her curiosity about Station 1 piqued now that she'd been there and had a look around. Madoc figured Gus had to be counting the minutes before he made his escape, but he surprised Madoc with an offer to clear the table while Madoc got Valerie cleaned up and into her pajamas.

"Want a beer?" Madoc asked him once Valerie was in her room with her tablet and Lemonade, reluctant to say goodbye to her new kitty friend the same way Madoc found himself wanting Gus to stay a bit longer too. "I have a decent IPA and there's more soda if you don't like to drink alcohol."

Gus smiled. "Beer sounds good. I like a drink now and then, but I can't consume much. Once my balance goes, I'm kind of screwed."

They brought their bottles to the couch and sat, Madoc staring out at the cityscape beyond the tall windows. He didn't know what he was feeling. Nerves because it was time to get real with Gus about a few things. But there was an odd sense of relief in him too, because this talk was long overdue.

"I'm sorry about the shit I said to you last week," Madoc said quietly. "I know you don't mean anything with the nicknames or think you're better than me. The only person bringing me down about the job is me."

"But why?" Gus frowned at him. "Your work is excellent, Madoc, and I see it every time we go on shift. If I need to say that more—"

"You say it enough, trust me, and I'm grateful you do," Madoc replied. "But my career lost momentum when I moved here because I had to start over and that hasn't been easy for me. Seeing opportunities like being promoted to medic slip away sucks and I get in my head sometimes about how much work I have to repeat or how I've lost literal years of progress. When you told me you were earning your A.S., I spun out more than usual."

"I'm sorry, man. That can't be easy."

"It isn't. But I had no right taking my frustrations out on you. You said once that you were just a guy standing in the way of things I wanted, like the job on P1. But that isn't true. You're a great partner Gus, and you deserve every break you earn on this job. I also think you're a badass getting a degree while working full-time *and* doing the medic field work."

The tips of Gus's ears turned red. "Thanks. I work hard at this job because I love it. But you weren't all wrong when you said I make it my life." He waved Madoc's immediate protest off. "The last couple of years have been chaotic for me too, losing my leg and firefighting, things falling apart with Ian. There were days I hardly recognized myself or what the hell I was doing.

"When I got into the EMS Academy, I was just incredibly grateful to have a new goal and a chance at a career I knew I'd be good at if I kicked enough ass. So, I put my head down and did my Super Gus thing, focused on the work and bulldozing past the stuff in my life that sucked."

Madoc shook his head. "You're more than just Super Gus. More than just the job too."

"I know," Gus said, though his eyes remained troubled. "But the work made me feel purposeful again and gave me back my independence. I needed that then and still do today. Maybe you don't believe it, but my confidence isn't always the best and the shit Ben pulled on me knocked me down hard."

The words—honest and real and raw—poked at Madoc's heart. In his eyes, Gus carried himself like the most centered, confident person in the entire city. But he wouldn't be telling Madoc any of this unless he really meant it.

"I hear you," Madoc said. "And I'm sorry Ben hurt you."

"Thanks." Sitting back, Gus regarded the beer bottle in his hands. "Look, I know I'm a lot. I've always been ambitious, and

I chase goals like the paramedic promotion and a degree you could argue I don't even need. But *I* am my own biggest competitor, and I would never try to sabotage you or hold you back for my own personal gain. While we work together, I will be focused on your success as much as mine. I want you out in the field as an EMT, not a recruit, because you are that good."

Madoc nodded solemnly. With each of them one-hundred-percent committed to growing their careers, they would have been true rivals if they'd been at the same level inside Boston EMS. And maybe there would always be a part of Madoc and Gus that welcomed healthy competition, no matter what level they happened to be at. But Gus was a decent guy and a good person who deserved his partner to be honest and real and maybe a bit raw with him too.

"I WANT to apologize for something else," Walters—*Madoc*, Gus reminded himself—said. "Namely, that I didn't correct you the first time you assumed I was married, because Noelene and I haven't been a couple for as long as we've lived in Boston."

Gus didn't reply. He wasn't sure what had spurred this confession, but if he'd learned anything today, it was that Madoc Walters was handling a whole lot of shit on his own and if the guy needed to unload, Gus could shut up and listen.

"Our divorce was finalized last fall, and I have sole custody of Val. Noelene and her brother Tarek help me make sure Val has what she needs to thrive and, most of the time, we work well together." Madoc licked his lips. "Noelene doesn't like parenting though, which can be challenging for all of us."

Well, that explained the aloof attitude Valerie had shown her mom. And the relief in Noelene's expression when she'd handed the spare keys to Madoc's apartment over to Gus. She'd had a meeting to get to, of course, but she'd known Gus less than an hour and been far too blasé in his opinion about entrusting him to take care of her daughter.

Gus cast a glance over his shoulder at Valerie's door to make sure it was still closed. "Has Noelene ever bonded with Valerie?" he asked.

"No." Pain crossed Madoc's expression. "We didn't plan to get pregnant, but Noels seemed truly happy about becoming a mom. Now, I wonder if I missed signs that might've tipped me off if I hadn't been so excited myself."

Leaning forward, he set his beer on the table. "Val was this tiny bundle of hangry and diaper changes who just wanted to be held. And I loved it." He gave Gus a small, sweet grin. "If keeping Val happy meant I ate with her strapped to my body, I did it. Spilled yogurt on her head more than once and ended up licking it off."

Gus chuckled gently. "That is adorably weird."

"I know." Madoc's smile faded. "Noels was cold toward Val. She took good care of her, don't get me wrong. But I could see her heart wasn't in it. She didn't like the mess or the chaos, or how you had to be 'on' all the time. Not being able to get more than a couple of hours' rest hit her a lot harder than it did me, and there were a lot of days I'd barely have time to put my stuff down after shift before she was handing me Val and taking off for hours at a time."

Madoc slid his fingers into his curls, mussing them before dropping his hands again. "I thought it was postpartum depression at first. But I'm sure it's something more profound now. Noelene never warmed up to Val or got better at dealing with the chaos, and that distance rubbed off on Val starting from early on. She ... *likes* her mom, I think, and Noels always takes good care of her. But Val isn't bonded to Noels the way she is me or even Tarek."

A mix of sorrow and pity panged through Gus's heart. His family meant the world to him, especially his ma, Layla, who made sure every day that Gus knew he was loved. He couldn't imagine not having her in his life. Or worse, being a six-year-old whose mom wanted nothing to do with parenting.

"Noelene is a sports agent and her hours and the travel are demanding," Madoc said. "After she went back to work, we got Val into a daycare and had a sitter, Marley, who'd step in if we needed her. Wasn't long before Val saw more of Marley than she did her mom, because Noelene always had an excuse to not be at home."

Anger brightened Madoc's eyes, but he also looked terribly hurt. "I started wondering if she was having an affair. Figured that had to be the reason she was gone all the time and didn't care that her daughter was more attached to the sitter than her own mom. Then I got an overdraft notice on our checking account and realized it was basically empty. And I figured out then that Noelene was spending most of her free time and our money gambling on blackjack and sports betting. That we were effectively broke because she'd burned through her savings and run up obscene amounts of money on our credit cards before moving on to the joint account that we shared."

Well, shit.

Stunned, Gus blinked several times before asking, "The money troubles you had back in Seattle happened because of her gambling?"

"Uh-huh. It was scary. And so fast." Weariness permeated Madoc's tone. "Noels cashed out her 401K to help pay down the credit card debts but that only went so far. And at the same time, she couldn't stop gambling. She'd try, then go off the rails, and it was like every time I turned around there'd be another hole to fill. When I found myself having to choose between paying rent or buying food to keep Val fed, I called Tarek for help."

"I can't imagine how hard that had to have been," Gus said. He'd endured a similar rollercoaster ride of financial uncertainty after his life with Ben had blown up. Gus'd only been responsible for himself though, and he'd been lucky to have a support system of family and friends to turn to. "But you know you did the right thing."

Madoc sighed. "I do. It *sucked* admitting I couldn't fix things on my own. But Tarek was incredible. He helped me find a rehab for Noelene and get us all moved here to Boston. He's been there for us ever since, pitching in a ton taking care of Val and giving us places to live."

"Is he some sort of tech bro?" Gus asked with another glance around at the apartment. "Figured he's gotta be if he owns this unit *and* a literal freaking penthouse."

"Tarek used to play pro hockey," Madoc replied. "His salary on top of his endorsement deals made him a fortune."

Gus cocked his head. He remembered then that a goalie with the surname McKenna had played for the Bruins, Boston's pro hockey team. The guy was a fitness pro now with an app and a website ... and he worked out of a gym in the Seaport.

Wait.

Gus's eyebrows went up. "Yo. Your brother-in-law is Tarek McKenna the *goaltender*? That dude is totally famous!"

"Ex-goaltender and yes, he is. Not my brother-in-law anymore now that Noelene and I are divorced, however."

"He'll always be Val's uncle, though," Gus said with a frown. "You know, I've learned more about who you are today than I did in the whole month we've known each other? I think that kind of sucks considering you're my partner."

"I'm sorry." Madoc grimaced. "I wanted to tell you about Noelene and me splitting up, but ... Honestly, it's embarrassing talking about all of this. Hard to not feel like a failure, especially since it really screwed up my career."

Gus softened at that. "Hey, no. I get that starting over is shitty, but you're nowhere near failing, Madoc. I'll remind you of that every day if you need me to."

"Thanks. I do feel like shit about what happened to you in that pub, though." Madoc pursed his lips. "Can't help thinking I should have done something differently."

"I figured. I've been doing the same," Gus admitted. "But we can't be blaming ourselves when we both know it was just shitty luck. Yeah, I got hurt, but we saved that kid's life."

"Please tell me you pressed charges against him," Madoc said, his voice going all low and growly and *why* was this asshole so hot? "Because if you didn't, I swear I'll kick you myself."

Stupidly, Gus snorted a laugh. And crap, laughing hurt.

Groaning, he dropped his hand to his chest, then startled a little when Madoc took hold of Gus's shoulders as if to steady him.

"Shit," Madoc murmured. "Are you all right?"

Gus kind of wasn't. Not with his chest aching and the rest of him very, *very* aware of how close his partner had gotten. When, glancing up, he saw for the first time that Madoc's eyes were slightly mismatched, a splash of brown interrupting the blue of his right iris along the outside edge, a rare and beautiful type of heterochromia. Madoc smelled delicious too, like soap and bacon and the IPA they'd been drinking.

If Gus leaned up a hair, their lips would meet. And the sheer insanity of the notion would have cracked him up again if he hadn't caught the expression of interest on Madoc's face.

That can't be right.

Except it was. Madoc's gaze drifted downward to Gus's

mouth and there was heat rolling off him in waves, the air around them crackling with promise.

The barn door sliding open behind them instantly broke the spell.

"Hi!" Valerie's cheery face appeared over the back of the couch. "Daddy, can I ask Mr. Gus if Princess Lemonade can sleep over here instead?"

Gus sat up, skin prickling as Madoc spoke with his daughter. What the fuck had just happened? Because it sure as hell seemed like Gus's *very* straight partner had wanted to kiss him. Again, a notion so ridiculous it was hardly worth entertaining.

Shifting focus, Gus packed the cat and her things up while also keeping an eye on Madoc. Who seemed very much his usual self. Not at all like he'd shared a supercharged ... *something* with Gus back on that couch.

So, maybe the whole thing had been in Gus's head. Wishful thinking brought on by an evening filled with unexpectedly intimate conversations with his partner-slash-crush.

However, Gus did not imagine Valerie looking dejected as he leashed Lemonade so the cat could climb into his backpack.

Getting down on his knee, Gus smiled at the kid. "Thanks for your help with the kitty today, Val," he said. "I know she loved meeting you."

"I loved it too." Valerie ran a hand over Lemonade's head where it poked up through the bag's zipper. "But what if she doesn't like your new house?"

"Oh, I think she will. Remember, Lemonade used to be a stray and she's a tough little chicken." Gus glanced up at Madoc who was watching them. "I could send a pic of her at my place to your dad and then he can show it to you."

"Okay." Valerie traced her fingers over the various Pride patches and pins Gus had attached to his bag, then stroked between Lemonade's ears one final time. "Have a good night, my honey."

Gus shifted his weight to stand but froze when Valerie stepped in and slipped her arms around his neck.

"Bye, Super Gus," she said, hugging him tight, and Gus only just managed to squeeze her back before she slipped away and ran off to her room.

"She really likes you," Madoc said when Gus'd climbed to his feet. "Did you mean it when you said you'd send a photo?"

Face absolutely on fire, Gus pulled his phone from his pocket and handed it over. "Of course," he said. "I wouldn't have said anything otherwise."

Once home, Gus didn't expect a reply to the pics he sent of Lemonade exploring the Fort Point apartment. Madoc sent one a few minutes later though with a pic of a grinning Valerie making a heart shape with her hands.

The messages didn't stop there either, Gus's and Madoc's shared thread filling up in the following days with photos, random thoughts, some links to online recipes, and snippets of silliness.

Madoc: *What would you tell your 21-year-old self?*

Gus: *Travel, have more sex, buy good pots & pans. You?*

Madoc: *Floss. Also, Beanie Babies won't be worth shit.*

Gus didn't think twice when a message from Madoc popped onto his screen at midday on Thursday. Until he read it and caught the urgency in its words.

Madoc: *I need your help.*

NINE

MADOC SLUMPED BACK against his front door. He felt fucking awful. Heartsore and so tired he wanted to sleep for a week. A luxury he didn't have when his girl needed him to make sure she was cared for and safe. Felt loved. Things Madoc wanted Valerie to have every day.

He wasn't sure how he was going to manage everything on his own now that Noelene ... Madoc sighed. A jumble of feelings hit him every time he thought of his ex. Disappointment so bitter it curdled his stomach. Genuine worry for her well-being. Dread knowing he was going to have to tell people why she wasn't around.

"Gus? Does it ever come off?"

Madoc glanced toward Valerie's room. Seemed she'd dropped the 'Mister' and was just calling Gus by his name.

"Not often," Gus replied. "If it does, that means it's time for me to see my doctor and probably get a new socket. My leg should stay on until I'm ready to take it off."

Oh, boy.

Madoc made a beeline for Valerie's door. Earlier in the

week, he'd talked to her about Gus's prosthesis and explained the basics about how he'd come to need it, but it seemed Valerie had saved some questions for the next time she saw Gus in person.

"How come you take it off?" she asked now.

"Well, I have to for showers and also for sleep," Gus said. "But sometimes I take off my leg because I feel like it."

"Ah."

Poking his head in past Valerie's door, Madoc took in the scene. He'd already known Gus would take good care of Valerie. But finding them seated on the purple throw rug by the bed, Valerie swiping a marker over one of Gus's drawings while Gus braided her hair was unexpected and adorable.

Gus had his back against the bed with Valerie stationed in front of him, the drawing pad on her knees. She wore pajama pants and an old hockey jersey, and Madoc had to smile at Gus's Pride bracelet around her left ankle.

His partner, in the meantime, looked slightly rumpled in his white undershirt, his hair a bit messy. Gus'd changed out of the brown cargos he wore on duty, and the prosthesis left visible by his long shorts drew Madoc's gaze.

He'd glimpsed Gus's ankle beneath the hem of his pants many times, but never seen the whole limb before now, and he knew it was fashioned from carbon fiber and fiberglass with a mix of metals including titanium. The black silicone socket that went over Gus's shorter right leg had been molded to match his muscled left calf, giving the whole prosthesis a sleek, powerful appearance. Even so, Madoc was more struck by Gus's expression, which was intent on his work while also at ease.

"Gus?" Valerie exchanged one marker for another. "Does it hurt when you wear your pos-thee-sis?"

"If everything fits me properly then no, it shouldn't hurt," Gus replied. "But if I get a wrinkle in even one of my socks or the liner, I have to fix it right away because that sh-*stuff* feels really bad."

Valerie snickered. "You almost said a potty word, huh? I won't tell Daddy, 'cause I don't want him to get mad at you."

"I won't be mad, honey," Madoc threw out, waving when two sets of brown eyes swung his way. "Gus is a grown-up and can say potty words if he wants."

They ate a one-pot pasta with red sauce for dinner with 'pizza bites', little twists of cheesy bread that Valerie and Gus had made up. And while Madoc didn't have much of an appetite, chatting with Valerie and Gus helped ease some of the anxiety twisting his insides. He still caught Gus watching him over the course of the meal and post-dinner cleanup, questions clear in his gaze.

"Will you tell me what's going on?" Gus asked once Valerie was in her room for some pre-sleep screen time with her door closed. "And don't say it's nothing, because I can tell you're stressed."

"I definitely am," Madoc muttered, then headed for the kitchen because it was the farthest point in the apartment from Valerie's room. "Thank you for picking Val up," he said. "I know I didn't give you much notice."

"No big—I was doing errands when you messaged. Did Noelene have another work emergency?"

"No. Well. Not that I know of." Pulling the refrigerator door open, Madoc stared into it. His voice sounded flat to his own ears. And, weirdly, he felt flattened too, like the air around him was pressing him down. "I talked to her last night after shift, and everything seemed normal," he said. "But this morning, there was a note taped to my door saying she had to go, and I guess that's what she did."

A ringing silence followed, stretching out and out before Gus spoke again.

“Go as in ... Did Noelene take off on you?”

“Seem like it, yeah.” Madoc gave himself a quick shake. “I went to Tarek’s and a lot of her stuff is gone from the room she uses up there.”

He didn’t like thinking about the empty drawers and clothes hangers he’d found in Noelene’s room. The note she’d written in her strong, blocky script.

I have to go, Madoc. I tried, and I think you know that better than anyone. But I can’t breathe when I’m here and I don’t want to live like this anymore.

“She planned it,” he said, looking at Gus. “Probably had been for a while.”

Gus swore quietly. “You called her?

“Goes to voicemail.”

“What about her office? Could you ask her boss where she went?”

“I went there today after dropping Val off at school. Her boss looked surprised to see me, so I don’t think Noelene told the people she worked with about what she was going to do. Her boss said Noels had business trips lined up for the next several weeks which I know takes weeks of planning. But it doesn’t really matter when Noelene’s schedule isn’t my business.”

“The fuck it’s not.” Gus set his hands on his hips. “Noelene’s supposed to be *here* helping you with Val.”

“I know. But I have sole custody, Gus, and Val’s care is on me. And if Noels is gambling again, I don’t want her seeing Val anyway.”

Some of the outrage went out of Gus’s face. “Shit. Do you think she’s relapsed?”

“It’s possible. Noelene’s a binge gambler. Long stretches

where she has some control but when she falls off the wagon, everything goes sideways fast."

Madoc pulled the pitcher of water from the refrigerator and let the door swing closed. "It was bad in Seattle toward the end. She called in sick to work a lot. Would go days without real sleep or food and she got careless with Val. Forgot pickups and to feed her. Would bring her places she shouldn't have. Or not bring her at all. Noelene left Val alone a few times," he said, "always when I was supposed to be headed home so Val wouldn't be on her own for long. But Val was just *three*."

He hated the acid in his own voice. That he'd been through this before and recognized Noelene's tells but had done nothing, despite his gut telling him she'd been acting strange.

"She's been distracted lately and staying out late more. When she showed up at the station Monday with Val, I knew something was off with her."

Madoc went into the cabinet for glasses, but then he set them on the counter and stood there, staring right through them. "I never thought she'd leave, though. Like actually walk out on her kid. Who the fuck does that? And how dumb am I not to have seen it coming?"

"Hey."

A hand came to rest on Madoc's shoulder, and when he glanced up, his heart squeezed at the concern shimmering in his partner's eyes. "I'm so fucking angry with her, Gus."

"You have every right to be." Gus shook his head. "I don't even know what to say."

"Same." Madoc's laugh hurt his throat and left a bitter taste in its wake. "I have no fucking clue how I'm going to explain this to Val. Like, what do I tell her?"

"You'll figure it out," Gus replied quietly. He pursed his lips, then stepped closer and slipped his arms around Madoc.

"I'm guessing you're not much of a hugger," he said, "but I'm here if you need me."

Madoc had no fucking clue what he needed just then. But God, it was so fucking good to be comforted. To not have to be strong, if only for a goddamned minute. To be held after so many months of being touch starved. Squishing his eyes shut, he wrapped his arms around Gus, his chest cracking wide open. And the storm in him shifted, anger and heartbreak becoming something Madoc didn't know how to name.

As a teen, he and his friends had sometimes gone cliff jumping at a state park near where they'd lived. They'd been too stupid-brave to be fully cognizant of the dangers that came with leaping into cold water from heights of thirty and forty feet. But a similar feeling of standing on the edge came over Madoc now, sending his pulse into overdrive.

Gus shifted, his hold on Madoc loosening as he started letting go. Madoc knew he should do the same. He had so much shit left to do tonight and couldn't stay wrapped around Gus like an octopus. Madoc didn't want to be away from the warmth Gus'd wrapped him in, though. Didn't want to let go of Gus, so he didn't.

Hardly daring to breathe, he turned his face until his forehead was against Gus's temple, relief pulsing through him when Gus leaned into the touch rather than pulling away. Gus'd dropped his arms to Madoc's waist and as his eyes fluttered open, Madoc glimpsed disquiet in them he knew he had put there.

This week, Madoc had disclosed more about the shitshow that was his life to Gus than he had to anyone, even Tarek, without warning or explanation. Rather than backing off, Gus'd offered support, twice dropping his plans to kid-sit Madoc's girl. He hadn't judged Madoc for his choices or secrecy and instead stayed and listened.

An urge to get closer invaded Madoc's blood. He wanted to smooth the furrow between Gus's brows. Erase the worry from his face. Change the pout on his mouth change into a smile. With a kiss.

Something Madoc wanted to do with Gus Dawson more than anything he'd wanted in a very long time.

Slowly, he angled his head until his lips met the laugh lines beside Gus's right eye. He kissed the top of Gus's cheekbone. The corner of Gus's mouth. And each tiny touch sent lust bolting through Madoc unlike anything he'd ever felt before.

Gus stayed very still the whole time, his gaze locked on Madoc's.

"Mad," he said at last, his voice a bare whisper. "What the fuck are you doing?"

"I don't know," Madoc replied just as softly. He'd never heard his partner so tentative. And knowing he wasn't the only one feeling unsure emboldened him. "Mostly hoping you don't want to punch me right now."

Gus's eyes warmed. "I definitely don't."

Leaning in, he covered Madoc's mouth with his own, movements slow and so natural. Madoc closed his eyes, his insides cartwheeling like he was in free fall as sensations both familiar and strange broke over him. Velvet soft lips and beard stubble. Muscular arms around him. A throaty, pleasured hum that went straight to Madoc's balls.

Gus.

Who cupped Madoc's cheek in his hand and kissed him with an intensity that had Madoc's bones going gooey, knees trembling so hard he might actually fall.

Gus didn't let him, though. He eased Madoc backward, then crowded closer and used his weight to pin Madoc against the counter. And fuck, Madoc was on fire. He'd been kissed plenty in his life, but none could match this one. He was getting *hard* for God's sake, just from kissing.

Kissing Gus, *you fucking idiot, and what the hell are you thinking?*

Awareness pricked up the back of Madoc's neck. Was he really doing this in the middle of the shambolic mess Noelene had left him in? With his *supervisor* from work, who was only here tonight because Madoc had begged him for help with Valerie?

Oh, Jesus, Valerie. How the hell would Madoc explain this if she came out of her room right now?

Instantly, Gus eased back, almost as if he'd heard Madoc's inner monologue.

"Hey," he said, his arms still around Madoc but loose now, his voice pitched low and soothing. "You good?"

Madoc nodded, unsure if the buzz in his chest was relief or rejection. A week ago, he'd never have imagined himself kissing a guy. Liking it a *lot*. The way Gus'd taken control, tipping Madoc backward and pulling a groan out of him had been hot as fuck and, oh my God, why was his brain doing this to him?

"I'm okay. Wait, are you?" An ugly thought pushed its way past Madoc's mini-freakout, and he quickly looked Gus over. "I didn't knock into your ribs, did I?"

"No. I feel only excellent right now," Gus said with a chuckle. He dropped his arms then, but kept hold of Madoc's right hand. "It's been a while since a kiss made my head spin."

Madoc's whole face went up in flames. "Been a while since I kissed anyone," he admitted. "But I've never kissed a guy before tonight."

"NEVER KISSED A GUY BEFORE TONIGHT."

The words were like a bucket of ice water over Gus's head. Kissing Madoc—fuck, just touching him—had been the single hottest thing he'd done in months. His body still buzzed with a craving for more contact, a thing Gus could not allow to happen.

He didn't know whether Madoc was bi-curious or closeted, or simply experiencing one hell of a stress reaction to his ex going AWOL—God knew, it might be some combination of all three. Gus was very certain Madoc was not in his right mind at the moment, however, and that adding sex hormones to the mix was the very last thing he needed.

Not to mention Madoc freaking reported to Gus on the job, which was the only reason Gus needed to keep his distance.

Inhaling, he gave Madoc's hand another quick squeeze before letting it go. "If you want to talk about it, we can. But if you need time to process, just know that's cool too. Whatever you're feeling right now is—"

"I don't know what I'm feeling, Gus, and that's kind of the problem. One of them, anyway." Madoc leaned back against the counter, his shoulders sagging.

"I've always liked women," he said. "How they look and feel and smell, all that. But sometimes, I notice guys. It's never the same level of interest. Like, I'll notice it and then it'll be gone the next second. Except ... that hasn't happened with you. I *keep* noticing you and the interest *doesn't* go away, and I don't know what to make of wanting to kiss you."

"You don't have to make anything of it," Gus said. "You had an impulse that you acted on and maybe even liked a little."

"I liked it a lot. Kissing you is the best thing I've felt in literal years, and I want to do it again." Madoc scrubbed a hand over his forehead. "But Christ, it terrifies me to even think that. Especially with my whole life already fucked, Noelene gone, Tarek away, nobody I can call for help with Val."

Stomach falling to his feet, Gus had to stop himself from taking Madoc's hand again.

Focus, Dawson. This isn't about you and your damned feelings. It's about your partner needing your help.

"You don't have any family who are local?" Gus asked.

"Not outside of Tarek, and he's gone for the summer, hiking the Appalachian Trail with friends." Madoc dropped his hand and looked at Gus again, his face lined with fatigue. "I could message, but what am I going to say? 'Hey, T, your sister took off, so could you come home and help me with Val?' He mostly leaves his phone off anyway which does me no good when I need someone right now."

"You have me," Gus said, "and I'm happy to help."

Surprise streaked across Madoc's face. "You've helped me twice this week already and I really appreciate it."

"No, I mean ..." Gus frowned. What did he mean exactly? That he could kid-sit his partner's daughter until Madoc found someone else? Because maybe that wasn't the greatest idea given all the boundary-stomping he and Madoc had done tonight.

Then Gus glanced across the apartment to Valerie's door, which now boasted drawings of a familiar-looking black kitty among the paper hearts, flowers, and cartoon ponies, and his chest went tight for reasons that had nothing at all to do with his ribs.

Gus didn't know Noelene McKenna and had no idea what kinds of complicated things went on in her head. But she'd made sure Valerie was someplace safe before fucking off, and that counted for something.

Turning to the pitcher of water Madoc had left on the counter, Gus picked it up and carried it to the fridge.

"We need something stronger than water," he declared, exchanging the pitcher for two bottles of beer. "And since you're stuck with the guy who needs to keep his head on straight to walk, beer will have to do."

"I don't feel stuck with you at all." Madoc got the opener from the drawer and popped the caps on the bottles. "I'm *glad* you're here, glad that you stayed after I almost freaked out."

"Then let me keep helping you with your kid after tonight," Gus said. "I know you still have to figure out what's going on with Noelene, but in the meantime, you'll need someone with Val while you're on duty, right? Monday and Friday before and after school, plus all day over the weekends?"

"Yup. I've been looking at childcare services."

"Like a kidcare-dot-com? Bro, you know that's going to kill your wallet. Besides which, I'm going to be free during those hours for at least the next month, and I'll kid-sit for free."

Madoc shook his head. "I can't ask you to do that."

"I'm offering."

"Gus."

"Madoc."

"Knock it off," Madoc said with a scowl that made Gus smile like a goof because he really had missed bugging his partner.

"You need the help until Tarek can get back here," Gus reasoned, "and I'm saying I want to give it you."

"I appreciate that," Madoc said, "and I'm genuinely blown away you'd even offer. But there's no way I expect you to be my kid-sitter and burn up all your free time."

"What if I told you I want to burn up some free time because I don't know what to do with it all?" Gus asked. "I can't exercise or work the way I normally would, and I hate having to sit on my ass knowing I'm letting you and the crews down—"

"That's not what you're doing," Madoc protested. "You need time to heal."

Sighing, Gus sipped his beer. "I know. But I still feel shitty about everything. You having to switch shifts, me being stuck at a desk. My doc thinks I may have a hairline fracture in rib three, which means I can't come back on regular duty until she clears me to do so."

"Damn, I'm sorry."

"Not your fault, remember? We just have to make it work. And I'm happy to watch your kid because if keeping busy with Val helps me feel less like I'm riding the struggle bus, then it's a win for me too."

Madoc frowned slightly, doubt still clear in his face. "I'm not convinced you understand what you'll be signing up for, man. Because keeping up with Val *and* work is a lot."

"You know, that started to sink in today after I hauled ass across town so I could freeze my balls off watching your kid skate around the ice rink like an absolute baller." That got Gus a laugh and he crossed his arms over his chest with a smile.

"You're right that I don't fully comprehend what it takes to watch a six-year-old," he said. "But it was good getting out of my head Monday and today doing stuff with her that wasn't about my stupid ribs. So, if you trust me, we could give this idea a shot and maybe both get something out of it."

Madoc fell quiet a couple of beats and Gus gave him space to think. A lot of guys in Gus's place might go to great lengths to avoid kid-sitting duties. But Gus wasn't most guys and he needed to keep busy to stay sane. Besides, stepping up for this tiny family felt like the right thing to do.

The door to Valerie's room slid open and she appeared, sprinting across the apartment with her tutu bouncing.

"My show's over, Daddy!" she said as Madoc scooped her up, and she made her face all pouty. "My favorite baker had to leave the tent."

"Are you watching the Big Summertime Baking Show?"

Gus asked, smiling when Valerie and her dad nodded in tandem. "I watch it, too! The judge with the blue eyes is my fave."

"He looks like a wolf!" Valerie cried. "But he's nice when people cry. I bet he'd even be okay with Daddy making cake from a box."

"Girl, box cake is yummy," Gus chided her playfully. "Almost as good as the kind from the supermarket with the huge frosting roses."

"Ooh." Valerie made an 'o' with her lips. "I love the vanilla kind with lots of sprinkles."

"Yes." Gus held up his hand and she smacked it with hers. "Cake rules."

"Uh-huh! Do you wanna watch baking with me?" Valerie cocked her head at Gus. "We can do that the next time I see you."

What a cutie.

"I'd like that!" Gus said. "And if your daddy says it's okay, I said I'd help get you to school sometimes in the morning."

Valerie beamed at Madoc. "What about after school? Is Gus gonna pick me up, too?"

Smile wry, Madoc looked between his daughter and Gus. "Well, I think Gus and I are going to work out a plan."

TEN

GUS ARRIVED at Madoc's doorstep very early the next day with a bunch of kid-craft ideas he'd found on the internet and a solid case of sleep deprivation thanks to his dumbass brain keeping him up thinking about kissing his partner.

Who looked phenomenally hot when he opened his door, all sleepy-eyed and barefoot, clad in a white t-shirt and blue jersey shorts. Gus's ability for rational thought went bye-bye as he followed Madoc into the kitchen because *Lord*, his partner's ass was glorious under that thin fabric, high and tight and beautifully round above a pair of thick thighs.

Thankfully, seeing a rainbow-spangled pony lunch box on the kitchen island snapped Gus back to reality.

Focus, Dawson.

They chatted over coffee and eggs, Madoc thanking Gus more than once for his help before producing an actual printed checklist that Gus took with a smile.

"It's more for Val than for you," Madoc said. "If she has questions, just show her the documentation."

"So, it's like that, huh?"

"Yup. She's paying attention to everything all of the time, even if it looks like she's not."

"Got it. What does she know about her mom?" Gus asked. "I don't want to flub anything if she asks."

"I told her Noelene's out of town on business. Which is true, as far as we know." Face serious again, Madoc picked up their mugs. "I have an appointment after shift with the attorney who handled my original custody agreement because I want to end Noelene's parenting hours. She's supposed to spend a certain number of hours with Val every week," he said, "but I don't feel comfortable with that arrangement anymore after the shit she pulled on me this week."

Frowning, Gus nodded. "Of course. Take all the time you need, and we can talk about where you want to go with the kid-sitting when you're ready."

"I want to talk about what happened last night too." Madoc set Gus's cup under the brewer and started a cycle though he kept his gaze down. "You know the, um, kissing and all that."

"We can talk about the kissing, of course. I just don't want you feeling pressured about anything."

"I don't feel pressured. But I also can't act like last night was nothing."

Well, shit that wasn't good. And here Gus'd hoped he'd be doing the right thing by not make a big deal about anything.

Standing, he walked around the island to join Madoc at the counter.

"It wasn't nothing for me, either," Gus chided gently. "I still need you to set the pace, so I understand what you're ready for."

Color stained Madoc's cheeks, but he met Gus's eyes. "That's fair. I'm not a child though, and you don't need to walk on eggshells around me."

Gus nodded. It was possible he was being overprotective,

and Madoc didn't seem as spooked today as he had the night before. Gus still wanted to tread carefully. His partnership with Madoc had crossed into a weird place over the last several days. They'd become ... involved in a way, their connection deeper than the more straightforward friendship that came from being colleagues.

An hour later, Gus had done some light yoga and donned his uniform and Valerie had slept through her alarm. Gus prodded the kid-shaped lump under the quilt on her bed until she rose, but while she was sluggish in body and mood, her brain came online quickly and the Q&A portion of the morning began over breakfast.

"Gus? Is a hotdog a sandwich?"

"Does your pos-the-tic leg have a name?"

"How come I can wear pants to school, but the boys don't wear skirts?"

"Do you call blueberries 'bluebs', Gus? 'Cause I do, and I think I invented a new word."

"Gus? How come you don't color your drawings in?"

Gus glanced down now to where Valerie lay on the floor by her closet. "Because you're better at coloring than me."

He was only half joking; Gus had never been able to get colors onto paper that were as vivid or true as the ones that lived in his head. Seeing his drawings take life under Valerie's fingers was wonderful though, her imagination taking them to fantastical places Gus'd never even imagined.

Smiling, he handed down a pair of rainbow-striped socks. Valerie attended a public school, but the students wore uniforms, and she'd spent ages deciding between navy blue leggings and a navy-blue skirt before deciding she'd wear both with a white polo shirt for her top. She looked pretty cute too, even lying flat on her back.

"How come you don't want to keep Lemonade?" she asked him now, waving a sock in each hand as she spoke.

"It's not that I don't," Gus replied, "but if I took her home, everyone at Station 1 would miss her, you know? So, she lives there most of the time and we all share taking care of her."

"Aw. That's wicked nice!"

"Lemonade seems to like it."

Taking a knee, Gus tied one of Valerie's sneakers while she worked on the other. "Okeedokee, artichokey," he said. "How about you brush your teeth while I braid your hair?"

"I can do that!" Valerie said brightly. "But Gus? If tomatoes are fruits, does that make ketchup a smoothie?"

Gus snorted. "I don't know, girl. But that one was kind of deep."

VALERIE HAD ENLISTED Gus as her partner in crime.

That much was obvious the moment Madoc walked into his kitchen and a pair of paper airplanes sailed past his head, chased by Valerie's giggles. He mimed hitting the deck, then laughed as his girl rushed to greet him, purple tutu bouncing with every step.

"How you doin', Daddy?"

"Doin' just fine, Valley Girl."

He scooped her up and she wasted no time launching into an excited tale about her project to build a fleet of paper aircraft. Madoc smiled at her bright eyes and admired the little flower-shaped clips adorning the thick braid hanging over her shoulder, noting Gus's bracelet was around her left upper arm this time.

"Whose idea was it to make planes?" he asked.

"Mine!" she chirped. "Gus brought lots of ideas, and I got to vote on my favorite. Ooh, and he made me a coloring book!"

"That was a lot easier than folding paper planes," Gus teased as he joined them. He wore the t-shirt and cargo shorts he'd arrived in that morning along with a smile.

Madoc had brought home pizza for dinner, and he quickly tasked Valerie with cleaning up her craft supplies so he could make salad and catch up with Gus.

"How'd it go?" he asked Gus, who seated himself at the kitchen island.

"Good, I think! I let her dress herself this morning, but we lost a pair of socks somehow." Gus glanced around, his brow creasing slightly. "Still not sure where they went, but I suppose they'll turn up again someday. We got out of the house in time to make sure Val wasn't late for school, and after pickup we walked around the fruit stalls at Haymarket before coming back here. There's a carton of blueberries in the fridge that Val wants for dessert."

He's enjoying himself.

Madoc could tell from the warmth in Gus's face. But the circles under Gus's eyes were also darker than yesterday and the way he kept rubbing his chest with his knuckles spoke of pain.

"She wasn't too much?" Madoc asked and Gus, God love him, shook his head.

"Not at all." Gus stole a glance at Valerie before looking back to Madoc. "Can I ask how it went with your attorney?" he asked quietly.

Madoc brought the salad ingredients and bowl to the island, then walked around it to take the seat next to Gus's.

"It was a good meeting," he replied. "We talked about my reasons for revoking Noelene's parenting time, and we'll talk again after the terms are re-drafted. The attorney's filed an emergency order to end the shared agreement in the meantime to get the ball rolling."

Concern clouded Gus's face. "I'm sorry, man. I wish Tarek was here, so you didn't have to deal with this on your own."

I'm not on my own, Madoc thought as another wave of that weird grief hit him, thick as mud. He hated what Noelene had done to their family, but he still worried for her.

For Gus too, who was rubbing his ribs again and looked startled when Madoc reached out and pressed his own fingers over Gus's.

"Is this okay?" Madoc nodded at Gus's chest. "I don't want you hurting even though I know it probably can't be helped."

"It can't. But it's not bad, I promise. Just achy today is all." Gus glanced away, ears going red, and Madoc hoped he hadn't embarrassed him.

"Daddy!"

Dropping his hand, Madoc turned a smile on his girl. "Valerie!" he exclaimed, mimicking her the way Gus so often did with him and, predictably, she rolled her eyes.

"I'm hungry," she said, then surprised him by crowding up against Gus's legs. Slinging an arm over his knees, she set her hand on Gus's kneecap, not far from the top edge of the prosthetic's socket. "Like, wicked staahving," she added, laying the local accent on thick, "and so is the Gusberry."

Madoc grinned at his girl. "The Gusberry, huh?"

"Because I'm sweet and tart all at the same time." Gus gently tweaked Valerie's braid. "Personally, I prefer Guszilla, but it's not like *I* have any say in the matter."

Tipping her head back, Valerie let out a monster roar, and Madoc was still chuckling as he headed off to shower and change while his daughter set the table and his partner finished the salad.

He'd missed this. Laughter and banter around chores. Place

settings for three at his table. Easy, caring touches from another adult, whether they came in the form of shoulder nudges or a hug that'd centered him instantly. And the kissing they'd done last night ... Christ. Madoc hadn't stopped thinking about how it might feel to do it again. To learn if sharing another kiss with Gus would feel as good.

"You still want to talk?" Gus asked later that evening when Madoc returned from tucking Valerie into bed. "I'm not in the mood for beer, but I saw some bottles of Mexicoke in the fridge."

"Cola's fine," Madoc said with shrug. "And yeah, I want to talk," he said, stepping into Gus's space where he stood by the windows. "Maybe kiss you some more too, if you want."

Gus's lips curled in a slow smirk. "I want." Gently, he pulled Madoc into a loose hug. "Haven't stopped thinking about the way you taste since you laid one on me last night."

Heat swirled in Madoc's belly, though he was sure his heart might actually jump out of his chest. "Same," he said, putting his hands on Gus's slim waist. "It's just ... I *really* have no idea what I'm doing, so please don't laugh if I fuck this up."

The amusement went out of Gus's face. "I would never laugh at you over something like that," he said. "It's okay to be unsure about what you're feeling. And to say no when I ask if it's all right to kiss you."

Madoc closed his eyes and set his forehead against Gus's. "It's more than all right."

The barest whisper of breath ghosted over his lips just before Gus slotted their mouths together. And oh, kissing was *absolutely* better than Madoc's memories. The beard stubble and Gus's throaty sound of approval. The power radiating from his lean frame. The way he held Madoc, taking control through touch.

Gus deepened the kiss, mouth opening wider, and Madoc

gladly fell into it, every inch of him clamoring to get closer. For more.

Delight thrummed through him, filling Madoc's chest. Then Gus teased his tongue between Madoc's lips and the jolt of pleasure that rocked through Madoc almost put him on his ass.

Holy fuck.

He couldn't have stopped his moan if he tried. He was on fire, every one of his nerve endings crackling and his dick straining in his boxers as Gus moved his hand to the back of Madoc's head. They moved the few steps separating the window from the couch, their lips never parting, and the second Madoc's ass hit the cushion, Gus climbed onto his lap and that delicious weight reduced Madoc's bones to water.

"This okay?" Gus asked him between kisses, chuckling when Madoc grunted and kissed him back harder.

This was much more than okay. This was everything. And Madoc felt only joy.

He reveled in Gus's weight pressing him down. The powerful thighs bracketing his. Gus's prosthesis against Madoc's left leg, hard and strange but not unwelcome. Gus holding him. Those drugging, irresistible kisses, Gus's mouth the best thing he'd ever tasted.

Madoc ran his hands up and down Gus's back, delighting in the way Gus's muscles flexed. Gus wanted this too. Wanted Madoc, an understanding that had Madoc's chest clenching. It'd been far too long since he'd felt desired. Since *he'd* wanted someone this badly. Basked in being embraced as he oh, so slowly fell apart, his balls throbbing and his cock hard.

Madoc's breath stuttered as Gus rolled his hips, a slow, tantalizing motion that brought their dicks together through the layers of clothing, sending fire rippling under Madoc's skin because Gus was hard too. Then Gus slid his fingers among

Madoc's curls, and Madoc melted a little further into the couch cushions. Purely on instinct, he reached down and cupped Gus's ass in his palm, then rocked up into Gus's next hip roll, pleasure blooming deep in his belly as he chased the pressure of Gus's body against his own.

Only for Gus to make a sound that was both hungry and pained before he broke the kiss.

"Christ," Gus muttered. "Not sure I believe what you said about not knowing what you're doing."

Madoc chuckled through the blush heating his cheeks. "I don't with guys," he said, "but I've always been a quick learner."

"I believe it." Slipping his arms around Madoc, Gus wrapped him up in a hug, his voice fond against Madoc's ear. "Seeing as I am about to lose what's left of my mind."

Same.

Closing his eyes, Madoc laid his cheek on Gus's shoulder and tried to get his thoughts straight. He'd always enjoyed being intimate with women, but this ... God, it was powerful. He'd never been so consumed by kissing. Gotten so hard he almost hurt. With a *guy*, for fuck's sake, who Madoc had wrapped up in his arms without hesitating.

And what did that say about the man Madoc had thought he'd been all these years?

"I like this," Madoc murmured. "But I don't know how to feel about that."

"It's okay not to know." Gus's lips against Madoc's hairline soothed him immensely. "You need time to get to know a side of yourself I'm guessing is new, and it's normal to feel jumbled up in your head while you do it."

Opening his eyes, Madoc sat back enough to see Gus's face. "Jumbled up sounds about right. But it's not just that I've never done this with a guy," he said. "Between work and Val, I don't have time for any kind of personal life beyond having ice cream and beer while I try to catch up on the TV that I've missed. I was being serious when I said it's been a *while* since I kissed anyone."

A soft laugh rumbled through Gus's chest. "I hear you, man. I haven't been dating either. Haven't really felt up to it since Ben blew up my life."

He pressed his lips against the apple of Madoc's cheek. "*This* could be nice though if you think you'd be up for it. Having fun with a friend, nothing too heavy."

Gus dropped kisses along Madoc's temple and forehead, retracing the route Madoc had taken along Gus's skin only the night before. And with each sweet, infinitely soft touch, Madoc relaxed a bit more.

"I like this," he said again. "And yeah, I think I'm up for it. Only with you, though. Not ready to talk about it with anyone else."

Madoc was sure he sounded ridiculous. Like he was clinging to a version of himself that had started to fade from existence the moment he'd pressed his lips to Gus's. But Gus took Madoc's uncertainty in stride.

"There aren't any deadlines," he said. "When you're ready to talk about who you are with anyone, you'll know. Until then, we'll do whatever feels right and you can talk or not talk to me all you want."

They sat a while longer, Gus rubbing warm circles into the space between Madoc's shoulders. And when Madoc finally sat back so Gus could climb off his lap, he felt steadier, especially because Gus kept hold of Madoc's hand.

ELEVEN

THANKS TO VALERIE and her boundless energy, Gus found himself doing more around the city just for fun than he had in years. They visited parks and playgrounds and looked at public art on their walks to and from school, while the weekends were reserved for kid-friendly tourist attractions like the New England Aquarium or Castle Island, a peninsula at the very end of the South Boston Waterfront that boasted beaches and a granite bastion fort dating back to the mid-1800s.

Gus had a blast doing all of it, even the more mundane stuff that came with a kid-sitting gig. Like supervising the morning and evening chaos of washing up, changing clothes, and taming of hair. Finding snacks for the bottomless pit in Valerie's tummy and activities to entertain her busy mind. Drawing and coloring and endless kid-craft, along with plotting out desserts to surprise Madoc.

Staying busy also helped to improve Gus's sleep, and with his ribs healing, he felt more himself every day. He didn't get all the way back to 'normal' in terms of rest though, thanks to

Madoc slowly driving him mad. And weirdly, Gus was enjoying losing his mind with his partner.

Once Valerie's door slid shut for the night, Madoc was on him, kisses hot and hungry and so fucking good. They never went further than making out and their clothes always stayed on, but Gus was quickly becoming addicted to being stoned on pleasure with Madoc Walters. He loved watching those blue eyes go glassy and hearing Madoc's sexy little groans. Kissing him until Gus's limbs were so soaked with pleasure he had to legit drag himself to the door.

Gus always did, his cock aching and his balls so full he'd head for the shower the second he got home so he could jerk off. But now Gus was dreaming about his partner, waking up ready to explode after only a few strokes. Which was *absurd* when Gus was too fucking old for sex dreams about a guy who wasn't ready to admit he was queer. Didn't matter that Madoc's touch set Gus on fire—they weren't a good fit and Gus knew it.

He tried to maintain some distance. Made time for family and friends on the non-kid-sitting days and supported his basketball club every week at practice and their scheduled games. And yet Gus always felt a pull toward Madoc's apartment.

To where Valerie would shriek as she kicked Gus's ass at Taco Cat Goat Cheese Pizza, one of the weirdest, wildest games he'd ever played. Where rainbow ponies decorated the shower curtain and bath towels in the main bathroom and a hockey stick and a banana-shaped cat toy were favorite playthings. Where Madoc would ghost his fingers over the back of Gus's arm while they cooked dinner. Only to get a hell of a lot closer than furtive touches once they were alone.

"You got a new someone?"

Gus glanced up from his phone as Felipe, his friend and basketball team co-captain, wheeled over for a quick break from shooting drills. The team was playing in Charlestown tonight, but Gus'd spent the last ten minutes going through the many video clips Valerie had been sending since Madoc had picked her up from school.

Shaking his head, Gus frowned at his friend. "Why do you ask?"

"Because you're smiling like a dork at that thing." Felipe nodded at the phone in Gus's hand, dark eyes dancing with interest. "Plus, you look all gaga the way people do when they're crushing."

Busted.

"It's not what you think." Gus ignored his hot ears. "I've been doing my partner on the truck a favor and watching his kid after school. Val's six and was catching me up on her day."

Felipe's grin softened and he reached over to pat Gus's shoulder. "That's very nice of you, *manito*," he said, voice fond the way it always got when he used the Spanish word to call Gus his 'pal.' "But how did I not know you're like a regular Gary Poppins?"

And yeah, Gus didn't like not knowing how to talk about the time he spent with the Walters. He'd told his parents and sister about kid-sitting, as well as Connor and Judah. But not that Gus dropped in to keep Madoc company at the hockey rink during Valerie's practice on the days he didn't kid-sit. That he typically stayed for dinner any night he was at Madoc's and then lingered afterward.

Definitely not that Gus couldn't wait to get back to the Seaport apartment the next morning so he could crowd Madoc up against the kitchen counter and make out with him some more, just as they were doing right now.

"You're going to make me late," Madoc chided, his lips curling against Gus's next kiss. "But I'll cook tots with dinner tonight to make up for having to leave. *If* you want to stay in with us again."

Gus liked the hopeful look he caught in Madoc's eyes. It made him feel like he was wanted for more than just the kid-sitting.

"I don't have any plans," he replied. "I'm going to grab Lemonade from the station this afternoon for another sleep-over, so if you won't mind hanging out with her too, ask me again after you get home."

"Okay." Sighing, Madoc dropped his arms from around Gus's neck and turned back to the coffee maker. "Hey, you know there's a bench in my shower in case you ever want to rinse off."

After he'd gone, Gus took himself to the couch with his coffee and pad to draw before the quiet was shattered by a small person needing food or who wanted to ask, 'Can you put Chapstick on a turtle?' But Gus was more tired than he wanted to admit and soon the lines on the page started to blur and he found himself erasing mistakes.

Sighing, he closed the pad. He had time for a quick nap before Valerie woke, but napping meant removing his prosthesis, and Gus wasn't sure how Valerie would react if she got up early and caught him without it. She knew Gus'd lost part of his leg of course, but he wasn't sure she genuinely understood he still had a real limb beneath the silicone socket.

Would Valerie be afraid of Gus's stump? Or worse, feel repulsed?

Gus let resentment burn in his chest. He'd learned not to fight feeling bitter over having to navigate a world not designed for his body. There were days he ran out of patience for doors that weren't wide enough for his chair or rickety, uneven staircases that were a nightmare to climb and descend with a mechanical ankle. But Gus couldn't and wouldn't hide every time he needed to use his crutches or chair or adjust one of his stump socks, all things he'd do in front of Valerie at some point and that she'd want to talk about.

Removing his leg and his gear, he stretched out on the couch and considered the hushed room around him. The faint sounds of traffic from the streets below as the city woke up. A coffee smell and the cushions cradling him.

Soft noises pulled at the gauzy feeling enveloping Gus, and the cushion to his right dipped. He peeled an eye open and found a pajama-clad Valerie parked by his side, having dragged the quilt from her bed and her brown eyes still sleepy. Without ceremony, she plunked her head down on Gus's stomach and he grunted, uncrossing his arms so he could steady her.

"How you doin', Bug?" he asked, and she yawned, her body a warm weight against his.

"Doin' fine," she replied. "Are you callin' me Bug 'cause of my ladybug tracksuit?"

"Nah. I'm calling you Bug because you're cute as a bug in a rug who is snug."

"Ahh!" Valerie giggled. "Can I have pancakes for breffast?"

Gus rubbed her back with his hand. "Sure. I just need to put on my leg."

Sitting up, Valerie turned her head to get a glimpse of Gus's lower half. "You took it off for sleeping?"

"Yup. But sometimes I take my leg off because I feel like it, remember?"

"Uh-huh."

Levering himself upright, Gus gave her his hand and she climbed over his knees while he swung his legs off the couch. Valerie kept a hold of Gus as she wiggled her way into the seat beside him, her own bare feet dangling over the cushion's edge a good six inches above the floor. She studied Gus from the knees down, gaze sweeping over his sound leg beside the short limb, which ended a few inches below his knee.

Gus watched her, pleased she simply seemed curious. "What are you thinking, kid?"

Tilting her head, Valerie angled a look up at him. "It doesn't hurt?"

"It shouldn't hurt if I take good care of myself," Gus hedged. Kids often focused on pain when they looked at his stump because they imagined it hurt, and in truth, Gus *did* hurt to some degree every day. He'd gotten lucky with managing phantom limb pain, but coping with missing a part of his leg exacted a toll on the rest of his body that made him ache and sometimes worse.

Straightening his knee now, he held the short limb out, running a hand over the skin and fading scars. "I have to take good care of the real leg under the prosthesis and keep it healthy," he said, "so I can wear my prosthesis whenever I feel like it."

Valerie reached out and copied Gus's gestures, smoothing her fingers over his scars. "Is that how come you wear socks on this part of your leg?"

"Yes. The socks and the liner protect my skin and also make it fit better." Relaxing his knee, Gus retrieved his gear from beneath the table and showed her everything, taking care to explain the purpose of each layer.

"Sometimes I have to put on or take off socks during the day because the shape of my short limb changes," he said, nodding as Valerie's eyebrows rose. "Making adjustments like that keeps the socket snug so my leg doesn't come off if I'm working, playing sports, or walking around."

"Cool." Valerie kicked her feet a few times, then pulled the quilt around her again. "Will you show me how you put on your leg so we can have pancakes?"

Gus smiled. "Yes. You know you can ask me questions if you have them."

"Uh-huh. Daddy says it's good I have lots of questions." She frowned. "Noelene doesn't like it, though."

Shit.

Gus licked his lips. "People are different," he said lightly, "and some have more patience for questions than others."

"I guess you're right."

Valerie swung her feet some more while Gus drew on his gear and leg, and when she started in with the questions, he did his best to answer them.

"HELLO, HELLO," Madoc called as he let himself in that evening with his bag and a grocery sack. He breathed in a luscious, sugary-baking aroma but stopped short after spying Gus camped out on the floor outside Valerie's bathroom in a t-shirt and shorts, a baseball game playing on the TV across the room while Lemonade sprawled out with her banana nearby.

"Well, hi," Madoc said with a small smile. "What are you doing down there?"

"Monitoring shower time while the Sox get their asses handed to them. Val and I got kind of dusty today and she didn't want to wait for you to get home," Gus said. "My leg is under the coffee table, in case you were wondering."

Brow furrowed, Madoc set his stuff down, then walked to Gus's side. Gus had a sketchpad on his lap, but it wasn't until Madoc had also gotten down on the floor that it truly registered Gus only had one leg stretched out in front of him, his left foot bare while the rounded end of his short right limb poked out of the bottom of his shorts.

Lemonade opened her eyes and blinked at Madoc a few

times, then rolled to her feet, quickly relocating onto Madoc's lap so she could make biscuits against his thigh. Madoc stroked a hand over her back, but he was also checking out the crutches by Gus's right side, which were fashioned from matte black metal with forearm cuffs to support a forward-leaning position rather than being propped up under the arms.

"How are your ribs when you use them?" Madoc asked.

"Only semi-terrible." Gus shrugged. "Val wanted to see how they worked," he said, "so I left my leg off."

Nodding, Madoc leaned forward and looked over Gus's short limb for the first time, knowing instinctively Gus wouldn't mind. With his gaze, Madoc traced the flat, pale scar running from Gus's shin to the back of his calf, bisecting the end of the stump with surprising neatness given the severity of the crush injury Gus had sustained.

A sudden need to touch Gus—to *feel* that Gus was all right—had Madoc setting his hand on Gus's left thigh.

"Do you wear a shrinker if you're not using your leg?" he asked. Shrinker socks were a type of compression sleeve that helped some amputees maintain the size of their stump and improve the fit of their prosthetic's socket.

"Pretty often," Gus said, laying his hand over Madoc's atop Gus's thigh. "They help with swelling if I eat stupid things and with pain when I have it. I've got a shrinker in my bag but figured I'd need to put my leg on again soon anyway, so I didn't bother with it."

Madoc met Gus's eyes. "You don't have to put it on for Val or me. Just do whatever's most comfortable."

Gus smiled, very small. "All right."

"Also ..." Madoc bit his lip. "Not sure how you're going to feel about this, but I didn't notice you weren't wearing your leg at first. Does that make me a bad friend?"

"Nah." The corners of Gus's eyes crinkled with his grin. "It means you're getting used to having me around."

Madoc smiled back. But his blood started to hum as he held Gus's gaze, and the world around them shifted focus, everything else fading while Gus stood out in sharp relief. And Madoc couldn't look away. Couldn't get over how incredible Gus looked in the last of the day's light coming in through the window, skin slightly sunburnt along the bridge of his nose and his cheekbones, his hair and eyes lit with gold.

Beautiful.

The timer in the kitchen pinged.

Gus nudged Madoc's shoulder with his own. "I need to get that thing out of the oven before it burns. Val and I made cake with a tub of bluebs that we picked up on our way back to the city."

Madoc chuckled at Gus's use of Valerie's word for blueberries. "Sounds fantastic. Where'd you two go today?"

"Golfing." Grinning, Gus spun the sketchbook and showed Madoc an enchanting doodle of Valerie, pigtails flying and smile luminous as she prepared to ... throw a frisbee.

Madoc glanced from the sketch to his partner. "Disc golfing, huh?"

"Yup." Handing the sketchbook and pencil to Madoc, Gus picked up his crutches. "I took some photos for you that I'll stick in our chat."

Short limb held out in front of him, Gus pressed himself vertical using only his left leg, a crutch in each hand, while a laughing Madoc scooted the cat off his lap and used all fours to scramble up.

"We went to a course in Quincy," Gus said on his way to the kitchen. "It's in this big wooded park and there are walking trails and a playground that we visited afterward. That's why I had the crutches out," he added. "I like to have them on hand when I walk trails or hike in case I need extra balance."

He pulled the cake pan from the oven and it looked truly luscious, juices from the deep blue fruits staining the yellow cake. Madoc was still more interested in watching Gus though, because his fussing over his baking was adorable.

"Your face is red," Madoc observed. "I've got some aloe vera gel you can use if you want." He paused, trying hard to sound casual as he asked, "You and your kitty-pal staying for dinner?"

Gus smiled. "Yes. Don't forget you said you'd make tots!"

Madoc worked at not smiling like a big goof. He knew Gus had a life of his own and probably a million things to do more interesting than staying in on a Saturday night. Still, Gus stuck around most nights and seemed content doing so.

He's a good friend.

A good friend who'd bonded with Valerie too. Madoc's girl was very tactile with Gus, patting his hair or shoulder when they were close, clearly enjoying talking with him whether they were setting the table or just chilling while Gus showed her how to brush Lemonade's fur. She was leaning into Gus's side now for a mutual half-hug as he wished her goodnight, a gesture that both warmed and tugged at Madoc's heart.

Valerie wasn't missing her mom; she'd only asked Madoc once about Noelene's extended absence and hardly blinked when he hadn't given her much info. And maybe that was to be expected given Noelene had always done so goddamned much to put distance between herself and her daughter.

These nights with Gus and his kitty, though ... Valerie would miss them when Gus went back to working the night shift and her life reverted to a new version of 'normal' that didn't include Noelene at all. Madoc still had no idea what that world was going to look like but knew it was time he set the stage for his girl.

"I want to talk about your mom," he said as he tucked Valerie into bed. "And about how she and I usually cooperate on decisions about who you live with and where you go to school."

Settling back against the pillows, Valerie nodded. "You talked to the judge when you and Noelene got a divorce," she said. "An' the judge said you and Noelene make a team but that I belong with you, right?"

Madoc forced a smile. His custody agreement with Noelene was layered and nuanced, thousands of words filling a thick document that laid out the painstaking details of how two people could work together to care for a child. A child who didn't care about nuances or details and simply wanted to be with the parent who made her feel loved.

"You have such a good memory! And I wanted you to know I've decided to go back to the judge." Madoc took a seat on the mattress. "I'm going to tell her it should only be me making the decisions from now on. That way, you and I can do our stuff on our own while your mom does *her* stuff on her own. Noelene wants to get her own place, away from Boston, and I think it's a great time for us to move everything out of your sleepover room upstairs down here to this room."

"Even the bed?"

"Well, no, not the bed or the furniture because you already have all of that here in this room."

"Ah! But what about Uncle T?" For the first time, Valerie looked concerned. "If Noelene moves away and I don't do sleepovers, is he gonna get lonely? Because I don't want that."

"Uncle T's going to miss your mom, but we'll still see him all the time. He'll just have sleepovers down here when he kid-sits you overnight instead of the other way around."

"Oh-h-h, I get it now." Valerie mulled that over for a few

beats, pointing and flexing her feet beneath the quilt a few times before she spoke again. "So, Noelene's not coming back?"

"I really don't think so, honey." Madoc took Valerie's hand. "And that's okay for us and your mom. She has stuff going on she needs to figure out, and if living somewhere else helps her do that, I want to support her."

"Because you're in love?"

The guarded expression on Valerie's face bruised Madoc's heart.

"I love your mom for giving me you," he said, running his thumb over her knuckles. "But no, she and I are not in love. Noelene is still part of my family, same way you and Uncle T are, and I always want my family to have good lives. Does that make sense?"

Valerie was quiet a beat, eyes searching Madoc's face, looking for what he couldn't guess. But she nodded at last. "Yah, it does."

"Good." Bending over, Madoc pressed a kiss to his girl's cheek. "I love you lots."

"I love you lots back, my honey," she said, then slipped her arms around Madoc's neck and dragged him down for a hug. "I'm glad you're my family."

Chuckling, Madoc gathered her close. "I'm glad of that too, Val, every single day."

TWELVE

"WHAT'S GOING on in that head of yours, Mad?"

Madoc smiled to himself. After leaving Valerie's room, he'd taken Gus into the master bath for a little sunburn treatment and now Gus was seated on the vanity, his face upturned and his eyes closed while Madoc smoothed aloe vera gel over sun-rosy skin. Gus always read Madoc well, however, and had clearly sensed something in his mood.

"Noelene messaged me." Madoc replied. "Said she's okay and the child support payment will be on time. That she hasn't been gambling. And that she's not coming back."

Gus's eyes fluttered open. "I'm glad you heard from her. I know you've been worried."

Nodding, Madoc screwed the top back onto the tube of aloe vera gel. "I was. She's not sure yet where she'll end up after this trip, but she promised not to go dark again so we can deal with court dates and stuff."

He set the tube on the counter. "I told Val about her mom leaving. Not every detail, but enough to understand Noels won't live upstairs anymore and that I'm revising the custody agreement."

"How'd she take it?"

"Fine." Madoc shrugged. "More concerned about how Tarek's going to feel about it, honestly, which is just pathetic. A part of me hates that my kid doesn't miss her own mom, but I get why that is."

Gus took Madoc's hand in his own and held it. "How do *you* feel, Madoc?"

Weirdly, Madoc also felt fine. He'd been an unholy mess after Noelene had fled but he'd righted his ship in the weeks following with help from Gus, who'd been there for Madoc in ways he'd never expected.

Who smelled of vanilla and sunshine tonight, mixed with his usual woody, masculine scent. And didn't hesitate to slip his arms around Madoc when he took Gus's face between his palms and slotted their lips together.

Madoc stepped closer, belly jumping when Gus opened his mouth and welcomed Madoc in with a low, pleasured noise. He felt each kiss *everywhere,* like painless fire, and tonight, he wanted to be brave about falling into those good feelings. Heart thumping, Madoc half lifted Gus off the counter, only to quickly set him down again when Gus groaned deep in his chest.

"Fuck," Madoc muttered. "Did I hurt you? I didn't—"

"Will you please shut up about that?" Gus scolded between more nipping kisses. "I'm not made of glass." He dropped a hand to Madoc's ass, fondling him through his joggers. "I'll tell you if I need to slow down as long as you promise to do the same."

Madoc would have agreed to anything just then because his body was blazing and he needed to chase more kisses, even as

Gus gently pushed Madoc backward so he could slide down off the vanity and grab his crutches.

"Come on," Gus murmured, tipping his head toward the door. "I'm going to make you feel good."

Oh, how Madoc wanted that. To feel Gus all over. Hear Gus groan and swear and to taste Gus's skin. But when they walked back into the bedroom, he had the oddest thought that his bed looked enormous, as if the king mattress had suddenly doubled in size. Or maybe it was Madoc himself feeling small and unsure. Like his anxieties around his attraction for this man would rise up and crush him.

As was so often his way, Gus seemed to sense Madoc's mood. "What are you thinking?"

"That I want more than kissing tonight," Madoc admitted. "But I'm in so far over my head here, Gus. I feel like a goddamned virgin all over again and I hate it."

Reaching up, Gus slipped an arm around Madoc's neck. "Just let yourself feel. You do that, and I promise you'll know what to do."

Madoc closed his eyes as Gus stroked his thumb over Madoc's cheekbone, and neither moved for a few beats. Then Gus kissed Madoc again, and it was as if a piece of Madoc that had been out of line for a long time slid back into place.

He groaned, aware too late that he hadn't been particularly quiet about it. "Shit, sorry," he muttered when Gus broke away.

"Love hearing you." Gus trailed small kisses up Madoc's cheek. "Like knowing you want me too."

"I really do." Madoc forced himself to step back. "Give me a second to shut the door and I'll show you how much."

The promise in Gus's eyes had Madoc practically scrambling, the urge to tackle Gus onto the mattress heating his body. But once the bedroom door was closed and locked, Gus set his crutches aside and grabbed hold of Madoc's shirt with both hands, tumbling *him* backward as they kissed through their laughter, limbs tangled together.

Lying beside Gus—feeling so much of him all at once—was incredible. They'd done their share of grinding on the couch but, again, everything felt different tonight. Electric, like a live current was buzzing all around them.

Madoc rubbed his hands over Gus's shoulders and back, eager to help Gus tug his t-shirt up and over his head. And *damn*, Gus looked good. Madoc had known his partner was fit under his clothes, of course. Gus needed core and upper body strength to support himself when he wasn't wearing his prosthesis and boxing was one of his favorite workouts. Gus's torso was sick though, with chiseled planes of lean muscle and a bona fide six-pack that spoke of more sit-ups than Madoc could ever imagine suffering through.

"Making me feel pretty smug," Gus teased, pushing Madoc onto his back. "You gonna show me some skin or what?"

"Not sure I want to, now that I know you look like *this*," Madoc snarked, though he was laughing as Gus helped him peel his own t-shirt off.

His chest was broader and fuzzier than Gus's and his stomach nowhere near as hard, but Gus ran a hand over Madoc's torso in clear appreciation, his eyes aglow.

"Gorgeous," he said softly, then stretched himself out over Madoc.

Instantly, Madoc's brain short-circuited. All that skin. Gus's fingers sliding around his, raising their joined hands over Madoc's head. Knees pressing hard into Madoc's thighs and caging him, taking control so Madoc didn't have to. Madoc's cock twitched and he groaned into a deep and dizzying kiss, Gus's mouth hot against his.

Gus rolled his hips, rubbing his groin into Madoc's through their clothes, and need rushed through Madoc in huge wave. He thrust up, trying to match Gus's rhythm, chasing that pressure and aching for more.

"You feel incredible," he near gasped when they finally came up for air.

"Yeah, I do."

Madoc would have laughed, sure Gus was giving him shit, but he caught an intensity in Gus's stare that had his pulse jumping.

"Need this," Gus said, so quietly Madoc wondered if he'd meant to speak. Madoc didn't know how to ask though and stayed silent as Gus untangled their fingers, then rolled off Madoc and onto the mattress.

He pulled Madoc close, winding one arm around his shoulders and running his free hand down Madoc's chest to his abs, fingers brushing the waistband of Madoc's pants as he caressed Madoc's stomach. Madoc got his arms around Gus, kissing him hungrily, and his cock jumped when Gus reached under the joggers and slid his hand into Madoc's shorts. But then Gus shattered the last of Madoc's sanity by pulling away only to dip his head and wrap his lips around Madoc's left nipple.

Lust bolted through Madoc so hard he gasped. He'd never felt more erotic as he did just then watching Gus suck and swirl his tongue, each lick seemingly hardwired to Madoc's cock. Gus was into it too, making the hottest sounds with his eyes closed tight, his groin hard and hot against Madoc's thigh.

Groaning, Madoc turned more toward Gus, a need to get closer gripping him. Gus responded immediately, almost growling as he kissed his way across Madoc's chest to the right nipple, and Madoc dropped a trembling hand to shove at his joggers, grateful when Gus quickly got with the program.

Together, they pushed Madoc's pants and underwear down

his thighs, and Madoc hissed as cool air hit his overheated skin. He clutched at Gus, sure he was holding on too tight, but Gus didn't seem to mind, kissing Madoc with disarming sweetness. He took Madoc in hand again, palming the head of Madoc's cock and spreading the moisture leaking steadily from the tip around.

A shudder rocked Madoc bodily.

"*Gus.*"

"Yes," Gus whispered. "Let go for me."

He stroked Madoc with exactly the right amount of pressure to drive Madoc wild. Looked at him like he was the only thing in the world that mattered. Like Madoc was the *best* thing. And when Gus leaned in and brushed Madoc's cheek with his lips, the tenderness of the gesture sent Madoc tumbling over the edge.

Pleasure coiled in his belly, tightening almost to the point of pain before it snapped, and Madoc was lost, groaning and shaking as his cock pulsed and Gus worked him through the orgasm, only slowing his strokes when Madoc was boneless.

"Damn," Madoc muttered. "I didn't know."

Gus lips curved in a smile against Madoc's cheek. "Didn't know what?"

"How fucking good this could feel." Madoc leaned back and caught Gus's gaze. "How good *I* could feel—"

With you.

Gus's eyes flashed with something Madoc didn't know how to interpret. "What the fuck am I going to do with you, Mad?" he asked with a wonder that made Madoc's throat tight.

Gus used Madoc's t-shirt to wipe Madoc down, but Madoc could feel the heat and tension thrumming through him and knew Gus had to be aching to get off. Madoc wanted that too. To get under Gus's skin and see him out of control.

After pulling his own pants back up, Madoc splayed his

hand over Gus's abs. "Will you show me?" he asked. "Show me what you like?"

"Yes," Gus said without hesitation. "But I'm telling you right now, I'm going to like anything that you want to do."

Kissing, they settled onto their sides, and Madoc was aware of the fine tremors running all through Gus's body. He helped Gus slide his shorts and boxer briefs down over his thighs but went still as he glimpsed Gus's cock for the first time, erect and red against Gus's abdomen, the tip shining wet. Madoc couldn't tear his gaze away. He took Gus in hand, hefting that hot weight with a sigh that matched Gus's.

"I'm clear, just so you know," Gus said, sounding wrecked. "I haven't been with anyone since knowing you."

"Thank you for saying that." Madoc kissed him softly. "I want to make you feel good, Gus, the way you did me."

"You do." Gus gasped. "You are."

He inched closer to Madoc, seeming to crave the contact, and hummed happily when Madoc wrapped his free arm around Gus's shoulders. Then Gus reached down and slid his fingers around Madoc's, and they groaned together as a drop of pre-cum welled up through Gus's slit.

"Fuck, that feels good." Tipping his head back, Gus's eyes fell mostly closed. "Touch me the way you like to be touched," he urged, shivering lightly at Madoc's next upstroke. "Yeah. Just like that. God."

Satisfaction swelled in Madoc's chest. He'd done that—reduced the guy people called Super Gus to a sweaty, needy mess. And Madoc loved it. Loved seeing Gus coming undone. Loved that *he* was getting hard again just watching Gus.

"Mad," Gus panted. "Gonna come. I—"

"Show me," Madoc whispered, his chest squeezing when Gus's eyes opened wide. "I want to see."

Gus shot hot and hard over Madoc's fist, his mouth falling open, and Madoc cradled him close, spellbound by the bliss in Gus's face. He slowed his strokes over Gus's cock as the tension in Gus's limbs faded, and Gus snuggled close, uncaring of the mess between them.

"That was so good, baby," Gus murmured, his eyes falling closed. "You feel fantastic."

Yes, Madoc did. He wanted to tease his badass partner for being a world-class cuddler who mumbled sweet nothings while sex drunk. But he couldn't say a thing past the rocks in his throat.

Madoc had just had some of the greatest sex of his life without taking his clothes all the way off. And it'd happened with a man.

With Gus, whom Madoc would never have guessed capable of such devastating seduction and tenderness. Who'd rewritten Madoc's world, getting him off harder than anyone in recent memory while making him feel adored and cherished, all at the same time.

EVEN IN HIS POST-ORGASM DAZE, Gus could feel Madoc starting to freak. That was on brand, given the guy had gone from his first same-sex kiss to a mutual jerk off in just over a week. On the plus side, Madoc didn't seem inclined to pound Gus into sand or kick him out of the apartment, neither of which Gus would have appreciated.

Gently, he stroked his hand up and down Madoc's back. They'd gotten cleaned up and settled back on the bed, Madoc with his face tucked against Gus's neck, hiding a little.

"How you doin', big man?"

Madoc's mouth curved against Gus's skin. "Doin' all right, thanks. Just trying to wrap my head around everything."

Gus didn't like the melancholy note he caught in Madoc's voice. "You want to talk about it? Or would you rather be alone?"

"Talking would be nice." Madoc sighed. "If you're sure you're not too tired."

Gus would've been perfectly content staying in Madoc's bed for the rest of the night. But he knew very well that his friend wasn't ready for that kind of intimacy, so they headed out of the bedroom and grabbed beers from the fridge, taking them to the couch as had become their habit.

"I was in high school when I first started noticing guys." Madoc eyed the bottle in his hand. "I'm attracted to women—that wasn't a lie. But I never told anyone I sometimes felt ... a *way* around men. Being the het guy always seemed safe."

Disquiet bubbled in Gus's gut. "Safe meaning easy?"

"Safe meaning without risk."

Gus slipped an arm around Madoc's shoulders. He hated the pain he caught in Madoc's eyes. Knowing that the hottest sex Gus'd had in a very long time had led Madoc to memories that hurt.

"My parents live in Doe Prairie, a town south of Spokane," Madoc said. "My father teaches theology at a small Christian college and my mother is a homemaker. They were—*are* conservative, politically and religiously. Community means everything to them and when I was growing up, the four blocks around our house seemed like the whole world." He licked his lips.

"I had a good life. We weren't rich, but I never lacked for things I needed. For a long time, I wanted to be my parents. Find someone like my mother who'd help me make a family and become a professor like my father."

Gus brushed his knuckles against Madoc's forearm. He couldn't imagine the guy beside him leading a bucolic, small town life with a cute nuclear family. The Madoc Walters Gus knew drove a big metal box through some of the worst traffic in the country and practiced emergency medicine like a champ, all while raising an amazing kid largely on his own.

"Can't say I don't dig the idea of auditing a class with Professor Sex Bucket Walters," Gus teased, simply to make Madoc smile. "But what changed your mind?"

"Lots of things," Madoc replied. "Until the sixth grade, I was homeschooled with a group of neighborhood kids in a co-op but started public school after turning eleven. That was the first time I truly got to spend time around people I hadn't known my whole life. Started to understand not everyone thought the same way as my folks." He winced. "Weird huh?"

"I don't think so. Lots of people grow up the way you did," Gus reasoned. "Church and community are important to them, and I respect that."

"I do, too, typically. The trouble is that *I* started not feeling at home in the church and community. Like I couldn't talk about things I was thinking or feeling."

Gus smoothed a curl back from Madoc's temple. "A thing like that you might be into guys?"

Madoc bowed his head. "It was always quick, a blip that disappeared right away. I knew my friends weren't feeling those blips, though. And I didn't dare tell anyone, especially my parents, because even thinking about that kind of life was not something they would've tolerated."

Gus winced at the bitterness in Madoc's voice.

That kind of life.

"A guy I'd known growing up came out the year before I graduated high school," Madoc said. "Keith was older and had already left the community to move to Portland. We'd never been close, but I'd known him my whole life. After he told his parents he was gay, they acted like he had died."

The intensity in Madoc's gaze raised Gus's hackles. "I hated the way people talked about Keith. And it scared me thinking my parents would do the same thing to me if they found out the truth about me."

Grief for the teenager who'd had no one to turn to with all of his complicated feelings rose in Gus's chest.

"I wish someone had been there for you," he said. "That you'd been able to count on your family and community."

Madoc hummed quietly. "Me too. But in a way, people being shitty about Keith gave me a push I didn't know I'd needed to get out of Doe Prairie. I enrolled in the business program at the University of Tacoma but was more interested in my roommate's pre-med program. Nagi had his EMT certs and was riding for a private service to make money, and the more we talked about the work he did, the easier it got to imagine doing it myself. I was sure I could, y'know? And I *wanted* to do it, way more than I wanted to be sitting in finance classes."

He shrugged. "Maybe there was a piece of me that wanted to get into EMS because it was so far outside of what my parents expected of me. But as soon as I started the cert course, I knew I'd found the right thing for me.

"So, that was it," Madoc said. "I got my certs then moved to Seattle so I could apply to ride with the fire department and in the process, I met Noelene. My parents hated everything about my decisions. Seattle's only an hour's drive from Doe Prairie, you know. But I may as well have moved to a moon colony. They just wanted nothing to do with us."

"What about Val?" Gus asked, his heart sinking when Madoc shook his head. "Have they ever met her?"

"I tried to set something up, but they never seemed interested. After a while, I gave up and went no contact. A part of me understands why they disapprove. My father is a tenured professor and my mother's a homemaker, and there I was, working a blue-collar job and married to a woman who makes three times my salary." Madoc grimaced. "They don't even know about the divorce or that we moved to Boston. But if they did, it'd just be more of the same in their eyes, because everything I've done since leaving Doe Prairie has reduced me incrementally as a man."

"Hey." Gus gripped Madoc's hand tight, his heart squeezing just as hard. "Nothing about you is lesser, Mad. You're one of the strongest men I know, and if your parents can't see it, they're the worst kind of judgmental assholes."

"Thank you for that," Madoc said. "It still took me years to unlearn the ideas my parents put in my head. And being attracted to men? God, Gus. I buried that part of myself deepest of all. Got so good at being the straight guy I started believing it. Until you." His voice cracked and broke Gus's heart along with it.

"I knew you were different from the first day we met. You weren't just a blip on the radar and the more time I spent around you, the more I wanted to know you," Madoc said. "But I wanted you to know *me* too. The man I always hid because I didn't feel safe with anyone knowing him."

Affection and protectiveness swelled in Gus's chest. "Thank you for trusting me. For letting me get to know the real you."

Color flooded Madoc's cheeks. "Not sure I'll ever be out and proud and wearing a rainbow bracelet like you. But I'd like to be able to tell the world I'm bi without freaking out."

"You will, when you're ready," Gus said, eyes prickling dangerously. "You just told *me* you're bi, Madoc, and you don't look freaked out at all."

"Shit, you're right!" The brilliant smile that lit Madoc's face quickly fell. "I can't believe I did that," he said, voice thick with the tears that were gathering in his eyes.

"I can." Gus wrapped Madoc up in a hug. "You're so much braver than you give yourself credit for."

THIRTEEN

FRIDAY, *May 10, 2:00 P.M.*

KID-SITTING WAS EASY PEASY, lemon squeezy. Until it wasn't.

Valerie was a fun child, full of light and laughter, and uncannily intelligent about the world around her. But like any human, she had shitty moods and sometimes got sulky when she didn't get her way. The scowl she showed Gus at pickup that afternoon, however, told him something had set her off, and actual dread trickled through him when her teacher, Ms. Jensen, asked for a word.

Gus waited for Valerie to stalk off to a swing set to join the blond and gangly Kenny Baker before he looked at Ms. Jensen.

"Is something wrong?" he asked, trying to quell the urge to squash whoever had made the Bug feel less than awesome. "And should you be talking to Valerie's dad instead?"

"I will speak with Mr. Walters," Ms. Jensen said. "But I

wanted to talk to you first because an incident happened today that involves you."

A creeping feeling came over Gus that he already knew what the 'incident' might be about.

"The students designed suncatchers today," Ms. Jensen said, pulling a craft project from the tote bag she wore over one shoulder. It was a heart-shaped frame fashioned from heavy paper, with pieces of brightly colored tape stretched from one side of the frame to the other, filling the empty space like pieces of stained glass. When Ms. Jensen held the heart up to the light, the tape glowed so prettily, Gus had to smile.

"That's much cooler than the tissue paper flowers I made back in the day."

"The internet is a wonderful resource," Ms. Jensen replied with a laugh. "Typically, we allow the children to make two hearts, but Val asked if she could make three. One for her father, one for her uncle, and one for her friend, Super Gus."

Gus was going to strangle Madoc for bringing that ridiculous nickname into Valerie's life.

"Please tell me Val didn't call me that in front of the class."

"She did." Ms. Jensen tucked the suncatcher back away. "And that sparked a conversation I should have expected."

"About my leg."

"Yes. Some of Val's classmates used words about your prosthesis and you that she didn't appreciate. Please remember the children were likely repeating words they heard from adults," Ms. Jensen added, "but regardless, we don't allow our students to use slurs or other hateful language."

Fire blazed up the back of Gus's neck. "And what did Val say to the kids?"

"A lot about how your prosthesis works and allows you to do your job." Ms. Jensen smiled. "She had great information to share that I assume came from you and her dad. However, she also told the other kids to shut their pie holes, and that wasn't so great."

Gus pressed his lips together against a wild urge to laugh. He loved that, at just six, Valerie had such a clear idea of how she wanted the world to work and wasn't afraid to say so.

The curly-haired Bug was pretty deflated as they headed out of the schoolyard a few minutes later, however, and Gus's insides twisted at the understanding that her day had been spoiled simply by knowing him.

"Ms. Jensen told me some of your classmates had opinions about my leg that you didn't like," Gus said. "If you want to talk about it, I'm happy to listen."

Valerie huffed through her nose but then reached up and took Gus's hand. "Tamberlyn said your leg was ugly and that you shouldn't wear shorts. And then Liliana said you prob'ly don't have a job because you're a freak except that you're *not*." Her face when she looked up at Gus was so miserable he stopped walking and took a knee.

"I'm sorry that happened." He rubbed Valerie's upper arms gently. "I get why you didn't like what the other kids said. Not everyone understands words can change depending on how you use them. Like, if I say I'm a pizza freak, that means I love pizza like crazy. But if someone calls me a freak because I have one leg and not two, it sounds like they think something is wrong with me when there isn't."

"I know!" Valerie's scowl was fierce. "Miz Jensen gave them a talking to but then she said I shouldn't have told Liliana to shut her big pie hole."

Somehow, Gus kept a straight face. "I heard about that too."

"And are you mad or sad 'cause I got in trouble?" Valerie poked her lip out, her eyes abruptly shiny, and her voice got very small. "I bet you are."

Gus drew her into a careful hug. "I feel a little sad because you're unhappy, Bug, but I am not mad," he said. "You did a brave thing speaking up about something that didn't feel right to you. And, just so you know, Ms. Jensen is going to talk to the parents of those kids about why what they said wasn't cool."

Sighing, Valerie slipped her arms around his neck, and Gus adjusted his hold so he could lift her up, sore ribs be damned.

"I don't think I like Tamberlyn or Liliana anymore," Valerie said. "They were mean, and they didn't listen when I tried to explain."

"Did that make you feel mad or sad?"

"Yes. But I didn't cry."

Gus couldn't help frowning. "It's okay to cry, Val. Sometimes, it's what people need to do."

Valerie set her head on Gus's shoulder. "I know. But, Gus? I'm kinda hungry. My tummy feels like it's eating my guts."

"Gross." Chuckling, Gus patted her back. "Good thing I know a place to grab snacks!"

He took her across the street to his friend Judah's yarn shop, and Judah supplied Valerie with wedges of cheddar cheese before suggesting they take Hank the wolfhound to a nearby dog park so Hank could frolick like the world's largest puppy.

"Dude, Val is so *cute*." Judah made puppy eyes of his own at Gus. "How long does this surrogate daddy gig last?"

Gus's insides wobbled. Surrogate what now?

"Um. I'm just the kid-sitter, Jude, and only until I'm cleared for regular duty. Her mom travels a lot," Gus said, straight-faced through the white lie, "but Val's close with the uncle and between him and Mad, they'll have it covered."

"Nice."

Judah's expression turned thoughtful as he watched Valerie with Hank.

"You know Con's grandmother raised him, right?" Judah

waited for Gus's nod before he continued. "He wasn't much older than Val when she took him and his brother in, and he's always said she was the best parent he could have had. But Con had other people in his life that he counted on too. Teachers and coaches, his brother especially, even though James was still just a kid himself. Having people she can count on—parent-y types like the uncle and you—probably makes Val feel like she has lots of support when her parents can't be around."

Biting his lip, Gus glanced back over at Valerie. She didn't see *him* as a parent-y type when they'd only known each other for a couple of weeks and he was just the kid-sitter. Valerie was in a much lighter mood by the time they left for home though, and that made Gus feel good too.

"Big Dog Hank was so nice!" Valerie said as they waited for the train at Haymarket Station. "And Mr. Judah. Plus, he had a rainbow pin that said 'Wicked Proud'. That was for Pride, huh?"

"Yup, it was. Judah's got a whole collection of pins."

Valerie swung Gus's hand. "And the colors are like the ones on your bracelet."

"That's right." Gus swung her hand back. "Do you know what Pride is about?"

"Daddy says it happens when you're happy with yourself and feel good about who you love. But is Mr. Judah your boyfriend?" Valerie turned a quizzical expression on him. "You hugged it out at the yarn place and then the park and I was just wondering."

"Friends can hug it out, hon. That's what Jude is, my very good friend," Gus said. "His boyfriend's name is Connor, and he works with your daddy and me."

"Ah! Then who is *your* boyfriend?"

"I don't have one right now. And that works for me."

Valerie hummed. "I wish you could be Daddy's boyfriend. You're nice and smart and you make real good desserts."

"That's the sweetest thing anyone has said to me all day, Valley Girl." Gus smiled down at her. "So, thank you for that."

Valerie preened. "You're welcome."

They boarded the train that arrived and took seats near the door, Valerie swinging her legs. "Gus?" she asked after the doors had slid shut. "Do you want to have a family?"

"I already have a great family," Gus said with a smile, though instinct told him to tread carefully. "I've got my ma and my pops and Donna, plus lots of friends. For some people, friends make the best kind of fam and I'm lucky that I have some of both."

"Uncle T is my friend and my fam," Valerie mused. "But I dunno when I'll see him again."

"Shouldn't be long now," Gus replied, sure the near month that had passed since Tarek's departure had to feel like an eternity to the Bug. "Your daddy said Tarek would be back as soon as he's done camping in the middle of nowhere."

The train pulled into State Street station, passengers walking by Gus and Valerie as they debarked and boarded. Valerie watched them with interest, and the doors were closed again before she looked back up at Gus.

"Do you think Noelene is camping in the middle of nowhere, Gus?"

I think I really hate the questions that don't have good answers.

Gus cocked his head at Valerie. "Noelene is on a work trip, remember?"

"Yeah. But Daddy said she's not coming back this time and I think that's okay for us."

"I see. Do you miss hanging out with your mom?"

"No. She seems sad all the time." Valerie frowned. "Uncle

T says it's up to us to make her feel good except I don't know how."

Gus regarded brown eyes that were far too knowing for someone so young. "Hon, you're not responsible for how your mom feels and neither are your daddy or uncle. The only one who can decide how your mom should be feeling is your mom."

"She feels like work is more fun than me." The ease with which Valerie spoke stole Gus's breath. "But that's because I make the drama nobody wants."

Gus tipped his head back and forth, pretending he had to consider his words. "I've only met your mom once, so I really don't know her. But I think she cares about what happens to you more than she cares about work."

"You do?"

"Yup. Because your mom makes sure your daddy is there for you when she isn't because she knows he's the person who loves you most in the world and who'll take the best care of you."

Valerie said nothing as the train sped along. But she smiled, very small, and put her head on Gus's arm.

Gus didn't mind.

His emotions were wobbly though, even hours later after they'd picked up some grocery store cake for that night's dessert and gotten Princess Lemonade from Gus's apartment, making sure to first hang up the suncatcher Valerie had made for him. One moment, Gus would be fine, and then he'd think about that heart-shaped piece of paper and colored tape in his window and his eyes would start prickling.

They talked with Madoc over dinner about Valerie's argument with her classmates, Madoc doing his dad thing while Gus stayed mostly out of it because he knew his place. But when Valerie's bedtime arrived, she wanted a hug, then took Gus's face between her hands as she said goodnight. That pure and wonderfully caring gesture—one she so often shared with her daddy—had hit Gus so hard his throat filled with gravel just thinking about it as he stood beside Madoc's windows, looking out at the cityscape.

"Are you okay?" Madoc asked, stepping up to Gus's side. "You've been kind of quiet tonight."

Gus gave his partner a small smile. "I can be quiet."

"I know. But you aren't, usually." Setting a hand against Gus's neck, Madoc furrowed his brow. "I'm sorry you had to deal with Val's classmates acting shitty about your leg."

My leg is the least of Val's worries.

Gus pursed his lips. "I didn't have to deal with anyone being shitty—that was all Val. And I don't like knowing people gave her a hard time because of me."

"I understand. But kids are kids, and sometimes they act like jerks." Madoc slid his hand down to Gus's waist. "If it helps at all, I'll say I've learned to follow Val's lead. As much as I want to jump in and slay all the dragons, there are times that I can't."

"Val shouldn't have to slay anything. She's just a kid."

"Yes. But she gave me an idea while we were talking during dinner. You and I could show up after school together on the truck. Give the kids a glimpse of you on the job, so to speak, so they actually see what Val was telling them about your leg not holding you back."

Gus grinned at his partner. "I love that you'd do that for her."

"*We* would be doing it for the whole class." Madoc tugged Gus closer. "Teaching them that while you're different because of your leg, you're also the same as anyone."

Gus kissed Madoc deep. He needed to be held tonight. To feel desired. And God, he wanted to see Madoc breathless and begging for more.

Still kissing, they stumbled toward the bedroom, knocking into furniture along the way, and after the door was locked behind them, Gus pinned Madoc against it and palmed him through his joggers.

Madoc tipped his head back with a gasp. "Oh, shit. I ... I bought some lube."

"Did you now?" Gus dropped kisses along Madoc's jaw. "We'll have to use it sometime."

"We can tonight. If you want, I mean." Madoc ran his hands over Gus's ass. "I know we haven't done a lot together—"

"I love what we do." Gus drew back and met Madoc's gaze. "And right now, I want to taste you because I haven't yet and am dying to."

He sank to his knees, watching Madoc's eyes widen, and nosed at Madoc's dick through the joggers.

Madoc set his hands on Gus's shoulders and groaned. "Gus."

Mmm, that throaty murmur did things to Gus. Easing the pants over the bulge tenting Madoc's boxers, Gus kissed Madoc's thighs, rubbing his cheeks into the muscles and reveling in the contrast of strength and softness under the coarse hairs.

He pulled the boxers down next, smiling at the shaky sigh that came out of Madoc when his cock was freed, the head already damp and deep red against Madoc's abdomen. Leaning in, Gus closed his eyes and inhaled soap and musk and man, humming when Madoc cupped the back of Gus's head with his hand. The sureness of Madoc's touch sent fire zigzagging down Gus's spine and damn, his whole body thrummed.

He pressed an open-mouthed kiss against the base of Madoc's cock, then gripped Madoc's hips so he could lick and tease Madoc's hard shaft. He sank into a haze of pleasure as he feasted, soon turning his attention to Madoc's balls as Madoc babbled softly, voice breaking over his curses.

Forcing his eyes open, Gus found Madoc watching him with an expression so blitzed Gus groaned. He pulled back, wrapping a hand around the base of Madoc's cock, then slid his lips over the head, reveling in the bitter-salt flavor and heft of the cock on his tongue. He'd always loved giving head and knowing he'd be the first man to do this for Madoc was an incredible turn-on.

He took Madoc deep, opening his throat until his nose brushed the curls of hair on Madoc's groin, and Madoc's eyes glazed over, his moaning now constant. He gasped as Gus swallowed around him and his hips bucked forward, driving his cock into Gus's throat. But Gus was prepared and pressed his weight against Madoc's thighs to keep him still as he sucked, his own cock straining against the fly on his shorts.

Soon, Madoc was shaking, and the desperation in his voice went straight to Gus's balls.

"Gonna come," Madoc whispered. "*Fuck,* I'm gonna come so fucking hard."

Gus slipped a hand under Madoc's balls, massaging the soft mound of his taint. Triumph flashed through him at Madoc's keen and Gus didn't let up, sucking hard as pleasure coiled in his belly.

Inhaling sharply, Madoc went rigid, every muscle drawing impossibly tight for endless seconds before he shuddered and his dick pulsed in Gus's throat. His eyes blazed blue and beautiful, joy mixed with wonder in them, and he cupped Gus's face with unsteady hands. When he traced his thumbs over Gus's lips, gently stroking them as they stretched wide over Madoc's cock, Gus lost it, right there on his knees, another man's cock in his mouth while his own went untouched.

Orgasm barreled through Gus and the world around him

lost color and faded, leaving just him and Madoc in stark relief. Gus lost the fight to keep his eyes open, aware of his own hoarse moans and that he was clutching Madoc's thighs. But Madoc was holding on to Gus too, keeping him steady when Gus finally pulled off and pressed his face against Madoc's leg.

"God." Panting, Madoc threaded his hands into Gus's hair. "That was ..."

"So fucking good," Gus mumbled.

He didn't care that he sounded like a guy whose brain had been blasted to rubble. Or that he had jizz in his pants and was too wrung out to do more than sink down onto his ass with his back pressed against Madoc's door.

Sliding down beside him, Madoc gathered Gus up. "Did you come?" He pressed his lips to Gus's temple. "Just from sucking me?"

"Uh-huh." Peeling an eye open, Gus pulled back and smiled at Madoc's fiery red cheeks. "Bet you're feeling proud of yourself."

Madoc didn't reply, instead kissing Gus hard, and Gus happily lost himself in it. They probably needed to talk about the things Valerie had said today about Tarek and Noelene. About what was going to happen with this ... thing between them once Gus was back on the truck and a new normal shaped their day-to-day.

But just then, all Gus wanted was to be with Madoc and bask in how good they could make each other feel.

FOURTEEN

SATURDAY, *June 10, 12:20 P.M.*

"JUST KEEP in mind that the flavored dams don't always pair well with vaginas."

Becca, the young woman Madoc had been talking to, peered into the Pride Safer Sex Kit he'd given her, a plain brown paper bag that held lube, condoms, and latex dams, some of each flavored.

"Hm." She glanced from the bag to Madoc. "Any thoughts on which flavors might be nicer than others?"

Madoc imagined Gus slicking his fingers with the lube they kept in the nightstand and smiled through his instant blush.

"This'll sound dumb, but vanilla tends to be fairly subtle," he said to Becca. "Might be fun to start there and experiment until you find one you like better."

"I like your style, my dude." Grinning, Becca headed off with a jaunty wave. "Thanks, and Happy Pride!"

"Happy Pride!" Madoc called back, then looked out over the thick crowd.

His adopted hometown turned out for Pride week with events all over the city including today's annual Pride Parade and accompanying festival, big, joyous affairs that drew up to a million attendees into the city limits. Boston EMS crews were there to support the celebrants along the parade route and at the festival sites in medical tents like the one Madoc was working today with Olivia, while one squad marched in the parade itself, queer-identifying EMTs and paramedics like Gus, who'd brought along his own very special guest in the form of Valerie.

Pulling his phone from his pocket, Madoc swiped through the photos Gus'd sent from the route and Olivia stepped up beside him to get a glimpse too. Sun and blue skies soared above the marchers, but Valerie's enraptured expression shone even brighter as she posed beside the ambulance and helped carry the Pride banner. She wore a specially sized t-shirt that matched the crews' with a rainbow Boston EMS logo on a black background, and along with the purple Red Sox cap Gus had gifted her, had acquired a pair of sunglasses with red heart-shaped frames from somewhere that made her look incredibly cute but also very grown up.

Madoc hadn't hesitated at all when Gus'd approached him about allowing Valerie to march with him. He loved knowing she could take part in a movement that honored the past while also looking forward to a future Madoc wanted for her. To a world where love was celebrated openly by people everywhere and Madoc's girl was free to carve out her own identity, whatever it turned out to be, without fear.

Madoc was slowly working on getting to that point too, at least in his head. He wasn't ready to live out loud and proud the way Gus and his friends did, but he was sure now that he wanted to do more than stand on the sidelines during Pride or any other day of the year. Madoc wanted to be his true self all the time and not only behind closed doors.

There isn't a deadline, he reminded himself, *I'll know when I'm ready.*

The passage of time seemed to have sped up over the last couple of weeks though, with Gus almost ready to resume regular duty and Valerie's school year nearly over, and Madoc worried all the time about the changes that were to come. Like how the family would need a new, dedicated kid-sitter, even after Tarek came back, and how much that would cost. That Valerie probably wasn't going to like the new kid-sitter as much as she did Gus. Definitely that Madoc needed to talk to Gus about how this … *thing* they had between them was going to work once they were back on a truck together.

"Daddy!"

Everything that didn't feel like joy and light and love fell away as Madoc walked out from behind the table and swung his girl up in his arms.

"Hey, Valley Girl! I hardly recognized you with those fancy glasses!"

"Ahh!" Valerie whipped the sunglasses off and beamed. "It's me, see? Mr. Owen gave me these glasses an' he's Gus's friend. Ooh, and these, too!" She proudly patted several strings of shiny beads that hung around her neck. "They're Yardy Graw beads."

"Very shiny. But I think you mean Mardi Gras beads."

"Oops!"

"Not a big deal." Madoc blew a raspberry against her cheek and made her laugh. "Where's Gus?"

"Yo, big man." Gus walked up wearing beads and sunglasses of his own and immediately pulled Olivia into a hug. "How you guys doin'?"

A swarm descended upon the table then, Connor, Heather, and Mark Mannix leading a group of friends and coworkers, all talking at once. Connor had Judah and Mark was with Owen, while Heather introduced her partner to Olivia and her husband who were chatting with Gus's ex, Ian, and *his* boyfriend Tris. And then another wave arrived, nurse buddies of Ian's and musician friends of Judah's, names flying fast and everyone coupled up.

Except for Madoc and Gus of course, the two unattached guys who did their coupling up in secret.

An odd melancholy ghosted through Madoc as he held his girl and took in the happy faces around him. He couldn't comprehend what it been like for Tarek and Tim, pretending to be only friends for the rest of the world. Because Madoc felt weird doing it now with Gus at his side, and all they'd done was fool around some.

"The parade was *so* fun, Daddy," Valerie said. "Gus and Mr. Connor gave me piggyback rides when I got tired, and I liked all the cheering and music. Miss Heather even let me blow the horn on the truck a whole bunch and I wish you could've marched with us!"

"I do too, sweetie." Madoc dropped a kiss on her cheek. "Maybe I'll be able to do that some time."

Looking up, he caught Gus's small smile. Madoc hadn't really come out to Valerie just then, but he wanted to think he was getting closer.

A roar went up from the crowd as the music changed and Donna Summer's *I Feel Love* rolled over them, beats pulsing fast and heady.

"Yas!" Gus crowed, high-fiving a brawny dude named Emmett who started herding the group out into the dancing throngs. Catching Valerie's outstretched hand in his, Gus followed along, leading Madoc and Valerie with him.

"Hey, I don't dance!" Madoc insisted "And I'm on duty!"

"Eight minutes!" Turning, Gus flashed him a megawatt smile. "That's how long this song lasts, Mad, and I know Liv can spare you that long."

Valerie kept tight hold of Gus's hand as she bounced in Madoc's arms. "C'mon, Daddy, dance with us!"

Madoc did of course, because he couldn't say no to two pairs of laughing brown eyes and music that sounded so good. And while there was no Pride miracle to give him more grace, he still had fun shaking his butt for eight minutes and making his daughter and friend happy while doing it.

"HI, BUG! HAPPY PRIDE!"

Grinning, Gus waved at the five-foot-nothing bundle of energy standing outside his apartment building.

"That's my ma," he said to Valerie and Madoc. "She's here to bless us with her famous Pride cookies that look like wee flags. Hey, Ma!"

Layla Dawson was dressed in jeans and a red *Free Mom Hugs* t-shirt, cloth grocery sacks in either hand and her smile beaming as Gus jogged over. "I'm so glad we caught you!" she exclaimed.

"Me, too!" Gus hugged her tight. "Val left her backpack here this morning and we're just picking it up. Where's Pops?"

"Inside with your cat. He built the princess a tower upon which to climb and I think she might even like it once she gets over its sheer size."

"I am ... intrigued."

"You're right to be," Layla replied with a laugh. "I had to come back out to grab your cookies from the car, so here you go." Stepping back, she handed Gus one of the sacks. "There are eggs in there too, since I knew you'd be out of them again."

"Thank you, Ma." Turning, Gus gestured to Madoc and Valerie who were watching with unabashed curiosity. "This is my partner, Madoc, and his girl, Valerie."

Layla's eyes lit up even brighter. "August has talked about you so many times this summer. I'm Layla, and it's so nice to meet you in person!"

"Great meeting you too, Mrs. Dawson." Madoc extended a hand and gave her the cute, toothy smile. "Gus talks about you often."

"He calls *me* Bug," Valerie said impishly, bouncing on her toes. "An' sometimes I call him the Gusberry."

"Do you now?" Layla raised an eyebrow at Gus. "I think I like that, hon."

Gus rolled his eyes. "Figures."

Inside, Steven Dawson was babying Lemonade in the crook of his arm, and he grinned when his son goggled at the *towering* cat tree that now stood near the windows. Styled to look something like a cactus, it stood at least as tall as Madoc with platforms for jumping and perching, a couple of enclosed 'condos' and a hammock for lounging, scratching posts to keep sharp claws under control, and several dangling toys to tantalize.

"Ho-lee cats," Valerie said, staring up at the thing with an awe that echoed Gus's perfectly.

"Happy Pride, August!" Steven bussed Gus's cheek. "What do you think of your kitty cactus?"

"I think it's a lucky thing my ceilings are high." Gus gave his pops a smile. "It's amazing. Thanks for building it."

"How come you're callin' Gus August?" Valerie asked, her squinty expression bringing a smile to Steven's face.

"Because that is the name his ma and I gave him," Steven

replied. "Gus is a fine nickname but to me he'll always be August, just like his sister is Belladonna instead of Donna."

"Bell-a-donn-a's real long to spell," Valerie observed. "My friends call me Val."

Steven nodded firmly. "Then so shall I. My name is Steven, by the way, and I like your hat!"

"Thanks! Gus gave it to me."

Valerie reached up and patted Gus's hip but quickly turned her attention to Lemonade while Gus introduced Steven to Madoc. Gus then left them all to chat while he took the grocery bag to the kitchen, and he ooh'd out loud as he unpacked two boxes of cookies.

"One of those is for Connor and Judah," Layla called over, "and if you talk to Ian before I do, tell him I have a box for him and his fella."

Steven set the cat down beside the cat tree, then looked to Layla. "We should go, hon. Did you give them the jars?"

"Just about to." Smiling, Layla turned to Valerie. "Have you ever heard of a fairy glow jar, Val? August and I used to make them when he was small so he and his sister could shine light in the dark." She held up the second grocery sack. "I thought maybe you'd like one for yourself."

Valerie's eyebrows went up. "That's for me?"

"Yes, if you think you'd like to keep what's inside." Layla cocked her head at the child. "How about I show you and your daddy how the jars work and then you can decide?"

She produced two Mason jars from the bag, each coated on the inside with purple glitters, lilac and orchid streaking through darker shades of violet and indigo. But the jars also held strings of lights that, when switched on, made the glitter shine in a truly magical fashion that had Valerie gasping.

"I love these," she said, eyes starry as she tilted a jar in her hands back and forth. "Thank you, Mrs. Gus's Ma!"

Everyone laughed, but Gus caught a complicated expression on Madoc's face. Amusement mixed with a wistfulness that made sense when Valerie's own grandparents couldn't be bothered to know her and strangers had gone out of their way to be kind.

An urge to take Madoc's hand squeezed Gus's chest, and he had to glance away before he did something dumb like get emo over glitter and fairy lights.

The tiny studio seemed quiet after his parents had gone, Valerie camped out on the floor by the cactus with her jars and the kitty, while Madoc glanced around at the room.

"This place is great," he said.

"Thanks. I'd show you around except I don't have to." Gus chuckled. "What you see is what you get."

"Well, I really like it. And your parents. Sounds like they're still close with Ian?"

"Uh-huh." Gus went to the couch and sat. "Ian's estranged from his family, so mine kind of adopted him when we were together."

Valerie turned a quizzical look onto Gus. "Was Mr. Ian your boyfriend?"

"Yes." Gus smiled at her, aware Madoc was watching them closely. "Now we're just regular friends and Ian's new boyfriend is Tristan."

"Mr. Tristan is the tallest person I ever met!" Valerie laughed to herself. "But how come Mr. Ian's esh-tranged?"

Gus flicked a glance at Madoc, whose smile bore a familiar wry tilt.

Always paying attention, even if it doesn't seem like she is.

"Ian isn't close to his mom and dad," Gus said, "and that's what I meant by estranged. Ian is good friends with *my* ma and pops though, and they get along great."

"Ah." Valerie turned her attention back to her glow jar.

"Your ma and pops are wicked nice," she observed. "I bet they want you to have your own boyfriend, huh?"

"I'm sure my ma wouldn't mind," Gus replied with a laugh. "But you know it's okay that I don't."

"Yah, but I was just checking." Valerie settled onto her back again. "Can I have one of your ma's cookies?"

"Dinner first, honey," Madoc said, then looked to Gus. "I thought we could do the noodle bar near my place if you, um, don't already have plans."

Gus did have tentative plans; invitations to Pride parties had come to him from all over. He'd join in at some point because Pride in his hometown was one of his favorite times of the year. At the moment, however, Gus had two sets of hopeful eyes on him and no urge to be anywhere else.

Back at Madoc's, they put on the baseball game and shared ramen and *bao* buns, and Valerie decided tamarind chicken wings were delicious.

"I love this day," she declared, cookie in hand and eyelids heavy as she rounded the table to hug Gus. "And I like your ma and pops a whole lot, my dear Gusberry."

Gus set his cheek against her curls. "They like you back," he assured her. "I'm glad you had a good day, Valley Girl."

While Madoc put her to bed, Gus checked his phone and found dozens of loving notes from family and friends, many accompanied by photos captured at parties and events held throughout the day. Flipping through his own photos, Gus chose one Olivia had sent of him dancing with his friends at the festival, Madoc with Valerie in his arms among them, and he sent it out to his people along with all the heart emoji on his phone.

"What's up?" Madoc had a beer in each hand when Gus looked up, and Gus happily traded his phone for a bottle.

"Just wishing the fam Happy Pride," he said. "Hope you don't mind me sending that."

"Oh, wow." Madoc traced Valerie's face on the screen with his fingertip. "She's in the photo Boston EMS put up on their socials too, and man, is she proud. Thank you for taking her with you today."

"Thank you for letting me," Gus replied. "Look through the rest of the pics and grab what you want."

Madoc did some scrolling and tapping but handed the phone back when it started chiming with incoming messages.

"You ought to be out having fun with Con and your friends," he said. "They're going to keep pinging until you answer."

"This is why we mute." Gus set the device to vibrate. "And I am having fun. I love this day, like your kid said, and I'm good right where I am."

Emotion flashed over Madoc's face, an intensity Gus didn't know how to read.

"Does Val ask you about boyfriends a lot?" Madoc asked. "Because she hasn't asked me about dating in a very long time. I'm not sure how to take that, honestly. Or what I'd say if she did ask."

"I wish you could be Daddy's boyfriend."

Gus licked his lips. "She's asked me about boyfriends a couple of times. And you'll figure out what to say if and when she asks you, too," he said gently.

Setting his beer on the windowsill, he slipped his hand into his pocket and pulled out a tiny enamel pin he'd bought from a festival vendor earlier in the day.

"I get that you're not ready to wear Pride colors," Gus said, handing the pin to Madoc. "But I figured you could hang on to that as a reminder."

For several long seconds, Madoc stared down at the little

bee in his palm, its thorax striped pink, purple, and blue with black instead of the usual yellow, colors Madoc already knew signified bisexual pride.

"A reminder of what?" he asked softly.

"That it's cool to just *be* yourself."

Madoc's lips quirked up at the corners. "That is the corniest thing you've ever said to me."

He met Gus's gaze, the expression in his eyes so tender and broken Gus had to kiss him. Madoc clung to Gus at first, seeming to draw comfort from being held, but soon his touches grew bolder, like he needed his hands on every part of Gus he could reach.

"Want you," he said in a gravelly voice that had Gus's dick going from 'totally interested' to 'fuck yes' in three seconds flat. "Been dying to do this all day."

Gus skimmed a palm over Madoc's belly. "Want you too. Did you buy more lube?"

"Uh-huh. It's in the nightstand." The color on Madoc's cheeks spilled over onto his neck. "I, uh, also bought condoms."

"Mmm, good to know."

They moved to the bedroom where Madoc set his pin on the dresser before they stripped off and Madoc stretched out on the mattress, his hand warm on the small of Gus's back while Gus removed his prosthesis. Gus barely had time to set it aside before Madoc was tugging at him, grinning as Gus slid his left leg over Madoc's torso and straddled his waist.

"Looking pretty smug up there, August," Madoc said. He stroked his palms over Gus's thighs and knees, tracing sweet fire into Gus's skin over the calf of his sound leg and the rounded end of his stump. "You want to tell me what's on your mind?"

Gus slid his fingers through Madoc's chest hair. He loved

the way Madoc touched him. That he'd used Gus's full name and was watching Gus with such warmth.

"I was thinking," Gus said, "that I'd ride that big dick of yours *if* you're up for it."

"Jesus. I'm up for that," Madoc said. "That's what you like?"

"To be fucked?" Gus thumbed Madoc's nipple and made him gasp. "Yes, I like it very much with the right partner."

In truth, Gus usually topped because that was what his partners had preferred. Gus didn't mind being owned, though. To surrender and be taken so thoroughly he forgot his own name. Knowing he'd have that with Madoc—a man for whom all this was new—had Gus's balls throbbing.

He slicked his fingers with the lube from the nightstand, then carefully stroked Madoc's shaft and balls, unsurprised when Madoc whined, gaze turning wild. Gus's hands shook as they sheathed Madoc's cock with a condom, and when Gus wet his fingers again, sudden warmth flashed under his skin.

"Need to get myself ready," he murmured, reaching back with one hand, only for Madoc to groan deep in his chest.

"Oh, fuck, Gus."

"Soon," Gus promised him, his eyes slipping almost closed when his fingertips met his rim.

He imagined the picture he painted, back arched as a soft noise fell from his lips. Gus slid one finger into his hole, heat instantly radiating outward from his ass and groin. His heart bounced as Madoc shifted beneath him and sat up, but it was good having that solid wall of body against his own. Then Madoc wrapped his mouth around Gus's left nipple and Gus had to bite back a cry.

Sweat sprang out on his skin, the combination of being sucked and filled at the same time incredible. The stretch and burn in his ass intensified when he added a second finger alongside the first, and though Gus forced himself to go slow, the only reason he stayed upright was because Madoc was holding him.

"You're shaking," Madoc muttered, trailing kisses up Gus's chest. "What do you need?"

You.

But that felt too heavy, so Gus kept his mouth shut as he pulled his fingers free from his ass, then lined his body up with Madoc's. Sinking down slowly over Madoc, Gus's breath caught, pain a bright flash when the ring of muscle in his hole gave way. And then Madoc was filling Gus, his arms coming around Gus like twin bands of iron.

"My God." Madoc sounded dazed. "So … *tight*."

Fighting a whimper, Gus dropped his forehead to Madoc's. He knew what Madoc was feeling. Profound heat and pressure around his cock, more intense and *so* much better than anything he might have imagined. But Gus was drowning in his own need. Aching in the best possible way and so fucking full, consumed as he was split open.

Emotion swamped him, the sheer intensity of *everything* stealing his breath. Being with Madoc like this, sharing another first. The way Madoc was looking at him when Gus peeled his eyes open, trusting and incredibly present.

A tingling started deep in Gus's balls as he took himself in hand, aware of Madoc's low hiss.

"Look at you." Madoc rubbed his palm over Gus's right ass cheek. "Does it feel good? Me inside you?"

"Yes. Like burning from the inside out," Gus whispered.

Madoc groaned. "Me too. God, Gus. I feel you. All of you, everywhere."

Gus started rocking, slowly at first as his pain became bliss, then faster with Madoc to guide him. Gus moaned into Madoc's mouth, his blood buzzing with ecstasy. He wanted to last and make it good for Madoc. But then Madoc slid a hand behind Gus and fingered his rim, and the touch dissolved Gus's bones. He panted against Madoc's lips, too strung out now even to kiss.

"Love this," Madoc was muttering. "Love it so much."

He thrust up into Gus, his movements gaining momentum and speed, rough in exactly the way Gus needed, nailing his prostate again and again. Fire bolted through Gus, and he was *there*, soaring high and fast with his heart lodged in his throat, shuddering as he came all over himself.

Madoc let out a broken moan and fucked hard into Gus, thrusts almost brutal. Gus fought to hang on, murmuring praise and encouragement and who knew what else, until Madoc fell apart too, his face buried against Gus's neck.

They fell asleep tangled around each other in Madoc's bed. And though the overnight hadn't been planned, when Gus woke up the next morning, Madoc was smiling at him.

FIFTEEN

FRIDAY, *June 16 1:30 P.M.*

"DID you see that guy's leg? I wonder what happened?"

Madoc shot a glare at a pair of moms seated not far away. He and Gus had driven A1 to the after-school pickup today and while the ambulance had drawn lots of attention, Gus's prosthesis was getting more because he'd rolled up his pant leg and left it visible.

"Ugh, that's so weird."

"Don't stare, sweetie."

"If that were me, I would legit off myself."

The voices from parents and caregivers around the playground were loud, like they believed Gus had lost all of his hearing along with part of his leg, and the pity, disapproval, and outright revulsion on some of their faces made Madoc angry.

"Quit with the death glare," Gus said out of the side of his mouth. "It was your idea to talk to the kids and you don't want to scare them, do you?"

Madoc raised an eyebrow at the small figures swarming Gus, Heather, and himself, all firing off questions with the ease of the very young.

"Are you really an ambulance driver, Mr. Gus?"

"Do you like working with boys, Miss Heather?"

"How come you're so freaky tall, Mr. Madoc?"

A dark-haired boy stalked up, looking Gus up and down with a critical expression that was almost comical on his little kid features, and this was Tamberlyn, one of the kids who'd pissed Valerie off some weeks earlier.

"Do you hop around when you don't have your fake leg?" Tamberlyn asked Gus. "And how come you gotta show off when that leg is gross?"

"I *can* hop around, but I'd rather use my crutches or a chair because they're faster and safer," Gus said. He rubbed the crown of Valerie's head through her ball cap while she glowered at her classmate. "And I think my prothesis looks rad. It helps me do my job and play sports, and if you think it's gross, that's not my problem because I'm not responsible for how you feel about me."

"Oh." Tamberlyn cocked his head, face uncertain now. "You can play sports?"

"Yup. I box and bike and go running, and I also play basketball in a league and swim when I go to the beach."

Tamberlyn lit up with laughter. "You can swim with only one foot?!" He cast another look at Gus's leg, and now his gaze held only interest. "That *is* rad."

Gus took a knee so he could pull his prosthesis off and show the kids how it worked, and though one child scooted around Heather's legs as if to hide behind her, the rest ooh'd and leaned in to get an eyeful of Gus's short limb.

"Dude, your partner is brave."

Madoc glanced over at Kenny Baker's dad, Joey, who'd

circled around the cluster of kids to join him. "What do you mean?" he asked, knowing he sounded wary. Madoc liked Joey, but if the dude said anything about Gus and his 'struggles' putting the world's problems into perspective, Madoc was going to get real.

"I mean that this bunch is tough," Joey replied. "They almost ate me alive when Kenny brought me in for Career Day, and I've been teaching sixth-grade science since before these munchkins were even born."

Joey pitched his voice high like a child's. "Mr. Baker? Will spiders run away when I fart? And how come dog treats taste so disgusting? What if I'm not even real and just someone's memory?"

Madoc laughed. "Val licked her own arm yesterday and told Gus and me she tasted 'neutral'."

"Fantastic," Joey said around more cackling. "Hey, do you need help with the pickups? I've been meaning to ask since Kenny said Val's mom and uncle have been out of town. Is that why you switched to days?"

Madoc read the questions in Joey's eyes. Knew he wanted to ask why Valerie's mother hadn't been around and why Gus'd had to step in. And abruptly, Madoc wanted someone to know what his ex had put him and Valerie through.

Slipping his right hand into his pocket, Madoc held on to the tiny bee pin Gus'd given him. He'd taken to carrying it like a good luck charm and, for whatever reason, the thing made it easier for him to relate some of his uncomfortable truths.

"Gus got injured and that's what landed us both on the day shift. But he took over the drop-offs and pickups because Val's mom left Boston this summer. Noelene and I divorced last year," Madoc said. "We'd been doing the co-parenting thing, but now it's just me."

Joey's cheeks and neck flushed a dark red. "Whoa, Madoc. I had no idea."

"I know. It isn't easy, especially since Val's uncle has been away too, but I got lucky with Gus having time to help out."

Not sure what I'd have done without him.

"You tell me if you need more hands, okay?" The humor in Joey's face had gone. "I know school's almost over, but Kenny will be here for summer camp like Val, and Bryn and I can do pickups if you ever need help. And we should meet up for dinner sometime, maybe out at one of those bougie places on the water out near you!"

That'd be nice. For all of us.

The dispatcher's voice came through his radio. "A1, what's your twenty?"

"A1 in the North End, Charter and Hanover Streets," Madoc replied. "You can show us clear."

"Copy. Water rescue in progress at 306 Congress Street, multiple persons reported stranded in the water at the Boston Tea Party Ships and Museum. 14-D-3, unknown status, BFD Marine 1 on scene. You can go Code Two with just lights."

"Roger that." Madoc nodded to Joey, then looked over at Heather and Gus. "Gotta go, Boss," he called, relishing the slight headshake he got from Gus in return.

"So we heard," Gus said, swinging Valerie up into a piggyback. "See you later, kids," he called to the crowd. "Madoc and Heather have to go fish people outta the haahbah!"

Valerie burst out laughing at Gus's exaggerated accent and they were all giggling as they jogged back to the truck.

"How about we go out for dinner tonight?" Madoc asked Gus. He'd liked Joey's idea of dinner on the water and, with the shift away from days imminent, needed to pounce while he could. "My treat to thank you for everything."

"That sounds fun." Gus went to the driver's side window so

Valerie and Heather could exchange a final high five. "Just shoot us a message if you run into a delay so we know not to wait."

Valerie patted Gus's hair while Madoc zipped around the front of the truck to the passenger side. "Is delay the same thing as late?" she asked.

"Yes, it is," Madoc called back, "but I won't be either."

Heather let out a lusty sigh. "I can't believe you said that." She aimed a droll look out the window at Gus. "Expect your date to be one-hundred-percent delayed, Dawson, 'cause your boy's jinxed us for sure."

Gus sauntered off with Valerie still on his back, but Madoc stared hard at Heather as he strapped himself in. "Dude, that wasn't cool."

Heather raised her eyebrows at him. "What did I do?"

"Said Gus and I had a date. I don't want Valerie getting any ideas, especially since she doesn't even know—"

"Oh, relax, straight boy." There was scorn in Heather's eye roll. "I doubt your kid even clocked my mistake."

Madoc ground his teeth as they pulled away from the curb. He didn't bother correcting Heather about Valerie clocking everything, including jokey throwaway comments. But he did feel a powerful urge to tell her she'd made a mistake when she'd called him a straight boy.

It's not right that she doesn't know about me. That Val doesn't know Gus and I are more than friends.

Madoc was still wrestling with his thoughts that evening as he sat with Gus and Valerie in a BBQ Shack located not far from Madoc's building. Because the night *felt* like a date but also like something more established and real.

Dusk had fallen and they were seated beside a glass door that opened onto a patio and gave them a stunning view of the Inner Harbor that even a romantically backward guy like

Madoc could appreciate. Despite not being ready to add romance or a relationship to his already complicated life.

A relationship with Gus, who smiled at Valerie when she slid down from her seat and walked around the table to him, fingers and answering grin sticky with barbecue sauce. Without asking, she picked a deep-fried pickle off Gus's plate and bit into it before Madoc could warn her.

"Oh, no." Valerie made a horrible face, eyes crossed and tongue protruding, clearly hating life. "I think these are poison," she said very seriously. "*Or* made from toads."

Amusement shone in Gus's face though he kept it straight. "It's a pickle, hon, not poison or toad," he replied. "I'm glad you tried it too, because now we know you don't like deep fried pickles."

A corner of Madoc's heart ached watching them. Noelene had always had a hard time dealing with Valerie in restaurants. She'd hated the inevitable mess and Valerie needing help with her food, and she'd had no patience at all when Valerie wanted to be part of the conversation, effectively making adult conversation impossible.

Gus rolled with it all. Answered the weird and wild questions and wiped saucy fingers without complaint, easily fielding requests to style Valerie's hair into a faux mohawk and to help her with a drawing project she wanted to share with her friends before summer vacation.

He's okay with the chaos and mess.

"Can we take some cake home, Daddy?" Valerie looked at Madoc over the table. "My bum is tired of these chairs and I wanna build a blanket fort with you n' the Gusberry." She grinned at him. "I like this date!"

And ugh, there it was.

Gus just tweaked one of Valerie's braids. "This isn't a date, Bug," he said. "This is adventure time for three!"

They built the fort back at Madoc's, stretching the quilt from his bed over the backs of the dining chairs to form the roof while his bed pillows and the couch cushions became the floor. Madoc cut slices of Ooey Gooey Butter Cake that they ate while watching Val's show, and when her bedtime rolled around, he assumed Gus would disassemble the fort. But Gus was still in the thing when Madoc slipped out of Valerie's room, his bare left foot sticking out of the fort's opening and his prosthesis under the coffee table while he watched that evening's Red Sox game.

"I live here now," Gus said cheerily when Madoc peered in at him. "I can pay rent in *bolos*."

Snorting, Madoc crawled back in beside him. "Sounds fair. I'm sure Val would also accept payments in cake."

"Mmm. Cake should be its own food group. As should pizza and cheese."

"Please do not repeat such things to my daughter."

Settling onto his back, Madoc studied the fort's ceiling. "Forts are usually her thing with Tarek," he mused. "They have a whole setup in the loft with this cool parachute thing that hangs from a hook in a ceiling beam."

"Maybe that's why she wanted to build one down here," Gus said. "So she could share it with you."

"Maybe." Madoc turned his head and met Gus's gaze. "I told Kenny Baker's dad about Noelene leaving."

Gus muted the TV, then rolled onto his side so he faced Madoc. "How did that go?"

"Fine. I didn't want Joey assuming she and I were together anymore."

You let Joey and everyone else assume Gus is only your partner on the truck.

Madoc looked back at the quilt overhead. Gus had never once given him shit for clinging to his straight guy act. But meeting Gus's parents during Pride—seeing how close and loving the Dawsons were with each other—had started Madoc wondering if it weighed on Gus having to play along. The same way putting on a fake happy family face while his marriage had been imploding had weighed on Madoc.

"I don't want to pretend everything's cool with Noelene anymore," he said quietly. "So, I told Joey I've been taking care of Val on my own with your help. Not about me being bi, though." Madoc bit his lip. "I wasn't ready."

Gus slid their fingers together. "You'll get there, Mad. No timetable, no deadlines, remember?"

Madoc wanted to believe Gus was right about him. But he knew his voice would break if he spoke, so he shut his eyes and hung on to Gus's hand, and for the moment that was enough.

When Madoc opened his eyes next, he knew instinctively it was late in the night. He was lying on his side and the TV was dark because it had shut itself off. The lights still burning beyond the blanket fort lent enough light for Madoc to see Gus beside him, however, eyelashes like dark smudges against his skin and that plush mouth slightly parted in sleep.

Gus's hand was still linked with Madoc's, and for a few drowsy seconds, all Madoc wanted was to tug Gus closer and wake him with kisses. But a soft sound by Madoc's feet drew his attention and he went from sleepy to fully alert in a heartbeat.

Letting go of Gus's hand, he levered himself up and held an arm out to Valerie as she crawled into the fort. She scooted into his lap without hesitating, her eyelids heavy, and Madoc knew she wasn't entirely awake.

"Why are you up?" Madoc asked her. "Did you have a bad dream?"

Valerie leaned into Madoc's shoulder. "Jus' wanted to see you and Gus," she murmured, already slipping back into sleep.

Madoc pressed his lips against Valerie's soft hair, breathing in traces of her raspberry-scented shampoo as he focused on calming the wild beating of his own heart. She hadn't seen anything out of the ordinary when she'd crawled into the fort—Madoc and Gus had merely been sleeping. Madoc couldn't help feeling he'd dodged a bullet though, because even if Valerie didn't recall these moments after waking up, he would with absolute clarity.

Aware of Gus stirring, Madoc bit his lip. He didn't know what to say to his friend. Hardly knew what he was feeling himself. But he didn't like the distant look he caught on Gus's face as Gus drew his prosthesis back on.

It's not right that Val doesn't know about us.

Standing, Gus peeled aside the fort's roof and helped Madoc up, remaining silent while Madoc carried Valerie back to her room. He appeared ready to leave by the time Madoc returned a few minutes later, shoes on as he disassembled the fort, every line of his body telegraphing his readiness to collect his cat and head out the door.

Madoc recognized the pulse of panic in his gut as ridiculous—it was already Saturday and Gus would be back in a few hours to kid-sit. Madoc didn't *want* Gus to go, though. Not before he could tell him ... what?

That he was addicted to the way Gus made him feel? To the time they spent together?

That sounded too serious in Madoc's head when he and Gus were just supposed to be having fun.

So, he said nothing and instead went to Gus and kissed him. Sighed when Gus responded hungrily, his hold on Madoc exactly right.

They went to the bedroom, undressing each other between kisses, and Madoc sat by the head of the mattress while Gus removed his prosthesis for a second time that evening.

Madoc didn't think he'd ever tire of watching him. Gus's lean muscles flexing with each movement. Erect cock bobbing slightly and all that glorious golden-fair skin that was Madoc's to touch.

Setting a hand on Gus's hip, he ran it down over the meat of Gus's thigh, cock twitching at Gus's low hum. Gus pulled the lube from the nightstand drawer, and heat flooded through Madoc as Gus climbed astride him with a few fluid movements. Gus was so hard against Madoc's belly, and his soft noise of pleasure when he kissed Madoc had Madoc's balls throbbing.

Pulling back slightly, Madoc brought a hand to Gus's cheek. Fire lit Gus's gaze but it was his expression—so tender and fond—that had Madoc's heart thumping hard.

"Need you," Madoc said, his breath catching when Gus angled his head so his lips met the heel of Madoc's hand.

"I'm here," Gus murmured, pressing more kisses along the palm and base of Madoc's thumb. He rocked his hips into Madoc's, rutting slow and so sexy, bliss on his face as he took Madoc's thumb into his mouth.

Lust seared through Madoc. Groaning, he held Gus more tightly, kissing along Gus's throat and desperate to get closer. When the need to feel Gus's mouth on his own overwhelmed him, Madoc carefully pulled his thumb free, then drew Gus into a scorching kiss that turned his bones to liquid.

Gus eased Madoc backward, shifting his weight so he could hold Madoc down. He kept up the slow grind, his movements driving Madoc wild without getting him off, until finally Gus sat up, his cheeks and neck flushed pink.

Smiling a little, Gus leaned back and plucked the lube up from the nightstand. "Gonna blow you," he said. "Been thinking about it all day and I'm not leaving here 'til you come."

Again, the idea of Gus leaving hit Madoc strangely. Maybe

because Gus had slept next to Madoc almost every night since Pride.

Quickly, Madoc levered himself up and slipped his arms around Gus's neck. "What about you?" he asked, dropping a kiss against Gus's throat. "Want you to feel good too."

"I will." Gus angled his head to give Madoc more access. "I love sucking you. But if you want to jack me at the same time, I won't complain."

Madoc nearly growled. Gus blowing him was one of Madoc's favorite things they did together. But he was just as much into the prospect of making Gus squirm.

They kissed some more and wet their fingers with lube, eventually winding up in the middle of the bed, Gus straddling Madoc's waist with his face aimed toward Madoc's feet. And Madoc couldn't get enough of touching Gus, running his hands over Gus's back and ass, his heart thumping at the sly smile Gus flashed over his shoulder.

Gus leaned forward and took hold of Madoc's hips, rolling Madoc right until they were both on their sides. He tucked his arm under Madoc's bottom leg and drew Madoc closer so he could rest his head on Madoc's thigh, and Madoc spread his knees wide on reflex to give Gus some room. He mirrored Gus's actions, heat zinging under his skin as the movements put Gus's dick mere inches from Madoc's face. Gus's cockhead was purple and shiny with pre-cum, and Madoc's mouth actually watered with sudden awareness.

I want that.

Gus took Madoc in hand, and the crazy-good heat Madoc craved followed a second later when Gus took Madoc's cock between his lips. Madoc gasped, desire rattling up his spine, and bucked his hips helplessly, but Gus was ready for him and groaned through his sucking.

Moving on pure instinct, Madoc took hold of Gus's dick in

one hand, then leaned in and pressed his face against Gus's groin. He breathed in soap and musk, and he dropped kisses along Gus's skin, slowly moving lower, exploring as he jacked Gus. When Madoc finally set his mouth on the tip of Gus's dick, Gus made a desperate sound above him.

Emboldened, Madoc pushed his tongue out and licked, gasping as bitter salt exploded across his tastebuds. Gus moaned again and Madoc licked a second time and then a third, so tantalized by the contrast of heat and velvet he didn't hesitate to open his mouth around Gus's cockhead.

A feedback loop of pleasure unfurled between them, invading Madoc's senses. His dick in Gus's mouth, the taste of Gus in his own. Gus's skin searing against Madoc's, his thigh muscles trembling, Madoc's arousal so potent he felt like he was floating.

He wasn't brave enough to take Gus very deep, but Gus's steady groans were the best kind of encouragement. Gus fondled Madoc's balls, rubbing warmth into the delicate skin, then slid his fingers along the cleft of Madoc's ass. Madoc tensed, his body on guard at the strangeness, but it fell away as Gus traced Madoc's rim with his fingertips.

Balls throbbing, Madoc moaned and thrust harder into Gus's throat, chasing his release as incredible sensation flooded through him.

He'd *never* felt anything like this with a partner.

Enraptured. Connected. Complete.

And then Gus pressed his fingers lightly across Madoc's hole and Madoc was losing it in huge shudders, his body screaming as he came and came and came.

Head spinning, he had to pull off Gus's dick just so he could breathe. He buried his face against Gus's thighs, holding on for dear life while Gus drank him down and when Gus let Madoc's softening cock fall from his mouth, Madoc reached down and took hold of Gus's shoulder, clumsily hauling him back up the bed.

New fire thrilled through Madoc at the taste of himself on Gus's tongue and as he reached for Gus's cock, he pushed away the realities that awaited them. Work and childcare, Noelene still gone and Tarek out of reach, Madoc no wiser about how things would play out after Gus started back on full duty.

For the moment, it was okay not to know anything and simply be here with Gus.

SIXTEEN

"ARE YOU DRAWING DADDY AGAIN?"

Cheeks flushing warm, Gus aimed a mock scowl at the Bug, who'd not only sneaked up on him but had Gus busted over who he'd been sketching.

"Yes, but I'm drawing you, too," Gus said, holding up his notebook so Valerie could see the image he'd captured of her and Madoc sharing cake inside the blanket fort. "See?"

"Oh, we look so nice!" Valerie exclaimed. "But how come you didn't draw you?"

Gus shrugged. "I never do. Just like I don't color my stuff in but leave that to people who are better at it than me."

He didn't like self-portraiture and was never satisfied with any attempt he'd made to capture what he saw when he looked in the mirror. While some people thought that just meant Gus was vain, the truth was he'd always found the world and people around him far more interesting to look at than his own face.

Madoc for instance, who was so gorgeous, and the bright-eyed little girl at Gus's side now who'd gone oddly quiet.

Closing the notebook, Gus set it aside, then cocked his head at her. "How you doin', Bug?"

Valerie leaned into him, setting her head against his shoulder. "Doin' fine. Lemonade didn't wanna get out of bed," she said, "but I didn't mind. I like it when you let her sleep over."

"Well, the small chicken princess likes the sleepovers too."

Gus ignored a prickling shame that rose in his belly as he and the Bug went to the kitchen. Strictly speaking, Valerie didn't *need* to know Gus'd slept over, too, and that was why Lemonade had spent the night. But spinning up half-truths to cover his tracks didn't sit well with Gus, particularly when Valerie was the one he had to lie to.

They made plans for the day over bagels and blueberries and cups of hot chocolate and coffee, and it was a Saturday just like all the others they'd shared since getting to know each other. Until it wasn't and the morning took a turn Gus'd never seen coming.

"Gus?" Setting an elbow on the table, Valerie propped her chin in her hand. "Is tomorrow when you go back to driving the ham-bu-lance with Daddy?"

"Tomorrow night, yes."

"Because your ribs got healed up?"

"Yup!" Gus stood and started collecting the plates. "Are you excited to have your daddy around for the before and after school stuff again?"

"Uh-huh! But are you going to be there, too?"

"If your daddy needs help, then yes, I could be there. Like, if he has an appointment or is running late and can't make it to you in time. But don't forget Tarek is coming back and you're going to have Clea around too, so your dad's going to have lots of help."

"Okay." Valerie took another bite of bagel. "I want *you*, though. And I think you should come live with us."

Gus kind of froze. "Um. I have my own place, remember?"

"I know. But upstairs is bigger than your place, so you'll have lots of room for your chair and stuff. Especially 'cause Noelene's not coming back and maybe Uncle T too." Valerie's expression clouded before she shook it off. "You can have my sleepover room," she said to Gus, "and that way I can see you every day and not only sometimes."

Oh, balls.

Gus set the plates back on the table and resumed his seat. He loved the enchanting, impossible direction the Bug's thoughts had taken her. Valerie just wanted the people she cared about to be happy. And if she was including Gus in her adorably impossible plan, that could mean she cared about him.

Which would have made Gus feel about a hundred feet tall if he hadn't lived in the real world.

"I would be happy to keep seeing you every day," he said gently. "But I can't take over Tarek's loft. He *is* coming back, and he will not be excited to find out he had a new housemate that he's never met."

The smile slipped from Valerie's face. "Yes, he will. Uncle T is nice! Maybe you could adopt him, so we can all be a fam."

"I love the way you're thinking so much," Gus said. His heart ached as he regarded the Bug across the table. "But making a family isn't that simple."

"Yes, it is. Daddy and me make one with Uncle T, easy peasy, lemon squeezy."

"Well, sure! Tarek is your family, Val. You're related to him through your mom and I'm just ..."

The kid-sitter.

The fuck buddy.

The guy who rides on the truck with your dad.

"... your daddy's partner," Gus finished weakly. "*And* his really good friend. The way you and I are good friends."

"You said friends can be family. Like Mr. Ian is with your ma and pops. Because they adopted him." Valerie narrowed her eyes. "And you called everyone from the parade your fam."

"I did." Gus reached over and set his hand over Valerie's where it lay on the table. "But I've known those guys a long time and we grew into being a fam as we got to know each other."

Valerie leaned forward in her seat, expression intent. "You've known me a long time. Does that mean you want to keep me?"

"As your friend, you mean? Of course I want to, for as long as you want me!" Gus's heart dipped when the light in Valerie's face faded. He'd said the wrong thing, but what? "Hon, even if we don't see each other every day, it's not like I'm going to forget you. I don't forget my other friends and fam who I don't see every day, right?"

"Yah, but you want to keep *them*."

Pouting furiously, Valerie pulled her hand away from Gus's, then plunked both elbows on the table with a huff. Unfortunately, her left elbow hit the side of the glow jar she'd set nearby and the thing went spinning off into space. Falling to the floor, it bounced once and shattered with a dramatic, glittery pop.

Valerie gasped, her horror immediate. "Oh, no!"

Gus was out of his chair in a flash. "It's fine," he said, rounding the table, one hand out to ward her off getting out of her chair. "It was an accident, and I'll clean it up—"

"But it's broken!" Valerie's dismay was palpable. She shifted her weight in the seat as if readying to launch herself from it. "I broke it, Gus, and I—"

"Don't move!" Gus barked, terror gripping him as images of glass cutting into soft little feet flashed in his head. His stomach bottomed out when Valerie startled badly at his hard tone though, and her eyes went shiny with tears.

"I'm sorry," she croaked, red splotches standing out on her cheeks and chin. "I didn't mean to break it."

"I know that, hon." Reaching her side, Gus scooped her up, his heart pounding so hard he nearly choked. "I'm so sorry I yelled."

Valerie sagged like her strings had been cut and the dam broke in a torrent of noisy sobs that she tried to muffle against Gus's shoulder. Rubbing her back, he carried Valerie to the bedroom and shut the door, aching as her tears wet his shirt.

"You're okay," Gus said again and again, hoping that it wasn't a lie and knowing he was going to hate himself a long time for this.

He got them settled on the floor by the bed to ride out the storm and, after what seemed like an eternity, the tears stopped, leaving behind mournful, hiccupping sighs that rocked Valerie's frame. She slid down from Gus's shoulder and into his lap, getting comfortable in the crook of his arm, and Lemonade picked that moment to descend upon them from the bed using Gus's shoulder and bringing a very small smile to Valerie's face.

Gus ran a hand over the Bug's hair. "How you doing, kid?"

"Doin' okay." She sniffled wetly. "But my head's all full of snot."

"Yeah, I can tell." Gus wrinkled his nose at her playfully, then looked toward the nightstand. "Let's see if we can do something about that."

They found a package of tissues, and he helped Valerie clean up, dabbing at her red-rimmed eyes and pink cheeks while she blew her nose.

"I'm sorry I yelled," Gus said again, a lump rising in his throat when Valerie dropped her eyes to her hands in her lap, her mouth drooping miserably at the corners. "I wasn't angry about the jar being broken or that it made a mess. I was afraid you'd cut yourself on the glass."

The doubt in Valerie's face when she looked back up at Gus made him feel even worse. "You were scared?"

"Yes." Gus licked his lips. "I'd never want to see you hurt, Bug, and the glass on the floor scared me a lot. I started to panic and the feeling got away from me, and then I was yelling without meaning to."

Sniffing, Valerie leaned her head back against Gus's shoulder. "My feelings got away too."

"Because of my yelling?"

"No. Because you don't want to live here with us."

Hiding a sigh, Gus rubbed his hand up and down Valerie's arm. "It's not about wanting to or not, hon. I already have my own place to live."

"So? You could still move over here. If you lived with us an' didn't go back to work, I wouldn't need a new kid-sitter because I could have you."

Once upon a time, Gus would have smiled over a declaration such as that. But today, the melancholy in Valerie's voice took up space in his chest and just made him feel sad.

"I need to go back to work, Valley Girl, because I'm your daddy's partner and it's part of my job to have his back when he's on the truck," Gus said. "And didn't you like Clea that time you met her after school?"

He'd heard a lot from Madoc about the sitter he'd found through one of the online services, an easygoing young woman named Clea who did freelance technical writing around her kid-sitting gigs.

"She was nice," Valerie allowed, "and we did some cool craft stuff, like making ladybugs outta pom-poms. But Daddy said Clea is gonna have to stay with me during the night sometimes though, and I don't think I like that at all."

"How come?"

"What if she leaves while I'm sleeping? 'Cause she could if she wanted."

The genuine concern in her expression had Gus's skin prickling. Did Valerie remember being left on her own as a toddler? Or was this fear rooted in the more recent past and Noelene finally walking out on her family?

Jesus Murphy.

"Clea will not leave while you're asleep," Gus said firmly. "She knows your daddy expects her to keep you safe while he's at work and if Clea doesn't do that, he'll find someone who will. Did you tell your daddy you're worried?"

He tried not to wince at Valerie's slow head shake.

"Well, I really think that you should, Bug. He'll want to know if you ever feel like you're not safe with a kid-sitter, no matter who that kid-sitter is, your uncle, Clea, or me."

Valerie worried her lip with her teeth for a beat. "But is he gonna be mad about drama?"

"Hon, this is not drama." With his first two fingers, Gus gently tapped Valerie's tummy. "If you ever get a bad feeling here because of a kid-sitter or anyone, I want you to tell your daddy as soon as you can. Can you do that for me?"

"Yes," Valerie said, very solemn. "I can do that."

"Good." Gus gave her a quick squeeze. "I promise you'll be doing the right thing."

They got to their feet then so Valerie could dress while Gus swept up the glass, and soon it was as if the storm of tears had never happened. Valerie's words continued to replay in Gus's head however, resonating even more deeply each time she took hold of his hand or gave him a smile.

"I want to see you every day and not only sometimes."

"We can all be a fam."

"Do you want to keep me?"

Gus'd been looking forward to parts of his life shifting back to his 'normal' when he resumed working nights. He wanted his paycheck to be less skimpy and to go back to playing basketball with his team and boxing with Connor. Gus definitely could not *wait* to put as much distance between himself and the desks in the office as possible too.

He was going to miss spending time with the Bug and her daddy, though. The after-school pickups with Valerie pelting across the schoolyard to him. The kid-craft projects and brain-bending questions. Making dinner with Madoc and the easy talks they had in the evenings once they were on their own. All that would be gone unless Madoc decided to keep Gus around.

And fuck, maybe *that* was what Valerie had wanted to know when she'd asked if Gus would want to keep her. If continuing to see her was important to him, or if he'd be the next person in her life who walked away.

Valerie didn't know Gus had no intention of walking away. That the Walters' family's happiness had become so intertwined with his own, that imagining not being part of their lives left him feeling lost.

Gus didn't doubt for a second that Madoc valued him as a partner and friend. But beyond work and sex, he wasn't sure what Madoc wanted from him and Gus had no one to blame for that but himself.

He'd played it light and no pressure so often this summer, mindful of Madoc still coming to terms with being bi while also shedding the baggage from his disastrous marriage. Gus hadn't expected Valerie to get attached to him, though. Or that he'd start to feel a similar way for Valerie and her daddy.

Gus bit his lip. He'd strayed without meaning to into dangerous territory that did not fit in the Gus-as-the-kid-sitter paradigm. But if Madoc wanted Gus even a little—to keep him around and build toward more than the hook-ups—Gus was damned if he'd let any of that shit, minor or major, hold him back.

They needed to talk about what each of them wanted. Gus would make it clear that he would be there for Madoc and Valerie, no matter who did the kid-sitting. Because he sort of liked the idea of forming a tiny fam of their own, just as Valerie had imagined.

It might take some work to figure out how all the pieces would fit together. But Gus wanted to put in the time, all of it with Madoc, every day that he could.

SEVENTEEN

MADOC SET his bag on the island chair beside Gus's, then bent to unzip his boots. They had a long night ahead of them starting the process of resetting their internal clocks for the night shift and had a plan to stay up late deep cleaning and doing food prep. And, Madoc hoped, wrapping himself around Gus until they were so high on pleasure Madoc hardly knew his own name.

He had a weakness for the way Gus looked at him when they were alone together. Like they were the only two people left in the world and had all the time they needed to laugh and be playful away from the pressures of work and life.

Madoc needed those moments to just be.

Peace crept over him as he glanced around. He took in the warm light cast by the lamps near the windows. The table set for dinner and the baking show playing on the TV. Gus's feet sticking out of the entrance of the new and improved blanket fort Madoc had designed. The pack of playing cards spread out on the rug beside the fort and a small yellow sock beside them.

Home.

Ambling over, he squatted down and peered inside the fort. Gus was reclined on his back with Valerie beside him, her head resting atop Gus's shoulder, and the cat was snoozing near Valerie's feet.

"Welcome home, Daddy!" Valerie waved both hands at Madoc. "How you doin'?"

Chuckling, Madoc got down on all fours and crawled in through the fort's opening. "I'm doin' good and glad to be home. What's going on with my people?"

Valerie levered herself up to make space for Madoc. "We went to the ah-quarium today," she said, "and then Gus and me did yoga and a whole bunch of rainy-day stuff."

"I'll bet your rainy-day stuff was more fun than mine. Oof." Madoc sprawled onto his stomach, smiling when the others laughed. "This is nice, though."

"Me and Gus made orange cake after lunch," Valerie said. She scooted over and draped herself over Madoc's back, and she pressed her cheek against his now, small fingers stroking his hair. "You can have a slice for snack and that'll make you feel better."

Madoc looked askance at his partner. "Because cake is a cure-all, huh?"

"Yes, silly." Rolling onto his side, Gus propped his head on his hand. "There'll still be plenty left for tonight's dessert too."

They chatted for a bit about the sea creatures Valerie and Gus had seen at the aquarium, but the whole time, Madoc thought Gus seemed off. When Valerie ducked out of the fort to use the bathroom, Lemonade followed her and Gus rolled onto his back again, seemingly studying the blanket stretched above them with a hangdog expression that told Madoc something had happened.

Bridging the small space between them, he ran his knuckles along Gus's upper arm. "Everything okay?"

"Val broke a glow jar this morning and I barked at her because I was afraid she'd cut herself on the glass." Gus huffed. "I hurt her feelings, she cried, and it sucked very much."

Shit. Valerie wasn't a big crier, but it was never easy to see her unhappy, particularly when you had no way to fix it.

"I'm sorry, man." Madoc squeezed Gus's shoulder. "She didn't cut herself, right?"

"No. But she said some stuff after the crying that I want to talk about."

"Okay. Though, I'd like to get off the floor before I can't."

They retreated to the kitchen while Valerie carried on watching her show, and Madoc tried the cake, which was stupid good, sweet and bright with citrus that made it hard to stop eating.

"What did Val say that you think I should know?" Madoc asked around a mouthful.

"She asked me to come live with you." Gus grimaced when Madoc goggled at him. "I told her I couldn't obviously, but then she said there'd be space upstairs at Tarek's because he might not come back."

Madoc frowned. "I don't understand. Val knows T's coming back. She made a 'Welcome Home' sign to hang in the loft and everything."

"Well, there's knowing a thing and then believing it." After scrubbing his face with his hands, Gus dropped them onto the counter. "I think Tarek's been gone long enough that Val's stopped believing he has a return date. She's said as much a couple of times."

She has?

That couldn't be right. If Valerie had questions about her uncle, she'd bring them to Madoc because they talked about everything.

Didn't they?

Heat slid up the back of Madoc's shirt collar. "When did Val talk to you about Tarek not coming back?"

"Today and a couple of weeks ago." Gus frowned. "She worries, I think. Like about Tarek not coming back and the new kid-sitter staying overnight with her."

"But ... Val met Clea, and they hit it off right away."

"I know. But I guess Val's got it in her head that Clea might leave her alone. Maybe because Noelene did that sometimes?"

Madoc felt sick. "Did Val tell you her mom left her alone?"

"No, you did."

"But Val *has* talked to you about Noelene?"

"Well, sure, a few times."

"And what did she say on those times?"

Madoc knew his voice sounded off. That the irritation building in him was misplaced and foolish when *of course* Valerie talked to Gus about all kinds of things, so why not her mom? The uncertainty on Gus's face had Madoc's back up though, and fuck if he could get a handle on it.

"What did Valerie say about Noelene, Gus?"

"That Noelene seems down a lot," Gus replied. "And that she'd rather be at work than be around Val."

Madoc's old friend grief swamped him then and he had to cut his gaze away from Gus as he replied. "You should have told me."

"You're right, I should have." Gus's voice was very quiet. "I thought Val was talking to you about the stuff with her mom. But now ..."

Madoc glanced back at the pause and saw Gus biting his lip, his face troubled. "What?"

"I'm starting to wonder if Val's not telling you things because she worries about how you'll react. That you'll think she's making drama nobody wants."

The air left Madoc's lungs. 'Drama nobody wants' was an

expression Noelene had used far too often around her family, particularly after their move to Boston. And if Gus was right, Valerie had come to believe Madoc viewed her through that same impatient lens. That Madoc might decide life with a six-year-old girl was so messy and complicated he needed to walk away, like her mom had.

A terrible, aching sorrow swirled through Madoc, pierced through with guilt. Valerie was the most precious thing in his life. She *had* to know Madoc would never leave, never turn her away.

Unless she didn't.

But how had that happened? And why the fuck hadn't Madoc noticed?

"You should have told me," he said again, the tears he couldn't shed hardening his voice. His outrage didn't waver at all when Gus's face fell even further. "Val is *my* daughter, and I need to know if she's hurting or upset. You had no right to keep this from me, Gus, none at all."

Gus's hands came up, palms out in a gesture like surrender. "I wasn't, I swear. I just—"

"Daddy? Are you and Gus fighting?"

Madoc had never felt lower. Valerie was on the other side of the island when he looked left, glancing between Gus and Madoc with wide eyes. Her hands were clasped in front of her, fingers entwined so tightly her knuckles were white. She looked stricken. Maybe scared. And fuck, Madoc wanted to throw up just thinking that.

"She worries about how you'll react."

"No, my honey, we're not fighting." Holding out a hand, Madoc was relieved when she immediately zipped around the island to him. He scooped her up and put his nose in her hair, eyes closed tight as he focused on breathing in and out. "Gus and I were just talking."

"You were talking really loud," she said against his shoulder, and Madoc tried to smile past the ache in his chest.

He didn't want his daughter or his friend feeling bad. Not over a mess that was Madoc's to own and clean up. Gus looked miserable when Madoc glanced over at him too, thanks to Madoc's big mouth.

But before Madoc could begin fixing things, he heard keys in the lock on the front door and a voice calling out, rough but dearly familiar.

"Madoc? Val?"

"It's Tarek," Madoc murmured to Gus, and Valerie perked up in his arms as a tall, broad-shouldered figure strode in. Tarek's jeans and t-shirt looked a bit dusty, and he was sporting a thick, overgrown beard, but his blue eyes were bright beneath his battered Bruins cap.

"Hello, my people!" Tarek crowed. "What's everyone up to?"

Valerie started giggling. "Uncle T, you got a rug on your face again!"

"That's what happens when you live the mountain man life, silly!" Laughing, he rubbed his palms over the beard. "I was going to shave but decided it's too glorious not to show off."

There was a flurry of activity, Valerie in Tarek's arms while he and Madoc exchanged hugs and Gus did his best to corral Lemonade who, oddly, seemed not to like the look of Tarek at all. She lashed her long tail as she eyed him, growling low when Gus picked her up.

"Ma'am," Gus chided quietly. "Why are you acting like you've never seen a beard in your life?"

"When did you get a cat?" Tarek asked as he eyed Gus up and down, unabashedly staring at his prosthesis.

An urge to tell Tarek to keep his fucking eyes to himself swept over Madoc. He 'saw' Gus's prosthesis, of course. Was never going to forget the socks and liners or the crutches and wheelchair Gus used when he felt like it or needed to. But Gus's prosthesis was *one* part of the whole person Madoc liked very much and who deserved better than to be gawked at behind his back.

"That's Princess Lemonade," Valerie said to her uncle. "And she's Gus's adventure kitty."

"Gus is my partner on the truck," Madoc added, hoping his smile looked more natural than it felt on his face. "He's been helping me out with kid-sitting while you were out of town."

"Ah." Tarek's expression lightened a little, polite now that he felt his family's attention on him. "Nice meeting you, man," he said to Gus, "I'm Val's Uncle T."

"She talks about you all the time." Gus's grin was easy, and now that Lemonade was in the crook of his arm with her feet up, she was much calmer. "My dad's a big fan by the way," Gus said, "and I'd shake hands if this beastie didn't need wangling. Madoc said you went northbound on the Appalachian Trail?"

"Uh, yeah!" Tarek set a wiggling Valerie back down on the floor. "My buddies and I try to hike the AT every year and this time we started in Georgia and trekked up through Tennessee and North Carolina. We reckon we clocked around four-hundred-fifty-six miles."

"Nice," Gus said with feeling. He stooped slightly so Valerie could treat Lemonade to some pats but flashed another interested glance in Tarek's direction. "A friend and I did the White Mountains in New Hampshire last fall but that was only nine days."

Madoc looked askance between his friends. Nine days? He couldn't imagine hiking for nine hours, never mind over a week, and four-hundred-fifty plus miles was so legitimately bananas, his brain rejected the number out of hand.

Tarek, meanwhile, was blinking, no doubt startled by the

idea of an amputee hiking up mountain ranges. "I love being up there during cool weather," he said, "but I wanted to get back to Boston so Madoc and my sis didn't think I'd defected permanently. Where is Noels, anyway?" He looked to Madoc. "Wondered if maybe she was down here with you all."

"She's been traveling," Madoc replied, though he felt Valerie's and Gus's eyes on him. "I can fill you in over dinner."

"I think that's my cue." Gus straightened up. "I'm going to get this grumpy chicken home to a beard-free environment so everyone can chill, including me."

Valerie stuck out her lip. "But Daddy's going to make sandwiches, remember? Then we were gonna have more rainy-day cake!"

"We can share sandwiches another time, Bug," Gus said, though he sounded somewhat uncertain. "And you can give my share of the cake to your uncle to welcome him home."

Gus got his and Lemonade's stuff together, Valerie grumbling the whole time about having to say goodbye before her bedtime, a sentiment Madoc silently shared. It felt wrong watching Gus leave when they had stuff to talk about. When Madoc still had to apologize for acting like a giant fucking jerk and they'd had plans to spend tonight together.

Madoc didn't know how to urge Gus to stay without making it weird though, particularly with Tarek eyeing them all, no doubt trying to decipher why Gus and his cat were in the apartment at all. So, Madoc let them go, knowing he couldn't put off bringing Tarek up to speed on where things stood with Noelene.

A conversation that went as poorly as Madoc had always assumed it would.

"I can't believe we don't know where she is," Tarek fumed. "Or that you haven't gone after her!"

"Will you keep your voice down? I don't want you waking

up Val." Madoc rubbed his hands over his face. "As for Noelene, she's an adult, T, and my focus has been on Val and keeping my job."

Tarek deflated instantly. "Shit. Why didn't you call me? I would've come back from my trip the second I'd known."

"And that is why I didn't call," Madoc said. "You needed the time away with your crew. We did okay too, once I had help with Val."

"From your partner, yeah." Tarek's face took on a pinched expression. "You really think he's the best choice of kid-sitter? You know, what with the fake leg and—"

"Don't go there, man." Heat flared in Madoc's chest. "Gus is more than capable of sitting for Val and he's done a ton this summer helping me out."

Been there for me in ways you don't understand.

Shame flickered across Tarek's expression but quickly disappeared. "Fine. I'm still going to talk to Noels about going back to rehab."

"I don't think rehab is what she needs this time, T," Madoc said. "According to her, she hasn't been gambling."

"And that's clearly bullshit. Why the hell else would she go AWOL?"

"Because she's happier away from us."

Tarek winced. "How the fuck can you say that? Noels cares about her family. I know she's had a hard time doing the mom thing, but that doesn't mean she won't get better at it."

Pain curled around Madoc's heart. He'd come around lately to thinking Noelene *did* care about them in her own way. But she'd still let them down, especially Valerie.

"Noelene doesn't want to get better at being a mom." Madoc held Tarek's gaze. "I know it and so does Val and I can't ..." He shook his head. "I'm not going to make my daughter live with someone who doesn't want her, T. I've petitioned to end

Noelene's parenting hours. She knows and we have a court date in August to make that final."

"God, Madoc." Tarek began pacing, face twisted and bitter. "Why would you do that? When the fuck did you get so cruel?"

The tears in Tarek's eyes sliced into Madoc. "I'm not trying to be cruel," he said softly. "Making that decision gutted me. But Noelene left without notice and broke what little trust I had left in her. I'm done looking back and wondering over 'what ifs.' I need to do the right thing for my daughter and myself and move us forward which, honestly, may be the best for Noelene too."

Pulling his wallet from his pocket, Madoc withdrew the note Noelene had left on his door and slid it across the table to Tarek. Madoc hadn't read the note since he'd found it. But he recalled its contents perfectly.

I have to go.

I tried.

I can't breathe when I'm here.

Madoc might never understand the demons Noelene was fighting, but the real cruelty would be to force her back into a situation where she felt crushed every day by her own life. To make Valerie live with a mother who couldn't love her.

Valerie deserved more. And so did Madoc.

"I need to move on, T," he said, "and so does my girl."

Tarek was staring at Noelene's note, a sick expression on his face. "I'll talk to her," he said at last, voice rough as he slid the page back to Madoc. "You just have to give me time to fix everything."

Refolding the note, Madoc slipped it back away. "Noelene not wanting to be a mom isn't a thing that needs fixing, T. Lots of people don't want to be parents," he said, "and there's nothing wrong with knowing that's how you're wired. But Val keeps getting caught in the middle of all this sad, heavy shit and it *has* to stop."

They went around and around, Tarek's outrage on his sister's behalf laced with guilt and regret and a sorrow Madoc recognized only too well. But while Madoc comforted Tarek through his heartache, his resolve didn't waver.

He would take care of his kid over everything.

EIGHTEEN

MONDAY, *July 30, 12:30 P.M.*

GUS JERKED, his heart in his throat. He grabbed at the thing pressed against his shoulder and hung on, voice shaking around his order. "I said fall *back*!"

"Hey." Madoc's voice was low and soothing, his fingers firm around Gus's. "You're all right, Gus. You hear me? You're safe."

And Gus was. There was no fire and he wasn't falling, and Madoc was beside him in the bed, his fingers caught in Gus's death grip. Pushing his sleep mask aside with his free hand, Gus forced himself to loosen his hold on Madoc without letting go entirely.

"Sorry," he croaked. "Nightmare."

"S'okay." Madoc threaded their fingers together. "What do you need?"

You, every day you'll have me.

Gus ignored the fluttery feeling in his belly and ran the

palm of his free hand over Madoc's lightly furred thigh. "This," he replied. "This n' more sleep."

"We should get up," Madoc murmured. "Bet you're hungry again."

"I can eat later." Gus moved his hand to Madoc's crotch, smirking as he fingered the outline of Madoc's hardening dick through the thin cotton boxers. "Besides, you're already up."

Madoc snorted at the dopey joke but quickly folded under Gus's petting. While never passive, it was clear he enjoyed Gus taking the lead, and he looked entirely content lying back with his legs spread so Gus could settle between them. Madoc grabbed Gus's ass and kissed him deep, and while Gus wasn't sure his brain and body would cooperate to let him get off, he soaked in the good feeling of skin against his. Of Madoc holding him close.

They ground against each other a while, Gus pulling away to get the lube from the side table when at last his own desire rose warm and welcome inside him. Hands slick, he took hold of Madoc and Madoc tipped back his head with a moan, so fucking sexy.

"Oh, wow." His hold on Gus grew deliciously tight, expression awed as Gus slid his own cock alongside Madoc's so he could work them at the same time. "How the fuck does this feel so good?"

The wonder in his voice had Gus's heart thumping. He loved watching Madoc lose himself like this, pupils blown wide and groaning as he lost it in hot, sticky splashes over the head of Gus's cock. And *man*, that did it for Gus. He went off like a rocket seconds later, the intensity of the rush leaving him boneless and gasping.

Madoc made himself the big spoon behind Gus in the aftermath, his body wonderfully solid. But then Lemonade hopped up on to the bed, tags clinking softly as she literally climbed over both of them on her way to curling up somewhere near Gus's knees.

"Whazzat?" Madoc muttered, already dozy again, and Gus had to laugh.

"It's nothing," he said, rubbing Madoc's arm. "Just go to sleep."

Gus tried to do the same in the silence that followed but gave up when echoes of the dream that'd woken him continued to flash through his head. He resorted to sketching awkwardly while lying on his side while his cat and partner slept on, something he'd done often since the change back to the night shift had disrupted not only Gus's sleep patterns but the rest of his life.

Being back on regular duty—treating patients, the adrenaline rush, bantering back and forth with Madoc—all of it had been like slipping into a favorite sweater the night Gus had boarded A1 again, the fit natural and so very easy. Gus'd been in his element immediately, almost as if his time away from the truck had never happened at all.

Unfortunately, that'd also been the vibe in the locker room after the shift ended because Madoc had started talking about needing to get home to Valerie before Gus had even finished changing into his street clothes.

Like Gus hadn't been a part of Madoc's complicated, beautiful life for over a month. Or that a mere twenty-four hours ago, they'd been in Madoc's bed, kissing each other awake instead of Madoc patting Gus's shoulder on his way out the door.

"Really glad we have this back," he'd said, throwing Gus a warm smile. "I'll see you tonight!"

Gus had waved him out, then headed for home because ... well, because what else was there to do? He'd expected to see less of the Walters family after his return to the night shift, of course. Just not for the time he shared with them to evaporate.

No more Q&A time with Valerie. No cozy dinners or intimate talks with Madoc over beers. No watching Madoc's face as they moved together in bed.

Every interaction he and Madoc'd had on the job in the days that followed was solid because they really *were* friends. But Gus'd felt ... not great. He'd missed the Walters family with a ferocity that'd taken him off guard and found himself avoiding going home to his empty place where the silence made it impossible to sleep.

Gus'd had no idea how or even if he could talk to Madoc about what he was feeling when everything happening had been the new 'normal' and Madoc had adjusted without missing a beat. Until a message had popped up on Gus's phone on the morning of the fifth day and had him wondering if he'd misjudged a few things.

Val wants to know if you'll have dinner with us, Madoc had written. *She misses you and Princess L.*

Gus'd stared at the words for a full minute before tapping out a reply. *OK. Can I bring anything?*

His buzzer had rung almost immediately, and Gus'd found Madoc on the doorstep with a bag of takeout and handmade cards from Valerie for every day she hadn't seen Gus.

"We'll come to you, if that's okay," Madoc had said almost shyly. "Even bring dessert to sweeten the deal."

Gus'd shrugged like his heart hadn't been about to bound out of his body. "Sounds like fun," he'd replied, "but how about I handle dessert?"

He'd smiled as Madoc had stalked through the door and kissed him and they'd spent the rest of the morning talking, eating, screwing around, and sleeping until Madoc had needed to leave to pick Valerie up from school. Gus'd tried to stay chill, but he'd been on tenterhooks until his buzzer had blared again a couple of hours later, repeatedly this time because Valerie had been the one punching it.

There'd been no discussion about why Madoc had seemingly pulled away or why Gus would want to resume spending time with the Walters. Gus and Madoc had continued to connect outside work from that point forward, however, whenever their schedules allowed.

It wasn't perfect. There was a lot of shifting of schedules and hustling between the apartments, Valerie complaining about not seeing Gus as much as she'd like while Gus kept similar thoughts about missing the Walters to himself. He told himself they all needed some time to become accustomed to this new normal.

Including Tarek, who seemed truly to struggle. Gone was the smiley uncle Gus'd met that first night, replaced by a grouch who was heartbroken over his sister having abandoned her family. Who was cold toward Clea and treated Gus like shit any time their paths crossed.

Gus knew Tarek was hurting; he had a sister of his own and would have been devastated watching Donna's life implode the way Noelene's had. It still *sucked* having to be around a dude who made faces when he caught Gus adjusting his leg and looked unbelievably tense anytime the topic of his queerness came up. Valerie simply asking to borrow Gus's Pride bracelet made Tarek's jaw go so tight it was a wonder the thing didn't snap clean off his face.

Gus truly hated knowing one of the city's beloved sports figures was an ableist homophobe. And how everything was infinitely more complicated because that 'hero' was someone Madoc and Valerie treasured. A family member Gus feared would flip out completely if he ever discovered Madoc was fooling around with Gus on the down-low.

And that was the part about the return to this 'normal' Gus struggled with most: sneaking around and lying to his crew-mates and fam, a burden that increased on the daily.

Hiding had been fairly easy when Gus'd been stuck behind a desk at the station. He'd rarely seen Madoc during the day, while the kid-sitting had given him the perfect excuse to be around Madoc during their off hours. Now that they were back to spending most nights together on A1, Gus felt on guard all the time.

He couldn't get too close or let his gaze linger on Madoc for too long, and simple gestures like sharing food in the canteen or inviting Madoc to a boxing workout with Connor and himself made Gus feel like he was under a microscope. He wondered all the time if he should just tell Madoc that he wanted more than fooling around behind closed doors but even more so if Madoc was at all ready to hear such a thing. Because Madoc didn't seem to struggle at all with this double life they were living, always so good at playing it straight.

Enough that Gus was starting to feel like someone's dirty little secret, a vibe he didn't like one bit.

"What are these?" Madoc asked as he peered at the contents of a plastic tub he'd pulled from Gus's freezer.

"Those were *supposed* to be a snack we'd eat on shift, you bum," Gus scolded. They'd dragged themselves out of bed at last and were making omelets in the kitchen, and he'd asked Madoc to grab a bag of frozen vegetables. "Val and I made them for you."

Madoc's eyebrows went up. "For me? When?"

"Saturday. You were getting your hair cut." Gus watched Madoc pluck several little purple-blue balls from the tub and pop them in his mouth. "They're blueberry bites," he said, "also known as bluebs dipped in yogurt then frozen."

"Yo, these are *good*," Madoc said around his chewing.

"Thank you for doing that with her," he added. "I already know that was Val's favorite part."

Gus went all gooey at Madoc's smile because he was a hopeless sap, and he quickly stuck some of the blueberry bites in his mouth to keep himself from saying stupid things.

"Since you brought up my girl," Madoc said, "can I ask you a favor?"

"Of course. You need me to pick her up?"

"Next Tuesday if you can. I have court that day and I'd like to talk to Noels after, make sure she's well."

Gus resumed his omelet making. "No problem," he said. "I'm having lunch with Ian and his beast dog that day, so I'll already be near the North End."

"Thank you." Madoc chewed some more before turning a thoughtful expression on Gus. "You guys really like each other, huh?"

Gus cocked his head. "Yes?"

Madoc scrunched up his nose. "Sorry, that came out weird. It's just ... You and Ian make time to hang out on the regular and I can't imagine doing that with Noelene."

"Ian and I split up for very different reasons than you and Noelene did," Gus reasoned. "And it took a while for he and I to get to where we are now."

Because it was just the two of us. Ian and I didn't have someone like Val making it harder both to let go and *come back together.*

"Can I ask what happened?" Madoc asked.

On reflex, Gus balked at answering. It wasn't easy for him, talking about why he and Ian had fallen apart. But he didn't feel right not answering when Madoc had been so honest with him about his own marriage breaking down.

Besides, wasn't this the kind of talk Gus wanted to keep

having with this man? The kind that went deeper than the surface stuff that always came so easily?

Gus poured the vegetables into the pan he'd heated and listened to them sizzle for a few seconds. Funny, the places he and Madoc chose to confide in each other. Beside the windows in Madoc's apartment. Under the blanket fort's roof. Nestled in Gus's bed. Perched on the truck's bumper beneath the night sky. The kitchens of the places where they lived and worked.

"Ian and I were so young when we met," Gus said, "and that meant we did a lot of growing up while we were together. We knew we wanted the same things. Each other and our careers, good friends, good lives. No kids." Gus watched surprise flash across Madoc's face. "After I lost my leg, it was like that life didn't fit me anymore. Or maybe it was me that didn't fit, no matter how hard I tried."

Madoc set the tub of frozen fruit aside and started breaking eggs into a bowl. "Are you saying you and Ian broke up over whether or not to have kids?"

"No. Ian might say otherwise if you asked him, but it wasn't about kids or no kids. It was about me being fucked in the head and not dealing with it."

"Gus."

"It's true. I wasn't myself after the accident. I was in pain, felt shattered." Gus ran his teeth over his bottom lip. "But I tried to pretend I was okay. That I could recover faster, come back harder than anyone predicted. That I was the Super Gus people imagined I was."

"Shit," Madoc said quietly. "I can't even imagine."

Despair whispered through Gus, familiar and terrible despite the passage of time, the losses he'd suffered raw all over again.

"Ian didn't expect me to be super anything," he said, stirring the vegetables in the pan. "He could see I was struggling and wanted to help. To talk wheelchairs and prosthetics and career options outside firefighting. And as dumb as it sounds, I couldn't because it felt like giving up and I was already fighting like hell not to drown. I didn't want to deal with my pain or fear, and I was incredibly tired of being a burden. So, I found people who made me feel like I wasn't."

"People like Ben?"

"People like Ben. I didn't cheat on Ian—I would never have done that to him or any partner. I wanted to feel normal though, whatever that means, and I had an easier time doing that around Ben. Ian thought I chose Ben over him."

"Did you?"

"No. I chose myself. Got caught up in my own head over the things I'd lost or couldn't do anymore, and didn't recognize I was taking Ian for granted. That he was scared and badly depressed and hurting in his own way. He needed help and I didn't see it. And maybe I needed to focus on me at the time, but I hate that I let Ian down." Gus frowned at Madoc. "That I hurt him so badly he had to walk away."

Madoc set down the whisk he'd been using to mix the eggs and took Gus's hand, sympathy pooling in his eyes. "I'm sorry."

"Thanks." Sighing, Gus looked down at their joined hands. "After Ian ended things, I made a colossal mistake with Ben, which you know. But I did work on myself. Got therapy for my pain and the stuff going on in my head. I've learned not to look past stuff that hurts. And I think I'm a better friend to the people I care about now."

"Good for you, Gus. I really mean that."

"I know you do." Gus squeezed Madoc's fingers and relished the small touch. "You trying to get to a similar place with your ex and stop fighting?"

Madoc shook his head. "I'm not sure where I want to be with Noelene. But I think it'd be good for my own mental health if the conversations we have didn't feel or sound like brawling."

"Makes sense to me," Gus said. "Fighting with Ian was hard on both of us, before and after we broke up. He deserved better."

"He did," Madoc agreed. "But so did you."

Tears Gus didn't want to shed made his throat thick. He hadn't expected a pass for his shitty boyfriend behavior, but Madoc's sympathy–the hug he pulled Gus into–was a balm Gus hadn't known he'd needed.

NINETEEN

TUESDAY, *August 8, 1:15 P.M.*

AS PROMISED, Noelene didn't contest Madoc's petition to remove her parenting hours and the change was granted without fanfare.

"Thanks for making that easy," Madoc said as he and Noelene headed through Downtown. They'd stopped for coffee at a coffee shop near the courthouse and taken their cups to go. "I know your schedule is packed and coming out to Boston was probably a pain."

"It's fine," Noelene replied. "I've been cutting back on the travel overall, so this trip wasn't a big deal. It's nice seeing the city again, honestly."

Her blonde hair was longer than it had been the last time Madoc had seen her, and she had a suntan that gave her a sun-kissed appearance. But the tension in Noelene's shoulders told Madoc she had a lot on her mind.

"How's Val?" Noelene asked. "She excited to go back to school?"

"Oh, yes." Madoc chuckled. "But she's still digging the summer camp thing. She finished hockey camp last week and started arts and crafts this week, so I expect to have lots of new doodads."

"Ha. Maybe she'll make you a much-needed new tie."

Madoc smiled at the old joke. He didn't get many opportunities to dress up and had exactly two ties to his name, both almost a decade old. He couldn't wait to show off the one he was wearing today for Gus though, who would appreciate Madoc's suit and pale blue dress shirt before peeling them off him piece by piece.

And wow, Madoc *could not* be thinking such things while he talked to his ex-wife.

Cheeks blazing, he slipped his hand in his pocket and held on to the bee pin Gus'd given him. "How have you been, Noels? Everything going okay?"

"With the not gambling, you mean?" Wariness filtered across Noelene's face as she exchanged a glance with him. "That's what you want to know, isn't it?"

Madoc stomped on an immediate urge to bristle. It felt like forever since he'd had a real conversation with Noelene instead of sniping. But once upon a time, he'd loved the person beside him and she'd loved him back. Noelene had been completely supportive while Madoc'd found his feet in emergency medicine and stepped up for him every time his parents had let him down. She was still doing her part even now to look out for Madoc and Valerie through child support, a responsibility she'd never once complained about.

"I wondered about the gambling at first," he admitted, "but you said you were clean, and I believed you."

Some of the brittle attitude Noelene had wrapped herself in fell away. "Why? We both know I've made your life hell."

"Yes." Madoc frowned. "It's not easy for me to be around you, and I'll never understand why you left Val and me the way you did. I still want you to be all right, Noels. Safe and well and all that."

Remorse flared in Noelene's eyes. "I want that for you too. And for what it's worth, I'm sorry I took off on you like that."

"It was a shitty time for me," Madoc acknowledged, "particularly with Tarek gone too. But I got lucky and had help from my partner, Gus."

"Tarek mentioned Gus has been around."

"Did he now?"

Noelene smiled slightly. "Yes. So, I know about Gus's leg. But I also already knew him from Station 1."

Right.

Madoc fought an urge to squirm. It was ... weird talking about Gus like he was only a work buddy and nothing more. Maybe because Madoc had traded lying about his marriage having imploded for hiding that he was screwing around with a guy he considered one of his best buds.

"Gus still helps me with the kid-sitting sometimes when Clea or Tarek can't," Madoc said. "He's picking Val up from camp today, actually."

"I'll bet she likes that. When I met him that one time, Gus had a black cat that liked to ride on his shoulder—Val took one look at them and boom, I may as well have not even been there."

Isn't that what you wanted?

Madoc swallowed past the instant heat that flooded his face. Noelene was probably just trying to keep things light. But Madoc's and Valerie's lives had started to change that early May afternoon and now so much was different. Thanks in part to Gus who'd put in too many hours being there for his Bug and for Madoc to be dismissed with a joke.

"Gus is good with Val. *To* her and me." Madoc watched amusement fade from Noelene's face. "I don't know if I'd have gotten through the last couple of months without him."

"I'm sorry it came to that."

"So am I. But I'm not looking for apologies, Noels. I just want to know how you've been doing. The note you left when you took off scared me a little."

"It scared me to write it." Noelene fixed her gaze on the sidewalk before them as they walked. "I feel less ... desperate these days, I suppose. But also like nothing in my life fits anymore. I look around and it's like everyone is speaking a language I don't understand, and I'm on the outside of everything."

Unease prickled up Madoc's spine. Gus'd said something similar a few days ago about losing his leg and feeling like his life hadn't fit him. Noelene was describing feelings that sounded a lot like detachment, however, which raised all sorts of red flags.

"So, you're not okay, huh?" Madoc asked, glad when Noelene immediately looked back up at him.

"No. When I was gambling, I could forget that I'd stopped feeling good about things I'd always loved. But it hit me this summer during one of my trips that I treat work the same way now. I use it to feel normal, whatever that means, and I know the behavior isn't healthy.

"So, I'm taking some time off. I found a little house in a resort town in Maine to rent, and I have a therapist who's helping me get a handle on ... whatever this is." Noelene gestured to her own head. "I know it'll sound weird, but I like talking to someone who doesn't already know my whole story."

"I get that." Again, Madoc's thoughts turned to his partner.

"Gus is the guy I spill my guts to," he said. "Turns out he's an excellent listener."

And my best friend.

Gus made Madoc laugh and think and feel heard. Like he was truly himself in so many ways. But more than anything, Gus gave Madoc support *and* space to fall apart and when they were together, Madoc felt like he had someone who was focused solely on *him* and what he wanted for the first time in years. And damn, Madoc was into it. Basking under Gus's attentions in and out of bed when it was just the two of them with no outside distractions. Watching Gus's gaze take on an intensity that made Madoc's heart ache in the sweetest way.

Things were more complicated now that they were back on the truck together, especially with Tarek acting so cold toward everyone but Valerie and pissed off any time Gus was around. Madoc continued finding ways to steal time with Gus away from work when he could anyway, needing to be close to Gus despite the hours they spent together on the truck. He was going to have to figure out what the fuck to do about Tarek's terrible attitude too, because it wasn't fair for Gus to get shit on when Tarek's anger should have been directed at Madoc and Noelene.

Yet here and now, Madoc couldn't admit to any of that.

"You're a good listener, too," Noelene said. "Definitely better at it than my brother."

"Tarek's too furious to listen, I think." Madoc shrugged. "But he's also hurting, and I don't know how to make it better. Not sure he'll ever forgive me for changing your custody."

"He'll have to since I agreed to the change," Noelene replied. "I think T believes he needs to take sides, and by taking mine, he's being a good brother. But that's not what I need or want to happen. And it isn't right for him to be angry at you or anyone else when I'm the one who walked out."

Brow furrowed, she turned to Madoc. "Do you mind if I head back to his place? I think it'd be good for both of us to talk in person for a change and I can pick up some more of my stuff while I'm there."

"Sure," Madoc said. "Gus and Val are making dinner at my place, so I'll walk you up on my way."

Nodding, Noelene ran her teeth over her bottom lip. "Should I ... talk to her?"

"She doesn't want to see you." Madoc kept his voice neutral. "Val knows we had court today and why, and I floated the idea of a visit if it was something she wanted. But Val said she didn't want to see you and I told her that was okay. She needs space, Noels, the same way you need it from us, and I want to respect that."

"Of course." Noelene hummed quietly. "I'm glad she knows what she wants. That she can talk to you and knows you'll listen."

A familiar pain settled over Madoc. People often told him that Valerie was his Mini-Me, what with her curly hair and features that were a near match to his own. But Madoc always saw his ex in his daughter's intelligent brown eyes, so like the ones Noelene turned on him now.

"I'm better with listening some days than others," he said to her. "But I'll always try."

GUS AND VALERIE were just leaving the Frog Pond wading pool on Boston Common when Gus's phone chimed with the message he'd been waiting for.

Court was good, home around 5.

Gus tucked his phone away. The news wasn't unexpected when Madoc had said all along that Noelene agreed with the removal of her parenting hours. The custody change would bring Madoc peace of mind, however, and maybe do the same for Valerie.

"All right, miss." Gus caught the Bug's eye under the brim of her purple Sox cap. "What do you think about making the lettuce cups you like for dinner tonight?"

Valerie skipped beside him. She'd put the flowered sundress she'd worn that day back on over her bathing suit and the spots that had gotten damp were already almost dry. "There's porks in them, right?"

Gus nodded; pigs, porks, close enough. "You fold them up like tacos, remember? And we can make peanut noodles to go with them."

"Ooh, yum. Can we make popsicles?"

"Great idea! I'm sure we can find stuff in your kitchen to make yummy fruity-toot popsicles."

"Yes!" Valerie grabbed onto Gus's hand. "Is Uncle T gonna eat with us?"

Ugh.

With noodles and a salad, Gus could definitely stretch the food they had to feed four. He was feeling kind of ragged today though, thanks to not sleeping well, and wasn't sure he had patience to deal with Tarek's shittastic attitude.

"I'm not sure what Tarek's doing tonight, hon," he said with a smile, "but there will be plenty for everyone if he decides to drop by."

Back at the apartment, Valerie changed into shorts and a pajama top, and once Gus'd gotten her hair into order, they worked together to prep their meal and tuck it all away in the refrigerator. They were in the midst of a drawing project when the front door opened and closed, but it was Tarek who strode in rather than Madoc, and Gus quickly schooled his expression.

"Valley Girl, hey!" Tarek called out with a grin that had Valerie setting her pencil down.

"Hi, Uncle T!"

She raced over, throwing herself at Tarek the way she often did her dad, and giggling when he engulfed her in his patented bear hug.

"Do you wanna eat dinner with us?" she asked her uncle. "Me and Gus are making lettuce cups with porks and noodles *and* there's fruity-toot popsicles."

Tarek looked impressed. "That all sounds yummy and yes, I'd love to have dinner with you and your dad. *After* I show you something upstairs."

"Like a surprise?"

"Yes, a surprise, and I think you're going to like it a lot!"

Tarek bussed her cheek loudly and scored some more giggles, but Gus thought something felt off. Madoc hadn't mentioned a kid-sitting hand-off to Gus for this evening, and nothing about a 'surprise' showing up out of the blue.

After Tarek had set Valerie down and she sprinted off to grab her shoes, Gus stood and walked out from around the table. "Hey, Tarek? Madoc didn't tell me you'd be picking up Val."

For the first time since he'd walked in the door, Tarek looked at Gus. And ugh, he looked annoyed and annoyingly good at the same time, all stern Viking with the beard and artfully tousled hair that somehow worked with the stupid expensive workout gear he liked to sport.

"I don't know what to tell you," Tarek said. "But I don't need your permission to spend time with my niece."

That hit Gus oddly. Because he had his marching orders from the guy whose opinion about Valerie mattered most. And then Tarek looked Gus up and down, gaze lingering several seconds too long on his prosthesis, and Gus went from feeling tired, rumpled, and sweaty to pissed the fuck off in two seconds flat.

"Val's staying here," he said to Tarek. "At least until Madoc gets home or I hear otherwise."

Tarek rolled his eyes hard. "Bruh, are you hearing yourself? You have no say here. If I want to take *my* niece upstairs to see *her* parents, I will."

Parents? But that had to mean ...

Gus frowned. "Madoc didn't say anything about Noelene coming back here."

"Why would he?" Tarek scoffed. "It's none of your business what my sister does, including a move back to Boston."

"She's not coming back," Valerie said from behind Gus.

She was by the door of her room when Gus looked over, a purple high-top sneaker in each hand. Valerie's focus was on Gus though, and her expression stonier than he'd ever seen it.

"Daddy talked to the judge today," she said. "An' he told her Noelene doesn't want to live here anymore."

"I know he did, Bug—" Gus started, only for Tarek to cut him off.

"That isn't true," Tarek said, sounding terse. "Your mom *does* want to live here, and you shouldn't be calling her by her first name, because that's very rude."

"I don't care." Eyes narrowing, Valerie's chin came up in a defiant tilt Gus recognized. "Daddy said I don't have to see her if I don't want to, because he is the parent who makes the decisions and keeps me safe."

Tarek's frowned deepened. "Valerie—"

"No!" Valerie's voice got louder with every word. "I don't want to see Noelene and you're not gonna make me! She's not coming back!"

Whoa.

Brushing past a stunned-looking Tarek, Gus walked up to

Valerie, only for her to back up several steps and put herself out of his reach, a move that had Gus's jaw dropping.

She didn't think he'd force her to leave the apartment ... did she?

Gus took a knee to get himself on Valerie's level. "Hon, you don't have to go anywhere," he assured her. "We'll just stay here and wait for your daddy to get home."

"Her dad *is* home and upstairs with her mom," Tarek muttered, acid in his tone and damn it, Gus wished the guy would shut the hell up for a minute.

Regardless of where Noelene planned to live going forward, her parenting hours had been removed by the court and she *couldn't* come back like nothing had happened, regardless of what her lump of a brother might want.

"C'mon, Val." Tarek's voice had turned coaxing. "You know it's up to us to make sure your mom's feeling good. You and your dad and me are responsible for her and—"

"No, I'm not," Valerie snapped. "Gus said I'm not ruh-sponsible for other people's feelings!"

"Yeah, well *Gus* is wrong."

The edge in Tarek's voice raised Gus's hackles. The big fucker had come around to Gus's right side and his eyes were blazing when Gus looked up at him.

"In this family, we take care of the people we love, and that includes your mom," Tarek said. "Now put on your shoes so we can go upstairs and see her."

"No!" Valerie stomped one bare foot. "I'm not going!"

"No one's going to make you go anywhere," Gus said, hands up as he tried to make himself heard.

Valerie was beyond reason, however, and kept right on with the yelling. "Yes, you are! You're gonna make me go because you're stupid and so is Uncle T and I hate you, hate you, hate you!!"

Without warning, she hurled her shoes, arms swinging wildly. One shoe flew off to Gus's right, narrowly missing Tarek, while the other skimmed the left side of Gus's head and caught his ear with enough force to sting like a motherfucker, heat and bite radiating immediately under Gus's skin.

Fucking ow.

Gobsmacked, Gus lost his balance and went sprawling forward before catching himself with his hands. Fire exploded in his left ear, though he heard Valerie's gasp perfectly as well as a door behind him slamming shut. And then Madoc was there, crouched beside Gus, his big, shocked eyes asking the same question that was flashing through Gus's own mind.

What the fuck was that?

TWENTY

MADOC COULDN'T RECALL A MORE chaotic scene in his own home. Valerie shouting and furious. Tarek staring, clearly shell-shocked. Gus on the ground.

Alarmed by the racket he'd heard from the hallway outside, Madoc had hurried into his apartment in time to witness Valerie launching her shoes, though the horror on her face as Gus'd fallen forward had scared Madoc even more.

Thankfully, Gus was already righting himself when Madoc reached them, though Madoc took hold of his shoulders anyway and scanned Gus's face for injuries.

"What can I do?" he asked, then winced at the angry color staining Gus's left ear. "Are you dizzy?"

Gus shook his head. "I'm okay. I was just surprised, is all."

Madoc got that. He was still trying to wrap his head around the idea his daughter had thrown things as he gave Gus a hand up, aware Tarek was hovering awkwardly nearby.

Schooling his expression, Madoc turned to Valerie. "What were you thinking?" he asked in his most serious voice. "We don't hit in this house, Valerie Mae, and we do not throw things at people."

"I didn't hit. "Valerie scowled, still angry and red-faced, her hands balled up at her sides. "An' I only threw stuff because Gus an' Uncle T said I had to go upstairs to see *her*."

"We'll get to that," Madoc said knowing without asking who the 'her' was. "Right now, I need to talk to Gus and your uncle, and I want you to go to your room while I do it."

"But, Daddy—"

"Please go to your room, Valerie." Madoc leveled a stern look on her. "Leave the door open and I will be there in a few minutes."

She wavered a second, no doubt fighting an urge to argue her case. But then Valerie's gaze flicked past Madoc, probably searching out Gus, and she heaved a full-body sigh before turning to go.

Madoc waited until she'd walked through her door before turning around, only to find Gus headed for Valerie's bathroom and Tarek glaring after him, arms crossed over his chest like every cell in his body had been emptied of patience.

Ironic given the shit show I just walked in on.

Jaw tight, Madoc got to his feet and made a beeline for the kitchen, gesturing for Tarek to follow. "What the fuck is going on?" he asked in a low voice. "Why are you here when I told you Noelene was going to meet you upstairs?"

"I came down to get Val. Who, thanks to your boy, wants nothing to do with her mom." Disgust colored Tarek's tone. "I don't know who that guy thinks he is, Madoc, but he needs to stay in his fucking lane."

Heat crept up the back of Madoc's neck. "Val decided all by herself not to spend time with Noelene," he said. "And even if she hadn't, I never said you could bring her upstairs."

Tarek's eyebrows went up. "Since when do I need permission to spend time with my own niece?"

"Since always. I make the decisions where Val's welfare is concerned."

"And no one else in the family gets a say, including her mother?"

"You and Noelene can weigh in if I ask you to, but otherwise no, and definitely not before Val."

"Val's only six," Tarek shot back. "She doesn't get to weigh in."

"Of course, she does." Madoc shook his head. "Val is a person with her own thoughts, Tarek, and if you think she didn't notice her mother took off and hasn't once reached out with a call or a message, you would be wrong."

Anger twisted Tarek's face. "I'm trying to fix that. God knows you don't give a shit, kicking your wife out and then going to court so it'd stick."

"Noelene is not my wife, Tarek, and she *left*."

"She also came back!"

"To sign off on removing her parenting hours!" Madoc knew he and Tarek were talking too loudly and he tried to shake off the exasperation gnawing at him. "Noelene doesn't want to be a mom," he said in a softer tone. "Maybe can't, at least not right now."

"And again, you don't care. How could you let this happen? I know you're still pissed about the money—"

"This is not about the money."

"—but tearing Noels down the way you do to Val is just wrong!"

A hand fell on Madoc's shoulder. "Guys, you need to chill."

Gus gently tugged Madoc back and away from Tarek, who

was standing so close their chests were brushing. Fucking A, what the hell was this night?

"Talk it out later if you want," Gus urged Madoc, voice hushed despite the intensity in his face. "After Val's gone to bed and—"

"Would you back the fuck off?" Tarek had turned his glare onto Gus. "Better yet, leave before I make you."

"T," Madoc began, reaching for Tarek only to have his hand batted away.

"No," Tarek ground out. "I want you to tell me why this guy is always around, acting like he's part of this family and sticking his nose where it doesn't belong."

He stepped forward into Gus's space, perhaps assuming his height and bulk would intimidate a guy who stood a full four inches shorter and was missing a body part. But Gus didn't blink, instead lifting his chin to meet Tarek's hard stare with his own. Madoc had seen Gus in the boxing ring at the gym; he was a good fighter and tough as nails, and if Tarek got it into this head to do something rash, it was not going to go well for him.

Tarek, unfortunately, was too busy running his mouth to read the room.

"I know he's your partner and you needed help with the kid-sitting while I was away," he said, eyes still fixed on Gus. "But that doesn't explain why he's *still* around now, way more than I am."

"Because I want him to be." Madoc swallowed as his friends turned his way, Tarek clearly surprised while Gus was harder to read. "Gus is my friend, and I owe him a lot."

Christ, the word 'friend' had never sounded so bogus. And Madoc was getting everything wrong too, because Tarek looked wounded and Gus dropped his hand from Madoc's shoulder, expression closing off even more.

Madoc had to force his focus to Tarek. "I was not in a good place after Noelene took off," he said. "I didn't know where to turn or what to do and it felt like I didn't have anyone in my corner. I was genuinely afraid I couldn't manage until Gus stepped up for me. He helped me keep Val's routines intact so I didn't lose my job trying to be in two places at once. And he backed me up every time I needed support or just someone to hear me out. He was there for us, T."

For me, most of all. The late blooming bi-guy with a shit-ton of single dad baggage.

Sighing, Madoc shrugged at Tarek who, if anything, looked even angrier. "Gus kept me sane. And maybe admitting all this makes me sound weak to you, but—"

"It makes you sound blind," Tarek bit out. "That's what you are if you don't see that Val's new fave person is just a fag who wants in your pants."

Madoc nearly cringed at the venom his friend was spitting. It wasn't the first time Tarek had cracked shit about a guy he perceived as weak or lesser or somehow different from himself; he and the dude-bros he hung out with talked like that all the time. Maybe it was all reflex borne from decades spent hiding within organizations that were often hostile to the LGBTQ community, a script Tarek followed to keep his own cover intact. But the slur hit Madoc differently now. Maybe because he could really see how Tarek was hurting himself any time he went after someone like Gus.

Or someone like Madoc.

In the meantime, Gus's eyes had taken on a dangerous gleam. "What is your damage?" he asked in a voice that could have chipped ice. "Are you the kind of homophobe who thinks queers are a danger to kids?"

"I—" Cheeks mottled like he'd been slapped, Tarek's

posture changed, his bluster gone in a flash. "That's not — I don't think like that."

"Bullshit," Gus snapped back. "I've seen the way you look at me."

"I am *not* a homophobe."

"Freaked out by the leg then?"

"I never said that!"

Madoc stepped forward. "Stop it."

There was distress in Tarek's face when he turned to Madoc this time, while Gus's expression remained rather cool. The same question was in both their faces, however, each asking without words if Madoc had their back.

And Madoc didn't know what to say to either of them. He couldn't out Tarek to Gus. Didn't *want* to out himself to Tarek because Madoc still wasn't ready for that.

Are you ever going to be?

Swallowing, Madoc looked directly at Gus. "Take it easy, okay? Tarek didn't mean that the way it came out."

Gus blinked and Madoc braced himself for the backlash he knew he deserved. But the blank, hard look that fell over Gus's features instead was a hundred times worse. Madoc could *feel* him withdrawing, the same way he had the night they'd walked into the pub on Province Street and everything had gone to hell in a handbasket.

"He meant it," Gus said quietly. "Guys like him always do."

"You don't even know me," Tarek began, only to cut himself off when Gus turned that flat stare on him.

Madoc quickly took hold of Tarek's arm. "Go home, T," he said firmly. "Talk to Noels and hear her out, and I'll catch up with you tomorrow."

"But what about Val?" Tarek asked. "We're not done here, Madoc, and she—"

"She is my daughter and you and I are *so* done." Madoc didn't fight his temper this time. "Jesus, Tarek, Val's not some toy the two of you get to fight over."

The instant dismay on his friends' faces had Madoc cursing the big mouth that had gotten away from him once again. But he couldn't deal with Gus and Tarek and their hurt feelings just then when his girl's were more important.

Madoc gathered up Valerie's sneakers from where they'd landed before going to her door, and he found her lying lengthwise across her bed on her stomach, the forlorn puppy eyes she turned on him making it clear she was done being angry.

"Hi, Daddy."

"Hi, Valley Girl." Crossing the room, he set the shoes on the floor, then slipped out of his suit jacket. "I'd like to talk about how you could have hurt Gus or Tarek when you threw your shoes."

Huffing, Valerie righted herself and sat cross-legged. "Okay. But is Noelene coming back?"

"No. Your mom's here to pick up more of her stuff from the loft and talk to your uncle, and I told her you don't want to visit with her."

"Then how come Uncle T and Gus said I had to?"

"Did Gus say you had to go anywhere?"

A beat passed before Valerie answered. "No. He said we should wait for you to get home an' that I didn't have to go anywhere." She frowned. "That made Uncle T mad because he doesn't like Gus."

Madoc loosened his tie and sat beside her. "I'm sorry I wasn't here so you could ask me yourself, like Gus said. I didn't tell anyone to take you upstairs." He held her gaze for several seconds in silence. "Do you understand me?"

Valerie took her bottom lip between her teeth a moment. "I

thought maybe you changed your mind about me and Noelene and a visit."

"I didn't change my mind." Madoc took her hand. "And if I had, I promise I would have talked to you about it first."

"Okay."

She leaned into Madoc's arm then and the tight band around his heart loosened slightly. They talked for a while, and he did his best to piece together what exactly had set Valerie off. She couldn't always find words to express the feelings she held for her mother, but they were complex and ran deep, and came with big insecurities that were scary to her six-year-old mind. When Valerie had decided the adults in the room were ignoring her fears tonight, she'd gone on the defensive and lashed out.

"You're allowed to have all these feelings, honey," Madoc said as she climbed into his lap, "and you can *always* talk to me about them. Telling Gus and your uncle they're stupid and that you hate them wasn't okay though, and you absolutely should not have thrown your things at them."

Red splotches sprang out on Valerie's cheeks and nose. "I know. I didn't mean to throw my shoes," she said, clearly crestfallen. "An' I don't hate anybody. I just got so mad. I felt like my head was gonna blow up."

"I understand." Heartsore, Madoc dropped a kiss on her curls. "I'm fairly sure Gus knows you didn't mean to hit him with your sneaker. But you owe him an apology anyway."

"Is Gus mad or sad because of me?" Valerie asked, her voice very small.

Madoc knew Gus was both of those things at the moment. But that was on Madoc, not Valerie.

"Gus isn't mad at you," Madoc murmured against Valerie's hair. "His ear probably doesn't feel very good though, and we're lucky his face is all right. That's why I'm going to put your sneakers in my closet for the next two days to remind you that they belong on your feet and not in the air."

Madoc rocked his girl back and forth while she cried and didn't let go until she'd calmed.

"It's only two days," he said, helping with the tissues while Valerie blew her nose. "And you can come and visit the shoes in my closet whenever you want. *If* I'm not sleeping or getting dressed."

Valerie's breath shuddered around a hiccup. "All right. Can I go say sorry to Gus?"

Madoc certainly hoped so. The apartment had been largely quiet while he and Valerie had been talking, but there were good cooking smells in the air and Madoc hoped that meant Gus had stuck around after Tarek had retreated upstairs. Relief still swelled in Madoc's chest when he glimpsed a familiar figure in the kitchen and Valerie immediately started wriggling in his arms.

Madoc set her down and she sprinted over to Gus, who got down on his knee to talk. He accepted her apology with his usual grace, then submitted to a careful exam of his still reddened ear, which Valerie kissed gently to 'take away the sting.' The gesture turned Gus's cheeks pink too, and he was smiling as Valerie cupped her hands around her mouth and whispered to him.

"Same for me, Bug," Gus said, taking Valerie's hands in his. "And thank you for making my ear feel so much better."

"You're welcome." Valerie swung their joined hands together before she looked to Madoc. "Are we gonna have dinner now?"

Before Madoc could answer, Gus spoke up. "I'm going to go, hon. You and your dad need some daddy-daughter time, and I want to give it to you."

Valerie's face fell. "But what about the popsicles?" she asked, new tears bringing a frown to Gus's face.

"I can't wait to hear how they turned out." Gently, he drew her into a hug, and Valerie cuddled in with a sob. "Oh, Val. We can make popsicles again some other time."

"Tomorrow?"

"Well, I'm playing basketball tomorrow, but maybe Thursday?" Gus flicked a glance up at Madoc that fell away again almost at once. "I was going to ask you guys if—"

"We're going on a boat that day." Valerie sat back in Gus's hold and rubbed her eyes with her fists. "I bet you could come with us."

"It's a harbor cruise for alumni of Tarek's ex-team," Madoc explained, heart heavy knowing there was no chance Gus would want to be around Tarek any time soon. "Some of the premium seat ticket holders will be there, along with former players and their families. Val's going to meet some of her favorite players, so she's pretty stoked."

Gus made big eyes at Valerie. "Ho-lee cats, that sounds so cool. And I'll be on a boat too, going to the Cape with my ma and pops. We're taking the ferry so no one has to drive, especially me since I'll be a zombie."

He tickled Valerie's ribs to make her giggle but fell quiet again while gathering his things. The silence weighed on Madoc as he walked Gus out and couldn't seem to catch Gus's eye.

"How's your ear?" Madoc asked when they reached the door, his hand on Gus's elbow. "Does it hurt?"

Gently, Gus pulled out of Madoc's grasp. "It's not too bad. But is Val okay? I've never seen her like that before."

Leaning his shoulder against the wall, Madoc sighed. "She's fine. Doesn't lose her temper like that very often but when she does, it's memorable. I probably should have seen it coming after everything she's been through this summer.

"We talked some about why she was so angry, but I think she's still trying to process her feelings and that's all on me. I've tried to be transparent about what Noelene's been up to, but I didn't want to flat-out say to Val that her mom doesn't want to be around us anymore. Maybe it was a mistake being vague."

Gus looked at Madoc then and the anger in his gaze took Madoc off guard. "You didn't do anything wrong. Val was upset because Tarek tried to ambush her. He walked in here saying he had a surprise for her at his place and she had no idea what she'd be walking into."

"Shit." Madoc closed his eyes, breathing in deeply then out before opening them again. "I didn't know that. For the record, Noelene came to get her stuff and talk to her brother, that's it. She knows Val didn't want to see her and never would have signed off on trying to trick her."

"That makes your buddy an even bigger asshole than I originally thought."

Tarek just wants me to take his side. But fuck, so does Gus, and I can't put Val in the middle again.

"I don't like what Tarek did tonight any more than you do," Madoc said, "and I am going to give him a lot of shit about it tomorrow. In the meantime, I think this a sign that we all need to take a step back and give Val some space."

Gus didn't respond straight away, but when he did, his voice sounded strange. "And by we you mean me, right?" he asked. "Like you want me to stay away from your family?"

"I didn't say that. You and I can spend time at your place like we usually do but—"

"But you don't want to see me unless it's to fuck."

A prickly feeling crawled up Madoc's neck. "Don't put words in my mouth."

"I didn't because it's what you meant." A muscle flexed in Gus's jaw. "That *I* should back off and not Tarek, the guy who's been treating both of us like crap."

Madoc was shaking his head even before Gus had finished speaking. "I'm not excusing Tarek's behavior, and I know he's been an ass. But he's my family, Gus, and I promise you he is a good guy."

"He isn't to me." The fight seemed to leave Gus all at once. "Tarek is not a good guy to *me*, Madoc, and I'm not going to be his punching bag, verbal or otherwise."

The sudden vulnerability—the raw hurt—in Gus's face stunned Madoc silent. Off the ice, Tarek was a sweetheart, gentle despite his size and wonderfully loving. Gus didn't know that version of Tarek at all, however, because the guy he got was cutting and rude. He stared at Gus's prosthesis and called him a fag, and he'd gotten up in Gus's *and* Madoc's faces tonight like he'd been itching for a fight.

Gus had his hand on the doorknob when Madoc snapped out of his stupor.

"Tarek's all talk," he said hastily. "I know he didn't mean even half the stuff he said tonight, and was just—"

A short laugh scraped out of Gus. "Being an asshole, I get it. But you know what, Madoc? I don't care about Tarek or whatever crawled up his ass and died. You want me out of your way, that's fine."

"That is *not* what I want." Madoc caught Gus's elbow again when he reached for the door handle, his face getting hot once again. Why was everything going so wrong? "I just think some distance right now would be a good thing for Val and maybe even for you."

"Honestly, I agree," Gus muttered, popping the door open. "But tell Tarek to stop bullying Clea, because she doesn't deserve it."

“Neither do you.”

“Good to know you think so. I’ll see you Friday.”

Everything in Madoc shouted that this wasn’t right and he couldn’t let Gus walk away angry and hurting. He reached for Gus again, but then Valerie called out for her daddy and drew Madoc’s glance. And in the span of a heartbeat, Gus slipped out, leaving Madoc with no choice but to watch him go.

TWENTY-ONE

GUS WENT to the gym and got in the ring with a trainer, sparring hard until he was streaming sweat and his knees shook from exertion. Nice of Tarek-fucking-McKenna to show his true colors at last. But it hurt that Madoc had too, by doing exactly nothing.

Gus didn't need defending—he put up with asshats all the time who wanted to ensure he knew his 'place' in their straight, able-bodied world. He'd still hoped Madoc would have his back with Tarek tonight. But that hadn't happened, and Gus was going to be mad and sad about it for a long fucking time.

"Val's not a toy the two of you get to fight over."

A heady mix of resentment and contrition washed through Gus as he stepped into the canteen at Station 1 after his workout. Images of Valerie's tearstained face battled with the look of disgust Madoc had thrown at him before storming off, and all Gus wanted now was to chill with his cat while he guzzled the mammoth peanut butter frappe he'd picked up on his walk over, because fuck it.

Unfortunately, Shift Commander Rivas was standing by

the coffee machine when Gus walked in and raised a questioning eyebrow at him.

"Something I can help you with, Dawson?" she asked.

"Oh, hi, Commander." Gus gestured to Lemonade who was already up on a chair and prepping to get airborne. "Came in to pick up the kitty."

Rivas chuckled as the cat leaped onto Gus. "You really ought to keep her at home, you know," she mused. "We'd all miss her of course, but it's obvious Lemonade is happiest in your presence."

Gus smiled at the gentle chiding but then Rivas's expression changed, and he got the feeling he wouldn't be going anywhere for a bit.

"Do you have time to talk?" Rivas jerked a thumb over her shoulder toward the doors that led to the offices. "I was going to message you about coming in before shift change on Friday but since you've so helpfully made yourself available on your night off …"

Gus reached up and stroked a hand down Lemonade's back. "Of course, ma'am."

He followed Rivas into the commander's office, setting his gym bag and Lemonade on the floor beside the guest chair before seating himself. The cat seated herself on Gus's foot, but when Shift Commander Marcel also walked in and closed the door behind him, Gus sat a bit straighter in his chair.

"We'd like your opinion on Recruit Walters." Rivas seated herself in the second guest chair while Marcel took a seat behind the desk. "Specifically, your impressions of how he's performed on A1, though anything else you'd like to add is welcome."

Gus glanced between the commanders. His assessment was always going to be part of Madoc's final evaluation, as would Billy Lord's, Madoc's supervisor back at Station 5, and probably Heather's too, given she'd partnered with Madoc for several weeks. But while Gus'd never delivered an eval verbally before, he didn't have to think hard about his response.

"Walters is an excellent EMT," he said. "He's smart and knows his medicine, and he's shown great instincts with the patients. I've also found him to be a creative problem solver who will work with me instead of going rogue."

Rivas looked interested. "How is he at taking direction?"

"He's professional and doesn't get in his head about it," Gus replied. "We all know Walters worked on crews in Seattle before moving here and his experience shows in how he approaches the job. While I'm always conscious of what he's doing on a call, I can give him space to manage himself because he's good at thinking on his feet *and* I know he can handle the autonomy. That said, he respects the chain of command and understands how to function as part of a team. We've only worked together a few months, but it feels like much longer."

"You trust him," Marcel suggested.

On the job, Gus trusted Madoc completely. Away from it, maybe not so much anymore.

"I do, sir," Gus said. "Walters has been a great partner."

One of the best I've ever had.

Folding his hands around his frappe cup, Gus again looked between his commanding officers. "May I know why you're asking me about Recruit Walters?"

"You may," Rivas replied. "But first, Commander Marcel and I wanted you to know that Bobby Stark submitted his retirement papers after his shift yesterday."

And there it was—the news Gus'd been dying to hear for so many months he'd lost count. Weirdly, Gus didn't know *what* to feel now.

"Good for Bobby," he said. "I hadn't heard it was official."

Commander Marcel nodded. "He'll start telling people

tomorrow and we'll begin the job of filling his spot on P1. And another at Station 3, as well as two at Station 16," he said with a rueful smile. "Change is in the air it seems, and just in time for a round of promotions. One of which will be yours, Paramedic Dawson, and please accept our congratulations."

Gus grinned for real this time and they all stood, Rivas and Marcel offering congratulations and handshakes while Lemonade complained about losing her seat and Gus tried to wrap his head around his emotions. He felt amazing knowing the hours he'd labored and studied and been an absolute baller on the job were paying off in a big way. But there was a hollowness in him too, turning Gus's happiness cool in his gut. Because regardless of who filled Bobby Stark's spot on P1 in the coming days, Gus's partnership with Madoc Walters on an EMS truck was at an end.

Marcel gestured for Gus to resume sitting. "Now, you've probably guessed that the promotion committee is weighing the idea of fast-tracking Recruit Walters, despite his short tenure with us."

More feelings buffeted Gus on all sides. Sincere happiness and so much pride for a guy who deserved not to languish on a BLS truck when he wanted and was capable of so much more. As well as a sinking apprehension that the space on Ambulance P1 might no longer be Gus's to take.

Madoc counted on working the night shift at Station 1 because location and timing meant everything to maintaining the tenuous balance between his work and life.

But Gus would not pass up a chance to ride on P1. Not even for Madoc.

Would you do it for Val? For the family you know you love?

And what the fuck was this madness? Gus didn't have room in his heart for people who could slip out of his life without warning. Who'd made it clear he wasn't a part of the family and instead was just a kid-sitter and fuck buddy, welcome in Madoc's home but still held apart.

The problem was that Gus loved Madoc and Valerie anyway, so much it hurt to breathe just thinking about it.

He loved that Valerie was zany and warmhearted and so fucking smart. That she showed Gus her kindness and imagination and that her heart mirrored her father's, one of the strongest, most real people Gus'd ever met. A man who'd made Gus feel like he was ready to put the shitstorm he'd been through with Ben behind him. Who'd set fire to Gus's body while giving him a glimpse of an ordinary, perfectly wonderful life Gus wanted with everything in him.

Partner. Daughter. Family. Love.

"You're my favorite person after Daddy n' Uncle T and I want to keep you."

That was what Valerie had whispered to Gus tonight as she'd fussed over his ear. Words that had lifted his heart and broken it into a hundred pieces. Gus couldn't imagine not having Valerie and Madoc in his life. But the truth was that he'd never truly had them.

"Walters deserves to be fast-tracked," Gus said to Marcel and Rivas. "The department is lucky to have him."

Marcel picked a folder off the top of a small stack on the desk. "The board agrees with you, provided Walters is open to the idea of a transfer or switching from night shift to days should that need to happen."

"Need to, sir?"

"Transfers and schedule changes are still in flux," Marcel replied, "including your own. Now, Commander Rivas and I have no doubt you'd do good work on P1. But we'd also like to offer up an alternate scenario for your consideration."

Gus cocked his head. "What kind of alternate scenario?"

"The kind we believe will make the best use of your skills

in both paramedicine and leadership." Rivas gestured to Gus. "You're good with the recruits, Dawson. You assess and change as needed without getting hung up on rank, and you act as a mentor to your partners while teaching them, a skill that doesn't come naturally to everyone who does this job."

"Thank you, Commander." Gus ignored his fiery ears. "I appreciate that."

"We appreciate you," Rivas said. "And we also believe you'd be an excellent fit in Rapid Response."

The excitement Gus'd been chasing since he'd walked into the office raised its head and his heart beat a touch faster. "You're talking about the Squad program," he said carefully.

"Yes, we are, Dawson," Marcel replied. "Would you like to hear more?"

Gus did. He knew all about the department's efforts to beef up its fleet with Squad cars, a type of tricked-out SUV that was dispatched to scenes ahead of an ambulance. Smaller and faster, the Squads moved more easily through traffic, allowing the paramedic on board to provide immediate treatment for patients or, if transport wasn't needed, connect them with the right services. The Squad car operators also supervised paramedics and EMTs in the field and carried the rank of lieutenant.

"So, if I'm hearing you right, you've got your pick of dream jobs," Felipe said as he and Gus wheeled into a Lexington gym to play basketball the next afternoon. "One you already wanted, the other as good if not better since it also includes a pay increase *and* a promotion."

"Basically," Gus said. "The job on P1 is mine if I want it, but there's also a Squad for me in Rapid Response."

"You are so fancy, *manito*!" Scooping a ball off the nearest rack, Felipe rolled it up and down the thigh of his own shorter limb, which ended about an inch above where his left knee had once been. "But help me out here, dude. Even though I appreciate you wanting to talk out the details, you've got to know what I think you should do."

"That I should take the Squad car with the extra pay and promotion?" Gus laughed at the 'duh' face he got from his friend. "Ian said the same thing."

"Is there a reason you're hesitating?"

"I don't think I am, really. More trying to be sure I'm making a good choice instead of just reacting to a shiny new thing." *Deciding for* me *and not someone else.* "Both jobs are great, and they'll kick my ass every day. Riding on a Squad car, though ... That'd be a step way outside of my comfort zone."

Bringing the ball to his chest, Felipe passed it to Gus. "That's the best argument I can imagine for you to take the Squad car. I think a challenge would be good for you, Gus. Unless you're going to feel weird ordering your buddies around."

"Eh, that doesn't bother me." Gus dribbled the ball and smirked without shame. "Everybody already knows I'm bossy, Felly, because that's my default."

"It's part of your charm," Felipe said. "Also, the reason we made you co-captain, so you can run your mouth at the refs and make up for how fucking slow you are taking the ball up the court."

With a wink, Felipe started wheeling past Gus. But then quick as anything, he snapped a hand out and stole the ball, cackling as he raced off with it and Gus chased after through his own laughter.

Basketball only distracted Gus for so long, however, the weight of his decision bound up with complicated feelings he couldn't discuss with anyone. Knowing that whatever choice he made would kickstart a shit-ton of changes for himself and a certain single dad who had no idea what was coming.

"Whassup, kid?"

Gus smiled at his pops. Every year for his birthday, the Dawsons traveled to Provincetown for the day to bike and go sightseeing, and to gorge without shame on a lot of great food. Today, they'd split up after lunch so Gus and Steven could hike the Causeway, a rock wall that spanned a mile-long section of Provincetown Harbor, while the others rode a ferry to the very tip of Cape Cod. There Gus would chill on a secluded beach with his parents, Donna, and Donna's boyfriend, Roan, toasting each other with cans of cold beer and peanut butter cookies his ma had made before they began the return journey to Boston.

The day had been fabulous, filled with laughter and affection, and now a stunning ocean landscape lay at Gus's feet. And *still* his thoughts kept straying back to the city, his partner, and the curly-haired Bug.

"Nothing much," Gus said to his pops. "Just have a lot on my mind."

Steven hummed agreeably. "Is it the work stuff? Or the guy stuff?"

"Guy stuff?" Gus leaned forward onto the handles of his crutches. "I haven't been—"

"Seeing your partner from the truck outside of work?" Steven suggested. "Because it kind of seemed that way to your ma and me that time we met Madoc at your place."

Oh, good.

Gus stifled a groan. He couldn't lie to his pops, not even for Madoc.

"We've been hooking up," he admitted. "It's all super casual and nobody knows."

"I don't think that's entirely true," Steven said in his dry way. "If things were truly casual between you and Madoc, you wouldn't be all Sulky McGee today because he and his daughter didn't show up to celebrate you."

"I am not Sulky McGee," Gus countered, aware he sounded like a big fucking sulker. "I didn't invite Madoc and Val because they already had a thing. Besides, it's probably best they couldn't come. People don't know Madoc is queer, not even Val, and he'd have been playing it straight the whole day."

Steven frowned. "That can't be easy for you."

"It's not."

"Because you have feelings for him." Steven shrugged when Gus eyed him. "I saw the way you were with him, Gus, and with Val too. And all I can say is that you need to be careful with her."

The edge of warning in his voice had Gus bristling. "We are being careful. Madoc always puts Valerie first."

"I don't doubt that he does—from what you've said, he seems like a wonderful parent. But Madoc and his daughter may not be on the same page about everything being casual." Steven smiled kindly. "Valerie may be just a little thing but she can't help who she loves any more than you can."

Gus's chest squeezed and he bit the inside of his cheek. "I know," he said, but something in his voice or expression must have given him away, because the humor went out of Steven's face.

"Oh, hon. I'm sorry."

"It's fine." Gus patted his pops on the arm. "I kinda ... fell into the deep end with a whole bunch of feelings. Might have dragged Val in after me."

"I know you don't really believe that."

"No. But Val doesn't understand I was never meant to be more than a kid-sitter."

"Or she doesn't care." Sighing, Steven put an arm around Gus. "Love isn't a thing you can make a person feel, son. If that's what Val feels for you, she got there on her own. *That's* why you have to be careful, particularly with her being so young."

The pressure in Gus's chest tightened terribly. "I don't want her to be hurt. But I also can't keep doing this casual thing with Madoc when I know I need more and if I walk away, I'll be walking away from her too, and letting her down."

"No one says you need to go poof all at once," Steven reasoned. "You and Madoc are friends, aren't you? So, figure out a way to make your withdrawal easier."

Gus stared out at the water again. "What if I don't have to withdraw?" he asked. "I do want a friendship with Madoc. Maybe we can work out a schedule where I still see them on the regular but make sure Val understands who I am to both her and her dad."

His pops stayed quiet awhile, and because Gus hadn't truly expected an answer, he didn't think that so odd. Until Steven ran a hand over the back of Gus's hair.

"In a perfect world, what you describe would be enough for everyone. But we both know the real world is complicated." The crease in Steven's forehead was deeper when Gus looked his way. "My focus will always be your happiness, especially after what you've been through the last couple of years. I worry that you won't be able to stop yourself from giving everything that big heart of yours has to offer, even knowing you won't get the same back. And you deserve more."

The gentle words had Gus's eyes watering. He did want more for himself. And he wanted more for Madoc and Valerie too. They all deserved to have people in their lives who'd be there for them and ensure they knew they were loved.

Gus wanted to be someone like that for the Walters family. He just didn't know if Madoc would let him.

TWENTY-TWO

FRIDAY, *August 11, 3:53 P.M.*

MADOC'S INSIDES buzzed as he walked into Station 1 and damn if his nerves weren't less about his final eval than they were about seeing Gus for the first time in days.

You asked for space.

Yes, Madoc had. He'd been so certain some chill out time would do everyone good after Tuesday night's drama. He just hadn't considered what it would be like for Gus to go dark. How Valerie would perceive her friend's abrupt absence or how unsettled Madoc would feel himself when the messages in their shared thread remained largely unanswered. Signs that Gus might be very pissed off over the way Madoc had handled things but was choosing to hide it.

Thankfully, Madoc had a whole shift ahead of him to fix things with his partner and would start right after his eval. He paused when he saw the crowd in the canteen though, firefighters from next door mixed in among office staff and a healthy number from the EMS crews.

"Walters!" Lucky Guzman from Station 4 waved Madoc over to where he stood with Amaya Monroe and a trio of firefighters. "Come eat some of this!"

Madoc spotted a massive sheet cake on the table then, and a banner hung on the wall congratulating Bobby Stark on his retirement.

Whoa.

"When did that happen?" Madoc asked when he'd gotten close.

"Tuesday, after shift." Guzman grinned. "I ran into Bobby on my way in today and the dude actually hugged me."

"He did the same to me," said Monroe with a laugh. "Would have hugged Gus too, if Gus hadn't had both arms full of cake."

One of the firefighters handed his plate to Guzman. "Where is the birthday boy, anyway?"

"In the office with Liv and Connor and the commanders," Guzman replied. He glanced Madoc's way, then gestured to the cake with the pastry server. "You want a piece? Gus's mom baked it and the frosting is psychotically good."

Madoc blinked, struggling to parse the onslaught of information, then shot Guzman a quick grin. "No, thanks. I have a meeting with the commanders too, and I don't want to go in there with chocolate all over my face."

He made his excuses and headed for the office, his brain still racing. Was today Gus's birthday? And why were Guzman and Monroe here instead of at Station 4? Did Bobby Stark have an actual retirement date on the books? Because if his spot on P1 was about to be open, that meant Gus would be—

"Walters, thank you for coming in early."

Madoc nodded to Commander Rivas, who was seated

behind the desk in the office with a small crowd of white-shirted crew around her, including Commander Marcel, Connor, Olivia, and Gus. Who was clad like the others in a uniform shirt that was white instead of his usual tropical beige. Was dressed like an officer, actually, complete with a badge and EMS pins on his collar that were gold and not silver.

What the hell?

Madoc blinked once at his partner before looking back to Rivas. "Of course, ma'am," he said. "Would you like me to come back in a minute?"

"That won't be necessary," Rivas replied, waving him in. "We were just wrapping up."

The others began to file out as Madoc crossed the threshold, and he exchanged quick smiles with Olivia and Connor before locking eyes with Gus. There was no time to speak in the two seconds it took for Gus to walk past, but he aimed a small smile at Madoc before stepping out into the hall, and there was a fondness in his gaze that hit Madoc square in the chest.

What the fuck is going on?

Madoc was still asking himself the same question ten minutes later, though his reasons were *very* different and far more exciting. Not surprising when he'd walked into this office expecting to graduate from Academy recruit to active duty and was about to step out with a promotion to paramedic and a spanking new assignment on Ambulance P1.

"I realize this is all unexpected," Rivas said once the handshakes and congratulations were over. "If you'd prefer to sleep on it and consider it further, please know you can."

"I don't need time to consider, ma'am," Madoc replied, trying hard not to flail. "I'm happy to accept the promotion and the spot on P1. Thrilled, if I'm honest."

Commander Marcel nodded, looking pleased. "Good. You

still have some hours left to complete for your field internship, so you'll shadow Bobby Stark aboard P1 for the next several weeks, and you can go ahead and make the switch to the medic shirts and patches in the meantime."

The station's alarm sounded, the dispatcher's voice quickly following.

"Boston P1, pregnant female with complications in labor at 3143 Melrose Street. 24-D-5, patient is thirty-two years of age, history of high blood pressure. Contractions ten minutes apart, delivery not imminent at this time. Although traffic's gonna be murder in and out of Back Bay," he added, "so you might want to step on it."

Marcel grinned at Madoc. "That's your cue, Walters," he said. "And I'd run if you want to make it onto your new truck."

Madoc hauled ass into the garage just as Stark climbed aboard P1 through the rear door.

"Let's go, Walt!" Stark yelled with a grin. "You're up to drive after Connor!"

"My name is not Walt!" Madoc called back out of reflex, but he was laughing as he got himself settled in the passenger seat.

He felt ... incredible. Almost high he was so pumped full of good feelings. He was graduating. Had gotten the promotion he'd wanted and would start making more pay. Madoc had the spot on P1 too, and shit, even his shifts were the same because he'd still be working the same nights. All of which had to make him one of the luckiest guys in the city and holy cats, he couldn't *wait* to tell Gus.

Who couldn't be Madoc's partner if Connor was still riding P1. The truck Gus'd always insisted would someday be his.

But if Gus wasn't aboard the Advanced Life Support truck at Station 1, where the fuck was he?

Heart stuttering weirdly, Madoc shot a look to Ambulance A1. Guzman was at the driver's side, the Toughbook in hand while Monroe spoke into her phone, their presence at Station 1 suddenly clear.

Madoc looked over to Connor who was pulling out past the garage's open doors. "Are they taking over A1?"

"Yup." Connor grinned at him before turning his eyes onto the street ahead. "And hey, congrats on your promotion, man! You must be so stoked."

"I am!" Madoc's own laugh surprised him. "Kinda shook, like the kids say, because how is this real?"

Chuckling, Connor guided the truck right. "I get it. The first week after promotions is always bananas with people shifting around to new posts. I think Station 1 got the most this cycle, what with Stark leaving, you moving over to P1, and Guzman and Monroe transferring in now that Liv and Gus have moved on."

"Don't talk like I'm not sitting right here, you bum," Stark called from the cabin. "Same place I'll be for the next month and a half until I can retire for real and chill full-time on the beach with a *cerveza*."

Madoc chewed the inside of his cheek, his head spinning with questions. Gus had moved on? But to where? And to do what?

How long had changes this big been in the pipeline?

And why the fuck hadn't Gus told Madoc about any of it?

Chatting with Connor and Stark over the course of the shift brought Madoc some answers. Namely, that Gus had indeed been promoted to paramedic *and* to lieutenant. That he'd transferred into the Rapid Response Unit where, along with Olivia, he'd help add Squad cars to the city's EMS fleet.

Madoc was so damned proud of his friend. But a hollow

feeling settled over him as he changed into his street clothes after shift. People came and went all the time on the crews of course, new recruits joining up and veterans retiring while promotions and transfers kept it all interesting. Seeing Amaya Monroe's name on Gus's locker still stung, as did knowing the empty corner that had once held Princess Lemonade's box-slash-bed would remain so.

That was the moment things got real for Madoc. When he knew Super Gus Dawson really wasn't coming back to Station 1, because he'd taken his kitty with him.

YOU UP?

Blearily, Gus eyed the message on his phone's screen. 'Up' felt like a relative term considering he'd lost count of the hours he'd been awake. But he didn't want to put this talk off when Madoc deserved better than to be low-key ghosted because Gus'd grown a whole bunch of complicated feelings.

Lemonade plopped her bum and her banana down on the couch cushion among the piles of laundry Gus had been folding, her orange eyes oddly intense.

"Dial back your judging," Gus muttered, "and quit being creepy."

He shot a message off to Madoc, then zipped around in his chair, putting laundry away and tidying up. He was setting out fresh water for the cat when the buzzer sounded and then Madoc was there at his door, bearing a tray of coffees and a paper bag of food, looking so fucking gorgeous it was torture not dragging him down for a kiss.

But no, that would make everything that had to follow even more difficult, so Gus invited his friend in, and they headed to the kitchen while he tried to figure out where to begin. Madoc beat Gus to it, however, speaking before Gus'd even gotten the tray of coffees from his lap to the counter.

"Con told me you were switching to days," Madoc said. "When does that start?"

Gus handed Madoc his mug. "Tomorrow. Liv and I have some training to get through with the Squad cars, and our official start is on Monday."

Warmth filled Madoc's expression. "I'm so proud of you, Gus. And my mind is blown too. Like, who gets a double promotion?"

"Well, there's you," Gus said with a playful roll of his eyes. "The board fast-tracked your promotion before you even graduated, Madoc, and that almost never happens. So, congratulations to you."

"Thanks." Madoc's cheeks flushed pink. "Still not sure I believe it's all real."

Gus got stuck for a second staring and had to turn himself toward the cabinets to snap himself out of it. Using the counter, he levered himself up so he could get a plate for their food. "What does Val think about her daddy's promotion?"

"I haven't told her yet, but I will today when I pick her up from camp." There was a slight pause before Madoc added, "About yours too, if you're cool with it?"

"Sure." Gus arranged the granola snacks and muffins Madoc had brought with him on the plate. "I know I'll need to explain why I won't be around, now that my job and schedule are changing."

"About that," Madoc said, his voice sober like his expression when Gus looked his way. "Why didn't you tell me? About the promotion and wanting to leave Station 1? Obviously, the Squad car gig sounds fantastic, but I really thought you wanted to ride on P1."

"I did. Never even considered transferring out until

Tuesday night. I went from your place to pick up Lemonade," Gus said as he got himself back into his chair. "Rivas and Marcel called me in, told me about the promotion, then said I had a choice if I wanted it—Stark's spot on P1 or a Squad car."

"And you decided to switch, just like that?"

"I think you know better. I told them I needed a few days to mull everything over, and then I did exactly that. But I had orders not to talk about it with the crews, so I went over it with my fam and some friends, again and again until I felt good."

"You could have gone over it with me." Pain flashed over Madoc's face. "Orders or not, I thought ... Listen, I know shit got weird Tuesday night—"

"You told me to back off."

"I asked you to give Val space for a couple of *days*, not disappear off the map. God, Gus, I was starting to worry."

Remorse pricked at Gus. "I didn't mean for you to do that. The truth is that you were the first person I wanted to tell about the promotion and the new job."

"So why didn't you? I'm your friend, aren't I? You should feel like you can tell me anything."

"I don't, though." Gus shifted his gaze to his lap. "Not after the other night."

"Because of what happened with Tarek? I know he made you feel shitty—"

"So did you." Gus looked at Madoc again. "I understand Tarek is your family, but I wouldn't let anyone speak to you the way he did to me. I'd step up for you and your girl every time you needed me to just like I did Tuesday night. That's what I was doing, Madoc—looking out for Val because she needed someone in her corner when Tarek was acting the fool." Heat flashed over Gus's face. "I do *not* use your daughter to score points with anyone and I'm honestly irate that you'd ever think that of me."

"I don't." Madoc grimaced. "I've never thought that of you, I swear, and I'd take it back if I could. I'm sorry, Gus."

Gus bit his lip. It helped, hearing that. But it also didn't change anything.

"Will you let me make it up to you?" Madoc asked. "We could do a birthday thing with Val, because you know she'll want to be part of it."

"My birthday was yesterday. That's why I went out to the Cape with my fam," Gus said. "I was going to ask you and Val to join us, but you had the NHL cruise."

He'd braced himself for the shock that flashed over Madoc's face, but it was still bruising to see it. To know that Gus simply wanting to bring the Walters along on a family outing freaked Madoc out.

"Uh. Well." Madoc cleared his throat. "Val and I can still celebrate with you over the weekend. And Clea will have Val during the day, so I can come over and see you in private."

The hope in Madoc's eyes pricked at Gus's heart. "I don't think that's a good idea, Mad," he said softly. "Not anymore."

Madoc looked troubled as he took a step closer. "What do you mean?"

Gus opened his mouth and shut it again, his resolve wavering. He could make something up and hold tight to what he already had. Keep loving this man and hope Madoc learned to feel something more than friendship back. Continue gambling with his own happiness. Then Gus's eye landed on the heart-shaped suncatcher Valerie had made that was still taped to the window and he remembered he wasn't the only one who stood to lose big when things inevitably went to shit between Madoc and him.

Reaching out, Gus ran his fingers across Madoc's knuckles, chest twisting when Madoc immediately turned his wrist and caught Gus's hand in his own.

"What are we doing here?" Gus twined their fingers together. "You and me, this thing we have going?"

Madoc stayed silent for several seconds. But then he got down on the floor beside Gus's chair, still hanging on to Gus's hand.

"I don't know," he said, sounding earnest. "I've never known what to call what we have or even if we needed to call it anything. I just know I like being with you."

Gus breathed through the ache building inside him. He didn't put much stock in labels himself. And he had no doubt Madoc cared about him. But while Gus'd been falling in love this summer, Madoc had not, and Gus knew he couldn't be truly happy if the most Madoc wanted with him was screwing around in secret.

"I like being with you, too," Gus said. "But I don't want to be a guy you spend time with until someone else comes along."

"That's not ..." Madoc frowned. "I haven't been looking to meet anyone. You know I'm not ready for dating."

"I do." Gus's attempt at a smile fell flat. "Hooking up with me was just for fun and good times. But I want more than hookups. I want something real."

"Meaning what, exactly?"

"A life with someone. Partner and kids. Family. I'd want that with *you* if I thought you'd have me."

Madoc blanched. "Fuck. I'm not ... I can't be someone's boyfriend. I'm not ready for that with anyone, male or female, and neither is Val. Christ, she and I are still working on understanding how I do my single dad thing now that Noelene's fully out of the picture."

"I understand. But I can't help what I want."

Raising his free hand to his chest, Gus rubbed his knuckles over his sternum. Funny how he ached there, despite his ribs having healed.

"You know Ian and I didn't want kids at first and that something changed after my accident. I was the one who changed. Who decided they wanted more than just career and partner and friends. Ian tried to get his head around it, he really did. But he couldn't and it pushed us further apart until we broke."

"Shit."

"Exactly." Gus huffed a laugh that caught in his throat. "I thought things would be different with Ben. But now I know he was good at telling me what I wanted to hear, and I was good at letting him do it. I don't know what Ben really wants, but he doesn't give a shit about starting a family. If he did, he wouldn't have stolen the money I was saving to help us get started doing it."

Madoc's face fell. "Meaning adoption or surrogacy," he murmured, not truly asking, though Gus nodded anyway. "Oh, Gus. I don't know what to say."

"You don't have to say anything. It's my fault I didn't see Ben for what he was. I see you though, and I like you so much. But to you, I'm just someone you fuck."

"That is *not* how I see you."

"Yes, it is." Gus drew an unsteady breath. "We're friends and partners and I'm happy we have that. But I think of you as *so* much more and you don't feel the same way. And I know it because having to lie and sneak around to see each other doesn't bother you the way it does me."

"Hey, I don't like it," Madoc protested. "But I'm not sure what you're asking for here when I already told you I'm not ready for more."

"I'm asking for space. I can't hide the way you do, Madoc, because I suck at it and the longer we do this, the easier it's going to be for people to guess that I've got a thing for you. Tarek guessed and so have my parents."

Madoc's eyes went painfully wide. "Your *parents*? What did they say?"

"Not much. Just that they could tell from the way I was acting that one time they met you and Val."

"Oh, God. What a mess."

Hurt flared in Gus's chest. "Is it really so bad if a few people know? Connor and Liv wouldn't care, especially now that I'm not your supervisor and we're not even in the same unit."

"Hold up." Madoc recoiled, dropping Gus's hand like he'd been burned. "Please tell me you didn't take the job in Rapid Response so we can screw around without you getting in trouble!"

The words hit Gus like a punch.

"No. I took that job for me," he said quietly, his empty hand cold. "But I'm done keeping secrets."

"There isn't a deadline. You've said that over and over." Madoc's voice came out thick. "That I'd know when I was ready to come out and that you had my back!"

"I do have your back. I'm not going to force you to do things you're not ready for and I would never, *ever* out you." Hearing the edge in his own voice, Gus took a beat to calm himself. "This isn't an ultimatum. This is me taking care of myself and making sure Val is all right too."

"Don't you do that," Madoc bit out. "You want to give me shit fine but do *not* drag my kid into this."

The mournful ache in Gus's chest turned cavernous. 'My kid', not 'ours.' Because Valerie wasn't Gus's child and Madoc wasn't his man, no matter what Gus's stubborn heart wanted.

"Love isn't an emotion you can make someone feel."

"I wish I could leave Val out of it," Gus murmured. "But I can't because she's become such a big part of this. I didn't fall only for you—I fell for your girl, just as hard."

The color drained from Madoc's face. "Gus."

"I know how stupid that sounds. All I had to do was show up to kid-sit until you didn't need me anymore, easy peasy, lemon squeezy." Gus studied his hands in his lap. "Except, I liked it. Playing house and feeling like I had a place with you and Val. When you still wanted me around even after Tarek came back, I started thinking that you and I could have something real. But we can't."

Gus had to pause because his stupid tears were making his voice wobble. Lemonade appeared as if by magic, leaping into his lap, and Gus buried his fingers in her fur.

"I can't be the guy you make time for when no one is looking. My feelings are bigger than screwing around and I want to be important to you and Val the way you are to me."

"You are important." Madoc looked even more stricken, no doubt because Gus was fucking crying. "You're one of the best friends I've ever had. And Val—"

"Is getting attached, the same way I am," Gus said, quickly swiping at his eyes. "I get that you're not ready for more, but your kid feels differently."

"I want to keep you."

Valerie wanted Gus in her life as a parent-y kind of person, maybe almost like a dad. And Gus had to bite his lip hard to keep his composure.

"Val wants things from me that she doesn't even know are impossible." Looking up, he blinked past new tears. "And it isn't fair to her or me to let her keep believing she'll get them someday when we both know she won't."

Pain filled Madoc's face, raw and so real. "You're right. I should have seen this coming and stopped it and I'm ... shit. I'm sorry."

"So am I. I know you don't need this emo shit in your life."

"Oh, fuck it, I'll be okay." Madoc ran a hand over his head, mussing his curls, regret written clear on his face. "But Val ... I don't know how I'm going to explain this to her. She *misses* you. And I don't want her thinking this is her fault."

"Neither do I. Maybe I could meet up with her and Clea after work one night every couple of weeks?" Abruptly, Gus recalled the concern he'd glimpsed in his pop's face during their talk on the causeway and he shoved it aside. "For dinner or to watch baking shows, that kind of thing, maybe a playdate with the cat. That way, Val doesn't get any ideas in her head about why I'm not around, but I can give her enough distance that she won't expect me to be more than a friend."

Nodding slowly, Madoc stared at his knees. "I think that would work. Let me talk to Clea and see what nights would be better."

He got to his feet then, every angle of his body broadcasting a 'don't touch me' vibe. But Gus knew Madoc well enough to guess the walls that'd gone up were about self-preservation rather than anger, which made a heartbreaking kind of sense when too many people Madoc had cared about had turned their backs on him.

"Hey, Mad?" Gus stopped his chair beside the front door and waited for Madoc to look at him. "I've still got your back, just like always. If you need anything, I'm here for you."

The color that stained Madoc's cheeks had Gus aching to hug him.

"Thanks for saying that." Madoc slid his hands in his pockets. "I meant it when I said you're one of my best friends. Maybe it's selfish, but I don't want to lose that."

Gus shook his head. "Not selfish," he said, "and you won't lose me as a friend. Just give me some time to get my head together so I know how to be that for you."

"Of course," Madoc said quietly. "Take all the time you need."

They exchanged almost smiles before Madoc opened the door and slipped out. And though it hurt like hell to watch him go, Gus did it anyway, knowing it was the right choice for both of them.

TWENTY-THREE

MONDAY, *August 21, 5:05 P.M.*

"BOSTON A1, A4, water rescue in progress at 66 Long Wharf. Multiple persons reported overboard near the Waterboat Duck House. Code Three, 14-B-1, parties are alert and, apparently, enjoying cooling off in the harbor."

Madoc paused in his work when a quiet 'quack' came over the radio, but didn't glance up from the Toughbook until a familiar voice replied, tone deadpan like someone hadn't just quacked at the dispatcher.

"Squad 84 at Fleet and Commercial," Gus said. "I can duck over, see what's going down."

Bobby Stark let out a groan from his spot by the rear doors. "Too far," he muttered, but snorted along with Connor when a pair of 'quacks' followed.

"81 in the Seaport," Olivia said next. "I can take this if you want to wing it back to HQ, 84."

"Roger that, 81," Gus replied. "84 out, have an egg-cellent shift everyone."

More quacks followed, audible this time in the ambulance bay beyond P1 *and* over the radio because it was Guzman and Monroe making duck noises as they hustled onto their truck. And when Connor and Stark broke up cackling, Madoc had to smile too.

The origins of the game the crews called Clusterduck were unknown, but quacking and puns followed any radio mention of the Waterboat Duck House, a tiny floating waterfowl shelter located in the corner of a large marina on Boston's Long Wharf.

Overhead, the alarm sounded, echoing out of their radios at the same time.

"Ambulance P1, person experiencing difficulty breathing at 2 Aguadilla Street, Unit 6. Fifty-three-year-old M2F, history of cardiac issues. 6-D-2, difficulty speaking between breaths. 911 call placed by a neighbor in the building, Boston Fire is on scene."

Even before the dispatcher had finished speaking, Stark was climbing aboard.

"I know that address," he said. "The patient has a pacemaker, so let's get a move on. Con, let's give Walters the lead and I'll walk you through her history on the way."

Madoc scanned Stark's notes from his last dispatch to 2 Aguadilla Street, appreciative but not surprised by the level of detail he'd captured about Miss Palagia, a male-to-female transgender patient Stark had been providing care to on and off for over five years.

"I saw her a couple of weeks ago," Stark said through the back window, "and it was a similar thing—shortness of breath with some fatigue that was out of the ordinary. We pushed fluids and she improved, but I'll bet you anything it's the battery in her pacemaker, either misfiring or low on power."

"How long has she had the pacemaker?" Connor asked.

"Going on eight years if I remember correctly," Stark replied. "Wouldn't be the first time we've seen a battery fail, though."

Madoc made more notes as he talked the call through with his partners. He really enjoyed working with these guys, who were both smart and talented and had an abiding respect for their patients but were also immense fun to be around. Madoc couldn't have asked for two better partners to guide him though the final hours of his field internship.

Except for Gus, of course. Whom Madoc hadn't spoken to directly in weeks.

He'd done his damnedest to respect Gus's request for distance and, fortunately, their opposite schedules left few chances for their paths to cross during a shift. He'd still glimpsed Gus a couple of times in the field, working alongside ambulance crews at scenes, his expression intent the way it got when Gus put his whole focus into something.

Madoc missed having that attention on him, on and off the job. Missed the banter he and Gus'd shared on the truck. The patter of Gus's and Valerie's voices back at the apartment. Gus cooing over the cat. Cooking and sharing meals and the talks that'd come so easily. Gus beside Madoc in bed and the feeling of ... *home* he'd brought into Madoc's life.

They'd gone back to messaging in their shared chat thread again, and while it wasn't as frequent as in the past, it felt good to swap photos, observations, and the odd dumb joke. Like the pic Madoc found on his phone after transporting Miss Palagia to Boston Medical Center, in which a half-dozen ducks sat around a little gray and white house atop a floating platform.

What time do ducks get up in the morning? Gus'd asked.

Madoc smiled. *The quack of dawn,* he replied. *Aren't you clocking out?*

Yup, Gus replied. *Figured your girl and Clea would get a kick out of these little dudes.* A pause and then, *Heading over there soon if that's still OK?*

A now-familiar ache stole through Madoc. He hated the caution in Gus's words. That he'd become oddly formal in his chats with Madoc, like they were strangers instead of friends. But then Gus'd bared his heart to Madoc the last time they'd met, and Madoc had recoiled like he had been slapped.

"I didn't fall only for you. I fell for your girl, just as hard."

Madoc wanted to be angry at Gus for ambushing him that morning and fucking up their friendship. For talking so earnestly about family and commitment and being there for each other. For talking about love. Gus'd never said the four-letter word aloud, but it'd been there in his eyes and touch. In the tears Gus'd shed as he'd told Madoc he needed to take a step back.

Biting his lip, Madoc turned his attention back to his phone. *Of course. Hug her for me.*

I will, came the reply. *Be safe tonight, Mad.*

Opening the passenger door on P1, Madoc paused when Connor and Stark walked up beside him.

"You good?" Stark asked with a nod to Madoc's phone. "You've been staring at that thing like you want to kill it."

Smiling, Madoc shrugged his partner off. "I'm cool. Gus is having dinner with Val and the kid-sitter tonight and I was just checking in."

"Nice." Connor's face brightened. "That'll be good for him."

Madoc could feel the smile slide off his face. Was Gus not all right? He hadn't said anything to Madoc, but maybe he wouldn't, given he'd stopped talking about himself to Madoc almost entirely.

He waited for Stark to head off to the hospital cafe with

their cups before turning to Connor. "Hey, Con? What did you mean when you said seeing Val would be good for Gus? Is he okay?"

A slight furrow formed on Connor's brow. "Honestly, I'm not sure. Gus has been off the last couple of weeks—very quiet and sticking close to home. At first, I figured he was wiped after the move back to days, but then Ian mentioned Gus wasn't himself, and I knew it wasn't only me noticing. A few of us brought him a bunch of takeout one night and got him talking, and it turns out he's been having some guy trouble."

The hackles on the back of Madoc's neck rose. With his guard down, Gus could *so* easily have given Madoc away to his friends, the way he'd inadvertently done with his parents. The funny thing now though, was the anticipation in Madoc's gut that was fast outpacing his dread.

Maybe Connor already knows about me.

"What kind of guy trouble?" he asked, biting his lip when Connor just shrugged.

"I guess he met someone," Connor said, "and they were hooking up on the regular over the summer. Gus didn't say a word to anyone though, which is definitely out of character." He furrowed his brow at Madoc. "Unless he told you?"

"No."

The denial slipped out effortlessly, followed by a hot jolt of shame that shriveled Madoc's insides. He didn't want to lie to his partner and friend, and knowing Gus'd done it for months to protect Madoc's cover made him feel sick.

Connor in the meantime was frowning. "Meh, I was afraid you were going to say that. Well, I guess Gus really liked this guy, but the dude wasn't into him the same way, so they called it quits. Which sucks obviously when it's hard feeling rejected. Gus played it down, but we all knew he was bummed."

"Boston P1, what's your location?" the dispatcher asked

through their radios and Madoc shifted his focus back to the job.

Connor's words lingered at the back of his mind though, surfacing throughout the rest of their shift and making Madoc's chest ache. Reminding him that Gus was hurting and that Madoc was the one who'd caused it.

"Welcome home, Daddy!"

Madoc scooped up his sleepy-eyed girl, mindful of the glow-jar she carried and a brightly colored headpiece he felt sure was new.

"Thank you, Valley Girl. How you doin'? And what is this fantastical thing on your head?"

"It's a crown!" Valerie beamed. "I made it with Gus and Clea, an' isn't it cool?"

Despite her initial reservations about a new kid-sitter, Valerie had bonded with Clea over a shared passion for kid-craft. The two regularly produced flowers and garden creatures fashioned from buttons, felt, and yarn, and Valerie preened now while Madoc admired the crown, which was really a head-band covered in soft mounds of pom-poms and decorated with little felt balls painted to look like ladybugs.

"Gus brought the bugs," Valerie said on their way into the kitchen where Clea was brewing coffee. "And we drew star maps for the fort. Ooh, Gus got me new pencils with kitties on them for back to school! And did you know we made cherry cake and that you and Gus are famous? 'Cause you are!"

Lost, Madoc looked to Clea, who was sporting a crown of her own boasting orange and pink pom-pom with matching felt beetles.

"The story about the Squad car program was on the local news and we recorded it," Clea said with a smile. "They focused on Gus a bit and how he started in EMS."

"And there was a pitcher of you!" Valerie yelped.

"A picture of me? Wow!" Madoc pretended to preen. "And what did Gus think of the video?"

"His ears got all red." Valerie giggled. "And then his ma called and after he hung up with her, he had to put his phone on mute because it kept dinging."

Madoc laughed along with her. The crews had known about the piece the local media had been working on to promote the Squad car program. Special focus on Gus was a new angle, however, and the interest Madoc'd had in checking the story out increased a hundredfold.

Clea and Valerie got the video queued up while Madoc loaded a tray with their cups and breakfast, then carefully slid the whole thing into the fort. He and Valerie were admiring the star maps with their fantastical constellations (*Lady Bug Girl*, *Wicked Clea Sky*, *Gusberry Major*, and *Daddyus Madocus*) when there was a knock at the door and Clea called out that she'd get it.

Madoc handed half a bagel to Valerie. "How many times have you watched this video?" he asked, and she chewed for a few seconds, eyes on the fort's ceiling while she tried to calculate.

"A whole bunch," she said at last. "I had questions and sometimes I missed stuff, and we had to go back and start over. Gus and Clea said they didn't mind."

"Didn't mind what?" Tarek asked out of nowhere, his bearded face suddenly in the fort's entrance but upside down, drawing a muffled shriek from Valerie and a yell out of Madoc that made everyone laugh.

"You're so loud, bro," Tarek chided. "But can I join the breakfast club if I bring something sweet?"

"Sure you can, Uncle T!"

Madoc smiled as his girl waved her uncle into the fort. Tarek had apologized to them both after the Night of the

Flying Sneakers, his grief over hurting Valerie's feelings clearly heartfelt. He'd been back and forth to Maine a few times helping Noelene move her stuff, but he checked in every day and sent Valerie postcards from the beach towns he passed to make sure she knew he hadn't forgotten her.

Reaching in, Tarek set a paper bag in front of Valerie. "I brought some *bolos*," he said, very smug. "Went to the hospital cafe your daddy and Gus buy them from because I wanted bread."

They arranged the muffins among the bagels and a smiling Clea scored two for herself before she headed home. Valerie, in the meantime, alternated between her bagel and a *bolo* topped with black raspberry jam that purpled her mouth and tip of her nose.

"We're watching Gus on TV," she said to her uncle, who'd plunked himself down on his side in the fort with his head propped up in one hand. "Him and Daddy are famous."

"In a PR piece for work," Madoc said. "A local news station interviewed the Rapid Response unit that Gus is part of now and somehow there is a picture of me."

"It's true!" Valerie hit Play on the TV remote and a Squad car appeared on the screen, zipping through the Theater District with its lights flashing.

"Boston EMS has pumped up its fleet of emergency vehicles this summer," the video voiceover said, *"adding eight new units called Squads to the city's Rapid Response Program, all operated by an elite team of paramedics."*

The Squad operators appeared onscreen next, everyone sharp in long-sleeved white uniforms shirts and dark ties as they stood in the garage at HQ. The focus quickly tightened in on Gus, whose face was composed in a 'listening' expression Madoc knew well. The gold pins at Gus's collar and epaulettes gleamed as bright as his badge, and Madoc thought he'd never looked more handsome.

"Among the Squad drivers is Lieutenant Gus Dawson, who came to Boston EMS after a distinguished career as a firefighter," the reporter said. *"As a captain of Boston Fire's Rescue Squad 1, Dawson survived a devastating injury during a partial house collapse in the South End that ended his firefighting career. Lieutenant Dawson found a new path in emergency medicine, however, and made history this year as the first amputee paramedic and lieutenant working for Boston EMS."*

Muffin in hand, Valerie climbed into Madoc's lap and fitted her back against his chest. "See?" she said. "Told ya he was famous."

Black and white photos from Gus's previous life with Boston Fire filled the screen next, achingly young in his full turnout gear and helmet at a scene with Beni at his side, a hydraulic spreader or 'jaws of life' in Gus's hand. Assisting an elderly man away from the scene of a fire. Supine on a stretcher as he was extricated from the house collapse that had changed his life, his fellow firefighters bearing Gus over the rubble. Recovering in a hospital bed, face drawn and unsmiling, his parents and Ian at his sides, Ian's hand around Gus's.

Madoc's skin crawled as he stared at the hospital shot. He'd found photos online of the accident that'd cost Gus his leg, and they never failed to unnerve him. Gus'd lost a crewmate and friend that day and it was only sheer luck that he hadn't died too.

Valerie looked at Tarek. "That's Gus's ma and pops in the pitcher," she said with a nod at the screen. "And Mr. Ian 'cause Gus n' him used to be boyfriends. And look, there you are, Daddy!"

Madoc managed a smile at the new photo that had come on the screen showing Gus and him picking their way out of a multi-vehicle collision, Madoc carrying a car seat with a baby in it while Gus held a little girl in his arms.

"Gus said you helped those kids," Valerie said. "That the baby was scared and crying and you made him feel better."

"I did." Madoc pressed his lips to Valerie's hair. "Gus and the little girl drew ponies, including one I brought home to you."

Madoc and Gus had bonded that night while they'd cared for those kids. Formed a partnership that would deepen as they also became friends.

Raising her hand, Valerie rubbed her knuckles against Madoc's chest, a small, easy touch that meant everything.

"Coming back after losing my leg was one of the most challenging things I've ever had to do," Gus said as the camera cut back to him and the crew. *"I had an incredible support system in the staff at Mass General and my family and partner and friends, and the amputee community here in Boston. It was never a question for me that I still wanted a career in EMS, even if it meant having to pivot from firefighting to emergency medicine."*

"This job will challenge you physically and mentally," Olivia added next, her name and rank appearing across the bottom of the screen. *"And you have to truly want it if you're going to succeed. I'm sure some questioned whether Gus would be fit for duty back when he started—people wonder the same about female EMTs and paramedics like me all the time."* She smiled. *"But our crews are highly trained and focused on working together to get the job done."*

That was the message the Squad car operators wanted people to take away from the story; that every EMT and paramedic in the city did their utmost to serve its people, whether they worked on a fire truck, ambulance, or Squad car.

"Is there anything you miss about driving an ambulance?"

the reporter asked the group and though most of the paramedics claimed that they didn't, joking about how much easier it was to maneuver the Squads through Boston's traffic, Gus and Olivia exchanged smiles.

"I miss having a partner," Olivia said, and Gus quickly nodded.

"We're all grateful for this amazing opportunity in Rapid Response," he added. *"But I've ridden with some of the best in the field and I know I miss that."*

Tilting her head, Valerie beamed up at Madoc. "Gus thinks you're the best," she said, so smug Madoc didn't mind that jam had migrated from her mouth to his jersey.

"I think the same about him," he said. "Gus was one of the best partners I've ever had."

Valerie's smile faded. "Do you miss our Gusberry, Daddy?" she asked, sounding quite serious, and Madoc matched her tone when he answered.

"Yes, I do, honey."

Every day.

"Me, too," Valerie said, before she reached for the remote to start the clip over. "But I was just checking."

She crawled out of the fort, claiming she'd be right back, and Madoc pretended not to watch Gus on the screen as he and Tarek chatted about Tarek's last trip to Maine. Valerie was back moments later though, colorful crowns in each hand and a big grin on her face.

"We made some for you, too! This one is for Uncle T—" she said, handing a black and yellow number to Tarek before she turned to Madoc. "And this one is for you, Daddy."

Emotions warred inside Madoc. The crown his daughter held was piled with blue and purple pompoms and rather than hosting a swarm of wee felted bugs held only two, a ladybug with a bee cuddled up beside it, its thorax striped pink and blue and purple with black. Like the enamel pin in Madoc's pocket, another tiny, gentle reminder that it was okay to just be himself.

Carefully, Madoc ran his fingertips over the little cloth insects. He wanted to say something—a thank-you certainly, and to tell Valerie how much he loved her. But his throat was too thick to utter even one word as he bowed his head, and she slid the headband over his hair.

The pom-pom crowns were left behind when it came time to drop Valerie off at her day camp, but Madoc's mind kept flashing back to the news story about the Squads and Gus. Oddly, it seemed that seeing Gus on a TV screen had also left an impression on Tarek.

"I get it now," he said as he and Madoc made their way back to the Seaport. "Why Val looks up to Gus like he's a hero. Because he kind of is, right?"

Madoc frowned slightly. "What do you mean?"

"The shit Gus went through losing his leg, working to get back out there with a new job." Tarek shook his head. "I never thought about any of that before today and I have to say, the dude is impressive."

"He is," Madoc allowed. "Gus is strong and determined and smart as hell. But he's also a guy just living his best life."

Tarek cocked his eyebrow at Madoc. "A guy who made history for the city."

"Sure, but that's not why Gus wanted to be promoted," Madoc said. "He does his job well because he's ambitious and cares about the patients and crews, not because he needs anyone's approval for living with a disability."

"That isn't fair." Red stained Tarek's cheeks. "I didn't say anything about Gus being disabled."

"Not outright, no. But you implied it when you said Gus impressed you because he still managed to thrive after losing his leg. Val doesn't care about that, mostly because she's just a kid. Sure, she thinks it's cool Gus was on TV and that he gets to drive a Squad, but she likes *him* because he's kind to her and fun to be around, and he listens when she wants to talk. You'd know all that too if you got to know Gus at all."

Expecting a rebuttal, Madoc was surprised that Tarek instead stared moodily off into space. Madoc let the silence hang between them until they paused at a crosswalk to wait out the flow of traffic.

"What's on your mind, T?" Madoc pressed.

Tarek sucked in a big breath, then let it go. "I keep thinking about that night Val threw her shoes. She looked at me like she hated me. And the stuff that Gus said? I feel sick knowing he thinks I'm—"

"Ableist and homophobic?"

"I'm *not*."

"Not sure I agree." Madoc stepped out into the crosswalk with Tarek at his side. "You *know* you're weird about Gus's leg, dude. And hey, I've been in your shoes. Had to adjust my own perspectives about people who live with disability and stop making assumptions, and God knows I'm still learning new shit all the time. But with you, it's like you won't even consider you're wrong, or that you've been acting like a total troll about Gus being gay."

Tarek rolled his eyes. "I couldn't care less about who he wants to fuck, Madoc. He doesn't need to be so open about wanting *you* though, especially around Val."

"Are you for real trying to sell me that shit?" Madoc scoffed. "Gus has never said anything remotely romantic about me to Val and I know it because she would have told me. And besides, I'm not talking about how Gus acts or doesn't—I'm talking about you being out of line so fucking often I've started to second-guess what's going to come out of your mouth every time you open it."

He cut a glare at his friend who had the good grace to look embarrassed. "I take Val to Gus's to hang out instead of Gus coming to mine because that way no one has to worry about how you're going to react when you see him. And the night of the harbor cruise with the NHL legends, I was on edge the whole time, braced for you and your buddies to start cracking jokes about queers."

Tarek stopped walking, his expression stunned when Madoc glanced back at him. "Are you being serious right now?"

Sighing, Madoc walked the few steps back to where Tarek stood. They were almost mid-way over a bridge that spanned the Fort Point Channel, and he knew they probably painted an odd picture to passing motorists and pedestrians alike.

"Yes, I'm being serious." Madoc kept his tone gentle. "I want to think you don't mean the shit you say about queer people and it's all just part of your het guy cover, but I'm at a point now where I'm not sure anymore. Maybe you do mean it. Maybe Tim was some kind of once-in-a-lifetime exception and if you'd never met him, you'd have just been a straight guy. But no matter what, the way you are around Gus has got to change."

Madoc folded his arms over his chest. "Val loves you, T, and she's always looked up to you. But she knows you don't like Gus and if she starts believing it's because he's queer or that you can't deal with his leg, she will be crushed."

"Shit. I'm sorry." Tarek's voice came out thick. "I'd never ... I don't want that to happen. I know I act like a jackass sometimes, but I am *not* a homophobe."

He looked so stricken, Madoc gently pulled him to the side of the walkway.

"Gus thinks you are. And worse, I let him believe it when I didn't call you out on your behavior," Madoc said. "I didn't want to out you, T, and I thought it'd be better for all of us if I kept the peace and gave you time to work through being angry at Noelene and me. The problem is that you turned that anger on Gus, who didn't deserve any of it, and I let him down by not having his back, especially after everything he did for me."

Tarek ran his bottom lip between his teeth, then turned and set his elbows on the bridge's railing.

"I can't imagine how nuts it's been for you this summer," he said, his gaze on the harbor. "Not knowing what was going on with Noelene and still having Val and the rest of your life to manage. You dealt with it the best you could and moved on, and so did my sister. But Madoc, you and Noels and Val are the only family I have left and when you all moved on, it felt like you did it without me."

Madoc's stomach bottomed out. "That isn't true."

"You sure about that? I was only away six weeks and when I came back, my sister was gone, there were empty rooms in the loft, and some dude I didn't know was standing in for me and doing things with Val that I can't."

"I don't understand. What did Gus do that you couldn't?"

"He took Val to Pride. Introduced her to his parents and friends. I've heard Val talk to Gus about his ex-boyfriend like it wasn't any big thing. And I know it's stupid, but I'm so fucking jealous Gus got to have those experiences. That's why I act like I hate him. A part of me *does* hate him for being able to do all that with Val when it should have been me. Would have been if I wasn't such a ..." Tarek's voice cracked and he closed his eyes, clearly trying to get back some control.

"I don't know what my life would have been like if I hadn't met Tim, either. He's the only man I've ever been with or even been interested in. But I did love him, Madoc. And now Val's never going to know Tim, just like she's never going to get to know my parents because all of them are gone," Tarek said.

"She'll never understand how much they meant to me and that hurts like hell."

Sorrow punched a hole in Madoc's heart. He'd known Tarek was grieving behind the strong front he put on. It still hurt watching him drop that mask. Understanding he'd been isolated in his suffering because he couldn't talk openly about the man he'd loved, not even with his family. Couldn't miss or grieve for Tim unless he was alone.

But now Madoc could see the lonely path *he'd* be traveling if he continued to hide who he was. Apart from Gus, no one knew the man Madoc hid behind his straight guy front, not even Madoc's own daughter.

"Do you miss our Gusberry, Daddy?"

Answering truthfully had been easy for Madoc to do without giving anything deeper away. But he couldn't keep that up forever. Could already feel in his bones that it was only a matter of time before Valerie asked him a question about Gus or girlfriends or how Madoc was living his life that would force him to choose between the truth and protecting his cover.

And lying to his daughter wasn't a choice Madoc was willing to make when the truth was right there in front of him.

Valerie deserved a daddy who liked himself and his life. To know he'd fallen in love with a man whose brown eyes shone with gold and who made Madoc's life better every day simply by loving him back.

Wait.

Madoc's knees actually wobbled. Two weeks ago, he'd told Gus he wasn't ready to be serious about anyone or talk families or partnerships or forevers. Now, all Madoc could wonder was how he'd missed the obvious.

Gus lit up his world. Grounded Madoc even as he lifted him and made Madoc want to shake off the past that was holding him back. Madoc trusted Gus more than anyone else in his life besides Valerie because Gus wanted him in spite of his baggage and big mouth and the responsibilities he carried as a single dad. Hell, maybe even because of those things.

Gus felt like home. And Madoc had fallen head over heels for him without even noticing.

When you're ready, you'll know.

Slipping a hand into his pocket, Madoc pulled out the bee pin and held it small and neat in his palm, its wings gleaming in the morning sun.

"I'm sorry Val won't get to know your folks or Tim," he said to Tarek. "And that it hurts you watching Gus do things with her. But it breaks my heart knowing Val's missing out spending that time with you. Because she doesn't have to, Tarek. Tell her about Tim. How much he meant to you and how happy you made each other. That Tim was the love of your life. Val should know all of that and who you really are. None of it is going to change the way she feels about you."

Tarek's sigh seemed to come from his toes. "I hope not. It's just ..."

"Hard to stop hiding," Madoc finished quietly. "I understand. How scared you have to be to get to the point where hiding feels like the safer option. You get numb enough you can almost forget the pieces of yourself that you're hiding. Except you can't because they're still a part of you."

He sensed more than saw Tarek turning toward him, and Madoc slipped the bee pin back in his pocket. "I don't want to hide anymore or ever lie to my girl about who I am. So, I'm going to tell her the truth."

"Which is what?"

"That I'm bi," Madoc replied, the words coming with stunning ease. "And I was too afraid until this summer to say that to anyone, even myself."

"Holy shit." Tarek grabbed onto Madoc's forearm, his eyes suddenly bright. "Are you okay? Can I do anything? Besides say 'holy shit,' I mean, which I know isn't helpful."

Madoc laughed, and though it was a touch shaky, it felt incredibly good. "I *am* okay, yeah. Sorry I'm springing this on you out of nowhere, but I haven't really figured out how to talk about this without blurting it out."

"Hey, I'm just happy you trusted me enough to tell me." Tarek's smile held only love, and he gave Madoc's arm a quick squeeze. "I'm so proud of you, bro."

Swallowing past a sudden threat of tears, Madoc pulled him into a rough hug, then just as quickly stepped back, a need to move driving him to resume walking. Tarek stayed with him, though he remained quiet, and they'd completed their journey over the bridge before Madoc trusted his voice to speak again.

"We need to talk about Gus, T," he said. "Because he's more than a friend. And that's another reason I need you to treat him better. I'm not naive enough to think I can convince the two of you to be friends, but I want to know you'll be able to handle Gus being around because *I* want him in my life."

A beat passed, then two, and Tarek exhaled loudly through his nose. "I can handle Gus. And I knew you and he were ... a thing. Think I have for a while."

Madoc straight-out gaped at him. "Say what now?"

Tarek shrugged. "You didn't seem surprised when I said Gus was into you, Madoc. And honestly, there's an energy between you when you're together that's hard to miss. The way you look at him sometimes ..." Tarek flashed a half-smirk. "You're not doing much to hide it."

Madoc didn't know whether to laugh or cry at that but something in his expression had Tarek looking at him with concern once again.

“What is it?” Tarek frowned. “Did I say the wrong thing?”

“No.” Madoc gave him a smile. “You said things I really needed to hear.”

TWENTY-FOUR

FRIDAY, *August 25, 4:43 P.M.*

“ALL UNITS, I need a Squad at Melrose and Charles, 27-D-6 G, two persons reported shot, male, early to mid-twenties.”

Gus flipped on his lights before replying. “84 in Chinatown, show me en route. Do I have a Code Four?”

“Negative, 84, BPD is still securing the scene.”

“Copy. How about an ETA on a truck?”

“That’s pending, 84—we’ll get one out to you ASAP.”

Jaw set, Gus put his focus on navigating through rush hour traffic while the dispatcher fed him the few details that’d come in about the victims. Gun violence was not common in Boston, but the crews had been slammed this afternoon with all manner of calls that kept the ambulances and Squads in constant motion. Being stuck with multiple potentially serious injuries on his own was bad luck for Gus, but keeping busy meant not having to think about the wreck that passed for his personal life these days.

Like how the only thing he looked forward to outside of work was hanging out with his cat while he sketched. How flat and colorless the world had become or how bone-achingly tired he was all the damned time. How much he missed—

You can't keep this up.

No, Gus really couldn't. But for now, he had patients to manage and needed to keep his shit together.

He got the Code 4 upon pulling up to the intersection of Melrose and Charles Streets and the scene was huge with a person down on either side of Charles and a ton of cops on hand. Traffic on the surrounding streets had been thrown into chaos, and there were a ton of onlookers gathered in the humid summer air behind the crime scene tape that cordoned off the area.

"Hey, guys," Gus called as he approached the cluster of people closest to him, a young female cop and a pair of civilians gathered around a young man who lay on his back. "How we doin'?"

"Doin' okay," the cop called back. "We've got a tourniquet on his arm, and he's been talking the whole time. He's in a lot better shape than the other guy."

Gus shot a quick glance at the second group across the street before dropping his bag and kneeling. He pulled out packets of gauze and gloves and handed them off to the cop, then quickly scanned his patient. The guy was young, probably mid-twenties, and slim with olive skin and dark wavy hair he wore short. His head and torso lay in the gutter while his legs had been propped on the sidewalk, and he'd been shot in the biceps muscle of his right arm, perhaps three inches above the elbow.

"Hey, buddy, I'm Gus and I'm a paramedic," Gus said to his patient. "Can you tell me your name?"

"Pascal." The guy met Gus's gaze, his hazel eyes wide. "I

don't even know what happened," he said, sounding dazed. "We were just walking, and I heard some pops and now this."

Gus frowned at Pascal's choice of words. "Did you hit your head when you fell, Pascal?"

"He might have," said one of the civilians. She had blood on her hands and looked completely freaked. "He went down like a ton of bricks."

"The shooter fled," the police officer said, tearing open a package of gauze. "These guys were in the wrong place at the wrong time."

Nodding once, Gus handed the civilian with the bloodied hands some wipes, then checked Pascal's wound, pleased when he found the tourniquet positioned well and tight, and that Pascal had a hole on the back of his arm too.

"You've got an exit wound here, buddy," Gus said, "and that's lucky because it means the bullet's not stuck in your arm."

"Yippee, I guess?" Pascal said and the mood shifted instantly, Gus and the cop exchanging amused glances while the civilians broke into nervous giggles.

"Trust me bro, you don't want that thing inside you," Gus said to Pascal. "If you think a bullet hurts going in, that pain is nothing compared to a doc having to take it back out."

Unfortunately, Gus's second patient had not been as lucky as Pascal and the second Gus got his ass across the street, his adrenaline cranked up several notches. Tyler was East Asian and stockier in build, with a bullet hole in his back just below the left scapula, a triangular bone better known as the shoulder blade. Gus couldn't find an exit wound anywhere on Tyler's torso, however, and the dude was sweating heavily and ashy-pale under the streetlights, too shocky for Gus's comfort.

"I'm going to start an IV in your right arm, Tyler," Gus said to him. "You're going to feel a big stick, and I need you to hold still. Don't you move, okay?"

"Oh, fuck." Tyler grimaced as the needle slid into his vein. He was older than Pascal, probably mid-thirties, and obviously terrified. "I feel like shit."

"I hear you, buddy, and I know this sucks really bad." Gus taped the line down against Tyler's skin. "I want to get some fluids in you while we wait on the ambulance."

"Am I gonna die?"

"No, you're not, Tyler, and I'm going to take care of you."

Gus did, traveling back and forth between Pascal and Tyler every few minutes to ensure both remained conscious, talking, and stable until more help arrived. The cops and civilians pitched in keeping both patients alert, and when A10 and P16 arrived with Olivia in Squad 81 just behind them, Gus shifted gears, splitting the crews so there was a paramedic on each truck and sending Tyler off first in P16 followed by Pascal in A10.

"That was good work," Olivia said as they headed back to the Squads. "You didn't leave me much to do."

Gus grunted. "Hope you didn't just jinx yourself," he said, "because today has been wild."

"Oh, good, that's just what I want to hear." Huffing, Olivia cocked her head toward a nearby cafe. "Feel like grabbing a coffee with me?"

Gus could have said no. Gone to the gym instead and worked out until his brain got the message he needed rest. Because Gus and sleep had become mortal enemies again and he was so wiped these days it was a struggle to get out of bed in the morning. Feeling depressed over Madoc wasn't helping at all, of course, nor were the thoughts that'd been buzzing around Gus's brain since Madoc'd sent a message asking to meet.

I respect that you asked for space, but I'd like to talk when you're ready.

Gus didn't know when he'd feel truly ready to see Madoc in person. When he was going to feel less like he was grieving the loss of a family that'd never even been his. Gus couldn't put Madoc off forever though, especially knowing Madoc wouldn't have asked to meet unless he'd had a good reason. So, Gus made up his mind to call him tonight. *After* fortifying himself with a jolt of caffeine.

"Michael and I want to adopt a kitty for Titus," Olivia said as she stood with Gus at the counter bar in the cafe with their coffees and snacks. "Would you be up for visiting a couple of shelters with me? I'd go on my own, but I'm afraid I'll want to adopt all of them, and I can*not* walk out of there with more than one cat."

Gus smiled. "Sure, I'd be happy to go along. Lemonade needs a new leash anyway, so I can pick one up from wherever we go."

"Maybe you could pick her up a new buddy while you're at it."

"Yeah, no. She's already up half the night playing in that damned cat tree and the last thing she needs is a partner in crime."

Chuckling, Olivia broke the snickerdoodle cookie she'd bought in half and handed a chunk to Gus. "Has she been waking you up?"

"No, but only because I'm not really sleeping," Gus said, then nibbled at his piece of cookie. "My body clock has been all over the place since the thing with my ribs. It was better for a while"—*when I was sleeping beside Madoc*—"but not so much now and it feels like my brain has been literally cooked."

"I hear you. I was a wreck after Titus," Olivia said, sympathy in her tone and expression. "Crabby and emotional and just *beat* down to my bones, especially after I switched to nights. Pretty sure I put most of the crews off the idea of having kids too, though you were the exception, as usual."

Gus frowned at her. "Me? What did I do?"

"Volunteered to act as a surrogate daddy to your partner's kid."

The cookie Gus'd been eating lost all its flavor. "I was just a kid-sitter, Liv," he mumbled, only for Olivia to surprise him with a shrug.

"That's not what I heard from Madoc."

"Madoc did *not* call me a surrogate dad."

"True. He did say there were days you spent more time with Val than he did, though. Said you baked stuff with her and taught her drawing techniques and that you froze your ass off at the hockey rink while she practiced. Even learned how to play the weird game with the goat cheese pizza and tacos."

Instantly, Gus pictured himself at Madoc's table, Valerie beating her chest after the Gorilla card had been thrown and gleefully collecting her winnings while Gus and Madoc laughed themselves sick.

"I was supposed to do all that stuff because I was the kid-sitter," Gus said.

"Okay. But can you tell me Val's favorite color?" Olivia asked.

"Purple."

"Any clothing she loves more than all others?"

"High top sneakers and a ladybug tracksuit. Also, she has this tutu she wears around the house."

Olivia smiled. "What foods does she hate?"

"Raisins," Gus replied promptly. "Because they ruin everything."

"Blasphemy. And what does she like for breakfast?"

"Bagels with cream cheese and fruit. And *bolos levedos* if

they're available." Gus bit his lip. "Where are you going with this, Liv?"

"Nowhere, sweetie. But I will say I've met dads who know less about the kids they've spawned than you do about Val, a kid you've only known for a couple of months. And that's because you were more than only a kid-sitter and it shows."

Gus stared at his snack. He'd sure felt like more than a kid-sitter to Valerie. And like more than only a friend to her dad. Which was why he knew Madoc's favorite color was green. That he kept an ancient *Blade Runner* t-shirt he'd had since college even though it was now at least two sizes too small. Gus knew Madoc sometimes got down thinking about his parents back in Washington but tried to hide it and that watching Gus in the boxing ring made him hot. And for as much as Madoc loathed olives, he adored marshmallow fluff to the point he refused to keep any at home.

A home that wasn't Gus's, no matter how badly he wished for different.

"Gus." Concern was in Olivia's dark eyes when Gus looked her way. "Are you all right? I feel like I said the wrong thing."

A series of rapid-fire beeps from her radio raised the hairs on the back of Gus's neck.

"Emergency Alert activated," a dispatcher said. "A1, what's your status?"

A chaos of shouts and curses came over the connection in bursts, voices yelling over one another because the mic on someone's radio had turned hot after they'd hit their emergency button.

"Just get the fuck out of here!"

"Stop!"

"Get your hands off him!"

Amaya Monroe's voice cut through the babbling, her tone

strident. "Mayday, mayday, mayday, EMTs and paramedics in need of assistance at 43 Concord Squa—hey!"

Gus and Olivia exchanged a single wide-eyed look before they were up and booking it back out to the Squads. Noises continued to broadcast over the open channel, voices issuing insults and threats and sounds like scuffling, but Monroe didn't reply to the dispatcher's requests for a status and the heavy silence that followed when her mic switched itself off was infinitely worse.

"Command 8, Boston A1 and P1 are mayday and requesting assistance at 43 Concord Square," the dispatcher said now. "Do you copy?"

"Command 8 copy," Commander Marcel responded. "Show me en route."

"Ten-four, Command 8. BPD is responding." A pause and then, "All units, be aware of reports of smoke coming from 43 Concord Square, Boston Fire ETA three minutes."

Anxiety twisted Gus's insides. Amaya Monroe was one of the most level-headed people he'd ever worked with. If she'd declared a mayday, something was very wrong at that scene she was working with Lucky, Connor, Stark, and ...

Fuck.

Quickly he pulled his phone from his pocket and dictated a message to Madoc. "Please respond," Gus said, trying for calm and clinical. "Where are you right now?"

He sent the same message several times, aware there was no point as dread trickled through him. Gus already knew where Madoc was, of course. And that whatever wild shit was going down in that row house at Concord Square, he and their friends were square in the middle of it.

An acrid smoke stink hung over the scene as Gus and Olivia quickly donned full bunker gear with heavy jackets, pants, and helmets, and they had to sidestep the engine and ladder crews who were already hard at work containing the fire. Amaya's mayday had drawn a ton of cops to the scene, many of them managing the neighborhood's residents and curious passersby, but through it all Ambulances A1 and P1 stood silent and still by the curb, lights off, clearly unattended.

Forcing himself to look past them, Gus jogged over to where Commander Marcel had stationed himself on the left side of 43 Concord with several other EMTs and paramedics.

"What do we know, sir?" Gus asked him. "Any word from the crews?"

"Not at this time," Marcel replied, expression stonier than was typical. "The building has four levels, and the fire has spread throughout the structure. Residents have been evacuated from all units with the exception of the back garden level, which is where we believe the crews from A1 and P1 are being held against their will."

Gus swallowed past the tightness that immediately rose in his throat. This was bad. Especially knowing no one had heard from anyone on A1's or P1's crews since the mayday.

"The number of persons inside the residence is unknown at this time," Marcel continued, "but Boston Fire has reported that a person in the unit threatened to discharge a firearm if the fire crews attempted entry, which is why Boston PD is stepping in."

A cluster of officials approached then, among them a senior SWAT officer, and Marcel stepped away for a confab while Gus waited on tenterhooks along with the others. When Marcel stepped back moments later, his eyes were steely.

"SWAT's going to breach the rear entrance," he said, then looked to Gus and Olivia. "Dawson, Park, take up position back there with Ellis, the rest of you hold here while we wait for a Code Four. *No one* moves until then, do you copy?"

Gus nodded sharply. "Copy, sir!" he chorused along with

the others, then set off toward a narrow cobblestoned passage between buildings 43 and 45 that connected Concord Square to Public Alley 502. Running behind the buildings on the block, the alley provided much needed space for resident parking, back gardens, and rear entrances for lower level apartments. A SWAT vehicle sat back there now competing for space with another engine truck and its crew, but the fire had spread farther too, flames licking out windows along the upper floors despite the fire hoses' spray, the smoke thick and much darker.

Gus exchanged a nod with the fire crew's lieutenant, then found a spot to wait at the rear of the engine truck. Glancing around, he noticed Olivia was red-faced, her expression bordering upon angry.

"Hey, they'll be all right," Gus said to her. "You know Lucky can charm the horns off the devil when he wants to, and he's probably already got plans to grab coffee with whoever is holding the gun."

Olivia grimaced. "I guess. I just ..." She shook her head. "I want our guys safe, y'know?"

Oh, Gus knew all right. His last day on the job as a firefighter—his final call beside Beni—had been in this very same neighborhood, inside a building much like the one his friends were now trapped in. He knew they were likely frightened. Feared they were injured or worse. And knew that if he'd just kept his dumb ass on P1, Madoc would be doing his thing on a whole other truck in a completely different neighborhood, then going home to his girl.

Oh, God, Valerie.

Gus's heart fell to his feet. If something happened to Madoc, what the hell was Gus going to say to her?

Focus, Dawson.

"Stand by for breach," Marcel said over the radio.

Tensing, Gus watched SWAT approach the back entrance of the apartment, crossing the minuscule yard in a straight line, while spray from the firehoses rained over them. A final command for the residents to exit was given by the lead officer, and when it went unanswered, a cop carrying a thick battering ram knocked the door in with a single swing.

Smoke poured out past the police darting into the apartment and Gus's heart thundered in his throat. Several figures were hustled out into the yard, gender and features unclear beneath the soot smudged on their pale faces, and then Marcel was in Gus's ear, calling Code 4 and ordering the EMS crews to approach.

Gus sprinted into the yard with the others. He registered the cold spray from the hoses and a chorus of voices as smoke filled his nose and throat and made his eyes burn. Then Gus's gaze was locked on the back entrance and the SWAT officers carrying out a tall, broad-shouldered male clad in a paramedic's uniform.

TWENTY-FIVE

"WHAT DID you think of your new teachers?"

"They. Were. Great!" Letting go of Madoc's hand, Valerie twirled around on the sidewalk. "Did you know Mr. Kenzie has a whole bunch of new books for the first graders? And I get to read them because *I'm* gonna be in first grade!"

Madoc grinned down at her. "Jeez, you're practically a grown up."

"Nuh-uh! I don't have a job, Daddy, an' you said I'm too little for a phone."

Madoc rolled his eyes at the not-so-sly hint. He *did* think his kid was too young for a smartphone, in spite of the growing up she'd been doing. Valerie was noticeably taller than she'd been last year at this time, and her cheeks and limbs had lost some of their plump baby softness. While Madoc didn't typically wax nostalgic over growth spurts or birthdays, he'd sulked alongside her when the ladybug tracksuit had become too tight and short overnight, struggling to grasp how his girl could be nearly seven when she'd been a newborn only yesterday.

Is Noelene thinking about back to school, too? he wondered now. *Or does it even matter since Val hasn't mentioned her mom at all tonight?*

"Daddy?"

Glancing up from his salad, Madoc caught Valerie watching him over her own plate. He'd assumed they'd pick an eatery close to Valerie's school for dinner, but she'd insisted they journey back to Flour Power, her still-favorite place that was only a block from Gus's apartment.

Madoc could have messaged Gus with a heads-up and asked if he'd like to join them. But he'd chickened out in the end, hesitant to reach out when Gus still hadn't replied to Madoc's last message asking if they could meet.

"What's up, my honey?" he asked his daughter.

"Can I use the pencils Gus gave me for back to school?"

"Of course. You can use those pencils however you want."

"Yay!" Valerie said. "I was just checking that you didn't mind."

Her choice of words hit Madoc strangely. "Why would I mind if you wanted to use the pencils Gus gave you?"

"Because you're mad at him, right?"

"Um. No." Madoc set down his fork. "Did I say something to make you think I was angry with Gus?"

"Nah." Valerie shrugged. "But you make a face when you talk about him, kinda like the way you do when you talk about Noelene."

Madoc blinked a couple of times before finding his tongue. "I make a face when I talk about Gus or your mom?"

"Like this." Setting her hands on the tabletop, Valerie creased her brow, then pressed her lips into a tight line. But she appeared downcast rather than angry and that was absolutely a state of mind Madoc had become familiar with over the last couple of weeks.

He swallowed a sigh. He'd tried really hard to hide the

unhappiness that'd dogged him since Gus's withdrawal. Valerie had seen through Madoc of course, because she knew him better than anyone.

"I'm not angry with Gus," Madoc said. "But I am a bit with myself."

"How come?"

"I hurt Gus's feelings. And I don't like knowing I made my friend feel bad."

Valerie picked up her egg sandwich and took a bite, then chewed for a couple of beats before speaking. "Is that how come Gus doesn't come over?"

Madoc eyed her askance. "Gus was at our place a couple of days ago, making crowns and cake with Clea and you."

"But *you* weren't there, Daddy." The 'duh' in Valerie's voice was withering. "I like it best when we're together," she said, "you, me, and Gus, because we make a family, just like me and you do with Uncle T."

Jesus, his heart. Leaning over the table, Madoc smoothed a wayward curl back from his daughter's forehead. "Is that what you want? To make a family with Gus?"

Valerie nodded, her dark eyes incredibly soulful. "He's one of my favorite people after you. An' I know Gus isn't oh-ficially family but I don't care about that. Friends can be fam too, right?"

"Right. Every family looks different. And sometimes, friends make the best kind of fam."

"That's why you have to do an apology with Gus, Daddy, so he knows you didn't mean to hurt his feelings."

"I plan to the next time I see him," Madoc vowed. "And just so you know, Gus is my favorite person after you too."

A smile crept onto Valerie's face. "I knew it. Gus makes you happy."

Pain mapped its way through Madoc's heart. "Gus makes

me very happy. And you know I was happy before when it was just you and me, right?"

"Uh-huh. But Gus makes you laugh and smile all the time when you're making dinner or talking on the couch, and you never get lonesome." Valerie shrugged. "I like that a lot."

"I'm glad. And you know you're right? Gus does make me do all of those things."

"Because you're in love?"

"Yes." Just like that with his girl, it was easy for Madoc to say. "I'm very much in love with Gus. But I hope you know that I love you first."

"I do." Pushing her seat back, Valerie got up and walked around the table to Madoc, who helped her hoist herself into his lap. "Gus says you love me most in the world out of anybody," she said with utter certainty.

Eyes stinging, Madoc took Valerie's hand. "I think Gus knows us pretty well. That's why I want to ask him if he'd like to try being boyfriends. I've never had a boyfriend before, you know. When I was growing up, I didn't know that some people like both boys and girls."

"But you know now, huh? And that's lucky." Valerie leaned into Madoc. "Just like if you ask Gus to be your boyfriend, he's gonna say yes because he loves us back."

Madoc was careful not to make promises he couldn't keep as he and Valerie finished their meal, then headed home. He didn't doubt Gus loved them, exactly as Valerie'd said. But Gus was also hurting, and it was up to Madoc to fix what he'd broken between them.

However, Tarek was pacing the hall outside Madoc's door when Madoc and Valerie stepped off the elevator and he wasted no time dashing up to them.

"There you are!" Beaming, Tarek scooped Valerie up in his arms. "It's about time you guys got home!"

"We went to the cafe for dinner," Madoc said, puzzled by the intensity in Tarek's gaze when he caught Madoc's eye. The guy looked almost relieved.

"We brought you a whoopie pie!" Valerie said. "Red velvet with extra goo in the middle, just how you like."

"That sounds delicious, thank you so much." Tarek dropped a kiss on her cheek. "You want to share it with me? I'll pour a big glass of milk to dunk it in and your Daddy can check some messages I sent him while you were at dinner."

Unease bubbled in Madoc's gut. He'd muted his phone before leaving the apartment with Valerie that afternoon and when he pulled it out now, he found a shit-ton of messages had piled up in those few hours. He ushered Valerie and Tarek inside as he started reading, noting that while many of the messages were from Tarek, Gus had sent several too, each one identical and only a few seconds apart.

Please respond, Gus'd written. *Where are you right now?*

I'm home, Madoc replied to the last. *Had a school thing with Val. Everything good?*

He flipped back to Tarek's messages while he waited for Gus to respond, and his disquiet grew as he understood Tarek had also been looking to know where Madoc was in between forwarding posts from a social media account run by Boston Fire.

Madoc was aware of Valerie and Tarek talking. But his eyes were on the photos attached to the posts of fire crews at work in the South End among a heavy police presence. There were shots of SWAT officers armed with shields, and a grouping of EMTs and paramedics in full bunker gear and helmets with Shift Commander Marcel.

A chill went through Madoc when he spotted Ambulance P1 in a photo, parked by the curb with A1 positioned ahead of it. And then there was a photo of three EMS personnel approaching an alley, a firetruck visible in the distance beyond them. The photographer had caught the EMS crew from behind, but Madoc recognized the badge numbers stenciled on the tails of two of the coats. 512 belonged to Olivia, 867 to Gus, and the two were headed into an active fire and police scene, probably to go after Connor, Stark, Guzman, and Monroe.

The messages Gus'd sent—*Where are you right now?* — flashed through Madoc's head and he bit back an urge to be sick. Gus'd gone to that fire thinking Madoc was there too, unaware he was across town at a cafe eating fucking salad.

7:40 P.M., Boston PD and BFD have extricated EMS crews and residents from lower level at 43 Concord Square. Multiple injuries, 2 arrests reported. Transports to Mass Eye & Ear/MGH completed by Boston EMS.

Thinking fast, Madoc grabbed the tablet from the dock in the kitchen and went to his room. He couldn't risk turning on the TV for fear Valerie would see something she shouldn't, and he was still pulling together information when Tarek found him a few minutes later.

"Shit, Madoc. I—"

Madoc held up a hand. "Where is she?"

"In her room with her coloring books," Tarek said quickly. "I asked her to wait until one of us came to get her."

"Thank you." Madoc exhaled hard. "I don't want her scared."

"I get it. Christ, *I* was scared." Shaking his head, Tarek closed the distance between them. "I got the alert on my phone and when I saw your truck in the photos, my brain started spiraling even though I *knew* you had the night off."

"Yeah. I think my partner was in that apartment, T." Madoc licked his lips. "And I know Gus was there too."

Tarek frowned at the screen. "I thought Gus worked days."

"He does. But the dispatcher I spoke to said a mayday call

came in right around shift change." Madoc held out the tablet and showed Tarek the video footage he'd found of Gus with Olivia and an EMT named Ellis stalking toward the alley, their expressions determined. "Gus must have heard it and headed over there instead of going off shift."

Madoc squished his eyes shut. "The news outlets are reporting that someone on the EMS crews may have been shot," he said, "and that several people were overcome by the smoke."

"Go." Tarek squeezed Madoc's shoulder, concern all over his face when Madoc looked at him. "I'll take care of Val."

"Are you sure you're okay to watch her? I know I'm kind of springing this on you out of nowhere but—"

"It's fine and I know you're worried," Tarek said, both hands on Madoc's shoulders now as he urged him toward the door. "Call and let me know what's going on when you do and I hope everybody's okay, especially your partner and Gus."

Much later, Madoc would acknowledge it'd been a mistake for him to drive to the MGH campus, because he'd spent most of the trip either speeding or leaning on his horn to get slow drivers to move.

There were familiar faces when he stepped off the elevator, Olivia seated in the waiting area with Heather and EMT Ellis, while Ellis's partner and other crew members stood in clusters, Commanders Marcel and Rivas off to the side with some other officer types. There was no sign of Connor, Stark, or the crew from A1, however, nor the face Madoc most wanted to see.

"Madoc!"

Breath catching, Madoc spun around, and there was Gus, expression fierce as he made his way over on his crutches. He looked worn out, hair messy and his white shirt stained with soot, but Madoc had never seen anything more beautiful.

Closing the distance between them in a few steps, he swept Gus into a hug that Gus returned with bruising force.

"Christ, it's good to see you," Gus muttered, his voice fervent. "I heard the mayday and I swear my blood froze."

Eyes shut tight, Madoc pressed his face against Gus's neck, breathing in smoke and sweat and hospital hand soap. "I was with Val," he croaked out. "She had a thing for school and I'm on vacation, didn't know any of this was happening until after we got home and saw Tarek. I'm sorry I didn't message you back before—"

Before you walked into a dangerous scene looking for me.

New fear clawed at Madoc's insides, despite having Gus in his arms, warm and vital and so very alive. "Jesus, Gus," he murmured, unsurprised when Gus squeezed him even tighter. "I can't believe you were there."

"I'm just glad that you weren't," Gus said. "Is Val with Tarek?"

"Yes, and she's good. But what about you?" Sighing, Madoc pulled back and scanned Gus up and down, frowning at his bloodshot eyes and damp hair. "What's going on with the crutches? And why are you wet?"

"Oh." Grimacing, Gus looked down at himself. "We were under the hoses at the scene, and I made it worse trying to clean up in the restroom. The crutches—"

"Are for balance because he's exhausted and his leg hurts."

Gus aimed a death glare at Zac, a nurse buddy of Ian and Mark Mannix who'd stepped up beside them.

"I told you, I'm fine," Gus said to him, only for Zac to shake his head.

"And I told you to put your ass in a chair and drink a bunch of water and yet, here you stand." Zac met Gus's stare head-on for several seconds before he flashed a small smile at Madoc. "Hi, Madoc."

"Hey, Zac." Without moving from Gus's side, Madoc held out his hand. "What does he need?" he asked with a nod toward Gus.

"Fluids, calories, and rest," Zac replied as he shook hands with Madoc. "His prosthesis is rubbing the wrong way, and I know he wants to take it off, but he checked out okay otherwise when he came in."

Gus huffed noisily, clearly annoyed at being talked about rather than to, and Madoc set his hand between Gus's shoulders in wordless apology.

"What about the others?" Madoc asked Zac. "Connor and Stark and the crew from A1?"

"They're smoky and banged up, Connor and EMT Guzman in particular," Zac said. "Right now, the priority is to get their oxygen levels back to normal but if you give me a second, I'll bring you a real update." Turning, he started for the nurses' station, then paused. "See if you can get Gus to sit down before he tips over, yeah?"

"I'll tip *you* over you keep talking about me like I'm not here," Gus almost growled.

Madoc wanted to laugh at the snarking, but his breath got stuck on the way out, so he just moved his hand to Gus's waist and started guiding him toward the waiting area. He knew Zac and the others could see them; that they'd already watched Madoc throw himself at Gus and hang on to him like a man about to drown. None of that seemed important now that Gus was beside him, sweating and cranky instead of choking past a lung full of smoke.

That could have been us.

As they moved, Gus gently knocked his shoulder into Madoc's. "I really am fine, you know," he said. "My leg only aches because my liner and socks got twisted."

"I believe you," Madoc replied. "I'm just not sure that *I'm* fine."

Once Gus was seated so he could deal with his leg, Madoc traded hugs and backslaps with Olivia and the others, listening as they talked through the details they'd scraped together about how a simple dispatch to treat a stab wound had devolved into utter chaos. It seemed things had started to go sideways after P2 had arrived to assist Guzman and Monroe, someone among the apartment's residents mistaking Connor and Stark for police officers. A fight had broken out, escalating to the point Monroe had hit her emergency button, but there was still no definitive word on what had started the fire.

"Stark said the apartment was tricked out like a party pad with strings of lights hanging from the ceilings and walls," Olivia said to Madoc. "He figured maybe a wire got crossed and threw a spark at some point and it spread from there."

"It may have started days ago," Gus said then. "Electrical fires sometimes burn slow when they're caused by damaged wiring that overheats gradually. A fire will smolder for a long while before it ignites fully and you'd never know."

He sipped the sports drink Madoc had pressed on him as everyone talked, all worried about their friends, particularly Connor, who'd sustained a concussion during the melee, and Guzman, whose shoulder had been dislocated.

That could have been us.

"You scared the shit out of me today," Madoc said as he drove Gus back toward the Seaport a couple of hours later. Their friends had been released after treatment and sent home, and still Madoc felt spooked. "Seeing you in those photos. *Not* seeing Connor and Stark and the others. Knowing some of you were injured and not having details. All of it was terrifying."

"I hear you," Gus replied. "And if it makes you feel any better, my ma's been blowing up my phone with all caps for the last two hours. She is, as my Gramps Dawson used to say, ragingly ripshit."

Madoc managed what felt like his first real smile since leaving his apartment as he looked at Gus. "You are so screwed."

"Yes, and you don't have to look so pleased about it, you smug motherfucker," Gus grumbled. "I'm going to give you a pass though, because you were nice and offered me a ride home."

He aimed a mock glare across the seat, but there was a softness in his eyes that nearly broke Madoc's heart. Because despite being so obviously wrung out and worried about their friends—despite the pain Madoc had caused him—Gus was looking at Madoc with love.

Reaching across the seat, Madoc took Gus's hand. "Can I make you dinner? I know you're tired and probably sore, and it'd mean a lot to me if I could lighten your load tonight."

It was torture watching Gus's smile fade, the light in his eyes shuttering. He didn't pull his hand from Madoc's, however, and Madoc almost didn't dare breathe for fear he'd break the fragile peace they'd managed to find.

"You're on vacation, Madoc," Gus said at last. "You sure you want to spend what's left of your night dealing with me?"

"More than." Madoc tried not to sound over eager. "I'd like to be there for you for a change, the way you've been for me so many times."

Gus's expression turned endearingly shy. But before he could answer, the driver of the car behind them tooted its horn.

"Light's green, bruh!" they yelled out their window, breaking what was left of the spell and cracking Madoc and Gus up.

Still, Gus kept hold of Madoc's hand the rest of the way to

Fort Point, and when Madoc pulled into the parking lot, invited him in.

TWENTY-SIX

NERVES TWISTED Gus's insides as he led Madoc into the studio.

"You want a drink?" he asked, going to his chair. "I have beer and Coke and some Korean energy drinks that Felipe's obsessed with."

Madoc closed the door behind them. "I'd love a beer. I'll grab one for you too, if you don't mind me helping myself."

"Absolutely, knock yourself out."

Propping his crutches and bag against the wall, Gus used the chair's arms for balance as he spun on his sound foot, then lowered himself into the seat. His groan was loud, but he didn't care when Madoc's hand between Gus's shoulders was a soothing weight Gus could lean into. It centered Gus and made the throbbing in his short limb that much easier to ignore.

"You good?" Madoc asked.

"Yeah." Gus sagged a little. "Just beat. My leg is sore. Plus, I stink like firepit, and I'm *so* done with this uniform."

Sighing quietly, Madoc squatted beside him. "Can I do anything?"

Gus opened his mouth, then shut it again. He was close to cracking with Madoc so near, his own emotions stretched thin after what had been a very long day.

"The cops had to carry Connor out of that house," Gus said softly. "For a second, I thought it was you."

Despite his terror, Gus had gone straight to work, Olivia and Ellis at his sides and more crews pouring into the yard as Stark, Amaya, and Lucky were brought out. Gus could still see Connor's eyes, the warm brown startling against his soot-streaked skin. Lucky's face twisted in pain, Amaya and Stark gagging for breath. Through it all, Gus's heart had been in his throat, his relief Madoc wasn't among the injured—that Madoc was somewhere safe—staggering.

Madoc moved his hand to the back of Gus's neck and Gus reached up, curling his fingers around Madoc's wrist. It helped, just hanging on.

Until the soft thump of a kitty dropping out of a cat tree with her tags jingling pulled him back out of his head.

"Uh-oh." Gus shared a smile with Madoc at Lemonade's plaintive meow. "Someone's big mad that I'm late with her food."

Madoc smoothed Gus's hair. "Guess we should feed her then."

The cat trotted up, excited by Madoc's presence, and though she made the leap onto Gus's shoulders for the quick ride into the kitchen, she complained steadily, chagrined at being left waiting.

"Let me take over," Madoc said to Gus over Lemonade's griping. "I'll deal with the small chicken princess while you go wash off the smoke and think about what you want for your own dinner."

Gus accepted the beer Madoc handed him, drinking deeply from the bottle before he set it between his thighs. "Might be too tired to eat," he said as he spun his chair around. "But I don't have to be at HQ for the debrief until ten tomorrow, so I'll have time for a giant breakfast."

He stopped by the closet to drop off his leg and grab a change of clothes, amused as he listened to Madoc chat with Lemonade. In the bathroom, Gus cleaned his prosthetic liner and socks first, and his beer was mostly gone by the time he got himself into the shower. He took his time basking under the hot spray, sluicing off smoke and sweat and God knew what else, and he babied his stump, carefully cleaning the reddened skin. By the time he emerged from the bathroom, he'd located his appetite, his stomach rumbling when a bunch of good smells hit him, herbs and meat and spices.

"Yo." Gus raised his eyebrows at a plate on his table piled high with sliced vegetables and cheese, crackers, and pieces of smoked turkey. "Did all that come out of my fridge?"

Madoc, who had the cat in his arms, huffed a laugh. "Yes. Thought maybe you'd get hungry once you had some time to chill. You want another drink?"

"Yes, please." Rolling up to the table, Gus traded his empty bottle and bundle of laundry for the cat. "Thank you for doing this."

"Thanks for letting me." Madoc gave him a smile before walking off.

Scooping meat and cheese from the plate, Gus broke off a small piece of cheese for the cat. When he took a bite for himself though, he saw the shades had been drawn and the bed pulled out of its cabinet. The extra pillows he kept in the closet were out and his phone was on the charger beside his sketchbook, and there was a movie playing on the TV with the volume turned down. Madoc had even set a bottle of pain relievers on the table and made sure Gus's crutches were on the left side of the bed, along with his prosthesis, a fresh liner, and socks.

"It'd mean a lot to me if I could lighten your load tonight."

Gus ran his knuckles over his lips. He understood the impulse to be close after the scare they'd had today, but this whole scene felt surreal. He'd been walking around for weeks feeling as if a big chunk of his life had gone missing, and now Madoc was loading the washer, looking every inch his stupid hot self and like he had no plans to be anywhere else.

Madoc had held Gus like a lover in full view of their friends and colleagues tonight, then kept him within reach when possible like he couldn't bear to lose contact. And God, the way he kept looking at Gus with so much tenderness and concern. Like he was seeing Gus with new eyes.

"How do you feel?" Madoc asked, setting new beers on the table. "Everything okay with your leg?"

"No blisters, thankfully, so I should be good." Gus popped an ibuprofen and chased it with beer. "And I definitely feel more human than I did an hour ago. How about you?"

"It's been ... a night." Madoc laughed, but he looked weary. The shadows beneath his eyes spoke of his own sleeplessness, and he nodded gratefully when Gus nudged the plate of food toward him.

"Val and I had a thing at the school like I said, so she could meet her new teachers and see their classrooms. And it really hit me as we were walking around that my baby's about to be a first grader."

Taking his phone from his pocket, Madoc flipped open the photo app to a pic of Valerie standing beside the school locker she'd been assigned and Gus had to swallow a sigh. He'd always loved hearing Madoc talk about his girl. Watching him light up with pride and affection.

"She's ready to be a big kid, huh?"

Madoc smiled. "Absolutely. She had a blast catching up with friends and exploring, and afterward we went to the cafe for dinner and talked about you."

For a second, Gus was sure he'd misheard. "Me? Why?"

"Because Val thought I was angry with you and that's why you only come over when I'm not around."

"Oh, balls. I'm sorry, Mad."

"It is what it is." Madoc studied his hands in his lap. "You needed space from me, and I've tried to respect that. Val noticed I wasn't myself though, and I should have anticipated she'd pick up on that. Considered how she was going to feel when you and I stopped being friends."

"We didn't stop being friends."

"I think it seemed that way to her."

Maybe to me too.

Madoc didn't have to speak the words out loud for Gus to know he was thinking them. And man, Gus felt like shit.

"We didn't stop being friends," he said again. "And if I'm honest, the space I said I wanted hasn't done shit for me." Gus huffed noisily through his nose. "I thought I could walk back my feelings if I wasn't around you. But every time I hear you over the radio or see you at a scene, all the stuff I'm trying not to feel hits me over the head. Christ, all it takes is Val saying your name when we're talking ..."

Madoc snapped his gaze up to meet Gus's. "I know. So, why are we staying apart when it's not working for any of us?"

Doing his best to ignore the flutter in his chest, Gus sat back in his chair. "I'm not sure what to say. I know I asked this the last time I saw you, but what are we doing here, Madoc?"

"Fixing things, I hope. And maybe starting over." Madoc folded his arms on the tabletop. "That's why I've been wanting to talk. So I could tell you how sorry I am for being a shitty friend. I should have called Tarek out for being an ass and I hate that I let you down there. That you think I only wanted you around because you got me off, which isn't true at all. I care about you, Gus, so fucking much."

"I care about you too. But I don't know where that leaves us." Gus shook his head sadly. He was so tired of hurting. "A couple of weeks ago, you told me you weren't ready to have someone in your life and now you say you want to start over. So, what the hell changed between then and now?"

"I did. I came out to Tarek."

Whoa.

Thunderstruck, Gus watched Madoc's cheeks flush red before his brain kicked back into gear. "You did?"

"Yes. I told him I'm bi and that you've been more to me than just a partner and buddy." Madoc heaved a big breath then blew it out. "Then I came out to Noelene and Clea too, since I was kind of on a roll and figured they deserved to know."

Gus took Madoc's hand in his. He'd hoped Madoc would find the courage to be honest with his family about himself someday. But seeing him now, eyes shining with equal parts excitement and trepidation, blew Gus away.

"That's a whole lot of telling, Madoc," he said softly. "How did it make you feel?"

"Incredible. And freaked out if I'm honest. But they were so good to me, Gus. T said he was there for me, no matter what. And Noelene needed a minute to process, but she heard me out. Listened to me talk for God knows how long about why I'd never told her the truth." Madoc's throat worked, and Gus knew he was fighting to keep it together.

"So tonight, I came out to Val," Madoc said. "And she was ... herself. Loving and kind and so much wiser than she has any right to be." Moisture sheened his eyes. "She just wants me to be happy."

"Of course, she does. Val will always want that for you

because she loves you with everything she is." Dropping Madoc's hand, Gus drew him in for a hug, a sweet ache in his own heart. "I'm so proud of you, Madoc, and I know your girl is too."

FOR THE SECOND time that evening, Madoc lost himself in Gus's embrace. It was selfish of him to seek comfort after he'd promised he'd be the one taking care of Gus, but damn it was good being close to him again, especially with his own emotions in an uproar. And Gus didn't miss the drying tear tracks on Madoc's cheeks when they parted, gently brushing over them with his fingertips.

"Are you all right?" he asked Madoc, his voice all caring concern.

"I'm good, I promise." Madoc cleared his throat. "It's still strange saying those words because I never have a plan or anything. But I'm *ready* to say them, like you told me I'd be. And now it's like I don't know what the hell I was waiting for."

"You were waiting to feel safe," Gus said. "It just took you some time to get there."

They lingered over the meal Madoc had constructed, catching up on easy topics that carried no heavy emotional toll and more pics, including some of Madoc and Valerie posing in their pom-pom crowns with Tarek. When Gus's eyelids started to droop, they cleaned up and moved to the bed to watch a movie where Madoc didn't pay much attention to the images on the screen, his own blinks getting progressively longer as a rosy, twilight space unfolded around them that was everything he needed and hoped Gus did too. Time to reconnect and rest and just *be,* hands entwined as the world beyond the studio walls continued on.

At last, Gus shivered lightly, then rolled toward Madoc, settling on to his side. "Guess we should talk, huh?"

"Yes. After you've slept." Turning his head, Madoc pressed his nose against Gus's hair. "You can't talk when you're not fully conscious."

Gus scoffed softly. "You're not exactly awake, bruh."

"Mmm, but I'm not the one who's been up for almost a full day at this point. We'll talk tomorrow when we can both think better." Madoc breathed Gus in. "Do you want me to go?"

"If you need to for Val—"

"Tarek's got her tonight, so I can stay if you want."

Gus inched a bit closer. "I want," he murmured. "But thanks for checking."

Madoc smiled to himself. He sat up and switched off the bedside light, then drew the quilt up from its place across the foot of the bed, and Lemonade appeared, climbing over Gus's torso to curl up between him and Madoc, her head against Gus's belly. Turning onto his side, Madoc cataloged the familiar features of the face that'd become so dear to him in the glow from the TV.

He had a lot of work left to do to fix things between them. But Gus had let Madoc in past the walls he'd put up to protect his own heart, showing a level of trust Madoc was sure he didn't deserve. To Madoc, that felt like real progress after so many weeks of missteps.

Blinking again, Madoc found the room quiet and dark, a sign he'd slept and been out long enough for the TV to power itself down. He was spooned up against Gus, his cheek against Gus's shoulder while Gus slept on, his breaths rhythmic and deep.

Madoc drowsed for a bit, soaking up being close as he breathed in Gus's clean, woody scent. Now and then, there were sounds from the direction of the cat tree as Lemonade did her thing, and Madoc's body was exquisitely aware of how good it felt to hold Gus again, that muscled back and ass warm and distracting, and more than enough to make Madoc's dick stir.

Carefully, Madoc extricated himself from the bed and started toward the bathroom, fully intending to splash some cold water on his face before he brewed some coffee. But there was sufficient light peeking under the window shades to illuminate the pages of Gus's sketchbook on the side table, and the lines on one page caught Madoc's eye as he passed by.

He'd clocked the sketchbook the night before but been more concerned with looking at Gus than his drawings. The face Madoc spied on the paper now took him off guard though, because it was undeniably his own.

Intrigued, he brought the book to the kitchen and turned on the light under the stove's hood, pleasure washing through him as he studied the sketch Gus had captured of Madoc studying a handful of cards.

There was nothing remarkable about the scene itself—Madoc played cards with Valerie most days of the week. But the style of the drawing held a realism that was almost startling, so like a photograph that Madoc ran his finger over the page to remind himself it was pencil on paper.

He'd known from early on that Gus wielded his pencils and pens with skill. But Madoc was still awed by the lines on the page that formed his own eyes, alight with good humor, and a grin curling the corners of his lips. Madoc's wonder only continued to grow as he flipped backward to the next sketch and then the others that preceded it, his face appearing on every page.

The tone of the drawings shifted between soft and dreamy and stark, Madoc's figure or face always standing out as the most vivid detail, the pencil strokes coming together like magic to show him at work and play and rest. Behind the wheel of the truck. Frowning over the Toughbook. Reclined beneath the roof of the blanket fort with Lemonade loafed on his belly. Brushing Valerie's hair at the bathroom sink while she brushed her teeth. Fast asleep with his arms around a pillow and his curls askew. Moments in Madoc's day-to-day he didn't think twice about but that Gus had seen and remembered.

More lights flicked on behind Madoc and he smiled to himself at the rhythmic creaks and taps that signaled Gus was using his crutches, a good sign he was feeling steadier now that he'd gotten some rest.

"You are so busted, big man," Gus said in a sleepy voice. "Having fun snooping through my private stuff?"

Heat splashed across Madoc's cheeks and he had to laugh. "Yes. And feeling a little conceited if I'm honest."

"Conceited?" Gus appeared at Madoc's side, hair wrecked as he frowned up at him. "What do you mean?"

"You made me look good." Madoc ran his finger over the book again, tracing the lines of his face in the sketch before them. "This guy in your drawings looks ... confident. Like he's got his life together and knows it. Like he's happy."

Gus glanced down at the sketchbook. "Well, I draw what I see, Mad," he said. "And you're all those things when I look at you."

Madoc nodded, considering. Then he turned from the counter and sketchbook and slipped his arms around Gus's waist, carefully setting his forehead against Gus's temple.

"I missed you," he whispered past his tight throat, his heart pounding when Gus didn't pull away. "I'm sorry things got so fucked up."

Sighing softly, Gus brought his right arm up and around Madoc's shoulders. "I'm sorry too." He turned his face so his nose brushed against Madoc's. "I missed you back, Mad. Every damned day."

They stood that way for a while, the damned counter and Gus's crutches making it tricky to get as close as Madoc wanted. But he held on to Gus anyway, soaking up his touch.

Gus saw a Madoc who was confident and happy because Madoc *was* both of those things and more when he was around Gus. He felt strong and sure of himself. Centered. Lighthearted in a way he hadn't been in far too long. And Madoc wanted so much to give Gus those same good feelings. He just hoped Gus still wanted him.

TWENTY-SEVEN

GUS HAD to stop himself from climbing Madoc and *damn,* it was hard when he was so fucking beautiful, smelling like sleep with a sheet mark on his cheek and his curls a bit wild. When he'd put his own life on hold for a time simply to be there for Gus.

Madoc had made Gus feel cared for. Like he was treasured and wanted. Especially knowing Madoc had come out to his family, not only about being bi but about his connection to Gus. That was all heady stuff for Gus, who'd craved everything Madoc had been giving and saying to him over the last twelve hours. It was scary too, when hope kept trying to bloom in Gus's foolish heart while nothing had been settled between them.

Reluctantly, he gave Madoc a final squeeze before letting him go. Gus tipped his head at the sketchbook on the counter.

"Before you get a big head, I do draw other people," he joked gently, smiling at Madoc's chuckle.

"I know—I've seen you do it." Madoc flipped through some more pages. "Still can't believe you'd want to draw *me*, though."

"I didn't at first." Gus turned the kettle on to heat water for coffee. "I tried to stop but it didn't work."

"What do you mean?"

"I don't get moony over guys who are married or straight. Particularly when that guy doesn't respect my work, wants my job, *and* thinks my leg is gross—"

"Yo." Madoc winced. "Jesus Christ, dude. Did you really think all that of me when we first met?"

"For a hot minute, yes." Gus patted Madoc's arm in silent apology. "You were all wrong for someone like me and I shouldn't have wanted to draw you. Except I did."

Reaching over, Gus flipped through the book until he reached a page dated April 1. The images there were just doodles he'd thrown down without thought, but there was no mistaking the eyes. Deep set and large with lush lashes, thick eyebrows conveying strength without being stern.

Genuine surprise filtered across Madoc's face. "April first was the first night I worked with you."

"Yup." Gus reached for the jar he used to store coffee. "Frankly, I had my doubts we'd make it past a second shift. But then I got to know you and figured out you weren't an actual asshole."

"I'm glad you gave me another chance." Madoc bit his lip. "And I know it's a lot, but I'm really hoping you can find it in you to give me a third one. The last time I was here—"

"I dumped a whole bunch of big feelings on you out of nowhere," Gus cut in. "That wasn't fair to you, and I'm sorry for that. I knew I was risking a lot that day. That you were going to feel like I was pushing you to choose me. I *did* want you to choose me. I couldn't keep going the way we had been when the sneaking around made me feel like you were ashamed to be with me."

"I was never ashamed of you, Gus—my shame was about me."

Expression troubled, Madoc put the small of his back against the counter. "I could tell you hated the hiding. And maybe you won't believe it, but it bothered me too, especially after you came back from your injury. It felt different then. More like I was actively lying to the people who knew us." He gave a shake of his head. "I can't tell you how sorry I am that you had to hide things from your friends and family because of me."

Fire touched Gus's cheeks. "Thank you for saying that. It helps knowing you didn't like playing it straight, either."

"I didn't," Madoc said fervently. "It sucked lying to Connor and Liv and Stark, and trying to avoid lying to Val. That was what sealed it for me—knowing a time would come when my daughter asked me something I wouldn't be able to answer without lying."

Gus frowned at his partner. "Did something happen?"

"No. But it hit me the other day that something was going to, probably soon." Madoc pursed his lips. "Tuesday at breakfast, Val asked me straight-out if I missed you. I told her I did, because it was the truth, but afterward all I could think was that if I kept hiding, it would mean having to lie to her someday. And I can't do that to Val. Not over who her daddy really is. She deserves better. And so do I."

Gus mulled Madoc's words over while he made their coffee. And he was awed by his friend's strength, knowing Madoc had feared telling his family his truth could mean losing them but that he'd done it anyway.

"So, Tarek was really okay with you coming out?" Gus asked as they moved back to the bed.

"He was." Madoc waited for Gus to get settled, the cups he'd carried with him in hand. "You should know he's not proud of the way he treated you. He's been angry at me and Noelene and bitter that we changed the way the family works. Resentful of you for stepping in for him when he wasn't around, even though that doesn't make any sense."

He handed Gus his coffee. "*Also,* it turns out that Tarek had already guessed about you and me which may be another reason he's been such an ass."

Gus's jaw dropped. "Get the hell outta here."

"I swear to God." With a helpless shake of his head, Madoc walked around the back of the couch. "Apparently, you're not the only one who's bad at hiding and he stopped believing my straight guy act a while ago."

Well, I'll be damned.

Gus doubted he'd ever be entirely cool with Tarek McKenna. But he respected the guy loving his family, and that Tarek worked hard every day to ensure their lives were good. That Tarek didn't want to lose them and, after Noelene had taken off, maybe it'd felt like he had.

"I'm glad you have his support," Gus said as Madoc sat down beside him. "I know you need that from him."

"I need your support just as badly." Sudden raw emotion passed over Madoc's face. "More than anyone, you've helped me wrap my head around things I struggle with. Like the idea I deserve a life of my own. Need time for me, away from child-care and the job, because I'm a better dad when I'm not cruising along on autopilot."

"Hey, you are never on autopilot with Val."

"I hope not but just hear me out." Madoc stared at his cup. "I had to shut down parts of myself after things started going bad with Noelene. Partly because I was hurt but even more because I was in survival mode every day keeping us afloat and I didn't have anyone else I could count on. I put my head down and made Val and the job my sole focus for a very long time and just kept my own stuff on hold.

"But I don't *have* to do that anymore. Val's growing up and I have people in my life now I can turn to for help. Tarek, Clea, Connor." Madoc glanced up. "You. And you *get* me, Gus, in ways no one else does." He flashed a small smile.

"You listen when I need to talk. Make me feel like ... me. Madoc the guy and not just Madoc the working dad who has no life. With you, I felt like I had a partner in the truest sense of the word because you were my best friend, work buddy, and lover rolled into one. I want that—want you—back in my life."

Gus's heart wobbled dangerously, that foolish hope rising again and scaring the hell out of him. Which was madness when he'd wanted to hear Madoc say things like this for such a long time.

"Oh, Mad." Gus swallowed hard. "I love what you're saying. But my heart hasn't been in great shape the last couple of weeks and—"

"Am I too late to fix this? Or ..." Madoc's face fell. "Maybe Val and I aren't enough?"

Startled, Gus stared at him. "How could you ever think that you and Val wouldn't be enough for anyone?"

"You told me the money Ben took was for adoption or surrogacy," Madoc said. "Val's almost seven, Gus, and we're never going to be—"

"Val is perfect," Gus cut in gently, "and the two of you are worth everything to me. But that's kind of the problem. Your life and Val's would be different with me in them as more than just a friend, and I can't promise the changes would always be easy. What if you decide that I'm the one who isn't worth keeping around?"

"That's not going to happen." Taking Gus's cup, Madoc set it on the side table with his own before he turned back, his gaze fierce, like he was looking *into* Gus and not simply at him. "Last night, Val said that you make me happy. That I laugh and smile more when you're around and don't seem so lonesome. She likes that we're friends and that you're special to me." Cheeks pinking up, he took hold of Gus's right hand. "I like it too."

Gus smiled past the ache that went through him. "Same."

"Good. I want that again, for both of us." Madoc squeezed Gus's fingers. "You make my life and Val's better every day we know you. You're good for me, Gus. You give me reasons to hope and play and kick ass on the job just to keep up with you. But you also remind me to stop sometimes and look at what's going on around me. Be present and grateful for what I have. You're the first person I think of when I have good news to share, and the only one I want to see if I'm having a crap day. Definitely the only one I want in my bed."

"Same," Gus said again, a near whisper this time thanks to the lump in his throat. A mere few months ago, Madoc had struggled to even talk about being bi. And now here he was, sounding so certain about how he wanted to live.

"I hate that I hurt you." Madoc brought their joined hands to rest over his own heart. "Hate that I hurt myself too, and Val, because I couldn't see what was right in front of me. That I want you desperately. Not because I need a kid-sitter or a buddy, but because you are the best thing to happen to me in a very long time and I fall in love with you more every day."

Gus's heart tried to beat its way out of his chest. "You think you're in love with me?"

Madoc gave him the most beautiful smile. "I know I am. I want to keep you, Gus, and so does your Bug. We want to make you part of our family, and you are the person we fell for."

'We' and 'our' were such small words. But they had Gus soaring high past his fear of being hurt.

Leaning over, Gus pressed his body against Madoc's and

closed his eyes. "I'm yours," he said. "Yours and the Bug's, for as long as you want me."

THROAT TIGHT, Madoc gathered Gus up in his arms. He wanted to say rash, stupid words that would have sent him spiraling only a couple of weeks ago. But right here and now, Madoc wasn't being stupid or rash; he was coming together with Gus, this time to stay.

"I know we still have stuff to figure out," he said. "So, this time, I'll follow your lead and just love you the best that I can."

Stars shone in Gus's eyes when he sat back, emotions writ clear on his face.

Affection. Joy. Pride, boundless and deep.

"I really like hearing you say that," he said, then climbed into Madoc's lap and sat astride his thighs. "Almost as much I like being able to tell you that I love you back."

Eyes shut tight, Madoc pressed a kiss against Gus's shoulder through his t-shirt. He'd come so close to losing this man. To missing out on something incredible out of fear. But Gus took hold of Madoc's face and kissed him, and it felt like '*Hello*' and '*Finally*' and Madoc's fear and guilt faded away.

They made out for a long time, pausing now and then to remove pieces of clothing or just run their hands over each other, neither in a rush to do more than feel. They were down to their boxers and Madoc was aching with need when Gus went into the drawer of the side table for a condom and lube and Madoc found himself unable to tear his gaze from that foil pack.

"I want to know what it's like," he blurted, sure this blush started at his toes. "You inside me, I mean. I don't know if I'm ready for ... everything yet. But I need to be close with you that way."

Gus's kiss was so sweet Madoc's eyes burned. "I love that you're asking me this," Gus said. "I'll make you feel good and take the best care of you."

Madoc didn't doubt Gus for a second. They stripped and he watched, his body humming as Gus slicked his fingers with lube, then fitted himself against Madoc's side. Only for Gus to stroke Madoc's cock teasingly, grip tight enough to get him ramped up without bringing him off, until Madoc started cursing at Gus to get on with it.

Face alight with laughter, Gus coaxed Madoc's knees up, then reached between them, using his elbow to nudged Madoc's right leg open wider. Goosebumps rose on Madoc's skin at being so exposed, but Gus's kisses quickly took the edge off until Madoc was once again melting into the mattress.

Reaching for Madoc's balls, Gus played with them for a time before moving his fingers to the soft skin of Madoc's taint. Madoc threw his head back against the pillow with a groan, his whole body on fire. When Gus coasted his fingers over Madoc's hole, Madoc gasped and let his knees fall open wider.

"Mmm." Gus's voice was wonderfully fond. "I think you like this."

Madoc was wild about everything that was happening to him. Gus holding him. The teasing touch against his rim that made it impossible to think. And then Gus pushed a fingertip inside Madoc and every nerve in his body blazed white hot all at once.

Groaning, he grabbed on to Gus. "Oh, God."

"I've got you. Bear down on me, Mad, and try to relax."

Forcing his eyes open, Madoc lost himself in Gus's stare. He'd never felt so vulnerable with any partner. But this was

Gus looking at Madoc like he was the best thing he'd ever seen and Madoc trusted Gus down to his bones.

Bearing down, he shuddered out a long breath as Gus slid his finger deeper. Indescribable feelings flooded Madoc's body, every cell lighting up. Pain edged the stretch and burn in his ass but in the best possible way, the pressure of being filled like nothing he'd ever experienced.

It hurt. It was *good.* And fuck, he wanted more.

Madoc's mouth fell open on a moan as Gus wrapped his free hand back around Madoc's cock. "*Fuck.*"

"That's it," Gus said, his own voice hoarse. "You feel incredible."

"Yeah, I do."

Gus huffed a laugh that set Madoc off too, but the ache in Madoc's hole was changing, morphing into a pleasure that soaked into his limbs. He whined as Gus eased a second finger in beside the first, then kissed Madoc soundly, driving his tongue deep into Madoc's mouth.

Madoc was trembling when they surfaced next, his skin too tight and hot for his body and his moaning near constant. With anyone else, he might have been embarrassed by his loss of control. But again, this was Gus, eyes shining as they locked with Madoc's, and he didn't flinch when Madoc's grip turned bruising.

"I didn't know," Madoc got out, his voice strange to his own ears. "*Gus.*"

"That's it, baby," Gus whispered. "Let go for me."

He curled his fingers and pleasure bolted through Madoc, radiating from his ass outward, drawing his balls up tight. Bucking his hips, Madoc bit back a cry but was unable to remain quiet when Gus tapped Madoc's prostate again.

Madoc whimpered and begged, the buzz inside him becoming a frenzy as Gus fucked his fingers in and out. When release came at last, it was like Madoc's body cracked wide open, his chest twisting hard as he unraveled in huge shuddering waves, cum on Gus's fist and striping Madoc's belly and chest.

Gus held him through it, crooning praise and sweet nonsense until Madoc floated back to earth. He didn't forget about Gus though, who was busy taking care of Madoc just as he'd promised.

Shaking off his stupor, Madoc pulled Gus into a deep, sloppy kiss and Gus moaned as the movement ground his groin against Madoc's hip. Madoc hauled him closer, humming approvingly when Gus shifted so he could frot his cock against Madoc's groin. And *Jesus*, Madoc had never seen anything more sensual.

Gus with his head back now, neck and upper chest stained dark red. Skin gleaming with sweat. That mobile mouth wet and kiss-swollen and so fucking tempting. Madoc hung on, learning the rhythm Gus set, his own cock hardening as he thrust up.

Loving Gus with everything Madoc had in him.

Madoc took Gus's face in his hand. "Love this," he said. "Love *you*, so goddamned much."

Gasping, Gus gripped Madoc tighter, thrusting hard and fast, his groan broken when he started to come, a plaintive sound that tugged at Madoc's chest. Wrapping Gus up in his arms, Madoc mirrored his slowing movements, Gus's cum smearing over their bellies and dicks, hot and messy and perfect.

They slept again, wrapped up in a warm cocoon beneath Gus's quilt until the world intruded again in the form of the small black cat that sat on Gus's head in a wordless demand to be fed. Messages from Valerie began popping up on Madoc's phone not long after, asking what time he would be home, if

Gus would be with him, how Gus was feeling, and would they please bring the cat along with them?

"Val said she wants pancakes with bluebs," Madoc said as he followed Gus onto the elevator in his building. "And also would like you to know that you are invited for dinner."

"I can do both." Shifting his bag with Lemonade in it slightly, Gus hit the button for Madoc's floor. "How do you want to play this around her?"

"What do you mean?"

"Well, I don't want to mess up and act like her daddy's boyfriend if Val isn't ready."

Reaching over, Madoc took Gus's hand in his own. "Don't worry about Val—she's known what she wants for a while. I was the one who needed to catch up because I wasn't ready for you when we first met. But I'm ready now." He wove his fingers around Gus's and smiled. "And I'm not letting this chance to make something good with you pass me by."

Gus's ears turned endearingly pink. "Me neither." He smiled and Madoc got slightly lost in those brown eyes that saw everything.

Then the elevator chimed, signaling their arrival at Madoc's floor and when the doors opened, Valerie was waiting for them by Madoc's front door, hopping from one foot to the other.

"Daddy 'n' Gus!" she called, a huge grin on her face as she sprinted toward them. "Welcome home!"

TWENTY-EIGHT

TUESDAY, *November 19, 10:15 A.M.*

"LOOKING GOOD, WALT."

Madoc huffed a soft laugh. Every time he thought that ridiculous nickname had faded from the crews' collective consciousness, it came back to surprise him.

"Thanks, Chen. You're looking sharp, too," he replied.

Madoc and Paramedic Regina Chen were in their dress uniforms, white shirts and gloves bright against their dark brown jackets and trousers while they waited for the ceremony to begin. Thirty-four Academy recruits would graduate and six department promotions announced that morning in Historic Faneuil Hall, while the mayor and Commissioner of Public Health looked on and someone special to each graduate or promotee pinned their badges to their uniforms.

"My wife's nervous about the badging," Chen said. "Which is funny considering she's a lawyer and stands in front of judges all the time. Is your kid badging you?"

"Yes." Madoc grinned. "She got to skip school for this, so it's a big deal for her, especially with Gus being promoted at the same time."

"Aw." Chen's smile turned indulgent. "That's really sweet. I'll bet you and Dawson have the biggest cheering section out there today."

"We could have the loudest," said a voice on Madoc's left and then Gus was there, eyes crinkling at the corners with his smile and so gorgeous in his uniform with his eight-point hat under one arm. "Madoc's girl and my ma are going to clap for everyone," he explained to Chen. "They know some of us can't have family here today and don't want anyone feeling left out."

Madoc took Gus's hand. He hadn't made a big deal about coming out at work. He'd simply been honest with Connor, Olivia, Stark, and a few others about who Gus had become to him and why they'd gone undercover at first. But Madoc didn't take moments like this for granted, very aware of how lucky he was to have the freedom to be open about who he was.

At 10:30 A.M., the doors at the front of the room were thrown open and Madoc, Gus, and the other promotees led the way into The Great Hall with the recruit class marching behind, their boots thumping against the hardwood floors. A market and meeting place since 1742, The Great Hall had seen the beginnings of the War for Independence and hosted impassioned speakers over the years ranging from presidents to abolitionists to women's suffragists. Today, however, its rows of wood seats on the main floor and second-story seating galleries were filled with the families and friends of the Boston EMS crews and the mood in the air was festive.

Madoc recognized faces on his march down the long center aisle to the stage, including Olivia and her son with Connor and Judah, and Bobby Stark with Guzman and a pack of Gus's firefighter buddies. But Madoc's pulse picked up when Valerie waved at him from her seat in the second row where she was flanked by Tarek and the Dawsons.

A cozy feeling wrapped around Madoc's heart as he watched Valerie whisper excitedly to Gus's ma. He was a big fan of Layla, Steven, and Donna, all of them as funny, smart, and loving as their son and loyal to their core. They doted on Valerie *and* Madoc, and knowing he had them in his corner—that he was safe being himself around them—still blew him away.

For a second, Madoc wished he was among the audience looking on as the promotees and recruits filed into rows of reserved seats at the front of the room and the honor guard followed behind, solemn as they bore the Massachusetts state and Boston EMS flags to the front of the room. He loved that Valerie got to be a part of this. That all the effort Madoc had put in to restarting his career was about to be recognized while he stood beside Gus, the person Madoc wanted to share everything with: his endeavors and passions, his struggles, successes, and home.

Madoc knew they were headed that way, though he and Gus had agreed not to rush into anything, both mindful of the emotional ups and downs they and Valerie had endured over the last couple of years. So, Gus had hung on to his studio, using it mostly as a study place now that he'd gone back to school. He spent the majority of his off-hours at Madoc's though and made sure the Walters saw him every day, knowing they wanted him there with them.

"History has been made in this room," Mayor Cesario said now as she surveyed the crowd, "and I'm delighted to know we're making it again here today. With thirty-three recruits, this is the largest graduating class in over a decade, more than half of whom are women, and we're recognizing two double promotions, a number I'm told is unprecedented."

Madoc smiled when Gus pressed the side of his knee against Madoc's.

"People who work in EMS often say that the work you all do is a calling," the mayor continued. "And as EMTs and paramedics, I know you step into difficult, often dangerous situations every day and meet people who are at their most frightened and vulnerable."

Setting her hand over her heart, Mayor Cesario looked along the rows of recruits and promotees. "You don't hear it enough, but I want to thank you on behalf of the citizens of Boston for caring so well for your patients while also preserving their dignity each time you put on your uniforms and ride out into our city."

A buzz rose from the crowd when it came time for the badging, the Superintendent of Boston EMS walking onstage with two captains who would assist with the proceedings. The promotees gathered on the left side of the stage and those pinning them on the right, and as each name was read out, Madoc imagined he heard Valerie's and Layla's cheers among the applause, their commitment to ensuring every promotee and recruit got some love going strong.

"Promoted to the rank of Paramedic, Madoc Walters," the captain at the podium said, "to be badged by his daughter Valerie Walters with assistance from Tarek McKenna. Paramedic Walters is also a member of the recruit graduating class and the first of today's double promotions."

There were whoops and applause as Madoc crossed the stage to Valerie and Tarek and God, he was so proud of his confident girl, the practice she'd put in for this moment with Madoc, Gus, and Tarek on full display. Valerie shook hands with the officials, then received Madoc's badge, and she was impossibly grown up when she turned toward Madoc. She looked heartbreakingly pretty, her curls falling loose over the shoulders of her scarlet dress, a soft knitted number Gus'd helped Madoc pick out that boasted a pattern of teeny cat faces.

There were murmurs and cameras clicking as Madoc took a knee, the presence of a former NHL star by Valerie's side perhaps generating some added excitement. Madoc didn't care about any of it though, too wrapped up in the pride he read on his family's faces.

"Congratulations, Daddy," Valerie whispered, badging him with a big smile. "Me and Uncle T and Gus are wicked proud of you."

"Thank you, honey," Madoc whispered back. He opened his arms so she could step in for a hug. "I couldn't have done it without you."

He kept her close when he rose to hug Tarek and shake hands with the officials, and they posed for the department's official photos before heading off the stage, just making it off as the last promotee's name was announced.

"Promoted to the rank of Lieutenant, August Dawson, badged by his parents, Layla and Steven Dawson. Lieutenant Dawson is also promoted to the rank of Paramedic today and is the second of our double promotions."

Cheers and whistles rang out, and Madoc quickly scooped Valerie up so she could see over the crowd and clap loudly for them both, her hands over her head and her smile broad.

Gus's face was easily visible above Layla's head, shining with a delight Madoc felt from across the room as she badged him. Lots of cameras flashed for Gus too because he was a little bit 'famous' among the EMS ranks. But then he stepped back and looked past his ma and pops and everyone else, searching out Madoc and Valerie. He smiled when he found them, his gaze locking with Madoc's and holding, all the pride and love Madoc felt for his man reflected right back at him.

"Proud of you," Madoc mouthed, and grinned when Gus did the same.

AFTER THE CEREMONY, the Dawson and Walters parties journeyed to the Seaport where they met up with more friends at the BBQ Shack on the water, and as Gus glanced around, his chest swelled with satisfaction.

His sister was sharing a basket of sweet potato fries with Felipe, Connor, and little Titus, while Judah and Lucky Guzman talked movies with Gus's pops. Gus's ma and Olivia were at the next table with Tarek, Ian, and Ian's boyfriend Tris, the group talking about Tarek's days playing pro hockey. And Madoc and Valerie were just returning from feeding money into the jukebox, the pair of them so fucking cute Gus could hardly stand it.

"Hello, my honey!" Valerie said brightly as she sidled up to Gus. "Are you having fun?"

"I'm having a blast, Valley Girl, and thank you for asking." Shifting slightly, Gus slipped his arm around her. "How about you?"

"I love this day." Valerie helped herself to an onion ring from Gus's plate and bit deep. "The ce-re-mo-ny for you 'n Daddy 'n everyone else was *super* cool," she said past her chewing, "especially the part with the radio."

Gus met Madoc's beaming expression over the table. Every graduation ceremony capped off with the recruit class being officially acknowledged via a formal radio communication with dispatch, an old-fashioned gesture that Gus had always loved.

"All units, please stand by for a special announcement from Command 4," the dispatcher said. "Command 4, go ahead."

An expectant hush hung over The Great Hall, every eye on

the superintendent at the podium with his radio. Gus's attention shifted to Madoc though, who was watching the proceedings with rapt attention.

"Command 4," the superintendent said solemnly. "Dispatch, please log on the graduates of Recruit Class Two, 2024. They have completed their assignment at the academy and are assigned to field operations at Boston EMS. We wish them good luck and godspeed."

The briefest of pauses followed before the dispatcher replied with equal gravitas, "Message received, Command 4. Congratulations and welcome to the department, Academy Class Two, 2024."

Hoots and hollers rang through The Great Hall, the applause joyful, and abruptly, Valerie was there with Gus and Madoc, having scooted past the knees of the people in the row behind them so she could squeeze her way into a group hug with an arm around each of their necks.

Gus found himself blinking back tears. Technically, Madoc had graduated months prior and received his badge and certificate in a much less formal ceremony held at Station 1. But the day still felt special to Gus, his chest swelling with pride for his guy. His own graduation had been profoundly bittersweet, his pride in his accomplishment shadowed by the losses of his firefighting career and Beni while his relationship with Ian hung in tatters. Gus had only happiness in him today though, particularly with Valerie there to share in her daddy's success.

After lunch, Gus and Madoc hugged their friends and fam goodbye, then walked back to the apartment with the Bug and Tarek, making plans to meet up for dinner and a game night in a few days. Tarek headed off to prepare for a new client, but he made a point of congratulating Gus once again with a friendly, genuine smile.

Things were much easier between Gus and Tarek these

days, Tarek having stopped with the snotty remarks while Gus worked at not bristling if the dude so much as breathed. It had to be weird for Tarek being around the person who'd stepped into the space his sister had chosen to leave behind, doubly so seeing as that person was male and Tarek wasn't quite cool with the gays. But Noelene checked in on the family often and, with the help of her therapist, was feeling more grounded, enough that Tarek had begun to move on himself.

Princess Lemonade Small Void Kitty, however, remained steadfast in her attempts to murder Tarek with her glares.

Gus bent now so his furry rebel could hop up onto his shoulders, and Madoc closed the apartment door behind them while Valerie sprinted off to her room. She surprised Gus with a quick return though, holding a flat package wrapped in rainbow glittery paper aloft like a prize.

"I have a present for you, my dear Gusberry!" she sang. "And I want you to open it!"

Gus raised his eyebrows at her. Together, they'd gifted Madoc a new tie bar bearing the city's seal and an engraving on the back to mark his promotion. But Gus hadn't expected any gifts for himself and said as much while Valerie herded him to the couch.

"The present isn't for pro-mo-tions," she explained when he was seated and had handed Lemonade off to Madoc. "It's for Tuesday because that's one of my favorite days of the week."

"Well, all right then." Gus chuckled as she laid the package on his lap. "And you're sure you want me to open this now?"

"Yes!" Boosting herself up onto the cushion beside Gus, Valerie waved at Madoc to get comfortable on her other side. "Daddy did the wrapping paper so it would look fancy."

"The idea was all Val's, though," Madoc said. "I just did my best to help."

"Nuh-uh, Daddy. You helped a lot because I told you what needed to happen."

Gus grinned at the banter as he unwrapped the package, which was sized and shaped like a school notebook. Under the glittery paper, however, was a pale green hardcover volume unlike any Gus'd ever seen.

Twelve Facts I Know About A Wild Gusberry

The title was bold and purple with grinning creatures Gus immediately recognized as drawn by Valerie gamboling on and around the words. Spangled ponies kept company with lady-bugs, honeybees, and butterflies, while a small black cat looked on from atop the 's' in 'Gusberry'.

Astonished, Gus stared wordlessly at the book for several seconds before looking to Valerie. "Did you make me a coloring book?"

"I made you a *story* book," Valerie clarified. "And it's all facts I know about you! Daddy helped me get all the spelling right an' I did the drawings," she said. "Then we put everything in a box and sent it away to the bookmaker people!"

"To a shop out in Northampton, really," Madoc said when Gus glanced at him. "They turn kids' art into keepsakes and were stoked to work with Val on her project."

"I colored you in on every page, Gus." Valerie leaned over and opened the book for him. "Because I know you don't like to draw yourself."

Gus smiled at her, but his throat was so thick it took him a second to reply. He could tell a great deal of thought and work had gone into this project and that significant time spent drawing and writing before the pages were organized into a package for printing.

"Thank you, hon," he said when he could. "This is one of the coolest gifts anyone's ever given me."

Valerie preened a little, then turned her eyes to the open page. "Fact One," she said. "Gus's favorite drink of all time is coffee."

A laugh immediately rose in Gus's chest. "I can't argue that."

Nor any of the facts that followed. From his ice cream of choice to his favorite rainy-day activity, each captured a detail Valerie had learned about him. That Gus liked to box and play basketball. Sometimes jumped around when he watched baseball games on TV. Made up silly songs while he did housework.

An adorable drawing accompanied the facts, a cute, smiley cartoon Gus with a nicely detailed prosthesis looking red-cheeked over breakfast in Fact Six (*Gus puts spicy ketchup on eggs so his face catches fire*), shaking the paw of a huge gray Hank in Fact Five (*Gus makes friends with giant dogs*), and bearing an ink-colored fur ball on his shoulder in Fact Ten (*Gus tamed a wild kitty who needed a home*). A square-shouldered, equally smiley Madoc also appeared in some of the drawings, as did a spritely, pigtailed Valerie whose expressions bore an uncanny resemblance to her real-life versions.

"Fact Eleven," she said now, turning to a drawing of the cartoon Gus and Valerie seated aboard a train car underground. "Gus is a really good listener because he always waits for his turn to talk."

Gus ran a hand over Valerie's hair. He'd come to regard the conversations they'd shared on their way to and from school as a turning point for them both. Valerie had learned that Gus didn't expect her to put on a happy face for him if she wasn't feeling it. And Gus'd started to fall in love with the Walters without ever meaning to.

He was falling all over again now, dazzled and truly moved

at the way this child had depicted him, all bright colors and strong lines, little face wreathed with sunny expressions. Happy, because that was how Valerie saw him.

Seeming to sense the change in Gus's mood, Madoc slipped his arm around Gus's shoulders and gave him a squeeze, a comforting touch he leaned into as Valerie turned the page to reveal a drawing of the blanket fort, three figures inside it and Princess Lemonade with her stuffed banana curled at their feet.

"Fact Twelve," Valerie said, her gaze no longer on the book at all but on Gus, and her smile the slightest bit shy. "Gus makes my family happy, and I love him a lot."

Gus's breath caught. He'd experienced some wicked highs today. Watched stars light Madoc's eyes as they'd helped each other with their uniform jackets. Shared Valerie's pride as she'd badged her daddy. Seen joy in his ma's and pop's faces as Gus'd presented himself to them on the stage.

Valerie saying she loved him, though ... that was the most incredible high of all. Gus already knew his Bug loved him because she did a dozen things every day that told him so without words. But this little girl had been through a lot and hearing her speak the words aloud—knowing she trusted Gus to care for her heart—was a gift he would never take for granted.

"I love you too, Val, and I love your daddy." Gus willed his voice not to shake. "Every day that I know you, I'll always be glad to have you in my life."

Gus went in to hug her at the same time Madoc pulled Valerie up onto his lap so she could embrace them both, and they ended up in a big group squeeze that was very much them, filled with elbows and laughter and murmured 'I love yous'.

Much later, after dinner and Valerie's bedtime, Gus locked the bedroom door behind himself and laid Madoc on the bed, his blood buzzing with the good feelings he'd soaked up throughout the day and Madoc's kisses.

"You looked fucking hot in your uniform today," Madoc muttered against Gus's lips. "That hat, oh my God. Wanna suck you while you're wearing it."

Gus chuckled. "That can be arranged," he said. "But only if I get to blow you beforehand."

He grabbed the lube from the nightstand, then spent time taking Madoc apart, his lust bound up with an overwhelming tenderness. Barely six months ago, simply admitting that he was bi would have sent Madoc spiraling. And now he was here with Gus, so much love in his eyes. His body practically melting into the mattress as Gus fingered him, though he kept a tight hold on Gus, like he couldn't bear to let go.

"More," Madoc murmured, his breath shuddering when Gus curled his fingers. "Oh, Jesus, Gus, please."

"Okay," Gus said with a smile. "I think you're ready."

He eased his fingers out of Madoc, then soothed his groan with more kisses, stroking Madoc's hip as he helped Madoc roll over onto his stomach. Gus moved his hand to Madoc's ass cheeks then, massaging and fondling the muscles while Madoc clutched a pillow to his chest and arched into the touch, his soft groans so fucking sexy.

"*Gus.*"

"I'm here."

On his knees, Gus lubed his cock, then nudged Madoc's legs wider as he lined up their bodies, his own body aching for release. He teased a few moments, tracing his cockhead around Madoc's rim while Madoc's pleas became increasingly desperate. Madoc *loved* being fucked, his need to surrender control intertwined with a desire to watch Gus take it. Gus faltered slightly when he finally pushed forward, however, the incredible heat and pressure of Madoc's ass around him almost too much.

Jaw clenched, Gus slid home with a long, slow stroke, his heart shaking when Madoc keened, low and forlorn. Lust sizzled up Gus's spine as he wrapped Madoc up in his arms and rocked into him, dropping kisses against Madoc's shoulders and neck, tasting the sweat that sheened his skin.

Madoc turned his head on the pillow, eyes closed tight and his cheeks and mouth tinted red. He rutted into the mattress, the slack expression on his face wanton and beautiful as he begged for more, for harder and faster, for Gus to please make him come.

And fuck, Gus wanted it all. For the bliss he had with his man to never end. To come inside Madoc over and over. Make Madoc lose it so hard he screamed.

Setting his forehead against Madoc's temple, Gus set a quick, rough pace that instantly had Madoc pushing back into the thrusts, his begging no longer coherent. When each exhaled breath caught like a sob in Madoc's throat, Gus knew he was close, so gone on pleasure that he'd be able to come without his cock being touched. So, Gus drove a little deeper, knowing how much Madoc relished the ache of being split open.

Grabbing tight to Gus's right hand, Madoc dragged it to his chest, his body starting to shake. "Don't let me go."

"I won't." Panting, Gus pressed his mouth to Madoc's ear. "I love you, baby," he growled. "I love you so fucking much."

Madoc went over the edge with a gasp, his body going stiff in Gus's arms before slowly relaxing again, frotting his cum onto the sheets. Then he bent his head and pressed an open-mouthed kiss against Gus's knuckles and without warning, Gus was there too, orgasm crashing through him in a breath-stealing wave. He unloaded into Madoc's ass, the world around him sliding out of focus as he came and came and came.

It was a minute before Gus's brain came back online and when it did, he found himself sprawled atop a very sleepy Madoc who grumbled when Gus made to pull out. But Gus soothed him with kisses and cleaned him up, unsurprised that Madoc quickly dozed off, the excitement of the day catching up with him.

Gus still felt too keyed up to sleep though, so he went to the dresser for some clothes and his sketchbook, intent on doing some drawing while his guy napped. But he found the Gusberry Fact Book there where he'd left it and quietly carried everything out into the apartment where he sprawled out on the couch and lost himself in its pages and his emotions.

"How you doin', my love?"

Smiling, Gus looked up at Madoc, who was clad like Gus in shorts and a t-shirt, his hair mussed up from sleeping. "Doin' just fine. I was too hyper to nap, so I thought I'd leave you to it. How do you feel?"

"Really excellent." Pausing to move Gus's crutches under the coffee table, Madoc eased himself down on the couch cushions beside him, chuckling when Gus closed the Gusberry book and turned onto his side to make room. "Starting to get hungry again and was thinking I'd make some eggs with too much hot sauce."

Gus's stomach let out a growl of approval that made them both snort.

"Guess I earned that," Gus said, then ran his fingers over the Fact Book's cover. "Still feeling amazed at all the work you and your girl put into this."

"Honestly, Val was halfway done with the drawing by the time she asked me to help her put it together." Madoc rubbed Gus's shoulder with his knuckles. "It got kinda dicey keeping the whole thing a secret when you switched back to nights though, so we took everything up to her old room at Tarek's and he gave us a hideout."

A laugh rose in Gus's chest imagining Valerie and Madoc walking a small truckload of art supplies into the elevator, but it got caught in his chest and abruptly Madoc was frowning, probably because he'd clocked Gus's reddened eyes.

"Hey." Taking Gus's hand in his own, Madoc snuggled in closer. "Are you okay?"

"Yeah. I'm … overwhelmed by today." Gus studied his fingers wrapped around Madoc's. "Being there with you at the ceremony. Seeing our fam all together. I really didn't expect to have this."

"Have what, love?"

"You. Val. Us." Sighing, Gus looked back at Madoc. "We both know nothing is promised, Madoc. That sometimes you lose people you care about and even the best laid plans just don't work out. I was in that kind of place in my head when you and I met. Thinking that I might be better off on my own, especially if I wanted a family."

Humming quietly, Madoc pressed a kiss against Gus's shoulder through his shirt. "I get it. You know I shut off parts of myself when we moved to Boston and thought being alone was better for me and safer for Val. But my life started changing the second I walked into Station 1 and met you," he said, such warmth in his eyes. "So, I guess I messed up both our plans."

"You really did in the best possible way." Gus smiled at his guy. "And I'm so glad you did."

The End

TWELVE FACTS I KNOW ABOUT A WILD GUSBERRY

BY VALERIE MAE WALTERS

1. Gus's favorite drink of all time is coffee.
2. Gus thinks peanut butter ice cream is totally dope.
3. Gus likes to box and also do basketball in his chair.
4. Gus jumps up and down sometimes when he watches baseball on TV.
5. Gus makes friends with giant dogs.
6. Gus put spicy ketchup on eggs so his face catches fire.
7. Gus makes up funny songs when he cleans.
8. Gus turns rainy days better with cake.
9. Gus will always share his *bolos*, even when he's wicked hungry.
10. Gus tamed a wild kitty who needed a home.
11. Gus is a good listener because he always waits for his turn to talk.
12. Gus makes my family happy, and I love him a lot.

AUTHOR'S NOTE

Thank you so much for reading! I hope you enjoyed meeting Gus, Madoc, and Valerie as much as I did. And if you recognized some characters from my Stealing Hearts series in this book, it wasn't your imagination!

While the EMS Station 1 stories are fiction, I did a lot of research into the hiring and promotion policies of Boston's Emergency Medical Services and the work lives of EMTs, paramedics, and firefighters working in urban areas. Information on the internet that helped me in this pursuit include Boston.gov and EMS wikis, discussion forums, and subreddits. Also invaluable is the advice from my proofreader, Barb, a retired paramedic who goes above and beyond with her fact checking.

Equally important for *Color You In* was gaining insight into the everyday experiences of amputees, particularly lower limb amputees. I found fantastic resources online from crutches reviews to papers about the construction of prosthetic limbs to amputee support subreddits, and some vlog and blog resources that were particularly helpful include *The Amped Life with Chris*, *Footless Jo*, *Adaptive Amputees*, and *Adaptive Athlete Jamie Gane*.

I'd also like to give a shout out to the creators of the highly entertaining TV shows *Boston EMS* and *Nightwatch*, to Albert Lin for his excellent National Geographic show, *Lost Cities*, and to the many creators out there who wrote about paramedics and EMTs like Noah Filer, Derek Eady, Cieran McKiernan, and David Kruysman, all amputees who have worked and thrived in their jobs in EMS.

ACRONYM AND CODE KEY

BLS Truck: Basic Life Support Ambulance. BLS is a set of life-saving medical procedures performed in the early stages of an emergency, typically administered by an individual who has basic medical training. The goal is to maintain the life functions of a person who is having a medical emergency until more advanced medical care can be provided.

For Boston EMS, BLS trucks are designated with an 'A' and are staffed by two EMTs. BLS trucks may be dispatched first to calls to perform triage and, if necessary, an ALS truck with paramedics will respond to lend assistance.

ALS Truck: Advanced Life Support Ambulance. ALS measures take BLS techniques to the next level with more sophisticated interventions and procedures. The goal is to stabilize critical patients who may have suffered a life-threatening event while preparing them for transport to a hospital. ALS techniques are typically performed by individuals who are highly trained.

For Boston EMS, ALS trucks are designated with a 'P' and are staffed by two paramedics.

Squad Units: In the US, Squads Units may also be referred to Sprint (Single Paramedic Rapid Intervention) Cars, Fly Cars, and Intercepting Paramedics.

Emergency Service Response Codes 1, 2, 3

In the US, response codes are used to describe a mode of response for an emergency unit responding to a call. They vary but often have three basic tiers.

- **Code 1:** Respond using lights and sirens.
- **Code 2:** Respond with lights only.
- **Code 3:** Respond without lights or sirens.

Police Radio Code 4

In the US, "Code 4" means a scene has been declared "safe" and indicates that officers who have responded are now in charge of the situation they were called to.

EMS Priority Dispatch Codes

Emergency Medical Dispatch Codes (EMD Codes) are part of the Medical Priority Dispatch System (MPDS). These codes follow a number-letter-number format to describe the nature of an incident, help categorize the severity of a patient's condition, and prioritize calls for emergency services.

The first component of a Code is a number indicating the type of complaint or protocol. There are currently 37 protocols in total. Examples: 1 = Abdominal Pain, 2 = Allergies/Envenomations, 3 = Animal Bites/Attacks.

The second component, a letter ranging from A to E, indicates the seriousness of the patient's condition:

- A (Alpha) = low-priority situation.
- B (Bravo) i= mid-priority condition.
- C (Charlie) = potentially life-threatening condition.
- D (Delta) = life-threatening emergency.
- E (Echo) = full cardiac arrest or imminent death
- Omega = lowest priority, may involve referral to another service or a non-emergency situation.

Alpha, Bravo, and Omega responses typically require BLS, while Charlie and Delta necessitate ALS. Echo responses demand ALS and specialized units with multiple resources.

The third component of the EMD Code is a number that provides further details about the patient's specific condition.

Examples:

- 6-D-2: Breathing problems, difficulty speaking between breaths
- 10-D-5: Chest pain without trauma, heart attack or angina history
- 23-C-5: Overdose/Poisoning, narcotics

- 27-D-6 G: Stab/Gunshot/Penetrating Trauma, multiple gunshot victims
- 29-D-1 M: Major traffic incident, multiple patients
- 32-B-1: Unknown problem (person down), capable of standing, sitting, moving, or speech

ACKNOWLEDGMENTS

Converse - Nike, Inc.
NARCAN (*Naloxone HCI*) - Emergent BioSolutions
Poop Bingo - Laurence King Publishing
Slapburger - Donut & Lola
Taco Cat Goat Cheese Pizza - Dolphin Hat Games
I Feel Love - Donna Summer
Free Mom Hugs - Sara Cunningham
Blade Runner - written by Hampton Fancher and David Peoples

THIRD TIME'S THE CHARM

If you enjoyed this book, check out *Third Time's The Charm*, available in paperback and ebook at your favorite retailer and Kindle Unlimited on Amazon

Third Time's The Charm

Sometimes you have to start over to get love right.

Luke Ryan's life is too chaotic for romance, what with running his business and being the legal guardian to his ten-year-old niece, but he's hopeful he'll find the right man.

Trauma surgeon Finn Thomason recently relocated from Chicago to Boston where his focus on medicine leaves him little space for a personal life. Making a commitment to find a better work-life balance, Finn hopes he'll also find a relationship.

Caught in an evening rainstorm, Luke shelters under a sidewalk awning...and encounters a handsome stranger. The two strike up a conversation and Finn offers to walk Luke under his oversized umbrella. Charmed, Luke accepts and asks Finn out for coffee in thanks.

Luke and Finn quickly grow close, but, as the summer draws to an end, Luke struggles to keep his connection with Finn while Finn tries to come to terms with caring for a man whose attention is pulled in many directions. Both men are scrambling to get it right, but only time will tell if they'll learn there is more than enough room in their hearts to go around.

ABOUT THE AUTHOR

K. Evan Coles is a mother and tech pirate by day and a writer by night. She is a dreamer who, with a little hard work and a lot of good coffee, coaxes words out of her head and onto paper.

K. lives in the northeast United States, where she complains bitterly about the winters, but truly loves the region and its diverse, tenacious, and deceptively compassionate people. You'll usually find K. nerding out over books, movies and television with friends and family. She's especially proud to be raising her son as part of a new generation of unabashed geeks.

K.'s books explore LGBTQ+ romance in contemporary settings.

For more books and updates:
https://kevancoles.com/

facebook.com/kevancolesauthor
instagram.com/k.evan.coles
amazon.com/K-Evan-Coles/e/B072L7L8BZ
bookbub.com/profile/k-evan-coles
pinterest.com/kevancoles
threads.net/@k.evan.coles

ALSO BY K. EVAN COLES

Wicked Fingers Press (Self-Published)

Stealing Hearts

Thief of Hearts (Novella)

Healing Hearts (Novella)

Open Hearts (Novel)

Hopeful Hearts (Novel)

EMS Station 1

Hooked On You (Novel)

Color You In (Novel)

Overexposed (Novel)

Flashpoint (Short Story)

A Hometown Holiday (Novella)

Moonlight (Short Story)

Pride Publishing (Totally Entwined Group)

Third Time's the Charm

Tidal Duology w/ Brigham Vaughn (Novels)

Wake

Calm

The Speakeasy w/ Brigham Vaughn (Novels)

With a Twist

Extra Dirty

Behind the Stick

Straight Up

Off Topic Press (Self-Published)

Inked in Blood w/ Brigham Vaughn (Short Story)

---

http://www.kevancoles.com

Made in the USA
Middletown, DE
02 April 2025

73698390R00203